10ͨ

Praise for
THE GRAVEYARD QUEEN series
by Amanda Stevens

"The beginning of Stevens' GRAVEYARD QUEEN series left
this reviewer breathless. The author smoothly establishes
characters and forms the foundation of future storylines with
an edgy and beautiful writing style. Her story is full of twists
and turns, with delicious and surprising conclusions. Readers
will want to force themselves to slow down and enjoy the book
instead of speeding through to the end, and they'll anxiously
await the next installment of this deceptively gritty series."
—*RT Book Reviews* on *The Restorer*

"*The Restorer* is by turns creepy and disturbing, mixed with
mystery and a bit of romance. Amelia is a strong character who
has led a hard and—of necessity—secret life. She is not close
to many people, and her feelings for Devlin disturb her greatly.
Although at times unnerving, *The Restorer* is well written and
intriguing, and an excellent beginning to a new series."
—*Fort Worth Examiner*

"I could rhapsodize for hours about how much I enjoyed
The Restorer. Amanda Stevens has woven a web of intricate
plot lines that elicit many emotions from her readers. This is a
scary, provocative, chilling and totally mesmerizing book. I never
wanted it to end and I'm going to be on pins and needles until the
next book in THE GRAVEYARD QUEEN series comes out."
—*Fresh Fiction*

Also by Amanda Stevens

THE DOLLMAKER
THE DEVIL'S FOOTPRINTS
THE WHISPERING ROOM

The Graveyard Queen

THE RESTORER
THE KINGDOM
THE PROPHET
THE VISITOR
THE SINNER

AMANDA STEVENS

THE AWAKENING

MIRA

JUN 8 2 2017

ISBN-13: 978-0-7783-1768-5

The Awakening

Copyright © 2017 by Marilyn Medlock Amann

THE AWAKENING

One

I came across the hidden grave my first day in Woodbine Cemetery. It was late October, warm and sunny with a mild breeze stirring my nostalgia and the colorful leaves that had fallen from the dogwood trees. Despite the temperature, I could feel autumn in the air—or at least in my imagination—as the sun settled toward the horizon.

Those fading days always brought twinges of melancholy and I was glad to have a new project to buoy my spirits. I was still in the early phases of the restoration—mapping, photographing and spending untold hours immersed in historical records. The hard labor of clearing brush and cleaning headstones would soon follow, but for now I luxuriated in the courtship stage, that heady, golden time of acquainting myself with the dead and their history.

Woodbine was one of the forgotten cemeteries in a whole community of burial grounds that fanned out from the Cooper River in Charleston, South Carolina. Tucked away at the end of a narrow lane and hidden from street view by a shrouded fence, this withering gem had languished in the shadow of the historic Magnolia Cemetery for decades until revitalization efforts in the area had uncovered it.

The grave was just as well hidden, secreted in the farthest corner of the cemetery and sheltered from the elements and the curious by the graceful arms of weeping willow trees. The graves of children always moved me, but this one affected me in a way I couldn't explain. Perhaps it was the stone monument cast in the shape of an old-fashioned baby crib that so intrigued me, or the likeness of the child that peeped from underneath the hood. Or the unsettling epitaph, which read Shush… Lest She Awaken.

There was no name on the memorial, but I could make out the birth and death dates. The little girl had passed nearly fifty years ago at the heartbreaking age of two. Setting aside my camera, I smoothed my hand along the edge of the polished stone as I studied her portrait. What a beautiful child she'd been, with a heart-shaped face and perfect bow mouth. The black-and-white image had been hand-painted to tint her lips and cheeks pink, her curls golden and her eyes a lovely violet blue.

She hadn't smiled for the camera and the solemnness of her countenance sent an inexplicable chill down my spine. It was strange to see such a serious expression on the face of an infant. Had she been ill? I wondered. Had her short life been filled with so much pain and suffering that death had come as a blessing?

I couldn't look away from that sweet, doleful face. The child captivated me. There was something so mesmerizing about her eyes…something almost familiar about the shape of her mouth and nose and the lines of her jaw and chin. I couldn't have known her. She'd passed long before I was born. I had only Mama and Papa and my aunt Lynrose in the area, none of whom had ever spoken of a dead baby. Despite the discovery of so many long-buried secrets, I doubted a familial bond, and yet I was drawn to that nameless child in a way that defied a real-world explanation.

Was she reaching out to me? Had my mere presence somehow awakened her?

It was not a comforting thought. I was a ghost seer, a death walker and sometimes a detective for the unquiet, but I did not embrace my calling. I took no pride in my abilities. I considered my gift a curse because all I'd ever wanted was a normal life. A quiet, peaceful existence, perhaps with a child of my own someday.

But ordinary was not meant to be, and I was coming to accept the painful reality that children were out of the question. I couldn't take a chance that I would pass on my gift just as it had been passed down to me. The ghosts were frightening all on their own, but the malevolent entities that had invaded my world—the Others and the in-betweens, the malcontents and the shadow beings—made for a harrowing existence. I wouldn't wish my life on anyone, especially a child. And as I had only just discovered, there was yet another danger lurking in the dark underbelly of the city. The *Congé* was a secret, fanatical group intent on ridding the living world of any force they perceived as unnatural. If they learned of my gift and the light inside me that attracted the earthbound entities, they would come for me and mine.

So, no, a family wasn't in the cards. I would never willingly subject a child to the horrors and dangers that came with my bloodline.

But…back to this child. Who was she? Why had she been buried in a nameless grave in this sheltered, forsaken corner?

Forsaken perhaps, but not forgotten. The grave had recently been tended. Someone had cleared away dead leaves and planted purple pansies in the bed of the crib. Someone remembered this child. Someone who still grieved for her, perhaps.

The breeze drifted through the willows, tinkling a hidden wind chime. I was so caught up in the mystery of the grave that at first I didn't take note of the melody. And it *was* a melody, distinct and haunting, as if an invisible hand tapped out the notes. Tearing my focus from the portrait, I lifted my gaze to comb the tree branches. The smell of woodbine deepened even though the blooms had long since faded. I felt something in the breeze— no longer a trace of autumn, but an ethereal chill that raised goose bumps along my arms.

Go. Go now, I told myself. *Go back to your work before you get drawn into yet another ghostly puzzle, yet another dangerous mystery.*

But I feared I had already lingered too long.

The sun hovered just above the treetops, but inside the grove of willow trees, a preternatural twilight had fallen. Here, the veil had already thinned and I could see a vague, timorous shadow in the deepest part of the shade. I shuddered, my hand still on the edge of the crib as a whispery missive floated over the grave and into my head. *Mercy...*

"Is someone there?" I called, and then chided myself for my stubborn naïveté. After all these years, after everything I'd seen and heard, I still wanted to believe the presence could be human and benign.

The shadow darted through the wispy strands of the willows and I heard a high-pitched giggle, followed by a muffled thump. Then an old, weathered ball rolled out of the shadows at my feet. I wanted to ignore the overture. I told myself to get on with the exploration of the cemetery, but before I could stop myself, I gave the ball a gentle kick back into the shadows. It was instantly returned, but this time I let it roll into the bushes.

The childish chortle died away and suddenly I sensed a darker emotion. The laughter that followed held no humor and only a remnant of humanness. Fear trickled down my spine as I searched the shade. "Who are you? What do you want from me?"

Mercy.

From who? For what?

It was time to end this game, time to heed the instinct that warned to distance myself from this grave and the specter hiding in the shadows. But when I would have turned to scurry back into the light, my feet tangled in a vine that snaked around the base of the tomb. I hadn't noticed the creeper earlier. It almost seemed as if the woodsy tentacle had slithered in while the ghost had caught my attention. As I bent to free my snared shoelaces, I heard the wind chime again, the sweet, haunting melody inharmonious with the darkness I felt from the entity and that high, mocking titter.

Instinctively, I reached for the key I wore around my neck, a talisman blessed by a divine hand and left to me by my great-grandmother Rose as protection against the ghosts. This provoked an even stronger reaction. A gust blew out of the shadows, so strong the blast felt like a physical assault. I was still bent and off balance, and as I staggered backward, the vine tightened around my ankles, jerking me off my feet. I fell in an ungainly sprawl, stressing my right wrist when I tried to catch myself.

I went down hard, gasping as pain darted up my arm. Cradling my tender wrist, I focused my attention on the shadows. I could see her there, watching me from the gloom. Her face reminded me of the embedded portrait, but she couldn't be the infant's ghost. This girl looked to have been at least ten when she passed. Sisters, perhaps. Dead but still clinging to their mortal bond.

I wanted to know her name, her history, her connection to the infant in the tomb.

I wanted to scramble to my feet, hurry from the cemetery and never look back.

The ghost's childish trickery disturbed me in a way I didn't yet understand. I found myself once again reaching for my talisman, but the key was gone. Frantically, I clutched my neck while tracking the mischievous entity. She giggled again before fading back into the shadows.

Two

I was still crouched on the ground with my gaze pinned to the spot where the ghost had vanished when I realized someone had come upon me. Not a ghost this time, but a human presence. I didn't jump at the intrusion. I'd learned long ago to keep my nerves steady, so I took only a moment to recover my poise as I turned slowly toward the cemetery.

A man dressed in a faded black jacket and tattered jeans stood no more than five feet from me, head slightly cocked as he observed me with surly indifference. I had never met him before, but I recognized him from the description I'd been given by my contact in the group that had hired me. His name was Prosper Lamb and he was the cemetery caretaker, a term I used loosely in his case because not much care had been given to Woodbine over the past several decades. The grounds were overgrown and littered with trash, the graves in bad need of weeding. He hadn't even bothered to pick up the empty beer bottles at the entrance, making me wonder how he managed to keep his job. I'd been told he lived across the road so perhaps proximity was the only requirement.

His gaze on me deepened and I suppressed another shudder as I took in his countenance. I guessed his age to be around forty, but a hard life had carved deep lines in his face. A scar at his neck and another across the back of his hand hinted at a violent past. He was tallish and lean with a hairline that had receded into a deep widow's peak. He hadn't said a word to alert me of his presence or to put me at ease. I had a feeling he enjoyed my discomfort.

I got quickly to my feet as I brushed off my jeans. "Mr. Lamb, isn't it?"

"You must be the restorer," he said in a countrified drawl. "They said you'd be stopping by today."

"Amelia Gray." I offered my hand, but then let it fall back to my side when I saw that his attention was already diverted.

He nodded to the ground at the base of the tomb where I had risen. "Looked like something knocked the wind out of you just now."

"Nothing so dramatic. My shoelaces tangled in a vine and I tripped."

"They're everywhere," he grumbled. "Briars, ivy, swamp morning glory. Pull one up, half a dozen more grow back in its place. No offense, ma'am, but this seems like a mighty big job for such a small woman." His eyes narrowed as he gave me a cool appraisal.

"I appreciate your concern, but I assure you I'm up to the task." I returned his frank assessment. "And what is it you do around here, Mr. Lamb?"

He merely shrugged at my pointed question. "They call me the caretaker, but I don't touch the graves. Not anymore. These days I'm more of a watchman. I keep an eye on things. Chase away the riffraff that has a tendency to gravitate to places like this." He put his hand on his waist, pushing back the wool jacket so that I could glimpse the gun he wore at his hip.

The knowledge that he was armed and quite possibly dangerous did nothing to put me at ease in his presence. I couldn't help noting the isolation of our surroundings. Despite our nearness to the hustle and bustle of downtown Charleston, I doubted a car had strayed this way in a very long time.

His expression turned sardonic as he continued to watch me. His speech cadence and manner of dress put me in the mind of an old-time traveling preacher, also not reassuring.

"You're off the beaten path and not in the safest part of town," he warned. "If you run into trouble, just holler. I'll be around."

"Thank you, Mr. Lamb, but I don't anticipate any trouble."

"No one ever sees it coming. And you can call me Prosper. Or Prop. We'll likely be seeing a lot of each other if you don't get scared off."

"Scared off by what?"

He grinned, displaying a toothy overbite. "Cemeteries can be frightening places, ma'am."

"Not to a cemetery restorer."

He shrugged, letting his jacket fall back into place as his gaze moved to the stone crib behind me. "That one there…she's a strange one."

For one crazy moment, I thought he meant the ghost and I glanced over my shoulder in dread. Then I realized he referred to the stone crib and the portrait of the dead child. "There's no name on the monument. Do you know who she was?"

"Never heard tell," he said. "But that's not the only grave in here without a name. Woodbine is where the well-to-do used to bury their secrets."

"What do you mean?"

His gaze turned sage. "Their bastards and mistresses, if you'll pardon my language. People they kept on the fringes of their lives. They erected all these fine monuments to honor the dead, but they couldn't or wouldn't give them their names. So they laid them to rest here in Woodbine, close enough to visit but separate from the respectable family plots in Magnolia Cemetery."

"I never knew that," I said, intrigued in spite of myself.

"Now you do. Who do you think pays me to watch over them?"

"I assume the same trust that hired me."

He leaned in. "Who do you think sits on the board? Who do you think made the donation to restore this place? Years and years go by and all of a sudden someone is mighty interested in getting this place cleaned up. That doesn't strike you as curious?"

"Not at all. The neighboring cemeteries have been undergoing revitalization for years."

"Maybe that's all it is," he said. "Then again, maybe someone has developed a guilty conscience."

I knew better than to encourage his gossip, but I couldn't help myself. "Who?"

"Well, that is the question, isn't it?" He lifted his head to sniff the air. "Smell that?"

I took a quick breath, drawing in the lingering scent that had been stirred by the ghost. "You mean the woodbine?"

"Nah, that stuff won't bloom again until next spring. I smell something dead."

My gaze darted inadvertently to the spot where the ghost had vanished.

Prosper Lamb walked all around the tomb, testing the air like a bloodhound. "It's fresh. Barely any rot. But I'm never wrong about that smell. I've had a nose for dead things since I was a kid."

My senses had evolved along with my gift, but evidently he was even more sensitive than I was. I didn't smell anything.

"Are you the superstitious type?" he asked suddenly.

"Not really. Why?"

"You're not bothered by corpse birds?"

"Corpse birds?"

"That's what my mama used to call dead birds found on or near graves. She claimed they were signs." As he talked, he reached inside the crib bed and carefully parted the purple blossoms. A second later, he extracted a dead crow, holding it up by the claws so that he could assess the glistening carcass. Even in the shade, I could see the sheen of black feathers and the dull glint in its beady eyes. There was something odd about the way the head dangled...

"Still warm," he said. "Must have just happened."

Foreboding tingled through me. "How do you suppose it died?"

"Sometimes they fall out of the sky without rhyme or reason. This one, though." He glanced up. "Something wrung its neck."

I suppressed another shiver as I quickly scanned the gloomy landscape. "I don't see how it could have just died. I've been here for several minutes and I didn't see anything."

He held the bird out to me. "Feel it for yourself."

"No, that's okay. I believe you. I'm just wondering what could have happened to the poor thing." I found my gaze flashing back to the place where the dead girl had vanished. I fancied I could still hear the echo of her taunting laughter.

My hand went to my throat again before I remembered that Rose's key had gone missing. "I've lost my necklace. If you find a ribbon with a key attached—"

"This one?" He shifted the dead bird to his left hand and reached out with his right to unsnag the ribbon from underneath the hood of the crib. How it had gotten there, I had no idea, unless the ribbon had been caught when I bent over the monument to study the photograph.

"Looks old," he said, dangling the key in the air in much the same way he'd displayed the dead crow. "A good-luck charm?"

"Something like that." I held out my hand.

He eyed the key for a moment longer before dropping it in my palm. "Better hang on to it then. A corpse bird isn't just any old sign. It's a death omen. Finding that dead crow likely means someone else is about to pass."

Three

That night I had the most disturbing dream, undoubtedly triggered by the ghost child's manifestation and by Prosper Lamb's death prophesy. I found myself walking through Woodbine Cemetery, a thick mist swirling around my legs as I searched for all those nameless headstones. I felt an urgency to find them. It seemed imperative that I visit each grave to let the dead know they hadn't been forgotten.

As I entered one of the ornate fences surrounding a plot, I saw my mother and my aunt Lynrose in wicker rockers drinking sweet tea at the edge of an open grave. They were dressed in summer finery, florals and pastels, rather than in heavy mourning attire. I could hear the murmur of their soft drawls as they peered down into the abyss. As I came upon them, Aunt Lynrose looked up with a stern admonishment. "Mind your manners, chile. Don't you go poking your nose in places it doesn't belong."

"Leave her be, Lyn," my mother scolded. "We

should have tended to this business years ago. Now it's up to Amelia to find out the truth."

My aunt worried the gold locket at her throat as she returned her attention to the open grave. "You should know by now, dear sister, that some secrets are best left buried."

I left them muttering to each other as I traveled on through a sea of headstones. Just when I thought I must be hopelessly lost, the mist thinned and I could see the willow trees that lined the riverbank. As I neared the water, the scent of woodbine deepened and I heard the distant tinkle of a wind chime. The haunting melody drew me deeper into the copse, where Prosper Lamb reclined against the stone cradle. He eyed me curiously as I came through the trees.

"That one there...she's a strange one," he warned. "A bad seed, you might say."

I turned to find the ghost child glowering at me from the shadows. She didn't taunt or try to play as she'd done before. Her anger was palpable. I could see blood on her hands and on the white drop-waist dress she wore. She stood upright, but her head dangled at an odd angle like that of the corpse bird she clutched to her chest.

As I started toward her, a powerful wind knocked me back. Struggling to remain upright, I called out to her. "Please stop. You'll hurt me."

Her surly expression never changed, but suddenly she lifted a finger to point at something in the mist over my shoulder. I thought Prosper Lamb must have come up behind me. Still battling that terrible wind, I turned in alarm but my feet tangled in a vine and I hit the ground hard, tumbling over and over as if rolling down a long hill.

I awakened before I hit the bottom, my heart pounding. For a moment I could have sworn I saw the dead child's face hovering over me in the dark, but nothing was there, ghost or otherwise. The night was calm and my dog, Angus, slept peacefully in his bed beneath the window. If he'd sensed an intruder, living or dead, he would have alerted me.

Clutching Rose's key to my breast, I settled back against the pillow. It had only been a dream. I was safe and sound in my own bed, protected from ghosts by the hallowed ground on which the house had been built, and from living intruders by the alarm system I'd recently installed. I was safe. Nothing could get to me here.

Yet my heart wouldn't be still. I checked the time on my phone, noting that it was straight-up midnight. I turned on my side and nestled under the covers, exhausted from the day's work but too unnerved to doze back off. No point in trying to analyze or dissect the disturbing visions. Likely, they didn't mean anything. But I couldn't bring myself to believe that. Dreams were often portents, and I couldn't forget Mama and Aunt Lynrose gazing down into that open grave or Prosper Lamb's warning that the ghost was a bad seed. I didn't believe that, either. A child wasn't inherently evil. Something must have happened in her short life to cause all that pent-up rage.

Outside I could hear the wind in the trees as I lay there sorting through my churning thoughts. I rolled restlessly onto my back and watched shadows flail across the ceiling as the chimes in the back garden jangled. I listened intently to that distant sound, dread seeping down into my bones. The discordant notes melded into a distinctive melody, one that I had heard in Woodbine Cemetery that very day.

I tried to ignore the haunting descant, drawing the quilt up over my ears. I wouldn't get up from my warm bed to go explore. I would not. It was the wind stirring the chimes and nothing more. But the melancholy strands floated through the house, luring me from under the covers and down the hallway to my office. I stood on bare feet at one of the long windows, arms hugging my waist as I peered out into the nocturnal landscape. I'd had security lights installed along with the alarm system and now I could peer into almost every corner. I trailed my gaze along the snowy beds of sweet alyssum, through the camellias and up into the tea olives. The leaves fluttered in the breeze, but no one was about. Nothing was amiss.

Go back to bed, Amelia. Stop borrowing trouble.

But I couldn't turn away from the window. I couldn't turn my back on the night. Something was wrong. I could feel it with every fiber of my being.

As I stood watching the shadows, something crashed into the window directly in front of me. I stumbled back, hand to my heart. At first I thought it must be a night bird disoriented by the reflection of moonlight on glass, but I hadn't seen so much as a darting shadow.

The sound came again and again. It was rhythmic and jarring, a steady *bam, bam, bam* that made me think of a ball being bounced against the window. And that made me think of the ball that had rolled to my feet in Woodbine Cemetery. Had the ghost child followed me home? Had she manifested in my garden? I couldn't see her. I couldn't yet feel her cold, but I sensed she was near.

The banging against the window increased, a hard, rapid volley that rattled the glass and set off my security alarm. Angus started barking and did not let up even when I hurried down the hall to deactivate the system. I returned to the window, my heart hammering a painful staccato as I stared out into the empty backyard. This was not a playful taunting; this was malevolent. I feared the ghost wouldn't relent until the glass shattered into a million pieces.

"Please stop," I pleaded.

Mercy, came the silent rejoinder.

"You'll break the glass. You'll hurt me."

Mercy, the ghost demanded.

"Mercy," I whispered.

The pounding stopped. Angus fell silent. The wind died away, leaving an unholy stillness in the garden.

Four

I awakened the next morning to the soothing sound of rain on my roof. I got up and dressed for the cemetery, but the deluge showed no sign of letting up. Work had always been my escape in times of stress and confusion, but today I felt a keen sense of relief that I could put off a return to Woodbine. The experience at my office window had left me unnerved. The ghost child wanted something from me and I hated to think what she might do next to get my attention.

But even apart from the dread I had of the apparition and her intentions, I had no desire to run into Prosper Lamb again. I had felt something in the caretaker's presence—an indefinable foreshadowing—that worried me. I wasn't comfortable with his proximity. I didn't want him watching over me. I would have much preferred a solitary restoration, but I had no control over his comings and goings.

Trapped inside, I spent the morning catching up on bills and invoices, and that afternoon, I worked on my blog, *Digging Graves*. The crib monument had so intrigued me that I decided to write about the history of such headstones. The more I researched, the deeper my fascination became until the single blog post I'd originally envisioned turned into a series of articles I called "The Loneliest Graves: An Exploration of Symbolism and Traditions Associated with Infant Burials."

Hours passed unnoticed as I became engrossed in my work. It was cozy in my office with the rain streaming down the windows and Angus curled up nearby. I sipped tea and contentedly typed away, stopping only when the drag of exhaustion called me to bed just before midnight.

Without any ominous dreams or ghostly interruptions, I slept the sleep of the dead and awakened to another rainy day. I returned to my writing, but by midmorning, I was starting to go a little stir-crazy. I drove down to Waterfront Park and then, grabbing my umbrella, exited the car for a soggy stroll along East Bay Street and the Battery. The weather had chased the tourists inside and I had the walkway to myself. I went all the way to the point of the peninsula and watched the waves for a few minutes before turning back.

The downpour shrouded the mansions along Battery Row, but even so, I stopped to admire them as I almost always did on my morning walks. The towering spectacles were a mixture of architectural styles representing the peak of Charleston's grandeur. Like most of the old houses south of Broad Street, they had been passed down from generation to generation. The Devlin abode was one of the largest on East Bay, a shimmering white Renaissance Revival with three stories of columns and a rooftop pavilion from which the family's ancestors had undoubtedly viewed the Battle of Fort Sumter in Charleston Harbor.

Once upon a time, I'd had a connection to that house, though I'd never been inside and had never met the current owner, Jonathan Devlin. Until a year ago last spring, I'd had a relationship with his grandson, John Devlin, a former police detective who was the heir apparent to the Devlin home and to the family fortune. Our breakup had not been mutual and I'd spent the past eighteen months brooding about his reasons and motivations when I should have long since relegated him to a distant corner of my memory. But no matter what I did or where I went, I couldn't seem to forget him. Scarcely a night went by I didn't ache for him, that I didn't dream about being back in his arms. Mornings were cold, cruel awakenings.

Not only had Devlin broken my heart, but he'd also returned to a life he once rejected. He'd resigned from the police department, taken control of the family's holdings and, rumor had it, he'd moved back into his grandfather's mansion. Sometimes in my weaker moments, I wondered if the reason he'd left was because I didn't have an acceptable pedigree. I wasn't a suitable match for someone who came from a world I could only gaze at from afar. The Devlin family was one of the old-

est and wealthiest in the city. They had been here
since the founding of Charleston over three hundred years ago. My people came from the mountains.

But that was too simplistic an explanation for
our estrangement and didn't take into account his
family's sinister connections—those dark alliances
and shadowy associations, some of which were
only now surfacing. It was hard enough to accept
Devlin's recent engagement, let alone the possibility that as a member of the secret and deadly
Congé, he might now be my mortal enemy.

As I stared across the street, the base of my
spine tingled. Little wonder, I told myself. For all I
knew, Devlin might be inside at that very moment.
Even the mere possibility of his nearness fluttered
my heart. But it was more than that. Someone
watched me.

My grip tightened around the umbrella as I
searched the windows and balconies and the rain-
soaked garden. I didn't see anyone until I shifted
my focus to the third floor and then my pulse
jumped. Devlin stood in an open doorway, arms
folded, one shoulder propped against the frame.
The moment our gazes collided, he came out onto
the balcony, leaning his forearms against the bal-
ustrade as he peered down at me.

I couldn't help but shudder at his intensity. I
knew the weight of that stare only too well. I had
felt the singularity of his focus in anger and in passion. As I stood frozen, rain pattering against my

umbrella, forbidden memories stirred to life—his husky drawl in the warm darkness...those obsidian eyes hard upon me as my legs locked around him...

I banished the images, reminding myself that Devlin was engaged now and some memories were best left buried. But even as I hardened my resolve, even as I tried to turn away from him, I could feel the pressure of his fingers around my arms, the feathery brush of his lips at my nape. It was as if he had come up behind me, coaxing me back against him as he wrapped me in a heated embrace. The sensation was so real and so powerful, I had the strongest urge to turn into him, to draw his face down to mine for a kiss. My hand lifted as if to touch him, but I quickly dropped it to my side and took a long breath to quiet my racing heart.

"Don't," I whispered.

He stared down at me for another long moment—almost defiantly, I thought—before he straightened and went back inside, leaving me alone and shivering in the rain.

I didn't like wallowing in misery and self-pity, so I drove over to the Charleston Institute for Parapsychology Studies for a quick visit with my friend and mentor, Dr. Rupert Shaw. He and Papa were the only ones I could turn to in times of paranormal upheaval, but today I wanted his company as much as his advice.

Once we were settled in his cozy but perpetually cluttered office with cups of soothing chamomile before us, I told him about my new project at Woodbine Cemetery and my encounter with Prosper Lamb.

"Do you know anything about Woodbine?" I asked.

"Most of the cemeteries in that area are on the committee's register of historic burial grounds," he said absently as he sipped his tea.

"Yes, some of the graves are pre–Civil War. According to the caretaker, Woodbine has a rather sordid history."

"Indeed?"

His response was so incurious I wondered if he'd heard me at all. Earlier when I'd called, he had seemed genuinely glad to hear from me, but now he appeared distracted and more than a little dispirited. He watched the rain through the garden doors with a brooding frown.

I set my teacup aside. "I have a feeling I've come at a bad time."

He gave a dismissive wave. "Nonsense. You're always welcome here. You know that."

"Yes, but I shouldn't take advantage of your good nature. I'll go now and come back another day."

"No, stay put, my dear. The rain has made me gloomy and reflective. Left to my own devices, I could easily become maudlin. Your company is a welcome diversion. No one can cheer me up the way you do."

"Which is surprising, considering the things we normally discuss," I teased. "We could talk about you for a change. I have the unfortunate tendency to dominate our conversations, but I am a good listener."

"That's a kind offer and I appreciate your concern, but I'm fine. I'd rather hear more about your work. What's this about a sordid history?"

I nodded as I settled back against my chair. It was obvious he had something on his mind, but I wouldn't press him. "It may be nothing more than gossip or an urban legend, but I'm intrigued by the caretaker's claim of buried secrets. He says Woodbine is where the city's well-to-do interred the people on the fringes of their lives. Mistresses, for example, and the children that came from those illicit unions."

"Cemeteries are more your domain than mine," Dr. Shaw said. "But I would never underestimate the decadence and callousness of the upper crust nor the extraordinary lengths they've gone to over the years to keep a stranglehold on their fortunes and legacies." There was an uncharacteristic bitterness in his tone that made me wonder again about his despondency.

"Like forming the Order of the Coffin and the Claw," I said. "And the *Congé*."

"Any number of closed and exclusive societies—the latter, of course, being far more sinister than the former."

I leaned forward, searching his careworn face

and feeling faintly alarmed by the sallowness of his skin and the dark circles beneath his eyes. He had the look of a distraught man, but perhaps his mood really was attributable to the gloomy weather. Still, his attire seemed more threadbare than usual and his thick cap of white hair wasn't as sleekly groomed as I'd come to expect. He had turned to the garden, watching the rain in glum fascination until I softly called him back.

He stirred and offered an apologetic smile. "I'm sorry, my dear. My mind keeps wandering but it has nothing to do with the company. You were saying?"

"I asked if you'd found out anything more about the *Congé.*"

"I've pulled back on my research. One of my sources became concerned that the inquiries had been noticed, and it seemed prudent to keep a low profile, at least for the time being. What I do know is that the *Congé*, with the exception of a very small and fervent faction, went dormant for a long period of time. As of late, there's been resurgence. A powerful reawakening, I'm told. Old connections have been reestablished, while new members have been recruited. The *Congé* remain rooted in the occult, but they are also deeply embedded in the mainstream—business, government, finance. Like the Order of the Coffin and the Claw, they favor their own and eschew the unknown. Their primary motivation is to protect and maintain the status quo. But the *Congé* take it one step further. They fancy themselves kingmakers with a divine mandate. They use the fears and superstitions bred by these turbulent times to satiate their lust for power."

"Who's behind the resurgence?"

His mouth tightened as he set aside his teacup with a clatter. "My sources either don't know or won't say, but I wonder if Jonathan Devlin might not be at the heart of it all."

I stared at him in shock. "Why would you think that?"

"It's nothing more than speculation, but the Devlin name features prominently on the list I told you about weeks ago."

"The membership list?"

He nodded as he twisted his pinkie ring, the snake-and-talon insignia all too familiar to me by now. "Think about what we know of their recruitment. They conscript from exclusive groups like the Order of the Coffin and the Claw, and there is no doubt whatsoever that the Devlins have had a long and intimate history with the Order."

"As do you," I pointed out. "You've never actually admitted your association, but you wear their emblem just as Devlin does."

"You're referring to my ring," he said with a twinkle in his eyes. "I believe I once told you that I picked it up at a flea market."

"That is what you said."

"Even if I had once been affiliated with the Order, someone with my background and interests would never have been allowed into the exalted inner circle. And after my unseemly dismissal from Emerson University, I would have been further marginalized if not outright ostracized."

"Is that what happened?"

He stared down at the ring. "*If* such a thing had happened, someone with my disposition, stripped of my reputation and power, might take a perverse pleasure in finding the venerated emblem at a lowly flea market. I might enjoy wearing said token, not out of vanity or misplaced loyalty, but as a poke in the eye at the elites. After all, they do like to keep their symbols unsullied."

"I can see how that would be satisfying," I said, not knowing whether or not I believed him. Claws were notoriously wily. "So the *Congé* recruits only from this exalted inner circle? Is that how they've remained under the radar for so long? Most of the Order wouldn't even be aware of them then."

"Correct. As I've said before, the elite chosen from the elite. The Devlin name carries the weight of aristocracy and tradition, perhaps more than any other of the old families. They've managed to remain virtually untainted through the generations, despite John's marriage to Mariama Goodwine. My guess is, Jonathan Devlin knows he isn't long for this world so he's putting his affairs in order and cementing his legacy."

"And he expects John to take over when he's gone?"

"He is the grandson and heir apparent. The only

other living Devlin so far as I know. That in itself adds cachet."

Once the conversation turned to Devlin, I found myself back on the Battery staring up at that third-story balcony. The intensity of his stare lingered in the prickle at my nape and in the sudden thud of my heart.

"I've always been very fond of John," Dr. Shaw said with a sigh. "I believe that, unlike his grandfather, he is at heart an honorable man. But if I'm allowed to speak plainly, the more distance you put between yourself and the Devlins, the better off you'll be."

"That is plainly spoken," I said.

"I've never made any secret of my disdain for Jonathan Devlin. He is a cold, ruthless man who destroys anyone unfortunate enough to find themselves in his path."

"That's a very bold statement. I wasn't aware you knew him that well."

His gaze hardened. "We haven't traveled in the same circle for years, but my opinion hasn't changed. And if I'm right about his connection to the *Congé*, he is also very dangerous. As I said, you should stay far away from that family."

"So it would seem," I murmured, still taken aback by the sharpness in his tone. I'd never seen Dr. Shaw like this, even during the time he'd been under the influence of a diabolical assistant. He didn't seem drugged or dazed today, but he was clearly preoccupied and not a little perturbed.

We both fell silent, lost in our own chaotic thoughts. Then Dr. Shaw let out another heavy sigh. "I've said enough about Jonathan Devlin. He is not a fit subject for such a gray day. We should get back to the subject of Woodbine."

"Because a cemetery is such a cheerful topic," I said with a smile.

"For us it is."

"Yes." I was happy enough to comply. For some reason, Dr. Shaw's animosity toward Devlin's grandfather made me uneasy, even though he was right to worry. Any member of the *Congé*, let alone the leader, could be lethal to someone like me and perhaps to Dr. Shaw, as well. "Here's something that might interest you," I said. "Woodbine has a ghost."

Dr. Shaw lifted a snowy brow. "Only one?"

"I've seen just the one, though I have a feeling the cemetery is a very haunted place. All those buried secrets." I shivered. "This ghost is the spirit of a little girl. And she appears to be a very angry entity."

"Do you know why?"

"I don't even know who she was. The only clue I have is an unnamed grave hidden within a copse of willow trees. The memorial is carved in the shape of a crib and the nameplate has only birth and death dates. The ghost seems to have a connection to this grave and I thought at first she was the spirit of the child buried there. But the infant died at the age of two and the ghost girl appears to have been ten or so when she passed."

"Sisters?"

"That was my second thought. The ghost child came to my house last night and almost broke a window. I didn't see her, but I sensed her out in the garden. She manifests with the smell of honeysuckle and a strange, haunting melody that I can sometimes hear in the wind chimes."

"Intriguing."

"Very. Before she appeared last night, I had a dream about her. The caretaker called her a bad seed."

"Do you think that explains her anger?"

"No. Despite what I've read about an evil gene, I don't believe children are born bad. Something happens in their life to turn them."

"Or someone."

Too late, I thought of his son, Ethan, a man with dark secrets and deadly tendencies. Ethan Shaw hadn't been born evil and Dr. Shaw had certainly been a benevolent if somewhat absentminded role model. They had always seemed close. And yet Ethan Shaw had fallen prey to outside manipulations and his own misplaced affections until one day he had brought a gun to my house and shot Devlin in cold blood before he, himself, had been shot and killed.

I wondered if Dr. Shaw was also thinking about his son and if I should openly acknowledge the tender subject. Or should I pretend the awkward silence was only a lull in the conversation?

"Looking back, you think you can pinpoint exactly when they made the wrong turn," he mused. "Where and why mistakes were made. And then years later you learn, quite unexpectedly, that you never really had a clue. Forces were at play you never saw coming." He picked up a silver letter opener from his desk and absently fingered the edge.

"I—yes, that's probably true." I felt bad that he couldn't open up to me in a more direct way. He had helped me through so many difficult times and he was obviously in the throes of rumination and regret. I wondered what had put him in such a state, the where and the why of his current deliberation.

Absently, he twisted the letter opener in his hand until the jewel in the handle caught the light. Something about his fixation chilled me. Then he rallied and gave me a tenuous smile. "Your ghost. Why do you think she tried to break your window?"

I shrugged. "She wants my attention. And like all the others, she needs my help."

"Will you help her?"

"Do I ever really have a choice? I keep hoping she'll just fade away. But they never have before." Now it was I who sank into gloomy contemplation. "I think other forces may be at play here, too, Dr. Shaw. I don't know how to explain it, but I've had moments of déjà vu lately. Callbacks to my past that I can't help but think have meaning. I have this looming dread that something is coming to a head. Or to an end. The caretaker found a dead crow in the bed of the crib. He called it a corpse bird. He said it was a sign that someone else was about to pass."

"Birds have been considered harbingers since the beginning of time. It's true that a dead bird is often thought to be an omen, but like the death card in a tarot deck, it may not signify a literal passing." Dr. Shaw observed me with kindly eyes. "It could be the death of something you've held on to for too long. An old relationship, for instance. Or the passing of an era. As with all things that end, the way then becomes clear for new opportunities. Perhaps a new destination."

On the surface, his words seemed hopeful, but for me, they dropped like anvils and I felt a keen sense of loss for something that had yet to go missing. "I'm not sure that interpretation makes me feel a good deal better."

"Letting go is a very hard thing," he said. "Grief and guilt, even loneliness, can become a comfort. A touchstone. The road behind us, littered as it is with mistakes and heartache, can often be more appealing than the open road in front of us."

"I hear what you're saying and I don't disagree, but in this case, I can't help thinking the omen may have a more straightforward implication. I've been having strange dreams. Premonitions. The corpse bird can be interpreted literally, can't it?"

"Oh, yes," he said, still toying with the letter opener. "A dead bird can most definitely be the harbinger of a physical death."

Five

I shook off the lingering effects of that unsettling conversation and rewarded myself with another long afternoon of research. Seated in my office with my back to the windows, I switched my focus from "The Loneliest Graves" to the business of restoring Woodbine Cemetery. I'd located a map in the local archives and had already begun a preliminary perusal of the records through the online databases of the main library and the county clerk's office. But the unnamed graves would require a more thorough digging.

As I worked, I was drawn back time and again to that stone crib hidden in the willow trees. I had the child's birth and death dates, so I felt certain I could eventually uncover her identity. But after a few hours at the computer, I remained stymied. Either the databases weren't up to date or her birth and death had been recorded in another county. Or—a more troubling prospect—the official records had been purged. That seemed a drastic action but one that might corroborate Prosper

Lamb's assertion about the well-to-do and their buried secrets.

I kept at it until early evening, when a phone call from Temple Lee drew me back out of the house for dinner. I'd once worked for Temple at the State Archeologist's Office in Columbia and we'd remained close after my relocation to Charleston to start my own business. I didn't often go out on weeknights, but a diversion was just what I needed, and Temple was always an entertaining dinner companion.

By the time I left the house, the rain had finally stopped, and the dripping city basked in a golden glow as the sun sank below the church spires. I decided to walk over to Meeting Street, taking time for a brief stroll through one of the city's churchyards before arriving at Rapture, a restaurant housed in a beautiful old building that had once been a rectory. I had learned on a previous visit that the place had been built on hallowed ground. No ghost could touch me inside and I was more than happy to leave the dead world behind me if only for the space of a meal.

But all through dinner, my mind kept straying back to that nameless grave and to the ghost child that had hovered nearby. I couldn't help wondering if she had manifested near the crib for a reason. She and the infant had a connection—to each other and possibly to me—that I had yet to discern. No matter how badly I wished to escape another netherworld puzzle, I could already feel the chill of her pull.

Thankfully, Temple seemed equally distracted and paid no attention to my pensive mood. The restaurant was crowded for a Wednesday night and even as she regaled me with a tale from a current excavation, her gaze darted now and then to the entrance and she seemed uncharacteristically fidgety. Lately, I seemed to have that effect on people.

Finally I put down my fork as I followed her gaze. "Are you expecting someone?"

"No, why?" she asked innocently, tucking back her hair. She was dressed in teal silk tonight, a lovely bold shade that complemented her coloring. Gold earrings dangled from her lobes and it seemed to me that she'd taken extra care with her makeup. She always looked fabulous but I didn't think her fine-tuning was for my benefit.

"You keep watching the door," I said.

She smiled and shrugged. "Just checking out the scenery. No harm in that, is there?"

"No, but I'm not sure I believe you. You have the look of someone who's up to something. Or hiding something." I was only half joking. Canting my head, I pretended to study her. "What's going on with you? The way you keep watching that door makes me wonder if you had an ulterior motive for your last-minute dinner invitation. And why, out of all the restaurants in Charleston, you asked me to meet you at this one."

"I didn't feel like eating alone and as to the

restaurant…lovely atmosphere, impeccable service and—" she motioned to her plate "—the best shrimp and grits in the city. Not to mention the lavender ice cream. Why wouldn't I choose Rapture?"

"I can think of one reason," I murmured uneasily, picking at my mushroom crepe. The rustic restaurant truly was beautiful. Candles flickered from wall sconces. Soft music played in the background. Our table looked out into the garden, where glowing lanterns seemed to float down from the tree branches. Without any hovering ghosts, the setting was dreamy and peaceful, but I couldn't stop thinking dark thoughts.

"Do you remember the last time we came here together?" I asked with a shiver. "You invited Ethan Shaw to join us. He's been on my mind today."

Temple grimaced. "Such a charming, elegant man, or so he seemed. Who would have ever guessed he had that kind of darkness inside him? I knew him for years. We worked together on a number of excavations and I never had an inkling."

"No one did. That's what made him so dangerous. And tragic."

She gave me a strange look. "John Devlin was here that night, too, remember? You'd only just met, but I could tell you were already falling for him. And I knew he would be trouble. I warned you about getting involved with someone like him."

"Someone out of my league."

"Someone with his past," she corrected. She searched my face in the candlelight. "Given how things turned out, do you ever wish you'd taken my advice?"

"That's a complicated question." And one I'd pondered often on sleepless nights when the house seemed too quiet and my bed too empty.

"Well?" Temple prompted as she regarded me across the table.

I drew a long breath and released it. "No, I'm not sorry. Not at all. Despite everything, I wouldn't trade a moment of my time with Devlin."

"Spoken like a hopeless romantic."

"Is that a bad thing?"

"It can be." She picked up her wineglass but didn't drink. Instead she stared into the dregs as if trying to divine an acceptable explanation. "You've created a fairy tale around that man. A romantic fantasy with which no ordinary mortal can compete. That's why you can't move on. This fascination you have for him has never been good for you, Amelia. I hope you can see that now."

Her words stung more than they should have, perhaps because they hit a little too close to home. "I did try to move on, and look where it got me."

She winced. "The police detective, you mean. The one down in Beaufort County. Yes, that was unfortunate."

Unfortunate? The man had tried to kill me. "Devlin's engaged now. I've accepted that."

"Have you?" A smile flitted. "You *sound* convincing, but I've known you for a long time and you've always been adept at putting on a good face." She paused as if contemplating whether or not to push on, but Temple had never been one to hold back. "Have you seen him since you've been back in Charleston?"

"Only in passing." I continued to pick absently at my food as I pictured him on that third-story balcony. Memories stirred yet again but I batted them away.

"He hasn't tried to contact you?"

"No." At least not in the way she meant.

"Doesn't his silence tell you something? You just came through a harrowing ordeal. You were nearly murdered by a madman and he can't be bothered to call and see if you're all right? Does he even know what happened to you?"

I shrugged off the question, murmuring something purposefully vague, but I knew Devlin was fully cognizant of the dangers I'd encountered during my last restoration. He had even whispered in my ear to warn me. I couldn't explain the how or the why of it to Temple because she would ridicule the concept of an astral traveler—someone who could separate the spiritual self from the corporal body.

My belief about Devlin's astral wanderings stemmed from something Dr. Shaw had told me during my Seven Gates ordeal: *I knew a young man once, a traveler who claimed to have looked into a hellish abyss. He was so shaken by the sight that he tried for years to convince himself what he experienced was nothing more than a nightmare. I don't think he ever traveled again—at least not consciously. He had a fear of being trapped in such a place.*

It was possible Devlin wasn't even aware of his ability, but it would explain so much about his younger days at the Charleston Institute for Parapsychology Studies and his subsequent rejection of all things paranormal. It would explain so much about *him*.

I rubbed a hand up and down my chilled arm. "This conversation has taken a bad turn."

"Yes, we've grown morose," Temple agreed. "Let's talk about something else, something pleasant. Tell me about this new project of yours. You said the cemetery is local, correct?"

I nodded and started to relax as our wineglasses were replenished and we drifted into more comfortable conversation territory. "It's located at the end of a narrow street off Algonquin Road, practically in the shadow of Magnolia Cemetery. But Woodbine is much smaller, only a few acres. And unlike the other cemeteries in the area, it's been badly neglected for decades. The fence is so overgrown with honeysuckle vines, you'd never know a cemetery lies behind it if not for the taller monuments."

"But didn't you mention something about a caretaker?" Temple asked as she shot another glance toward the entrance.

"That's what I was told, but now that I've met him, I think that job description was greatly exaggerated. By his own admission, he doesn't touch the graves. He's more of a watchman. According to him, he's there to chase away the riffraff."

"Which may not be a bad thing if the cemetery is as isolated as you say," she pointed out.

"True. But I don't know that Prosper Lamb's presence makes me feel a good deal safer."

"Prosper Lamb. What an interesting name."

"He's an interesting man and he does seem to know quite a lot about the cemetery. He told me that Woodbine was once used by the well-to-do to bury their secrets. Their mistresses and bastards, people they kept on the fringes of their lives."

"Well, that's a rather sleazy concept, isn't it?" Temple's eyes gleamed and I could tell that I'd hooked her in a way that I hadn't been able to engage Dr. Shaw. She was itching to know more, but we both fell silent as the waiter approached and the table was cleared. We ordered after-dinner drinks—a cordial for her and a cup of tea for me. Once we were alone again, she leaned in. "Go on. I want to hear more about these buried secrets. You know how I relish the salacious."

"At least you admit it." I cast a quick glance around, more out of habit than any real fear of being overheard. "Mr. Lamb said that's the reason Woodbine has so many unnamed graves. The wealthy benefactors bought the finest monuments to commemorate the passing of their loved ones, but they wouldn't allow their names to be inscribed in the stones. Whether any of it is true or not…who knows?" I looked up with a smile as a cup of tea was placed before me.

"It wouldn't surprise me," Temple said, cradling her glass. "Image and reputation were once everything to the blue bloods in this city. People would do anything, including commit murder, to protect their status. To be honest, I'm not sure times have changed that much."

Dr. Shaw had said much the same thing, but I didn't want to get into the *Congé* can of worms with Temple. I had no idea how to go about explaining the organization to a nonbeliever.

"I'm inclined to agree, especially since I can't seem to locate some of the records. If I were the suspicious type, I might think someone had purposely removed them." I sipped the tea absently as my thoughts drifted back to the cemetery. "I ran across one of the unnamed graves the other day, that of a little girl who died at the age of two. I haven't been able to find out who she was."

"Hers are the missing records?"

I nodded. "I may be jumping to conclusions. It's possible her birth and death were recorded in another county. But, Temple…" I paused on an inexplicable shiver. "Something about her burial won't let me go. I know it sounds strange, but finding her grave has had a powerful effect on me."

"In what way?"

"I can't explain it, really. Maybe it's because she

died so young or because her memorial is shaped like an old-fashioned baby crib. There's even an embedded portrait of her beneath the hood. The whole presentation haunts me."

"How very sad it sounds. But you know why it haunts you, don't you? It's our inherent fear of children."

"What?"

"It's true. We all have it. We fear their vulnerability because it forces us to face the prospect of our own mortality. If a child can die, what's to bind the rest of us to this mortal coil?"

"That may be profound and a bit muddled all at the same time," I said. "I do agree that every tiny grave is affecting. This one, though—" I broke off, still trying to analyze my reaction. "It almost seems as if I have a personal connection to her. I don't see how. She died long before I was born." Although in my family, the impossible was never out of the question, and I labored under no delusion that all our secrets had been uncovered.

"And there's nothing else on the stone to identify her?"

"Just her birth and death dates and an inscription that reads Shush... Lest She Awaken."

"You've given me goose bumps." Temple held out her arm so that I could see her pebbled flesh in the candlelight.

"I know. The phrasing is unsettling," I agreed. "But sleep and rest references are common on graves, especially those of children. I mean, think about where the word *cemetery* comes from. Literally, dormitory or sleeping place in Greek."

"That doesn't make the epitaph any less creepy."

"No, but it helps to put it in context. Remember, rural cemeteries were originally designed as parks where families could congregate with their children. In *that* context, sleep imagery was considered more appropriate for young eyes. I've been researching infant burials in general and..." My words faded as I realized I'd already lost her attention.

Her focus had once again shifted to the entrance and something about her expression, a subtle flicker of emotion, made me turn to see who had come in. A man stood just inside the doorway, his imperious gaze sweeping the dining room. He seemed to vector in on our table and something unpleasant crawled up my spine as our gazes briefly locked.

Until recently, I had never considered myself clairvoyant or psychic or even particularly intuitive, but the evolution of my gift had introduced me to any number of new sensations and abilities. For that reason, I didn't discount the uncanny premonition that suddenly gripped me. My heart thudded as I stared back at the stranger. His features seemed to eerily morph into the beady eyes and gaping beak of the corpse bird Prosper Lamb had plucked from the stone crib. I even detected an iridescent gleam in his dark hair. It was a very disconcerting vision and I quickly blinked to dispel the image.

The man's face settled back into its normal appearance, but my nerves bristled with unease. He looked familiar and I wondered where I might have met him. He was tallish and trim and I judged his age to be mid to late fifties. I could see a sprinkling of silver throughout his dark hair, and his face was a healthy golden shade that no tanning bed or spray could replicate. I couldn't place him, but I recognized the cut and drape of a well-tailored suit and the carriage of a man who had unquestionably been raised in the lap of luxury.

He gave a surprised, pleased nod when his attention moved across the table to Temple and she looked suitably taken aback by his arrival even though I suspected he was the reason we had come to this restaurant in the first place.

"Who is that?" I asked, thrown off guard by the man's disquieting presence and by my bizarre reaction to him.

Temple glanced at me in surprise. "You don't recognize him? That's Rance Duvall."

His back was to me now as he turned to greet someone beyond my view. Released from his gaze, my pulse steadied, but I still felt quite shaken. "Rance Duvall," I mused. "Why do I know that name?"

"In Charleston, you would be hard-pressed not to know his name." Temple lowered her voice. "He's one of *the* Duvalls. As in Duvall Island.

His family has been around for generations." She waited for me to make the connection and when I appeared suitably impressed, she continued. "He's also active in local politics, especially on issues regarding zoning and historic preservation. I wouldn't be at all surprised if your paths had crossed at some point."

I watched as others joined him and the party was guided into a private dining room. "He does look familiar, but I can't remember when or where we may have met. How do you know him?"

"One of the burial mounds we're excavating is located on Duvall Island. He's given us unlimited access and even arranged for the use of some very expensive equipment. Considering all the resistance and red tape that we're usually up against, his cooperation has been refreshing, to say the least."

Somehow I didn't think professional collaboration or cooperation was the extent of Temple's appreciation for Rance Duvall. I felt the need to warn her about what I'd seen in his visage. But what had I seen—or sensed? "Did you know he would be here tonight? Is that why you chose this restaurant?"

She smiled. "Happy coincidence."

"Sure it is. And your fixation on the entrance was just my imagination."

"It was." But she didn't try very hard to convince me. If anything, her smile turned self-satisfied as she picked up her napkin and dabbed at the corners of her mouth. "As long as we're both here, you don't mind if I go say a quick hello, do you?"

I did mind but I could give her no good reason for my objection. "Would it do any good if I said yes?"

She scooted back her chair and stood. "None whatever."

"That's what I thought. Temple—" Her name came out harsher than I'd meant it.

She lifted a querying brow. "What?"

I shook my head. "Nothing. Be careful."

She gave me an odd look before turning away from the table.

Six

I used Temple's absence for a trip to the ladies' room, where I applied a layer of lip gloss and tightened my ponytail. I examined my reflection as I washed my hands and dried them on a paper towel. Like Dr. Shaw, I had dark circles under my eyes from stress and lack of sleep. A ghost visit always took a toll and I didn't think I'd seen the last of this one. A part of me did wish she would fade away without further contact, but my curiosity had been roused despite my dread.

Leaning in, I stared at those dark circles as if I could somehow wish them away. And then I focused even more intently until the tiny motes at the bottoms of my pupils took on the look of keyholes. How many times had I wished for the ability to see into those openings, to peer so deeply into my psyche and soul that I could somehow divine my destiny?

The prospect of knowing the road ahead was at once intriguing and terrifying, I backed away from the mirror, turning my attention once again to the smudges beneath my eyes. Poor Dr. Shaw. I'd tried not to dwell on our conversation, but his mannerisms and vague musings about wrong turns had left me disquieted. And then how strange to already have Ethan Shaw on my mind when Temple had called to invite me to the very restaurant where the three of us had spent our first evening together.

The universe was aligning in strange and disturbing ways, and somehow at the center of it all was Woodbine Cemetery. Ever since I'd been awarded the project, there'd been so many references to my past.

I was still brooding about all those niggling moments as I left the ladies' room, but none was quite as unnerving as the sight of John Devlin standing in the alcove blocking my path just as he had done once before, in this very space, in this very restaurant. He leaned a shoulder against the wall and managed to look surprised, but my suspension of disbelief only extended so far. He must have seen me leave the table and followed me into the alcove to wait for me. Why, I couldn't imagine, but a happenstance meeting this was not.

I faltered, but only for a moment. Then I mentally braced myself as I moved forward, already feeling the heady pull of his orbit. His eyes were just as dark and perhaps even more mesmerizing than I remembered. He was tall, lean and still otherworldly handsome though his looks had changed. The five-o'clock shadow had become a perpetual feature, it seemed, as had the longer hair and his more casual attire.

My throat tightened as I approached and I hoped I wouldn't embarrass myself, either by being tongue-tied or blurting something far too revealing.

As it happened, Devlin was the first to speak. "Amelia," he drawled. "Just like old times."

He spoke softly, intimately, and yet I had no trouble at all hearing him over the din of the restaurant. His voice drew a quiver and I closed my eyes briefly, steeling myself against his unfair ambush.

"Hello" was all I could manage, along with a brief smile. I clung to my poise, but it was a feat hardly worth celebrating because I should have been over John Devlin a long time ago. I should have been dining with a new lover rather than an old friend, and I set my chin with an accusing jut, as if the blame for my bleak love life rested solely on Devlin's shoulders.

He said, "This seems to be quite the popular place tonight."

"Doesn't it?" My smile turned wry and I added an edge to my voice. "I'm still reeling from the coincidence of it all. You. Me. This alcove."

"One would almost think it planned."

And just like that, poise shattered. I made a nonsensical gesture toward the archway. "I was just on my way back to the table."

He made no move to allow me passage. "You

look good," he said, searching my face and then dropping his gaze for a more subtle scrutiny.

Good, not *well*. I hated myself for taking note of the distinction.

I had on a simple black dress with my mother's pearls. Perfectly safe and acceptable attire, but that dark gaze made me feel as if I had on nothing at all.

"You, as well," I said. "I mean, good. You look good. Different, but…good." Why did that scruff on his lower face appeal to me so? Or those silver strands at his temples? I had the strongest urge to run the back of my hand against the stubble and then plunge my fingers into his hair. Instead, I toyed with the string of pearls at my neck. I could feel my great-grandmother's key beneath my dress and I wondered if I should pull it free and hold it in front of me to ward off Devlin's magnetism.

As we stood there with very little else to say to one another, it occurred to me that perhaps this moment was the essence of Dr. Shaw's explanation of a death omen. Not a literal passing, but the end of something I'd been hanging on to. I'd been carrying a torch for Devlin for far too long and I waited for that moment of supreme revelation when the weight of unrequited love lifted miraculously from my shoulders, saving me from all those sleepless nights and liberating me for the open road ahead.

Instead, I found myself jostled by someone

passing by in the corridor. I was pushed up against Devlin and my heart jolted.

His arm came around me, so fleeting I might have imagined the caress. But for a moment, I felt the pressure of his fingers against the small of my back and I closed my eyes, drawing in that delectable, indefinable essence that was so uniquely John Devlin.

"Sorry," I mumbled and pushed away.

"You're here with Temple," he said.

"And you? You aren't dining alone tonight, are you?"

The question was a throwback to that first night when he had come to the restaurant alone, but I instantly berated myself. What a stupid thing to ask of an old flame that had recently gotten engaged. I'd momentarily forgotten about his betrothal. Now it all came rushing back to me and as an image of Claire Bellefontaine's perfect face flashed before my eyes, I did have a revelation.

I thought about the other time Devlin and I had stood here in this alcove and the conversation had turned to Ethan Shaw. Devlin and I had only just met, but I'd had the thrilling notion that he was jealous of my dinner companion. I'd known very little about him then, other than his profession and that two ghosts haunted him. Now I knew quite a lot about his past, about his dead wife and daughter, about his upbringing, his legacy, his affiliation with the *Congé*. If my hunch was true about his astral travels, I might even know something about him that he wasn't aware of himself. But for all those discoveries, he was more of a stranger to me at that moment than he'd been upon our first meeting.

He hadn't answered, I realized, so I gave him a reprieve. "You're here with—"

"There's a group of us."

A meeting of the *Congé*?

I said very casually, "I heard about your engagement. I should congratulate you."

Something flickered in his eyes, an emotion I didn't dare name. "Thank you." Unlike his eyes, his tone was impassive to the point of dismissive. I tried not to read anything into it.

I started to ask if they'd set a date, make the proper small talk about his upcoming nuptials, but instead I shrugged. "I really should get back."

"I won't keep you. But I'm glad I had a chance to say hello." That beguiling flicker again and a little half smile that made me wonder once more about the unlikely coincidence of our meeting.

Despite his engagement, a part of me wanted him to protest my departure. In the back of my mind floated a vision. His hand sliding up my bare arm as he pulled me farther into the shadowy alcove where he would stare deeply into my eyes for a long, heart-stopping moment before he kissed me.

He was already staring deeply into my eyes, I realized, and his gaze lingered on my lips as if he had read my mind. He straightened languorously, reminding me of all those long, dreamy mornings in bed. I might not know his motives or intentions or even the content of his heart, but I knew his body, all the angles and shadows. The ripple of sinewy muscle.

"I—nice to see you again," I murmured.

"Good night," he said, and as I brushed past him, I could have sworn I heard an ominous whisper in my ear. "Watch your back, Amelia."

I went back to the table and sipped my cooling tea as I glanced around the dining room. I didn't see where Devlin had disappeared to or Temple, either, for that matter. Which was just as well as far as I was concerned. The last thing I wanted was to see Devlin with his gorgeous fiancée, and as for my dinner companion, I needed a moment before facing her. Temple's ability to read me bordered on the uncanny. She would know something was up the minute she sat down across from me and I wasn't prepared for another grilling about Devlin. My only hope was that she would be sufficiently distracted by her apparent infatuation with Rance Duvall and wouldn't notice the high color in my cheeks or the slight tremor in my hands.

As I waited for her return, I tried to distract myself by going back over everything that had happened at Woodbine Cemetery. Staring into my cup, I conjured the infant's face floating on the surface of my tea. The expression captured by the photographer still distressed me. The big eyes, the button nose, the soft cheeks—common attributes of almost any two-year-old. But behind that sweet countenance something dark lurked. Or was that merely my imagination? Was I searching for something in the child's violet eyes that existed only in my head?

I sank so deeply into contemplation that the music didn't register at first. The canned melody was soothing background noise, nothing more. Then slowly the haunting strands wove into my consciousness as familiarity teased me. What was that song? I still couldn't place it. The tune seemed *right there* at the edge of my memory. Eerily pervasive and yet maddeningly elusive.

The room grew frigid, a dank, seeping bone-frost that often preceded the dead. I rubbed my arms and glanced around yet again. The other diners seemed impervious to the chill, but the cold wasn't my imagination. The corners of the window had rimed and I could see my breath on the air.

I turned to the garden in fear. Twilight had deepened to nightfall and the candles on the tables sputtered in a draft. My spine crawled as dread mingled with the cold. I told myself to look away. A manifestation in the garden was nothing to me. No ghost could touch me on hallowed ground and the talisman I wore around my neck was added protection. I was safe inside this former rectory. Safe inside my consecrated bubble.

But I couldn't tear my gaze from the window. Even as I watched the frost spread and crackle across the glass, even as my hand crept to Rose's key, I could feel an insidious presence tearing at my fingers, stealing my will as my defenses crumbled.

The scent of woodbine oozed in with the cold. The cloying perfume leached through the glass to whorl around my senses like smoke. I sat enthralled—trapped—as my gaze darted about the garden, searching for the ghost child even as I tried to recoil from her icy tentacles.

She was well hidden and nearly transparent. If not for the faint glow of her manifestation, I wouldn't have noticed her at all. But as soon as I focused on her, she grew more substantial, as if the warmth of my concentration imbued and emboldened her. The last of the shadows melted away and she stood exposed, an ethereal vision bathed in silky moonlight.

She had manifested in the same white dress as before but I could see more detail now. A row of black buttons set against a scalloped seam decorated the bodice, and a plaid ribbon trimmed the drop waist. She wore patent leather shoes with white tights, and another ribbon dangled from her long blond hair. Her attire was obviously from another decade. Late sixties to midseventies, perhaps, though I was no expert on fashion. She looked to be dressed for church, but her young features were twisted in angry defiance—and a touch of fear, I thought—as she stood with her hands behind her back hiding something in the folds of her skirt.

I became so fixated on her shimmering form that I felt myself slip deeper into enthrallment. She had my undivided attention, but she seemed unmindful of me. She didn't peer at me from the shadows as she'd done in the cemetery. She didn't taunt me or try to make contact. It was as if I'd somehow entered her memory, a voyeur to something that had happened in the past. The ghost wasn't aware of me because I didn't yet exist. I didn't belong in her world.

For the longest time, she stood motionless, hands behind her back, face tilted. Still defiant, still angry, still hiding her fear. Someone was with her, I realized. Someone invisible to me. Her companion must have said something to her for she tried to back away only to be drawn up short as though forcibly restrained. Her wrists were pried from her back, but whatever she had locked in her fist remained hidden from me. Her companion shook her hard, may even have struck her. The child's eyes widened in fear and shock as she flew backward, bouncing and tumbling as if rolling down a steep flight of stairs. Her body came to a jarring halt, arms flung wide, head tilted at a sickening angle.

I half rose from my chair even though I could do nothing. The tragedy had occurred long ago, before I was born, before I had discovered that nameless grave hidden deep inside the willow trees. I couldn't go back in time. I couldn't save the child because she was already dead.

My heart continued to pound and I grew dizzy with emotion. I didn't want to be in that child's memory. I didn't want to see any more of her past. Surely she had revealed to me all that she had intended.

But no. She wasn't done with me yet.

As I sat pressing my great-grandmother's key to my breast, the apparition floated up from the ground, limbs and head dangling as if carried by her unseen assailant. As they neared the edge of the garden, the ghost child's nebulous form pivoted back to me briefly as if the attacker had turned to make certain no one had witnessed the crime.

For one terrifying instant, I could have sworn I felt those invisible eyes upon me, warning me away, cautioning me to say nothing. Reminding me that this was not my business.

The scene faded. The ghost child vanished as a curtain of shadows once again lowered over the garden.

Seven

I sat stunned, my gaze riveted to the spot where the ghost had vanished as the frost on the window receded. The air around me warmed, but my bones felt cold and brittle. I drew a shaky breath as my every instinct tingled an ominous warning.

Forget what you saw. Ignore what you feel. Don't get dragged into another dead-world mystery.

But it was too late for caution. Too late to seek asylum in denial. The ghost child had already latched on to me, robbing me of warmth and energy, and in due time she would usurp my vitality unless I could help her move on.

Now I knew why my presence in Woodbine Cemetery had awakened her. Now I knew what she wanted of me. She had been murdered and no matter how much I might wish to believe otherwise, she wouldn't return to her grave until her killer had been exposed.

It wasn't the first time a ghost had come to me seeking justice, but a murdered child was an entirely different level of horror. Who would have done such a thing to that little girl? And how could I uncover a killer when I didn't even know the identity of the victim?

I touched a finger to the window. It was cool from the night air and nothing more. The temperature inside the restaurant was pleasant, but I couldn't stop shivering. I reached for my sweater, draping it over my shoulders and clutching it to my chest as I searched the garden for the specter. She was gone, melted back into the shadows of the dead world.

I picked up my tea and then set down the cup with a clatter when I realized someone had approached the table. I assumed Temple had returned and arranged my expression so as not to give away my distress. But when I glanced up, another shock rolled through me and my fingers tightened reflexively around Rose's key.

The woman who stood over me was a stranger, but I knew her name, knew her face, knew that smile tugging at her ruby lips as she stared down at me. I knew the sound of her voice even though we'd never spoken. She was Claire Bellefontaine, Devlin's fiancée.

Even if I'd never seen her in person, I would have recognized her from the engagement photo that had run in the paper. A photo that I had regarded far longer and far more often than I should have, truth be told. But I had seen her in person and recently.

Only a few weeks ago I'd been walking back to my car on Tradd Street when the lights of an oncoming vehicle had startled me into a recessed doorway. From my hiding place, I had observed first Devlin and then Claire Bellefontaine enter a shadowy courtyard. Their clandestine behavior had seemed peculiar to me and I became convinced the shrouded carriage house beyond the courtyard was, in fact, the inner sanctum of the powerful and deadly *Congé*.

I had no proof, of course, but I trusted my instincts and by then Dr. Shaw had informed me of the infamous list and had warned me of the Devlins' connection to the nefarious group. If Claire Bellefontaine was also involved, I now found myself in the presence of a very dangerous and cunning enemy.

Before either of us spoke, two thoughts ran simultaneously through my head. One: no matter that I still reeled from the shock of the ghost child's revelation, I couldn't give myself away to the woman standing over me. Two: now that I had the opportunity to observe her up close, she was far more attractive than I could have ever imagined. Easily one of the most beautiful women I'd ever encountered. A cool, ethereal blonde. The physical opposite of Devlin's late wife, Mariama, a fiery Gullah temptress. I didn't like to think where I fell on that spectrum.

Claire's silvery-gold hair was pulled back into a tight ponytail, highlighting her near-perfect bone structure. Her eyes were blue, her lips full and her skin tanned and flawless. She wore a simple white sheath, exquisitely cut and adorned with a single gold chain.

"Please forgive the intrusion," she said in a cultured drawl that reminded me of Devlin's, but the tentative note in her voice took me aback.

"Yes?" My heart fluttered a warning as another thought came to me. Had she seen me with Devlin in the alcove? Nothing had happened but a cordial conversation, so why did I suddenly feel like the other woman? The role didn't sit well with me and I tried to shake off the lingering effects of that brief encounter.

Her fingers curled around the back of Temple's chair. I couldn't help but note that her nails were clipped short and perfectly manicured. I didn't see a ring on her finger and hated myself for looking.

"We've never met, but I know you by reputation. I'm Claire Bellefontaine." She extended her hand and I could do nothing but offer mine in return. Her grip was appropriately firm and she didn't linger awkwardly as if to prove a point, yet I felt an intense relief the moment she released me.

I dropped my hand to my lap and threaded my fingers together. "Amelia Gray."

She smiled. "Yes, I know who you are. As I said, your reputation precedes you."

Surely she hadn't come over to my table to make a scene, so why was she here?

"I'm on the board that administers the Woodbine Cemetery Trust," she said. "I wanted to tell you in person how happy we are that you'll be overseeing the restoration."

She couldn't have caught me more by surprise, but I managed a courteous reply.

"Other firms were recommended, but your work speaks for itself," she went on. "And of course, you have an ardent admirer in Rupert Shaw. He's an acquaintance of yours, I believe."

"We're friends, yes, but I had no idea he was involved in the Woodbine project." Yet more alarm bells sounded. Why hadn't Dr. Shaw told me earlier about his involvement? Why had he pretended to know so little about the cemetery? I supposed it was possible that he could serve on the board and still be uninformed about the day-to-day details, but why not at least mention his recommendation?

Claire's expression remained guileless, but something hard lurked beneath that cool surface. "Perhaps he didn't want you to think that he had influenced the outcome. But I assure you that despite his wholehearted endorsement, the board would never have awarded you the contract if we hadn't been unanimously impressed by your résumé and portfolio."

"Thank you."

"That's all I wanted to say. I won't keep you any longer." She produced a card from her bag and placed it on the table. "I know you already have a contact on the board, but if you ever have a question or problem that can't be resolved to your satisfaction, please feel free to call me. This project means a great deal to me. You see, I have family in Woodbine."

"I understand." She had family in Woodbine? In one of the unnamed graves?

"Good night, Miss Gray."

"Good night."

She walked away, trailing the faintest scent of sandalwood and privilege. The other diners watched her. Men and women alike. Her beauty and charisma were palpable. What a magnetic couple she and Devlin must make.

I picked up her card. The stock was thick and creamy. Expensive and understated. Claire Bellefontaine. Attorney at Law.

The restaurant had grown cold again. I thought perhaps my suspicions regarding Devlin's fiancée had chilled me. It wasn't every day I found myself in such close quarters with a possible member of the *Congé*, someone whose mission it was to stamp out unnaturals like me.

But the frost was otherworldly. I turned to the garden, startled to find the ghost child hovering directly outside the window, so close I could have touched her cold face if not for the glass between us. I could see her features clearly now, could sense her powerful emotions. Her pale hands were clenched at her sides and as I sat there riveted by her nearness, her mouth dropped open and she emitted a piercing howl. The inhuman sound was so ear-splittingly shrill that I thought the window might shatter.

I resisted the urge to cover my ears, but the sound sliced like a blade through my nerve endings. The pain became so intense I felt physically ill. I glanced around at the nearest diners. How could they not hear that scream? How could they remain impervious to such bone-chilling rage?

She remained right outside the window, but she wasn't looking in at me, I realized. Her anger was directed elsewhere. When I followed her icy gaze to the front of the restaurant, I saw that she was staring at Claire Bellefontaine.

And Claire Bellefontaine stared back at me.

Eight

I said good-night to Temple and left the restaurant alone. She didn't seem to mind. She headed off to the bar for another drink and I suspected she'd already made plans with Rance Duvall. I didn't like the idea, but there was nothing I could do about it. Temple had a mind of her own and even if I could have offered a cogent argument for staying away from Duvall, she wouldn't have listened to me. I comforted myself with the reminder that she'd always been a savvy judge of character and could take care of herself. Right now I had other issues to worry about.

My head swirled with everything the ghost child had revealed to me in the garden. The sound of her scream still echoed in my ears. As stunned as I'd been by that dreadful howl, an even greater shock came with the realization that the ghost's focus had been trained on Claire Bellefontaine. What was *their* connection?

Claire's attention had been directed at me, but something in her frozen expression made me wonder if she'd seen or heard the apparition for herself. Or had at least sensed a supernatural presence. Dr. Shaw had once told me that he believed many of the *Congé* were sensitive to the other world, thus making them adept at ferreting out the unnatural. Had she read something on my face or in my eyes that aroused her suspicions? Or—an even darker thought—had Devlin told her about me? Had he confided his own suspicions regarding my gift?

Whatever the case, the encounter had left me trembling and dazed. Her involvement with Woodbine Cemetery couldn't be a coincidence and I had to wonder why Dr. Shaw, knowing what he knew of my gift, knowing what he knew of the *Congé*, hadn't at least warned me about her. Instead, according to Claire, he'd recommended me for the job and until I had a chance to speak with him again, I could only speculate as to his motive. Surely it would have been best for everyone if I'd stayed far away from Devlin's fiancée.

I turned on Queen Street, walking all the way over to Rutledge Avenue. It was still early and the streets buzzed with traffic. I passed any number of pedestrians on my way home, mostly tourists and a few students from nearby UMSC. Despite my uneasiness over the evening's events, I wasn't frightened. I had my phone and pepper spray handy. Even so, I kept a watchful eye on my surroundings as my mind continued to spin.

Not surprisingly, my thoughts eventually turned back to Devlin, as they almost always did. Why couldn't I move on? Why couldn't I accept once and for all that he was gone from my life and was never coming back? I didn't want to think of myself as a woman who pined. I'd been alone for most of my life. I knew how to endure, even to flourish, on my own so why couldn't I forget him?

Maybe Temple was right. I'd created a dangerous fairy tale around him, one that kept me clinging to the past. He was my one and only serious love affair, so instead of facing the reality of our breakup, I'd allowed myself a bittersweet hope that his departure had somehow been a noble gesture. I'd convinced myself that because of his reluctant involvement with the *Congé*, he'd distanced himself in order to protect me. Why else would he have found a way to warn me of the danger I'd faced in Seven Gates Cemetery? I told myself that no matter his association with that deadly faction, no matter his engagement to Claire Bellefontaine, he still cared for me.

My thoughts continued to churn as I turned right on Rutledge Avenue. The palm trees lining Colonial Lake cast long shadows across the moonlit surface. The water looked eerie and mysterious, and as I hurried along the street, the long row of Charleston-style houses seemed to crowd in on me. At the intersection of Rutledge and Beaufain, I paused to glance in the direction of the lovely old Queen Anne where Devlin had once lived with his dead wife and daughter. I couldn't see the house clearly from my vantage, but I had no trouble conjuring the turrets and arches and the shimmer of ghosts at the front window.

Up until that point, I hadn't felt a sense of urgency to get home, but as the memories faded, a vague worry descended. A nagging premonition that something wasn't right.

The steady *drip-drip-drip* of the rain-soaked trees niggled at my nerves. A streetlight hummed and sputtered and I turned anxiously to survey the shadows as a dog barked in the distance. Traffic had dwindled. Suddenly, I felt very alone in the dark and I continued on down the street, glancing over my shoulder now and then until my house came into view.

I couldn't deny a sense of relief as I pushed open the gate and entered the garden. I sailed up the porch steps and unlocked the front door, but I didn't go in. I wasn't sure why. Maybe some instinct warned that I should remain vigilant or my heightened senses had picked up an uncanny vibe. Or maybe it was as simple as wanting to enjoy the fresh air from the safety of my front porch. Whatever the reason, I moved to the corner where the shadows were the deepest and I could watch the street without being seen.

I drew calming breaths and focused. The night came alive for me. The waxing moon hung just above the treetops, and here and there stars peeked through a translucent veil of clouds. I could smell the tea olives at the side of the house and the last of the fall gardenias in the front garden. The perfumes mingled and drifted through my senses like a dream. Awash in that heady aroma, I stood there thinking of Devlin.

Where was he now? I wondered. Still at the restaurant with Claire and the others? Or had the two of them slipped away to spend the rest of the evening alone?

A night bird called from a treetop, coaxing me out of my reverie. The air had grown cooler and I pulled my sweater around me as I turned to go inside. Then I halted at the sound of an approaching car. Normally, this wouldn't have alarmed me. Rutledge was a busy street. But I was certain the vehicle had slowed as it neared my house.

I was still hidden at the end of the porch, but I found myself sinking even deeper into the shadows as I peered across the garden to get a look at the long, sleek sedan with tinted windows. The vehicle pulled to the curb and stopped in front of my house. I caught my breath as the driver cut the engine. Was I being followed? Watched?

I wanted to believe paranoia was getting to me. After everything I'd been through, it would hardly be surprising. But was it really paranoia? I had enemies among the living, the dead and the possessed. All those malevolent faces flashed through my mind as I huddled in the dark and waited.

The back window slid down. I could see the shadowy profile of the passenger as he leaned forward to speak to the driver. I had the impression of a rigid posture and a sleek cap of silver hair.

When he turned his head to stare up at my house, I caught my breath in astonishment. I knew him. As with Claire Bellefontaine, I'd never met him, had never even heard his voice. But I would have recognized Devlin's grandfather anywhere.

This was turning out to be a night of unnerving firsts.

I pressed back against the wall as I tried to make myself invisible. I heard the click of a car door and a moment later, the driver came around to the open passenger window. He was a big man with wide shoulders and a menacing presence. I heard the soft murmur of their voices in the dark, but I couldn't make out the conversation.

The driver left the car and came up the walkway, pausing with his hand on the gate as he tilted his head to stare up at the second-story windows. His behavior troubled me. I had the notion he was trying to determine whether or not the upstairs tenant was home. Another moment passed and then he opened the gate and stepped into the garden.

The night had gone deathly still. Even the songbird fell silent. Oddly, the scent of the gardenias deepened, as if Jonathan Devlin's arrival had somehow stirred the heavenly scent. The driver's footsteps were muffled as he strode up the walkway and climbed the porch steps.

I didn't move a muscle as I tracked him. If he peered into the shadowy corner, he would spot me huddled and quivering, but he didn't even look my way. Instead he paused on the top step as Angus barked a warning from inside. Then he turned to glance over his shoulder at the car.

"You hear that?" he called softly.

"You mean the dog? Yes, come away from the porch before the whole neighborhood is awakened," Jonathan Devlin said gruffly. "We'll wait until morning."

The driver immediately turned and exited the premises as quickly and as quietly as he had come.

I cowered in my hiding place as my heartbeat thundered in my ears. Only when the sound of the car faded did I rise and clamor down the porch steps, rushing along the walkway, through the gate and out to the street. I even took a few steps toward those receding taillights before I came to my senses and halted. What was I doing?

If Dr. Shaw's research and conjecture proved correct, then the elderly Devlin was not only a member of the *Congé,* but perhaps the leader. He could be every bit as dangerous as Claire Bellefontaine, perhaps even more so.

Why else would he have come to my house? Why now, if not on a mission for that dastardly faction?

Nine

Once inside the house, I calmed Angus as I locked the door, reset the alarm and then stood at the window for several minutes watching the street, my breath catching at the sound of every car engine. I didn't see the black car again but I could imagine the sleek lines gliding through darkened alleyways back to the exclusive enclave south of Broad, back to that towering mansion on Battery Row.

Letting the curtain fall back into place, I knelt to stroke Angus's back and scratch behind his battered ear nubs. Now that the outside threat had passed, he relaxed and pushed up against me. Since our time in Seven Gates Cemetery, we'd returned to our old friendship and I welcomed the ease and affection with which he now greeted me.

"I'm glad to see you, too," I murmured, dropping all the way to the floor so that he could nuzzle my face. "You've no idea."

After a few minutes in his calming company, I began to think a little more rationally. I even managed to consider the possibility that I had overreacted. The unexpected visit from Jonathan Devlin had thrown me for a loop, but if he were up to no good, would he have had his driver park in front of my house? Would he have sent the man up to my door? He was far too smart and seasoned to leave that kind of trail. No, whatever his motive, he hadn't come here on business for the *Congé*. So why *had* he come?

My nerves still thrummed as I headed down the hallway to the kitchen, Angus at my heels. I put on the kettle and fixed a cup of chamomile before letting him out in the rear garden for his evening activities. I sat on the back steps and sipped the soothing brew as he made his rounds through the bushes and flower beds, sniffing here, pawing there before disappearing into the shadows to do his business.

The night was still clear, but the wind had risen since I got home, and I snuggled my sweater around me as I listened to the tinkle of the wind chime. The discordant notes were a comfort because they didn't settle into a melody. I hoped that meant the ghost child hadn't followed me home from the restaurant.

Even so, I remained jittery, my disquiet too easily summoning the images that had unfolded in that garden. I shuddered as I thought back on that horrifying tableau. Someone had killed that child. Murdered her in cold blood. I wondered about her assailant, why he had remained invisible to me.

Was he—she—still alive? Had he gone unpunished all this time?

As I sat there puzzling over the child's death, bits and pieces of last night's dream mingled with the ghost's revelations. In the back of my mind, I could see Mama and Aunt Lynrose at the edge of that open grave, rocking and sipping sweet tea as my aunt warned me not to poke my nose in places it didn't belong.

Leave her be, Lyn. We should have tended to this business years ago. Now it's up to Amelia to uncover the truth.

What business? What truth? How could that child's murder be connected in any way to my family?

It couldn't, I told myself firmly. Sometimes a dream could portend the future or unlock the past, but sometimes a dream was just a dream. It was pointless to try and infer anything from those disjointed images when I had concrete clues to decipher.

The prospect of another investigation so soon after my harrowing experiences in Seven Gates Cemetery overwhelmed and exhausted me. What choice did I have, though? The ghost had already latched on to me and she wouldn't fade away of her own accord. I had learned that the hard way. Her tricks would only become more pernicious if I tried to ignore her. The sooner I started putting the pieces together, the sooner she would go back to her grave and we could both rest easy. That was the hope, at least.

Succumbing to my weariness, I yawned and called to Angus. He appeared at the edge of the shadows, head cocked as he regarded me across the garden. When I called to him again, he took a step toward me and then halted, his tail going up as he fixed his gaze on the steps beside me.

"What is it?" I murmured even as a thrill skirted along my spine. I turned to stare at the empty space beside me. There was no ghostly chill, no shimmer from a manifestation, only a quivering certainty that I was no longer alone.

"John," I whispered. It wasn't a question. I knew he was there just as I knew if I put out my hand, I would feel nothing but air.

The night became unbearably still, so quiet I could hear the sigh of the wind in the trees. Or was that my own sigh? I swallowed and touched my face where I could have sworn I felt his lips.

A moment later, the wind chime tinkled as if brushed by an invisible shoulder. I heard the gate creak as if a flesh-and-blood entity had gone through it.

Then all was silent in my garden.

I had another strange dream that night. I was a child again, no more than nine or ten, wandering through the familiar terrain of an abandoned cemetery. The air smelled of old death and fresh earth, a scent that I did not find unpleasant. As I walked on, the breeze picked up, swirling the mist at my feet as the leaves overhead started to whisper my name. *Amelia. Amelia.*

I wasn't at all frightened of those whispers or of my withered surroundings. I was at home here. The eerie sights and sounds were a comfort.

On either side of me, angels with broken wings rose up out of the mist and I wanted to stop and read the epitaphs as I had always done with Papa. But the plates on the monuments were blank, as if the inscriptions had somehow been scrubbed clean.

A memorial without a name seemed very sad to me. I didn't like the notion of the dead being hidden away and forgotten. Everyone had the right to be mourned and remembered, even those who had dwelled on the fringes of someone else's life.

I walked on, the paving stones cool beneath my bare feet. The shadows grew longer and a tingle up my spine warned of the coming twilight. But I didn't turn back. Something awaited me in the cemetery, something important. Something I needed to see. A part of me knew that I was dreaming, but it was more than a dream. Deep in my subconscious, memories were stirring.

Eventually, I came upon Mama and Aunt Lynrose still rocking beside that open grave as they sipped sweet tea from frosted glasses. They were dressed in cool linen, hair precisely coiffed, makeup and nails done to tasteful perfection. I caught the whiff of lemon sachet on the breeze and more faintly, the green notes from their perfume.

The familiarity of those fragrances wrapped me in the warmest embrace and I hurried forward, eager to be drawn into their circle. They whispered to one another, their expressions anxious and didn't even glance up as I approached. I went right up to the fence and called out to them through the wrought-iron gate, but they didn't seem to hear me and for whatever reason, I couldn't enter. The gate was locked tight.

I sank down in the mist and closed my eyes, letting their voices drift over me. I heard my name now and then, but mostly they were reminiscing about their girlhood days. The murmur of their soft drawls and clinking glasses aroused a dreamy nostalgia. I hugged my knees to my chest as I thought back on all those overheard conversations, all those sisterly secrets that intrigued and mystified even as they deepened my loneliness.

Mama said with a little sigh, "Lyn, do you know what I've been thinking about lately? That dress Mother made for your sixteenth birthday. The midnight blue one."

Aunt Lynrose clutched her hands to her heart. Her voice grew soft and unbearably wistful in the twilight. "Oh, how I loved that dress! I wore it to the spring dance, remember? The crystals on the skirt twinkled like starlight when I twirled."

"You wore your hair up that night and Mother

let you borrow her diamond earbobs. You looked just like a princess."

"And I felt like one, too."

"I remember how happy you were when you left the house. How you couldn't stop smiling."

"It was a night like no other."

"If only we'd known—"

"Don't, Etta."

"When you didn't come home—"

"Oh, don't let's talk about that part," my aunt pleaded. "I just want to remember the music and the moonlight and the scent of honeysuckle drifting in through the open doors."

"But we have to talk about that part," Mama insisted. "That's why we're here. When midnight struck and you didn't come home or even call, Mother was beside herself with worry. It wasn't like you to miss curfew. And Father—" Mama shuddered. "I'd never seen him so angry. He paced the floor all night and when you finally came home at sunrise, you had that terrible row."

"You don't need to remind me." My aunt's voice sounded resigned as she lifted a hand to her cheek. "I'll remember every word he said to me until my dying day."

"Nothing was ever the same," Mama said sadly. "We were a happy family until that night. At least it was easy to pretend that we were. Then Father sent you away and I wanted desperately to come with you. The tension in the house had become so oppressive by that time. But I suppose I had it easy considering what you had to put up with Aunt Rue. She was such a spiteful person. So pious and judgmental. I don't know how you stood it."

"I stood it because I had to. It was my penitence, Father said."

"It was cruel of him, what he made you do."

"And I've never forgiven him," my aunt said. "But what good does it do to dredge all that up now? Haven't we both learned that some secrets are best left buried?"

"Have you been able to bury it, though?"

"Yes, until I hear that song. You know the one I mean. And then everything comes back as though it were yesterday. All that pain and suffering. The guilt and the loneliness. Oh, Etta, the loneliness…"

The faint tinkle of a wind chime came to me as I knelt there clinging to the fence. The melody drifted through my senses, tugging at more memories until I had the strongest sense of déjà vu. I knew that I had overheard this very conversation just as I knew the secret my mother and aunt spoke of wasn't meant for my ears. I would be in trouble if they caught me eavesdropping and I couldn't abide Mama's disapproval. She and Papa were everything to me, so I tried very hard to never, ever displease them. I stood to alert her of my nearness, but when I called out to her, she dissolved into the mist without even acknowledging my presence.

"Where did she go?" I cried. "I need her to see me."

My aunt stared pensively into the open grave.

"Leave it alone, chile. You can't change the past. What's done is done. You of all people should know that no good ever comes from all that digging."

And then my aunt vanished, too, leaving me with a terrible foreboding. *What's done is done.*

I knew that I was still dreaming, but the realization gave me no comfort because I couldn't rouse myself. Not yet. The dreams and the ghostly visits were somehow connected and everything had meaning. The mist, the open grave, my mother and aunt's conversation. Even the beady eyes of the corpse bird that watched me from atop a headstone. If the crow wasn't a clue, then it was surely a sign or an omen. *It means someone else is likely to pass.*

I pulled myself up to my full height, shaking off those lonely bondages of my childhood so that I could continue the journey as an adult. As I moved back into the cemetery, I realized the scene had shifted and now I found myself behind the crumbling walls of Oak Grove Cemetery, that darkest of all burial places, where even the dead didn't wish to linger.

The mist thickened and the air grew colder. An unnatural wind tore at my hair and the hem of my nightgown. I covered my nose and mouth as the smell of fresh death rose up from a sea of open graves.

Straight ahead, the Gothic spires of the Bedford Mausoleum peeked up over the treetops. The distant tinkle of a wind chime lured me into the woods and when I emerged into a clearing, I found myself at the bottom of a long staircase. At the very top, light shone through an open doorway where shadows danced upon the walls.

I didn't want to go up there. I didn't want to see inside the mausoleum. But the melody of the wind chime wrapped around my senses, drawing me upward as if a string around my wrist had been tugged.

The air grew steadily colder as I climbed. The night became crowded with ghosts. The diaphanous beings drifted up behind me on the steps, brushing their frigid fingers through my hair, pressing icy lips to my ears as they whispered about unspeakable secrets.

I could feel my energy wane as their appetites threatened to consume me. But I kept climbing, on and on until I reached the summit. A silhouette appeared in the doorway blocking my way into the mausoleum. It was Devlin, barefoot and shirtless, his hair unkempt, his eyes inflamed with an emotion I didn't want to name.

I put out a hand, thinking he would dissolve the way Mama and Aunt Lynrose had, but instead I felt the warm ripple of muscle. I closed my eyes on a shiver.

He caught my wrist and I thought he meant to pull me against him. I wouldn't have resisted no matter his betrothal. But he held me away, the intensity of his stare deepening my unease until

I suddenly found myself wanting to break free of him.

"You shouldn't have come here," he said harshly, holding me fast. "You don't belong."

"Where are we?" I tried to look around him into the mausoleum but he stepped in front of me, shielding my view with his body. I could hear all manner of sounds inside, inhuman screams and groans that chilled me to the bone. "What is this place?"

"Go," he said. "Before they find you."

"Who?"

"You can't be seen here. This is a place for the dead."

"Then why are you here?"

He said nothing to that, merely stared at me longingly before he turned in resignation to go back inside. I stepped across the threshold into that cold, dark space filled with shadows and torchlight and noises that lifted the hair at my nape. But Devlin was nowhere to be seen.

I wasn't alone, however. Claire Bellefontaine crouched on the stone floor before a pool of blood. Light shimmered in her silvery gold hair and something dark and feral glinted in her blue eyes.

She lifted a finger to her ruby lips. "Shush. Lest she awaken."

Then she pointed to the doorway and I whirled. The ghost child hovered at the top of the stairs. She wore the same clothes as before, but now I could see a flash of silver in her fist.

Familiarity tugged at me again, but the memory flitted away as her face morphed into a corpse bird. I could see the iridescent sheen of her feathery hair and the dead gleam of those beady eyes in the torchlight. Her head hung at a sickening angle, but when I would have moved to help her, she emitted a high-pitched scream that knocked me back against the wall.

I crumpled to the floor, hands to my ears as I cried in horror, "Please stop. You're hurting me."

"Mercy," she said before she tumbled backward down the stairs.

I rose and rushed to the doorway. She was already gone, but she'd left something behind on the top step. A charm bracelet gleamed in the torchlight, but when I bent to pick it up, my fingers found nothing but mist.

I awakened with my fingers tangled around the ribbon at my throat. The weight and purpose of Rose's key should have reassured me, but my heart pounded so hard, I had to sit up in bed to catch my breath. I searched the shadows, all the darkened corners. Nothing was amiss. Angus snoozed on in a puddle of moonlight, oblivious to anything but his own dreams.

Shoving back the covers, I rose and padded into the hallway to check the alarm system. The activated light glowed reassuringly, but I still found myself glancing over my shoulder as I walked to the kitchen for a drink of water. Then I took a quick look around the house before returning to the front window to glance out at the street.

It was well after midnight and traffic had long since died away. The night was quiet and peaceful, lit by a crescent moon and the streetlights along Rutledge. I saw nothing untoward. Even the shadows were static. There was nothing inside or outside that should have kept my heart racing, and yet my uneasiness mounted the longer I stood at that window.

My scalp prickled a warning as I suddenly vectored in on the cause of my disquiet. Halfway down the block a sleek black sedan with darkly tinted windows was parked at the curb. The headlights were off, but I could see the silhouette of the driver behind the wheel. As if prompted by the fierceness of my concentration, he opened the door, briefly illuminating the interior of the car. He appeared to be alone. He got out and came around to recline against the front fender.

I could see him clearly underneath the streetlight. Even from this distance, there was no mistaking his identity. I'd seen him on my front porch only hours ago.

And there was no mistaking his intent. He had been sent to watch my house.

Ten

I managed a few more hours of sleep and arose early in a resolved if not entirely upbeat mood. A cool gray light seeped into the bedroom, but the warm edge of sunrise glowed just above the horizon. While I dressed, Angus roused and padded off down the hallway to wait patiently at the back door. After a quick look out the front window to make sure the black car had moved on, I turned off the security system and followed him outside.

Plopping down on the steps to tie my walking shoes, I let my thoughts amble while he went about his morning routine. Naturally, my mind went back to the dream and to Mama and Aunt Lynrose sitting beside that open grave in their rockers. Time and my subconscious may have embellished the dialogue, but I had no doubt I'd overheard a similar conversation sometime in the distant past. The memory had been pushed to the back of my mind until recent events had called it forth. But why? I still couldn't imagine how my mother and aunt were connected to Woodbine Cemetery any more than I understood Devlin's warning that I didn't belong in the dead world. And he did?

The way he had turned away in resignation to walk back into the mausoleum had chilled me most of all, but maybe I was making too much of that scene. Not every element in a dream had to have meaning. Maybe some of the images were nothing more than fragmented memories and disjointed worries knitted together into something indecipherable.

I called Angus back inside and poured nuggets in his bowl. I topped off his water before heading out on my morning walk. The air was cool, but I set a brisk pace and soon warmed up from the exertion. Traffic was still sparse and I met only a handful of early-bird pedestrians. As I strode along the cracked sidewalks, I kept a vigilant eye, but if the black car tailed me, the driver was skilled enough to avoid detection.

Turning left on Broad Street, I sailed past banks and law offices housed in centuries-old buildings as I headed toward the water. The pastel houses along Rainbow Row glowed softly in the morning light. I crossed the street to the Battery, telling myself to keep moving, to avert my eyes when I passed the Devlin mansion, but that was asking too much. I slowed my steps as my gaze darted across East Bay. The sun was just rising over the harbor and the light reflecting off the windows blinded me.

Shielding my eyes, I scanned the elegant facade,

searching the balcony where I had seen Devlin. He wasn't outside today. No one was about. The family slept on while I stood watching their house.

Abruptly, I turned and made my way to the bottom of the peninsula, crossing the street once again to White Point Garden. No one was about in the park, either, and I was glad to have the space to myself. I followed a trail past the gazebo and canons to a remote spot where I often came to think.

The camellia blossoms hung heavy with dew, and the smell of brine drifted on the sea breeze, which ruffled my hair. It was one of those clean, clear mornings when Charleston shimmered like a diamond. I headed for my usual bench only to find it occupied. I started to move on, then stopped dead as a quiver went through me.

The man's head was turned so that I could only see his profile, but I recognized the jawline, the rigid posture, the gleaming silver hair—not a strand out of place. Even at so early an hour, Jonathan Devlin was formally turned out in a three-piece suit and wingtips. A gold watch fob hung from his vest and a precisely folded pocket square adorned his coat. He could have been on his way to a funeral, so somber his attire.

I hadn't made a sound. I was certain of that. But before I could make my escape, he turned and pinned me with a gaze every bit as dark and intense as his grandson's. I was awestruck by that glare. It was as if his eyes had the power to hold me in suspended animation.

In that frozen moment, I suddenly became acutely aware of my own apparel—walking shoes, leggings and a faded hoodie. My hair was pulled back in a ponytail, but the wind and the exertion of my walk had loosened damp tendrils. I wore no makeup or perfume and my nails were clipped short so that I could more easily scrub away the graveyard dirt. A less appealing presentation I could hardly imagine, but why should I be so concerned about my appearance? Jonathan Devlin was nothing to me. I had no need to impress.

Even so, I couldn't dispel the echo of my aunt Lynrose's censure. *You must always wear gloves when you work, Amelia. On that there can be no compromise. A woman's hands never lie.*

Neither of us spoke for the longest time, which only prolonged the awkward encounter. Finally, I cleared my throat and shrugged. "I'm sorry. I didn't mean to disturb you."

"It's a public park. I don't own this bench." He had Devlin's drawl, I noted. That cultured cadence rarely heard these days and only ever south of Broad Street.

I tried to suppress a shiver as I inched back a step. "That's true, but you were here first. I can find another bench."

"No, don't run away, young lady." His voice softened though not without effort, I wagered. He rose from the bench to face me.

He was tall, with the trim physique and resolute demeanor of a man who cut himself and those around him very little slack. I wondered what it must have been like for Devlin, a rebellious teen losing his parents so suddenly and forced to live with a man who wore a three-piece suit and polished wingtips for an early-morning stroll in the park. But then, I didn't delude myself into thinking that this was a coincidental meeting. Not after the episode last night in front of my house.

"I may have beaten you to the punch this time," Jonathan Devlin allowed. "But you come here often enough that I imagine you think of this as your place." He gave a little wave as if to encompass our surroundings.

I stared back at him, trying not to show my nerves. "How would you know how often I come here? Or that I come here at all, for that matter."

"There is very little I don't know about you, Miss Gray."

Apprehension quickened my breath. "That sounds ominous."

"Yet you're still here." The light slanting down through the leaves caught him in such a way as to magnify the lines and creases in his face and the slight sag of his jowls. Despite his military posture and fitness, I detected a slight quake in his voice, a chink in his armor that he undoubtedly abhorred. A man such as he would cling to his vigor until his dying breath.

"Do you know who I am?" he asked, his dark gaze taking my measure.

Mentally, I drew myself up as I faced him. "Yes."

"Then you must wonder why I'm here."

"I'm wondering a lot of things," I said and then blurted, "You were at my house last night."

"Was I?"

"I saw you when you lowered your window. I heard you speak to your driver. He came back later without you and parked down the street. I can only assume, given your earlier visit, that you sent him back to watch my place. What I can't figure out is why."

"You see a great deal, don't you, Miss Gray?"

A tiny thrill slid up and down my spine. "You were not exactly discreet."

"I've nothing to hide."

"Then tell me why you came to my house last night. And why you were waiting for me here this morning. I'm curious about this sudden interest in me. Why now?"

"You mean now that you and my grandson are no longer lovers."

So he knew about my time with Devlin and he knew about our breakup. Of course he would know. I doubted anything that affected his family's status got by him. "Yes, that's exactly what I mean."

"My business with you has nothing to do with Jack."

I said coolly, "He doesn't like to be called that."

A brow lifted as he continued to regard me.

"Oh, no, he does not. But it hardly matters. As I said, this isn't about him."

"Then what is it about?"

He seemed at a loss all of a sudden, but his reticence only deepened my unease. I felt a sinking sensation in the pit of my stomach as he motioned to the bench. "Will you sit with me?"

I didn't want to. I couldn't help but believe the encounter was as dangerous as it was awkward. That every polite word he uttered concealed a perilous subtext. I didn't know Jonathan Devlin as he claimed to know me, but I didn't trust him. I'd heard too much about him from his own grandson over the years and from Dr. Shaw only yesterday. The man who stood before me was cold and ruthless, and his affiliation with the *Congé* made him a threat.

I searched for an excuse to end the conversation, wanting nothing more than to be on my way, but instead I found myself taking a seat on the bench.

"If this has nothing to do with your grandson, then what's it about?" I asked.

He sat down beside me, keeping a mannerly distance between us. He wore no aftershave that I could detect, but for some reason my imagination conjured the rich combination of lime and basil. "Before we go any further, I need your assurance that nothing of what we say will go beyond this bench. You mustn't repeat a word to anyone, even to my grandson. Especially to him."

"Your grandson and I don't talk."

Which wasn't exactly true after last night, but my assurance seemed to mollify him. One of his hands rested on the seat beside us and the other reclined on the arm of the bench. I could see a slight quiver in the fingers that curled around the curvature of the metal.

He took a moment to gather his thoughts as he glanced out over the water. In the ensuing quiet, I heard only the whisper of leaves overhead and the distant sound of the church bells. But the silence was weighty and portentous. Even as the sun rose above the harbor, igniting the sea, a black cloud settled over the bench where I sat with Jonathan Devlin.

When he finally turned back to me, something shadowed his eyes. A haunting darkness I'd seen staring back at me from the mirror. I found myself folding my arms across my middle, hugging myself tightly to ward off another chill.

"There's a ghost in my house," he said softly.

He could have confided nothing that astounded me more. The shock prickled at my nape and up through my scalp. I summoned every ounce of my composure to subdue my reaction.

Careful, a little voice whispered. *This could be a trap.*

"You don't seem the type to believe in ghosts," I said.

"But you don't really know me, do you? Although I'm sure you've heard my grandson's assessment." Was that regret I heard in his voice? More like disdain, I decided.

"No, I don't know you, which makes your revelation and this whole meeting even more extraordinary. Why are you talking to me about this?"

His gaze on me never wavered, but where he gripped the edge of the seat, his knuckles had whitened. "You may not know me, but I'm familiar with almost every facet of your life. Where you come from and who your people are. Your childhood, your education, your life's work." He paused. "The gift that has been handed down to you."

"The gift?"

His gaze hardened as he gave an impatient flick of his hand. "Please, let's not play games. I'm too old and there is too little time and too much at stake."

I said nothing to that, merely waited for him to continue.

"I'm not accustomed to having to vouch for myself," he said. "But I assure you, I mean you no harm."

"And I'm to take your word for that?"

"If my intentions were nefarious, would I have approached you in a public place? The gardens are open and the tourists will be stirring soon. Anyone could come upon us at any time."

I glanced around, wondering where his driver was at the moment.

"I came alone," he said, correctly interpreting my apprehension.

I drew a sharp breath. "All right. I'll take your word that you mean me no harm, but I still don't understand why you've come to me with your... problem. What is it you expect me to do?"

He faced straight ahead for a moment as if overcome by a sudden wave of emotion. "I want you to send her away."

"Her?"

"It. The apparition. The entity that has invaded my home."

"You've seen it?"

"Nothing more than the dart of a shadow out of the corner of my eye, but there is a cold spot in my bedroom and another in my study. Things have been misplaced or gone missing altogether. I hear voices at night and footfalls when no one is there. I've awakened to a cold breath upon my cheek." He paused. "And just this morning, the mirror in my bathroom cracked for no apparent reason."

"I can see how that would be unnerving."

"Unnerving? You've no idea. Normally, I'm a rational man, but this..." He trailed off. "I believe the correct terminology for such a disturbance is poltergeist."

He seemed to expect acquiescence, but my inclination was to say nothing at all. However, like the ghosts that wandered in and out of my life, I didn't think Jonathan Devlin would rest easy until I gave him what he wanted. "Contrary to your apparent perception of me, I'm no expert in such matters. But people who study the paranormal often draw a distinction between ghosts and poltergeists."

"People like Rupert Shaw?"

The derision in his voice made me harden my defenses. "Dr. Shaw is certainly the most knowledgeable person I know in such matters."

"Is he, indeed?"

"You would be far better off speaking to him about this disturbance than to me."

"What makes you think I haven't?"

I stared at him in surprise, instantly flashing back to Dr. Shaw's animosity. "When did you talk to him? And what did he say?"

"I'm more interested in what you have to say. Perhaps you could enlighten me about this distinction." He watched me carefully.

"Ghosts are considered to be the spirits of the deceased that, for whatever reason, linger in our world. Poltergeists are thought to be forms of energy. A manifestation of *negative* energy oftentimes left by a sudden and violent death."

"Like a murder, you mean."

I tried not to show my reaction. "Possibly."

"Please go on," he urged, but I didn't think it a good idea to pursue the conversation. He'd gone very pale and the tremor in his voice became even more pronounced.

"Are you okay?" I asked in concern. "You don't look well."

"I'm fine," he said, but I could hear a ragged note in his cultured tone that gave away his distress. "I'd like you to continue."

"I really don't know what else to tell you other than to provide a more simplistic explanation. Some consider ghosts passive and poltergeists aggressive."

Despite his alarming pallor, his dark stare was as intense as ever. "Is that what you believe?"

I knew from personal experiences that ghosts could be extremely aggressive, like the child in Woodbine Cemetery. Jonathan Devlin's description of his haunting reminded me of her impish behavior, but it seemed too far-fetched to believe there could be a connection. Then again, I really didn't believe in coincidences.

"Like most Southerners, I've heard ghost stories and folktales all my life," I said. "And in my line of work, someone always has an experience they wish to share. I've come to believe that if ghosts truly exist, most linger in our world because they want to be among the living again."

"If they exist." He smiled at that and my blood turned cold. I was reminded of who he was and what he might really be after—proof that I was an unnatural.

I clasped my fingers together in my lap. "Has anyone else in the household experienced these disturbances?"

"Not that I'm aware. The malice seems directed at me."

"*Malice* is a strong word."

"I can think of no more fitting a description."

"Do you know why you're the target?"

"No," he said, but he couldn't quite meet my eyes.

"Earlier you referred to the entity as a she. Do you know who this spirit was in life?"

"Not for certain, but I have a suspicion."

"Then you must also have some idea why you've been chosen as the recipient of the entity's hostility."

He paused as a curtain came down over his expression. "I won't answer any more questions until you agree to help me."

"Help you how? You say you want me to make the ghost go away, but how do you propose I do that?"

"Use your gift. Whatever it is you do to summon them. Then you can find out what the ghost wants."

I gave him a doubtful glance. "Even if I had that kind of power, I assure you I would never knowingly summon a ghost."

He fell into another deep silence. In the interim, I noted the pulse that throbbed at his temple and the infinitesimal twitch at the corner of his left eye. If he had fabricated the story as a lure to gain my trust or a trap to prove my true nature, he was certainly a very good actor. By all outward indications, Jonathan Devlin was a troubled man.

"Would you at least be willing to come to my

house and experience the cold spots for yourself?" he finally asked. "Perhaps your presence alone will be enough to entice the entity. If we can somehow placate the spirit, I can be done with this business once and for all."

His voice had risen in agitation and I tried to say in a calming tone, "I don't know if that's a good idea." Apart from willfully attracting a ghost, I wasn't so sure I wanted to run into Devlin. Not there. Not in the place that seemed to embody the chasm between us.

"You still think I mean you harm?" Jonathan Devlin demanded.

I returned his relentless gaze. "No, not really. Not in this instance. But I'm not wholly convinced your motives are just as you say. What you're asking…you must realize how all of this sounds to me. How taken aback I am by your request."

"You refuse then." He rose stiffly. "I suppose there is little more for us to say. I've come to you with only one intention…to enlist your assistance in expelling what I believe to be a malevolent and supernatural force from my home. A force I'm convinced means me harm. If anything happens in that house…if anything happens to *me*, my blood will be on your hands."

I stared at him in shock. "You don't really believe that."

"I'm a desperate man, Miss Gray. As you well know, desperate men say and do desperate things."

Eleven

The walk home seemed to take forever, and the conversation with Jonathan Devlin echoed in my head every step of the way.

There's a ghost in my house.

There is very little I don't know about you, Miss Gray.

If anything happens to me, my blood will be on your hands.

On and on and on. The more I replayed the dialogue, the greater my anxiety. I wasn't surprised a man like Jonathan Devlin would have me so thoroughly investigated that he could anticipate my visit to White Point Garden that morning. The greater shock would have been a passive acceptance of someone like me in his grandson's life.

No, what worried me—what absolutely petrified me—was his seemingly effortless ability to uncover a legacy that my family had kept secret for generations. And if he could so easily discover the truth…who else might know?

My heart beat faster and harder as I contemplated the implications of his revelation. Suddenly, I felt an overwhelming need to be home safe and sound in my sanctuary and I became increasingly paranoid as I hurried along the awakening streets, certain that shadowy figures lurked in every recessed doorway or that a long black car awaited me in the next alley. With sunrise the city had come alive, but I took no comfort in the rumble of delivery trucks and the occasional blast of a horn. I might have been alone, the sole survivor of a devastated city, so utter my sense of isolation.

Since childhood my aloneness had been a part of me. My instinct had always been to hide myself away behind the walls of my beloved cemeteries, but at that moment, I had a strong urge to seek out a sympathetic ear. I desperately needed to talk to someone about everything that had happened, but who to call? Devlin was out of the question for many reasons, and Temple knew nothing about my gift. She had a progressive point of view, but I didn't see her opening her mind to the possibility of ghosts.

Normally, I would have gone straight to Dr. Shaw, but for some reason, I felt hesitant to tell him about my encounter with Jonathan Devlin. Maybe it was Dr. Shaw's animosity toward the man or the fact that he hadn't told me about his involvement with Woodbine Cemetery. Or maybe it was nothing more than his moodiness. He'd obviously had something preying on his mind during our last visit and I was hesitant to add to his burden.

I didn't want to go to Papa, either. Despite our shared gift, we didn't always communicate well, and the revelations from so many of our visits often made things worse. So for now, I had no choice but to keep my worries and fears to myself.

Maybe that was for the best. I hadn't made a verbal promise to Jonathan Devlin, but he was undoubtedly counting on a tacit agreement to keep me quiet. So be it. I would honor his wishes so long as he kept his distance.

The safe harbor of my home beckoned and I entered the garden eagerly, letting the wrought-iron gate clang shut behind me. But as I bounded up the steps, a movement at the corner of the porch caught my eye and I turned with a start. A sparrow had alighted on one of the window ledges looking—I could have sworn—into my house. The tiny brown head rotated at the sound of my footfalls, but the bird didn't seem frightened—quite the contrary. The sparrow remained perched with head slightly tilted as if befuddled by my sudden appearance.

The action and expression were so bizarre that I remained rooted to the spot as the bird eyed me for an uncomfortably long time. The thought crossed my mind that I should shoo the creature away from my house, but I couldn't seem to utter a sound, let alone flap my arms. Because another thought had also entered my head. There was intelligence behind that stare. A normal bird would have flown away the moment I came up the steps. A normal bird would not have been looking into my house.

Was I going crazy? I wondered. Had I finally followed my great-grandmother into the ultimate sanctuary of insanity? How else to explain the peculiarity of that sparrow?

A car went by on Rutledge and the bird flew over to the porch rail where it gazed out across the yard toward the street. Then it hopped around to face me before fluttering back to the window ledge. All the while I didn't move so much as a muscle. The sparrow's unlikely behavior stunned me and for a moment, I wondered if those beady eyes had actually bewitched me.

I said aloud, "What is going on here?"

My voice should have scared it away, but instead the head cocked and the beak opened slightly as if the bird meant to answer me, which would have indisputably signaled the final stage of madness.

"Are you even real?" I muttered.

Through the front door I heard the click of Angus's claws on the wood floor as he propelled himself toward the sound of my voice. A moment later, he popped up at the window. The bird hadn't seemed in the least concerned by my presence, but the dog's sudden appearance behind the glass startled us both. The sparrow took flight, lighting briefly on the rail before soaring up into the treetops.

Released from the spell of my own shock, I

quickly unlocked the door and dashed inside. I peeked out the window again, but the tiny visitor was gone for good this time. Or at least I hoped so.

My intense relief at the bird's absence was so irrational, I once again questioned my stability. Maybe the encounter with Jonathan Devlin had left me more shaken than I realized, so much so that I had attributed humanlike qualities to a sparrow.

Get a grip, I told myself sternly as I got ready for work. But I felt off-kilter even inside my own home. The dreams, the sparrow, the strange encounters…it was as if the universe was trying to tell me something that I wasn't yet prepared to accept.

By the time I arrived at the cemetery, the sun was just peeking through the live oaks, burnishing a tin roof in the distance and dappling the headstones. Out on Morrison Drive, sirens screamed toward some dire emergency, but here in this tucked-away corner of the city, all seemed well. The ghosts had crossed back over at dawn and the cemetery slumbered in peace.

Grabbing my backpack, I climbed out of the vehicle and headed toward the gate. Two days of rain had softened the ground and just inside the entrance, I spotted a trail of footprints meandering through the graves. Normally, I wouldn't have given the tracks a second thought. People visited cemeteries all the time, even graveyards as old and neglected as Woodbine. There was no lock on the gate and no posted hours, so visitors were free to come and go as they pleased. But it was still very early and the impressions were fresh.

Unease niggled as I stared down at the prints. They led only one way—into the cemetery—so whoever had arrived before me was either still inside or had left by way of the side gate.

I hadn't noticed another vehicle parked near the entrance, so my first thought was that the caretaker had walked down from his house to make his rounds or to chase away trespassers and vandals. But there was only one set of prints and I didn't think they belonged to Prosper Lamb. He'd been wearing work boots when I met him on Monday and these tracks were smallish and narrow, leading me to wonder if the visitor was female.

Kneeling, I took a closer look at the prints, even going so far as to snap a couple of shots with my phone, though I couldn't say why exactly. An inclusion across one of the heels, possibly a cut or worn place in the sole, caught my attention, but other than the one anomaly, I found nothing unusual about the footprints.

Still, the notion of a woman wandering around Woodbine at such an ungodly hour intrigued me even though I told myself to forget about the tracks and get on with my work. People were entitled to their privacy, especially someone who had come alone to a cemetery to visit the grave of a loved one. I was the last person to intrude upon something so poignant and personal.

Yet I found myself making excuses as to why caution necessitated a quick trek through the cemetery. It only made sense to be aware of anyone in my immediate vicinity. Hadn't the caretaker warned me about the unsavory element that gravitated to places like Woodbine? Hadn't I been caught unaware before in an overgrown cemetery? I would be foolish not to take stock of my surroundings.

Shoving aside my conscience, I hitched my backpack over one shoulder and followed the tracks all the way to the rear of the cemetery where the willow trees grew along the riverbank. The footprints seemed to pause at the edge of the grove as if the visitor had stopped there to gather her courage.

Possibly I was projecting my own emotions onto the situation, but as I stood beside those footprints, gazing into the shadowy recesses of the copse, I felt the coldest of chills sweep across my nerve endings. Hidden inside those willow trees was the nameless grave I'd happened upon my first day at Woodbine. I could still picture the infant's forlorn little face peeking from beneath the hood of the stone crib. I could imagine the ghost girl lurking in the shadows nearby, keeping guard, watching and waiting, perhaps plotting some new trick to lure me into her mystery.

I told myself I would go no further. If the ghost

hadn't drifted back through the veil at dawn, I wouldn't risk another confrontation. If the visitor still lingered, I wouldn't intrude upon her solitude. Maybe she had come to the cemetery so early because she didn't wish to be seen.

But no good intentions or self-recriminations could make me turn away from those willow trees. Instead, I found myself edging closer, searching the ground for the telltale footprints. A mild breeze stirred the wind chimes and I tilted my head to listen. The melodic notes were random, but for me, a siren's song nonetheless. Parting the willow fronds, I followed the sound into the copse. I wouldn't have been surprised to hear the ghost's mocking laughter, but except for the mournful clinking of the chimes, all remained silent.

I stepped into the sheltered enclave and shivered. Something lingered. Not a ghostly presence this time, but human emotions so deep and pervasive they settled over me like a shroud. I was trespassing on something very personal here and I had the strongest urge to retreat. Instead I closed my eyes and focused, drawing those feelings deep into my being. Sorrow…loneliness…betrayal. I sensed an old bitterness, too, and a trace of fresh anger.

Suppressing another shudder, I moved to the stone crib, my gaze dropping to the bed from which Prosper Lamb had plucked the corpse bird. Nestled against that soft blanket of pansies was an old-fashioned teddy bear that hadn't been there on my last visit. The seams had been clumsily re-

paired and the mohair fur worn thin in places. One
of the button eyes was missing. The toy had obviously been well loved, possibly for generations, but
who had left it in the crib? The fabric was dry, so
I assumed it had been placed in the bed only that
morning. By the female visitor? Had she made
good her escape through the side gate or did she
dawdle in the shadows, having been frightened
into hiding by my arrival?

I lifted my head to scour the trees before returning my attention to the teddy bear. I wouldn't pick
it up or even touch it. Tampering with gravesite
offerings was anathema to everything I believed
in, but cemetery etiquette didn't preclude a closer
look. As I bent over the stone crib, a scent drifted
up to me. I closed my eyes yet again and drew it
in. Beneath the expected funereal smells of flowers and damp earth trailed a perfume that took me
back to the loneliness of my childhood. A tantalizing and nostalgic fragrance that reminded me of
my dream and of my mother and aunt whispering
beside that open grave.

Familiarity tugged at me and I straightened
once more to search my surroundings.

"Is someone there?" I called out.

Silence.

"I'm sorry if I disturbed you. My name is Amelia Gray. I work in the cemetery."

As I spoke, I turned in a circle, peering deep
into the shadows. The leaves ruffled as if whispering my name back to me: *Amelia. Amelia Gray.*

I saw nothing, heard nothing amiss, but I had a very strong sense that someone was there, watching and waiting, this time a human protector of the stone crib. I could feel wary eyes on me, tracking my every move.

Striking a conversational tone, I said, "When I saw your footprints at the gate, I got worried. It's so early and the cemetery isn't the safest place. I wanted to make sure you're okay."

Still no response. Nothing but the chattering leaves and the soft tinkle of the wind chimes. And yet I *knew* I wasn't alone. The feeling of being watched deepened, lifting the hair at my nape.

"Hello?"

A sparrow flew down from a tree branch and lit on the hood of the crib, looking so much like the one from my front porch that I gasped and took a step back. The sudden movement should have frightened the bird away, but instead the sparrow merely resettled its ruffled feathers, staring at me so intently that I felt utterly entranced.

It couldn't be the same bird. My house and the cemetery were miles apart. The notion that the sparrow had followed me was too insane to even consider. And yet there that tiny creature perched, eyes gleaming, head cocked, daring me to defy logic.

"Are you following me?" I murmured even as I acknowledged to myself the madness of such a question.

Thankfully, the bird didn't answer.

I lifted my arm. "Shoo!"

The sparrow never moved. The eyes didn't blink. For a crazy moment, I wondered if the bird was even alive.

"What are you?" I muttered. "Why are you here?"

The wind picked up, jangling the chimes. The sparrow's head swiveled as if tracking the sound. I started to do the same, but before I could turn, a dark blur at the corner of my eye diverted my attention. Then something hit the ground beside me with a thud.

I spun as another bird fell from the sky and then another and another until a dozen or more dead starlings formed a nearly perfect circle around me. Instinctively, I covered my head with my arms as I stood in the center, frozen in shock. What on earth…?

None of the birds moved, not so much as the blink of an eye or the twitch of a wing. I stepped from that gruesome ring, staring down at the ground in horror as I wondered what could have caused the mass death.

Out in the cemetery someone coughed, a human sound that should have reassured me, but instead goaded my fear. My voice rose in alarm. "Who's there?"

"Who wants to know?" came the surly reply.

I recognized the voice of the caretaker and I had visions of Prosper Lamb storming through the willow trees wielding his weapon, perhaps shooting first and asking questions later.

I called out quickly, "Mr. Lamb, is that you? It's Amelia Gray."

He paused as if trying to sort my name. "The cemetery restorer?"

"Yes!" My heart continued to thud as we conversed through the trees. "You've no idea how glad I am you happened along just now!"

"Why? What's wrong?" He sounded closer now, just outside the copse. "You didn't fall again, did you? I warned you about the vines."

"No, I'm fine. But something odd has happened. I'm just through the willow trees where we talked last time. Can you come back here?"

A moment later, he charged into the enclave, stopping cold when he saw the dead starlings at my feet. He gave a low whistle. "What happened?"

"I've no idea. I was just standing here watching a sparrow when all these birds fell from the sky—"

"A *sparrow*?"

I blinked at his emphasis. "Yes, it lit on the hood of the crib. I know this sounds crazy, but it seemed to be looking at me as if…" I trailed off, waiting for his reaction.

"As if what?"

I shrugged.

"A sparrow was looking at you? Looked you right in the eyes, did it?"

"Does that mean something?"

He didn't answer, just stood there gazing down

at that ghastly death ring. It was only then that I noticed the burlap bag he carried in one hand as if he had already been out collecting trash from the cemetery. Or other dead birds.

"These starlings fell in a circle like this?" he asked.

"Yes. I didn't move them. I never even touched them."

I could have sworn I saw a shudder go through him before he crouched and put a finger to the nearest corpse. "Still warm."

Wrapping my arms around my middle, I watched as he moved from bird to bird. "What could have happened? Why would so many die all at once like that? Disease? Disorientation?" I spoke half to myself.

He continued his examination without glancing up. "I saw something similar when I was a boy. A whole flock of starlings raining down from the sky like the end of days."

"The end of days," I repeated numbly.

"But these birds…" He glanced at me over his shoulder, his gaze dark and avid. "Their necks were wrung just like the crow we found the other day."

"No disease caused that."

"No, ma'am, it did not."

I thought about the odd angle of the ghost child's neck in my visions. Had the bad seed entity somehow caused the death of these birds? It was a terrible thought, but I couldn't dispel the image of the bloody and battered crow she'd clutched to her chest.

"Isn't it possible their necks were broken when they hit the ground?" I asked.

"All of them?"

"It's the only logical explanation," I insisted.

He rose without comment, his gaze moving past me to the stone crib. I turned, thinking the sparrow or perhaps the teddy bear had caught his interest, but his eyes had taken on a faraway look, as if his thoughts had traveled a million miles away from the enclave.

"Mr. Lamb? Are you all right?"

His head rotated slowly back to me and he blinked, as if reorienting himself to the here and now. "There's another explanation for these dead birds, but you won't like it."

"Why is that?"

"It's not a *logical* explanation."

"I'd still like to hear it."

"Remember I told you the other day that the crow we found was a corpse bird."

I swallowed and nodded. "I remember."

He lifted his gaze skyward, but whether to search for storm clouds or a flock of birds, I didn't know. "My mama used to say that right before someone died, a door to the other side opened so that the soul could pass through. If the dying lingered too long or the door opened too soon, things could come through from the other side."

I said with a shiver, "Like ghosts, you mean."

"Like bad, bad things."

"What kind of bad things?"

"Things that don't belong here. Things that look normal but aren't. Their presence in the living world throws off the natural order. Strange occurrences start to happen…" He trailed away, his gaze dropping to the dead birds. "People, animals…they don't act like they're supposed to."

I thought about the sparrow on my front porch looking into my window and then later on the hood of the crib staring into my eyes. "You mean like the sparrow watching me? Like these starlings falling from the sky without rhyme or reason?"

"There's always a reason if you know how to read the signs." His gaze was still on the circle. "Mama told me a story about an owl she saw once. White as snow with an uncommonly wide wingspan. She was out in the backyard bringing in the laundry when it swooped down out of nowhere and lit on a fence post. It just sat there and stared at her. Like it *knew* her, she said. Like it had some kind of message for her. Owls are common in the country, but something about that one scared her half to death. She wanted to run into the house and lock all the doors, but she was afraid to turn her back on it. So she stood there and watched it for hours, until darkness fell and the moon came up. Then the owl took flight over a nearby field, but before it got to the woods, it up and vanished, just like it had gone through a doorway. The next day, my mama learned that her mama had been in a bad accident. She'd been crushed by a tractor, but she was a fighter and had lingered far longer than she was meant to."

"That's quite a story," I said, thinking about all the strange things I'd seen come through from the other side. The ghosts and the malcontents. The Others and the in-betweens. And now a strange sparrow with humanlike behavior. *It likely means someone else is about to pass.*

He looked up slowly. "You wearing your good-luck charm?"

My fingers lifted to Rose's key. "Yes. Always."

He nodded. "Birds are messengers. The sparrow, these starlings, even that dead crow…they're coming to you for a reason."

"What reason would that be?"

His gaze darkened. "Just don't take off that charm. Especially when you're here in the cemetery. This is where they're gathering." He opened the burlap sack. "You go on about your business now. I'll take care of the birds."

I gazed down at the forlorn circle. "Before you dispose of them…please make sure they're dead. I wouldn't want them to suffer."

"Oh, they're dead all right. Good and gone. I can smell them already."

Twelve

I left Prosper Lamb to dispose of the birds and I got right to work, throwing myself into the tasks at hand so as not to dwell on the dead starlings and especially on my conversation with Jonathan Devlin. That he knew about my family legacy was a potentially life-changing revelation, but what could I do except carry on? I would warn Papa, of course, and I would continue to be cautious, but I wouldn't run away and I wouldn't hide in fear. I would get on with the restoration of Woodbine Cemetery just as I had been hired to do.

To that end, I spent the rest of the morning staking the cemetery with colored flags that corresponded with the grid I'd carefully laid out on the official map. Once the grid was completed, I walked the squares, checking off the graves on the map, making note of any historical monuments or topographical anomalies and starring the unnamed sites for further research.

Before moving on to the next section, I photographed the headstones from various angles using a mirror when needed to project light upon a blackened or weatherworn stone so that the inscriptions could be read. The map, the images and all my research materials would be included in the postrestoration package presented to the client upon completion of the project. It was tedious and time-consuming work and I enjoyed every minute of it.

I worked steadily all morning and then come noon, I gathered my belongings and headed for my vehicle. Normally, I wouldn't have taken any time off after losing two days to inclement weather, but my mother was in town for a doctor's appointment and I'd promised her and my aunt Lynrose over a week ago that I would make time for a visit.

Truth be told, I looked forward to seeing them in a normal setting instead of sipping tea beside an open grave. Those dreams still bothered me because I couldn't figure out what they meant. Old memories had been brought to the forefront, but how did that conversation between my mother and aunt tie in with the other happenings?

The puzzle was getting larger and more complicated by the moment. Obviously, my arrival in Woodbine Cemetery had awakened more than a ghost.

The questions continued to swirl in my head as I drove home for a quick shower and change of clothing. I dressed in jeans and a comfortable jacket because I would be returning to Woodbine after my visit, and by now, my mother and aunt were used to my casual attire. Despite the example they set, I took little time with hair and makeup, settling for a tightened ponytail and a thin layer of sunscreen on my already sunburned nose.

They were in the backyard soaking up the autumn sun when I arrived. It was a warm day and a little steamy after all the rain, but a light breeze made the outdoors pleasant. I could hear the silken rustle of the palmettos and banana trees that grew in profusion inside my aunt's garden. The scent of her tea olives drew me through the gate and I paused just inside to enjoy the tropical paradise she'd created.

She and my mother were seated side by side on a glider, swaying to and fro as they spoke in low tones. They hadn't seen me come in yet and I stood there wondering how, after all this time, I could still know so little about the two most important women in my life. My mother had always been a gentle, timid caregiver who had held me at arm's length even when she embraced me.

My aunt was much more demonstrative, but looking back now I realized that in her own way, she'd remained just as guarded as my mother. Her gregarious nature had made her seem more open and approachable, but I didn't know a single intimate thing about her. She'd never shared any of her secrets, never confided any of her hopes and dreams. The only thing I really knew about her was her profession. She was retired now but for most of her life she'd been a teacher and headmis-

tress at a private school not far from where I lived
on Rutledge.

Why had she never married? I wondered. Why
had she not wanted a family of her own? I had
never spoken to her in any detail about these issues, not from lack of interest or self-absorption,
but because in my family, personal questions were
not always welcomed.

Since my early childhood, Aunt Lynrose had
lavished upon me intriguing gifts and uncondi-
tional affection, and it pained me now that I could
see the distance between us so clearly. She'd always remained just a little enigmatic, but my
mother's reserve and my father's withdrawal had
made me cling to her easy hugs like a lifeline.

I'd grown up with so many secrets, apparently
in all branches of my family, and I'd carried every
last one of them into my relationship with Devlin.
Was it any wonder that things hadn't worked out
for us? Was it any wonder that my first instinct in
times of turmoil or trouble was still to retreat behind the sanctuary of my cemetery walls?

The gate swung closed behind me and my
mother and aunt glanced around with a start. For
a moment they appeared bewildered by my presence, as if they had forgotten all about our plans.
Or all about me, I thought uncomfortably. And
then they rose to greet me, smothering me in
lovely fresh-scented embraces and showering me
with praise and admonishments until I felt a little

ashamed of my earlier assessments. They truly did love me in their own way. Of that I had no doubt.

We stood in a patch of sunlight while my mother fussed about the dark circles under my eyes and my aunt clucked her tongue at my sunburned nose. She examined my hands and nails and shook her head in resignation, but with a fleeting smile to let me know that, for all her scolding, she found my carelessness endearing.

The two of them looked as elegant as ever in sweater sets and slacks, makeup perfectly applied, hair perfectly coiffed. They were both in their sixties but could have easily passed for ten years younger.

After the preliminaries were done and I'd asked about Papa and inquired about my mother's checkup, I sank down on the porch steps while my mother resettled in the glider and my aunt brought out a tray of frosted glasses.

"Are you sure I can't make you some lunch?" she asked for the third time.

"No, thank you. I had something to eat when I went home to change. The tea hits the spot, though." I took another sip of the iced brew. I preferred hot tea even in warm weather, but like most Charlestonians, my mother and aunt had been brought up on sweet tea.

"If we can't interest you in lunch, why don't you stay for an early dinner?" Mama said. "We could all go out before I drive back to Trinity."

"I'd love to but I have to get back to the cemetery in a bit."

Mama sighed. "You work too hard. Just like your papa. It wouldn't hurt either of you to take a day off now and then."

"I just had two days off due to rain," I said. "I don't like to fall too far behind. You never know when something else could come up. At least I'm working in town for a while. It's nice to sleep in my own bed at night."

"I'm sure Angus is happy to be home, too," she said. "Although that mutt is so devoted to you, he'd happily sleep in a ditch so long as it was next to you."

"He is a wonderful companion," I agreed.

"Will he go with you to the cemetery? I always worry about you alone in some of those old graveyards you take on."

"I can't have him with me this time. The cemetery is too near traffic and the gates are always kept open. And Angus likes to chase squirrels too much. He's very good at holding down the fort while I'm at work, though."

My aunt had been uncharacteristically silent during the exchange. Maybe it was my imagination or a lingering suspicion aroused by my dreams, but she seemed nervous to the point of fretful. I thought about Dr. Shaw's odd behavior and Temple's preoccupation and then I thought about Prosper Lamb's claim that when a door opened too soon, people and animals didn't act as they should.

That was an improbable explanation for the unusual behavior of three such disparate people, but they all had one thing in common—me.

"Where did you say this cemetery is located?" Mama asked as she folded her hands in her lap. By contrast, she looked restful and elegant, an understated foil for my aunt's unusual disquiet.

"I didn't say, but it's near the river, about a half mile or so from Magnolia Cemetery. It's called—"

"Oh, *must* we talk about cemeteries on such a beautiful day?" Aunt Lynrose broke in.

Her outburst took my mother and me by surprise and we stared at her for a moment as though an alien had been dropped into her backyard.

"I—no, of course not," I stammered. "I'm sorry. Mama seemed interested so I just thought—"

"Don't pay her any mind, Amelia. Lyn has been in a persnickety mood ever since I arrived." My mother turned to her sister. "What's gotten into you? We've seen so little of Amelia lately and I want to hear about her work."

"It's okay," I said. "We've other things to talk about. And I'm sorry I haven't been around much lately. Maybe when I get caught up, I can take some time off and we can make a day of it. Lunch, a movie, maybe some window-shopping on King Street."

"That sounds wonderful," Mama said. "Doesn't it, Lyn?"

"What? Yes, divine." My aunt smoothed an invisible wrinkle from her slacks. "You know what

I'd really love to do, though? We should make an appointment with a photographer and have our portrait taken. We haven't had one since Amelia was a little girl. People always talk about doing things like that, but they never get around to it. Then one day you wake up and it's too late. Someone close to you is gone and all you have left are regrets and memories and an old snapshot or two if you're lucky."

"Oh, Lyn, how morbid," Mama scolded. "And what a thing to say to someone who just came from the doctor."

My aunt looked chastised. "I didn't mean you. You're as healthy as a horse. You said so yourself. And now that you look your old self again, there's no reason to put off having our picture made."

"I'm not my old self," Mama said. "My hair has grown back and my skin is looking better, but no one is ever the same after cancer."

"Maybe not the same," I said. "But you've never looked lovelier."

"Thank you, Amelia."

"You and Aunt Lyn are still the most beautiful women I've ever known."

My aunt put a hand to her heart. "Chile."

"And you're right about that portrait, Aunt Lyn. Pictures are an important keepsake. When I was little, I adored nothing more than poring through all the old photo albums of you two when you were girls. Remember, Mama? I knew so little about either side of my family and those photographs made me feel connected even though I had a tendency to make up my own stories about your past. For a while, I convinced myself that you were long-lost princesses. All those gorgeous party dresses and formals you wore. I created a whole fantasy in my head about foundlings and an evil stepmother."

"We did have beautiful dresses," Mama mused. "But only because Mother could sew like a dream. We certainly weren't wealthy."

"She did have a way with a needle," Aunt Lynrose agreed. "Unfortunately, I didn't inherit her sewing or cooking skills."

"You never had the patience to learn," Mama said. "You were too much of a free spirit."

"Was I? That was so long ago. I hardly remember what I was like as a girl."

I listened to their back-and-forth with remnants of my dream still floating through my head. Melancholy settled over me as I pulled up my knees and hugged my legs. I felt like a little girl again, hearing their soft drawls as if through an open window.

"I had a dream about you last night, Aunt Lyn."

She looked up in surprise. "About me?"

"You were talking to Mama about a dress. I suppose that's why I remembered those old photo albums."

"What an odd thing to dream," my aunt said.

"It was very vivid. You said the crystals on the skirt twinkled like starlight when you danced."

"The midnight blue one," Mama murmured.

My aunt looked stricken. "Of all things. Why would you dream about that dress? How could you even know about it?"

"I must have heard the two of you talking about it when I was little. It seemed more like an old memory than a dream. I recalled whole chunks of your conversation."

Now both my mother and aunt looked troubled.

"What else did you dream?" Mama asked.

"You were sitting in rocking chairs drinking sweet tea by an open grave."

They both look horrified.

"What an awful dream!" Mama exclaimed.

"I suppose it was a little macabre, but it wasn't a nightmare. I wasn't frightened, at least not at that point. Maybe the open grave symbolized Rosehill Cemetery. Remember the way you used to sit on the front porch reminiscing? Sometimes I would hear you through the open front window. The cemetery was so close. I could smell the roses on the evening breeze."

My mother and aunt exchanged a glance.

"Anyway, you were talking about that dress. And I remember something about a missed curfew and Aunt Lynrose being sent away." I watched their faces carefully. I'd taken them by surprise, that much was obvious.

My aunt said in a strained voice, "I had no idea you'd overheard all that."

"I must have been very young. I had no recollection of the conversation at all until it came back to me in a dream. Even then it was interwoven with other scenes and vignettes so that I couldn't really distinguish between dream and memory. But it seems from your reactions that my recall must be fairly accurate."

"What I don't understand is why it would come back to you now." My aunt's hand crept to her throat. "Oh, Etta—"

Mama said softly, "It was just a dream, Lyn."

"No, she remembers. But the timing…" She put her fingers to her chin and glanced away.

"What about the timing?" I asked in confusion.

"You've never said anything about it before and it does seem odd that you would have such vivid recall of an obscure conversation," Mama said, which did not at all answer my question.

I set my empty tea glass aside and leaned forward. "What happened back then? Why was that dress so important?"

My mother gave me a warning look. "It wasn't the dress and none of it matters now anyway. It all happened a long time ago. Lyn went through a difficult time when we were younger, but there's no point in dredging it up now."

"We both went through difficult times," my aunt said as she reached for my mother's hand. "But we made it through, didn't we? Somehow."

"And now it's all in the past," Mama said.

"If only."

"It is," Mama insisted. "You're just going through one of your blue times."

My aunt gave her a wan smile and then turned to me almost shyly. "I know it must seem as if we're speaking in riddles, but I've never been one to dwell. What happened…happened, and that beautiful gown became symbolic of my unhappiness. And that was a real shame because Mother worked so hard on that dress. Each crystal sewn so precisely and so lovingly by hand. She called it my starlight gown."

They drifted back, murmuring softly to one another and leaving me once again on the outside looking in. I watched and I wondered. Why *had* that memory surfaced now? Why had my aunt been sent away? And why did the memory of her starlight gown still haunt her after all these years?

"You're out of tea," Aunt Lynrose said as she nodded toward my empty glass. "There's a pitcher in the kitchen. Shall I bring it out?"

"No, let me. I want to see how Binx is getting along anyway," I said as I got to my feet. I had a feeling they needed a moment alone to speak freely with one another so I used the tea as an excuse. Besides, I wanted to see the kitten I'd brought home from my last restoration. I'd found the poor thing huddled at the bottom of a hellish hole, his only company the remains of a murdered woman and her ghost. Aunt Lynrose had named the kitten Binx after a character in her favorite book and given him a home on her screened back porch. But we all knew it was only a matter of time before Binx would have the run of the whole house.

He greeted me at the door, attacking my foot and balling himself around my hand when I knelt to play. As with Angus, proper nutrition and a loving home had transformed him in a matter of weeks, and I hoped that dark abyss where I had found him was just a fading memory.

My mother's and aunt's voices drifted in from the garden and I realized they couldn't see me where I crouched on the floor, trailing a spindle of twine for the kitten.

"What else do you think she remembers?" my aunt asked in alarm.

"I doubt much else. She must have been very young when she overheard us. We haven't talked about that night in years."

"And yet she dreamed about it now. That can't be a coincidence coming so soon after I received the newspaper clipping I showed you."

"That clipping may not mean anything," Mama said.

"It means everything! When I think of all the time that was lost to me...to us..."

"That time wasn't yours," Mama said.

"No," my aunt said bitterly. "He and Father saw to that, didn't they?"

"Shush," Mama said. "You're getting yourself all worked up and that's not like you. Has something else happened that I don't know about?

Something's weighing on you. I could tell the moment I walked in the door."

My aunt paused. "He's asked to see me."

I sensed my mother's shock all the way through the screen door. "You won't go! Oh, Lyn, you can't confront him. Not in your state."

"Why not? You don't think it would be interesting to hear what he has to say for himself after all this time?"

"It's been nearly fifty years. Half a century. How can anything about that man possibly matter to you now?"

"He's old and sick. It's never too late to develop a guilty conscience. Maybe he's the one who sent the newspaper clipping. Maybe he wants the truth to come out before he dies so he can ask for forgiveness."

"And if he does?" my mother asked in resignation. "What will you say to him?"

"That all will be forgiven the moment hell freezes over."

I left Binx unspooling the twine and wreaking havoc on the back porch as I eased inside the house and made my way down the hallway to the bathroom to wash my hands. The overheard conversation with my mother and aunt was possibly even more distressing than the one I'd dreamed about.

Whatever had happened in my aunt's past obviously still haunted her and now I was haunted by the cool, calm way she'd talked about withholding forgiveness. It was almost as if she had come to a resolution while she and my mother talked. Maybe I was making too much of that conversation, but I felt the weight of another dark premonition pressing down on me.

Prosper Lamb was right. The birds were coming to me for a reason. I was having those dreams for a reason. Something bad was about to happen. A door had been opened because someone close to me was about to pass.

I splashed cold water on my face until the darkness receded.

When I came out of the bathroom, I heard music playing from one of the bedrooms.

Standing motionless in the hallway, I turned an ear to the sound. The strands were very faint as if a music box had been wound behind one of the closed doors. Slowly, I walked down the hallway, pausing at each room to listen. When I got to the end of the corridor, I pressed my ear to the door. The sound came from inside and I had a sudden vision of a mobile over a crib, stirring gently in a draft.

Where that vision came from, I couldn't imagine. My aunt didn't have children and if there'd been a mobile over *my* crib, I certainly couldn't remember it.

I glanced around the hallway, trying to ground myself in the here and now. To my right was a wall of artwork, mostly serene gardens and seascapes, but no portraits. To my left was a wall of floating shelves on which my aunt had displayed a variety of collectibles—vases, figurines, a bowl of potpourri. I studied the curios, not realizing that I was searching for something until my gaze lit on a pale blue porcelain box on the top shelf. The keepsake was only a little higher than eye level for me now, but as a small child it would have been well out of my reach.

Something about that porcelain box bothered me. I knew without picking it up that it would have a white cameo on the lid and that it meant something special to my aunt.

The faint tinkling drew my attention back to the door. I pressed closer and concentrated my senses. I couldn't make out a melody, but those random notes intrigued me. As I put my hand on the knob, my gaze lit again on that blue box and the memory that had been trapped at the fringes of my subconscious finally broke free.

I remembered standing on the other side of the door as a child. I even had a vivid image of the room—small but beautifully appointed with a dainty white crib, a rocking chair and shelves of books and toys. Over the crib, a butterfly mobile stirred in a draft, triggering the music box.

Even as a little girl, I'd been mesmerized by those faints strands. I hadn't been able to tear myself away even though I knew the room was off limits. The door had always been kept closed and so when I'd seen it ajar, the lure had been irresistible.

I sank deeper into the memory, recalling my delight at all those hidden treasures…until I'd sensed a presence behind me. I'd turned to find Aunt Lynrose on the threshold gazing down at me in shock. "What do you think you're doing? You know you're not allowed in here."

My aunt had never so much as raised her voice to me and her anger startled me so badly that I dropped the doll I'd been admiring. Why she would have a roomful of toys that no one could play with, I didn't know. It never even occurred to me to ask.

"I'm sorry," I said as I backed away. "I didn't mean to be bad."

Her face crumpled. "You aren't bad and I should never have spoken to you in that tone. I'm sorry, too." She picked up the doll and cradled it to her breast for a moment. "But you shouldn't be inside on such a lovely day. Come out to the garden with me. You can help with the tomatoes."

She took my hand and led me from the room. Then she locked the door and placed the key in the blue porcelain bowl high up on a shelf where I couldn't reach.

The memory floated away and I was left standing in the hallway with my ear pressed to the door. For some reason, I didn't have the nerve to turn the knob, let alone remove the key from the blue porcelain box. It had been one thing to breach forbidden territory when I was a child, but as an adult, snooping into my aunt's private affairs was unforgiveable.

But it wasn't just my conscience or ethics that kept me from that room. I didn't want to validate my memory. That ominous premonition was pressing down on me again and I somehow knew that if I opened the door, there would be no turning back.

I didn't know why I was dreaming about my mother and my aunt beside an open grave. I didn't know why birds were gathering in Woodbine Cemetery or why the ghost of that murdered little girl was tethered to the baby crib in the willow copse.

If I opened the door, I might find the answers to all of my questions, but I had a terrible feeling that something else, something precious, would be lost to me.

Thirteen

A little while later, I left my mother and aunt in the garden and returned to the cemetery. As much as I needed to make up for lost time, I had an overwhelming desire to blow off the rest of the day and head to the library for research. I had a feeling there was so much more about Woodbine Cemetery that I had yet to uncover. My dreams were deeper clues than I had first realized. How my mother and aunt tied into the overall mystery, I still didn't know—didn't want to know—but it was safe to say they had secrets. One of those secrets might even be buried in Woodbine Cemetery.

I didn't see the caretaker again for the rest of the afternoon, nor did I notice any other visitors. I had the cemetery to myself and I was grateful for the solitude. The hours passed peacefully.

Late in the day, though, when the light began to fade, my thoughts turned once again to the ghost child. I braced myself for another manifestation as my gaze swept the cemetery. If a hint of woodbine drifted on the breeze, I didn't smell it. If an ethereal hand tapped a melody on a wind chime, I didn't hear it. But just before sunset, I did happen upon another disconcerting find.

At the very back of the cemetery, enclosed in a wrought-iron fence, was a space designated for infants and children. A perimeter of live oaks wove a thick canopy over the area, protecting the tiny graves from summer's heat and winter's chill. Within that cool, deep grotto, a lush oasis of bromeliads and ferns had cropped up.

I stood shivering beneath the branches as I gazed across that sea of lonely graves. A section for children wasn't unusual, especially in older cemeteries, but I'd never run across one quite like this. The headstones were all a similar design—open cockleshells large enough to shelter a sleeping babe. The striking visual of the seashells, coupled with the gentle sway of the Spanish moss, created an eerie, underwater feel that deepened the air of loneliness.

"So you've found the enchanted garden," a female voice called behind me.

I whirled in shock, taken aback by the sight of Claire Bellefontaine picking her way across the damp ground toward me. My mind instantly reeled back to the ghost child outside the restaurant window as she'd screamed out her rage. The sound of that unnatural howl seemed to echo across all those lonely graves as Claire Bellefontaine lifted her hand to wave at me.

She wore tall boots and a sensible cotton jacket

that protected her from mosquitoes and brambles, but she looked no less striking in her casual attire. She had her hair down today, a silvery-gold curtain that billowed gracefully in the breeze. My hands had involuntarily clenched at my sides and as I relaxed my fingers, I made an effort to assume a nondescript smile.

"I've startled you," she said as she moved closer. "I apologize. I wasn't trying to sneak up on you. I thought you would have heard me tramping through the weeds."

She had moved as silently as a ghost across the landscape. "I was lost in thought, I guess."

"It is a place for contemplation," she agreed. "I hope you'll forgive the intrusion."

"Of course."

She patted the small cross-body bag that rested at her hip. "I've come armed with a camera. I wanted to get a few shots of the cemetery before you're too far into the restoration."

"Then you should probably hurry. The light goes quickly once the sun sets. And I've been told the cemetery attracts an unsavory element after dark."

"The unsavory are everywhere if one knows where to look." She gave me a sly smile as she looped her fingers through the strap of her bag. "Not to worry. I've come armed with more than a camera. I know how to take care of myself and I suspect you do, as well."

"Let's hope it doesn't come to that," I said, dis-

mayed by the notion of an armed Claire Bellefontaine. Suddenly, I found myself wishing for a more
effective arsenal than the cell phone and pepper
spray I kept in my pocket.

Was I in danger from her? After my conversation with Jonathan Devlin that morning, there
could be no doubt that at least one member of the
Congé knew about my gift. Who was to say he
hadn't shared his findings with his grandson's fiancée? Maybe she had come here to observe me
up close or to throw me off guard. Even if I were
to believe our encounter at the restaurant had been
a chance run-in, a second meeting in so short a
time could only be deliberate.

"What do you think about this place?" she
asked.

"The cemetery?" I studied her profile, searching for a hint of her true intentions. Her voice and
mannerisms seemed open and friendly, but her
eyes were cold and I could detect a hint of cruelty in her smile. One thing I knew for certain—
I wouldn't be turning my back on her. "There's a
lot of work to be done, but I've seen much worse."

"I mean specifically the children's section," she
said. "I call it the enchanted garden because it's
always so quiet back here and so lovely and cool
beneath the trees. It's like being a million miles
from anywhere."

I was all too aware of the remoteness. "Do you
visit these graves often?"

"Not really, but when I was little, my nanny and

I came every week. Pearlie had a thing for cemeteries. You would have liked her, I think. She was
a peculiar woman, God rest her."

"Is she buried here?" I inquired gently.

"Pearlie? No. She wanted to be with her hus-
bands in the old Good Hope Cemetery down in
Colleton County. It's a very restful place. Maybe
you've been there?" I shook my head and she fell
silent as she glanced skyward. "Listen," she said
in a hushed tone. "Can you hear them?"

Something in her voice made me shiver as I
turned my ear to the breeze, detecting the faintest of tinkles.

"The chimes are all over the cemetery, hidden
high up in the treetops. When the wind blows just
right, they sound like a pipe organ. Pearlie used to
say they were the music of the ghosts."

"They do sound ethereal," I said, thinking of
the murdered child's spirit and the haunting melody that always seemed to preface her manifestation. Was she here now? I wondered. Glowering
from the shadows as her rage continued to build?
I didn't see or sense her, but a tingle at my nape
warned that twilight was coming and we might
not be as alone as we seemed.

Claire Bellefontaine seemed oblivious to the
sudden nip in the air. She said dreamily, "We used
to drive out here after church. Pearlie had loved
ones in a nearby cemetery, but she always insisted
that we visit the enchanted garden before we went
home. She said it was important that the babies

knew they hadn't been forgotten. I can still see her sitting over there in the grass reading aloud from a storybook while I gathered wildflowers for the graves."

She had so perfectly described a scene from my own childhood that I wondered if she'd fabricated the memory in order to foster a kinship. How she had found out about my early days, I didn't know, but if Jonathan Devlin could uncover my family's darkest secret, I didn't put anything past the *Congé*.

I mustered another benign smile as I wondered how best to extricate myself from Claire Bellefontaine's company. She seemed in no hurry to get to her photography, leading me to wonder again about the real reason for her visit. Engaging her in conversation might be the best way to protect myself. At least I could keep an eye on her while we talked.

"Sounds like a pleasant way to spend a Sunday afternoon," I said.

She nodded, giving no hint that she was aware of my internal machinations. "For the most part it was. I adored Pearlie and I loved spending time with her. I felt closer to her than just about anyone, except perhaps for my brother. But I didn't share her fascination for the dead. This place..." She paused as she gripped one of the wrought-iron pikes. "Sometimes after we left, I'd fall into a deep funk. It seemed so unbearably sad that the children were buried so far away from their families, isolated and alone, locked inside this fence. I was afraid the same fate awaited me even though Pearlie assured me that when my time came, I'd be placed in a vault in the Bellefontaine mausoleum in Magnolia Cemetery. Amazingly, this did not comfort me," she said with a soft laugh.

Despite her air of aloofness, she had a way of drawing one into her orbit. Like a spider, I thought. Or the beguiling Venus flytrap. "It does seem sad and there is a sense of isolation back here, but the burials were probably a matter of practicality. If no family plot was available or the means to buy one, parents were offered an affordable alternative, which had the added benefit of saving space in the main cemetery."

"But that's even sadder. That the burial of a child would come down to a matter of economics."

Spoken like a woman who had never had to worry about her next couture gown, let alone the feeding and clothing of a family. "Cemeteries have the same hierarchy as the living world. That's just the way it is."

She gave me a quick scrutiny as she tucked back her hair. "You certainly know your business. I admire passion in one's work. It's a rare thing these days to find a calling." She paused. "So now that you've explained the purpose of the enchanted garden, perhaps you could also enlighten me as to why all the gravestones are so similar. I've always wondered."

"I can only give you a guess. At one time, there

may have been a benefactor, someone who took it upon himself or herself to provide headstones for children of the less fortunate. I can tell you that the open cockleshell design was very popular from the late eighteen hundreds all the way up to the Second World War. The Victorians, in particular, were fond of death as fantasy motifs."

"Death as fantasy?"

"A seashell large enough to shelter a sleeping child is a fantasy image, one that softens the hard reality of death. Some historians believe that the popularity in whimsical cemetery art in the nineteenth century corresponded to the rise of illustrated storybooks—Lewis Carroll, Beatrix Potter and so on." I nodded toward the fanciful headstones. "This style in particular became so fashionable that it could even be acquired through mail-order catalogues. In cemetery jargon, it's sometimes referred to as babies on the half shell, but I've never liked the term."

"It does sound a bit too frivolous." She closed her eyes as if listening to the distant melody of the wind chimes. "May I ask you something else?"

"Of course."

Her eyes were still closed, her lips curled in a slight smile. "Do you believe in ghosts?"

I didn't outwardly react. I'd spent my whole life hiding behind cemetery gates and a placid demeanor. And since my encounter with Jonathan Devlin that morning, a part of me had been waiting and preparing for the next shoe to drop. So, no,

I didn't react, but my every instinct warned that we were entering dangerous territory.

"Doesn't everyone?" I said lightly.

She gave me a sidelong glance. "You're teasing me, but it was a serious question. I'd love an honest answer from someone in your line of work. If ever a place could be haunted, surely it would be one of the abandoned cemeteries that you restore."

"The only thing to fear in most cemeteries is the human element I warned you about earlier."

She smiled—knowingly, I thought—before glancing back up into the treetops. "I've always wondered about Woodbine. Even as a child, I sensed… I don't know…a restive air. Maybe it was only my imagination. Pearlie did love to fill my head with the folklore and wives' tales from her own childhood. Still, this cemetery has a history, not all of it seemly."

I could certainly understand why the ghosts of those in the unnamed graves might be restless. "To answer your question, I don't *not* believe," I said carefully. "But I think most hauntings can be logically explained with a proper investigation."

"I'm not sure I agree with that. I'm not sure I *want* to believe that." She watched me in the same way that Jonathan Devlin had observed me that morning and I felt more strongly than ever that I was somehow being taunted or tested.

"Why not?" I asked, still in that colorless tone.

She turned back to the fence, her gaze moving aimlessly over the tiny graves. Now it was I who watched her. At the restaurant, I had thought her complexion flawless, but I found myself zeroing in on a tiny birthmark at the corner of her mouth and a sliver of a scar along her jawline. She wore a lighter shade of lipstick than the night before, but I could detect a note of the same perfume, a faint trace of sandalwood that reminded me of the cedars at the front of the cemetery. The woodsy scent conjured an image of a coffin, which I did not take as a good sign.

"I've never seen a ghost," she finally said. "As frightening as I would probably find such an encounter, I'd like to think there are things in this world that can't be explained away with a *proper investigation*." The exaggerated enunciation of my words seemed to mock me. "How much more thrilling it would be if we could experience life beyond our five senses."

Thrilling? She had no idea. Then again, maybe she did. Maybe she was one of the *Congé* whose sensitivity to the unseen world made her particularly dangerous to people like me.

"I've never really given the matter much thought," I said.

"I find that hard to believe. Surely you must have seen and heard things in some of your old cemeteries. Things you can't explain no matter how deeply you investigate."

"People have the wrong idea about cemeteries. They're built for the living, not the dead. If ghosts do exist, I think they are much more likely to attach themselves to people than places."

"An interesting thought," she said.

I didn't want to appear overly eager to change the subject, so I turned to glance back into the cemetery, letting my gaze travel leisurely over the headstones and monuments, perhaps searching unconsciously for traces of a manifestation now that the sun dipped beneath the horizon. There was still a lot of light in Woodbine, but dusk seemed to steal in from all the remote corners.

"You're right about one thing," I said. "This cemetery does have a fascinating history. You mentioned last night that you have family here."

"Two maiden aunts, Claire and Sybilla. Both died many years ago, long before I was born. I was named after them and so I've always felt an affinity. But the cemetery looks so completely different from the way I remember it, I'm not sure I would be able to find their graves now." She gazed around. "I had no idea this place had fallen into such a sad state."

I said in surprise, "You didn't visit before you awarded the contract?"

"There wasn't time. I was out of town when the donation came in, and the board had to contend with a deadline. We're fortunate you had an opening in your schedule so that we didn't have to forfeit the contribution."

I thought about Prosper Lamb's suggestion that a guilty conscience was likely the catalyst behind the Woodbine restoration. "I guess it's lucky for all of us, then, that my next job was postponed."

Her voice sharpened infinitesimally as she lifted a brow. "Is a postponement unusual?"

"Not really. Projects get delayed for any number of reasons. Why? You seem concerned."

She hesitated. "Perhaps I shouldn't say anything. I don't want to alarm you."

But, of course, that was exactly what she had done. "What do you mean?"

"I wasn't entirely forthright with you at the restaurant last night."

My apprehension deepened. "No?"

"I failed to mention that the donation was anonymous."

"Is that important?"

She shrugged. "Probably not. But in addition to a deadline, the donation came with another stipulation. That you and only you be awarded the contract."

I frowned. "But the project went out for bids. I submitted one."

"The bidding was by invitation only and you were the only one who received a notice."

I stared at her for a moment. "I don't understand. Why go to all that trouble? Why not just hire me outright?"

"That I haven't figured out yet. Maybe it was another way to ensure anonymity or maybe the donor thought you'd be more inclined to submit a competitive price if you thought others were vying for the contract. But let me make one thing clear. I didn't misrepresent Rupert Shaw's enthusiastic recommendation or the board's unanimous approval. If your references and credentials hadn't checked out, we were prepared to submit a counterproposal to the donor's representative."

"And you have no idea the donor's identity?"

"None."

I contemplated her revelation for a moment. "Why are you telling me this now?"

"I felt guilty for all the subterfuge."

"Is that why you came here today?"

"No, I really did want to see the cemetery one last time before the restoration. But finding you out here all alone and knowing how isolated this place is…" She trailed away. "I'm probably being overly cautious. I doubt there's anything more than eccentricity behind the odd stipulations, but I wouldn't feel right keeping you in the dark."

I didn't like the sound of any of this. I felt very much manipulated and set up. Until that moment, I hadn't given the postponement of my previous project much thought. Delays and rescheduling came with the territory when one's business depended on the capricious nature of weather and the bureaucratic slog through permits and red tape. Now doubt started to niggle as I wondered who might be pulling the strings.

One thing remained the same, though. I still didn't trust Claire Bellefontaine.

"This is all very curious," I said.

"I agree. And no one could blame you if you were to have second thoughts."

Was that a hopeful note in her voice? After playing along with such an elaborate charade, was she trying to get rid of me for some reason? Did her family have secrets in Woodbine they wanted to keep hidden?

My imagination was getting ahead of me. I took a breath and said, "The circumstances of the contract are unusual, I'll admit, but I see no reason we can't proceed. That is what you and the rest of the board want, isn't it?"

She didn't answer. Her head tilted as if she were listening to the chimes, but I had a feeling her attention had strayed elsewhere. She said without inflection, "Someone's coming."

I whirled toward the path, expecting to find Prosper Lamb making his way toward us, but instead I spotted two men walking in single file through the graves. They were both tall and fit with the privileged, predatory bearing of those who had known their rightful place in the world since birth.

Hunters was my first panicky thought. Elite zealots from the *Congé* on a mission to rid the living world of the unnatural elements like me. What better place to trap me than at the back of an overgrown and abandoned cemetery?

A part of me acknowledged that I was jumping to some pretty incredulous conclusions, but something about this whole situation set off warning bells.

The alarms grew even louder as the men advanced and I recognized the one in the lead as Rance Duvall. Was that why I'd had such an unpleasant reaction to his presence in the restaurant last night? Had my senses picked up a vibe or a tell that had alerted me of his true nature?

First an unexpected encounter with Jonathan Devlin in White Point Garden and then Claire Bellefontaine in Woodbine Cemetery. And now Rance Duvall. I felt cornered and I wanted nothing more than to bolt, but I was outnumbered and outgunned by at least one of the three.

I tried to convince myself that I was overreacting, but this was no happenstance gathering. How could it be? These people—members of a deadly faction—could be here for no other reason than to confront me. The cemetery was off the beaten path. No passing cars. No prying eyes. They could bury me in one of the graves and no one would be wiser.

At that moment, I would have welcomed the enigmatic caretaker's presence so that I didn't feel quite so alone. But no one was coming to my rescue. No one had my back.

Untying the jacket from around my waist, I pulled it on and slid my hands into the pockets so that the cell phone and pepper spray were within my grasp. Puny weapons, to be sure, but I wouldn't go down without a fight.

As I inwardly braced myself for battle, a chilly breeze blew through the trees, raising goose bumps at my nape and stirring the wind chimes all through the cemetery. The faint strands of a familiar melody filtered down through the leaves as the scent of woodbine invaded my senses.

Fourteen

The ghost child was nearby—whether drawn by the coming twilight or by the two men approaching, I had no idea. Or perhaps Claire Bellefontaine's visit to the cemetery had precipitated the manifestation. I couldn't yet see the apparition, but I felt her all around me. Her presence was like an icy hand trailing down my back.

I glanced over my shoulder at the enchanted garden. Crimson clouds scuttled across the western horizon where the sun had gone down, but the cockleshell headstones were still bathed in a golden glow. In that fragile in-between light, the ghost child was nearly invisible.

She didn't try to make contact or even to look at me. She sat cross-legged in the grass, head bowed so that I couldn't see her pale countenance. I thought at first that I had slipped into another of her memories. For whatever reason, she wanted me to witness this fleeting moment from her past. Was it another clue? Was she still trying to lead me to her murderer?

Not a comforting thought as the two men continued to advance and I became aware once more of how alone I was, how isolated this section of the cemetery. As much as I deplored the injustice of that child's death, I wanted to look away before I learned too much. Self-preservation ran deep. Searching for a killer was a dangerous business, and no matter my experience with ghosts, no matter my previous encounters with the depraved and the possessed, I was no hero. I was an everywoman trapped by my family's legacy and the circumstances of my birth. Where once I had been enticed by the vicarious thrill of police investigations and the dark seduction of an old mystery, I now craved peace and quiet. All I wanted was to be left alone, but I couldn't avert my gaze from that diaphanous form no matter how hard I tried. The shimmer of the ghost's manifestation enthralled me.

I waited, tense and breathless, but nothing happened. A memory did not unfold. The ghost remained immoveable, a gossamer statue, and it finally occurred to me that this wasn't a memory at all. This was her existence, her earthbound reality. She came to the enchanted garden to be with the other children because she had nowhere else to go. The loneliness that swept through me was dark and clawing, devastating in its intensity. She must have been waiting a very long time for someone to come along who could see her. For someone who could acknowledge her pain and give witness to her rage.

I almost put out a hand to her and then caught myself as Papa's imaginary caution drifted through my head. *Careful, Amelia. A ghost is a ghost.*

As if intuiting my reluctance, the entity rose and floated over to the fence, glaring through the pikes with churlish impatience.

I took a step back from the fence as I turned toward the main cemetery. The newcomers were momentarily hidden by a stand of laurel oaks. When they emerged on the other side, I finally caught a glimpse of the second man's profile. I had been shocked to recognize Rance Duvall in the lead, but now I was utterly devastated to realize that his companion was none other than Devlin.

He didn't so much as glance in my direction as they approached, but instead raked his gaze over the headstones and memorials as if memorizing the terrain.

My heart flailed as my every nerve ending bristled a warning. Why was he here? Surely he meant me no harm, but how could I be certain? I had to judge him by the company he kept, and my initial impression of Rance Duvall had been damning. I felt a spidery crawl at the back of my neck as I remembered the effect he'd had on me at the restaurant. He was a handsome man, but I couldn't help wondering what lay hidden behind his compelling visage. I couldn't dispel the image of beady eyes and a gaping beak as he halted on the pathway to say something over his shoulder to Devlin.

Devlin nodded, his gaze shifting in my direction and just like that, he took me in with the power of a physical punch. Once again I felt trapped, this time by the sheer magnetism of his presence. I couldn't look away. I could barely even catch my breath. The pulse in my throat throbbed as a thrill of excitement raced through my bloodstream.

In that moment when our gazes clung, treacherous memories besieged me. The intensity of his stare…his body as he moved over me…in me…the feel of his lips, his hands, his hair… The whisper of my name…

Amelia… Amelia…do you have any idea how much I want you?

Then take me.

My resolve weakened along with my knees. I was aware of his fiancée at my side and the impropriety of my thoughts. But I was only human and Devlin would always be Devlin.

Still in a state of shock, I'd momentarily forgotten about the ghost child. I didn't know if she wanted my attention or if her rage could no longer be contained, but her bloodcurdling scream cleaved the silence, ripping apart the last vestiges of my composure. I physically flinched. I may even have gasped. The pain of that howl became so intense I wanted nothing more than to drop to my knees and cover my ears.

"Mercy," I whispered.

An uncanny silence fell over the cemetery. The scream faded along with the tinkling of the chimes and I could hear nothing beyond the catch in my breath and the pounding of my heartbeat in my ears. I felt dizzy with relief, but I didn't think the ghost had vanished back into the ether. Not yet. Not for good. The game wasn't finished. She still had plans for me. I could sense her behind me in the enchanted garden, floating through those tiny graves, lurking among the seashell headstones. I didn't dare turn to seek her out.

Beside me, Claire said sharply, "What did you say?"

"Nothing."

"You mumbled something. I heard you." She looked at me through narrowed eyes.

My heart was still pounding, but I couldn't let her sense my agitation. I couldn't let her know that I'd just seen a ghost.

I took a breath and tried to recover my poise. "I recognize the man in the lead. He was at the restaurant last night. I was startled to see him in the cemetery, especially at this hour."

Whether she bought my explanation or not, I didn't know. She didn't challenge me and for that I was grateful. "You mean Rance?"

I turned in surprise. "You know him?"

"Know him?" She gave a soft laugh. "He's my brother. You didn't see us together at Rapture last night?"

"No, I—no." My fingers slipped to the key at

my neck. Rance Duvall was Claire Bellefontaine's brother? "I had no idea you were related."

"He has a lot of experience in restoring and preserving historical properties," she explained. "I asked him to come out here and take a look at Woodbine. I hope you don't mind."

I swallowed. "No, it's fine." Normally, I welcomed interest and even participation in my restorations, but all I could focus on at the moment was being trapped at the back of an overgrown cemetery with people who might well be my mortal enemies.

I searched Claire's features, this time for a family resemblance. Rance Duvall was older than she by at least twenty years, but even beyond the age difference, they looked nothing alike. He was as dark as she was fair and they didn't even share the same last name. The one thing they did have in common was my wariness of them. I knew very little about either of them, but I'd learned the hard way not to discount premonitions and intuition. I thought about Prosper Lamb's door and the bad, bad things that sometimes came through. I thought about the sparrow and the dead starlings and the dreams I'd been having about my mother and my aunt. What any of these events had to do with the three people who stood before me in Woodbine Cemetery, I had no idea. The connections and alliances made no sense to me...yet.

I tried to file everything away to be analyzed later in the safety of my sanctuary. For now, I needed to stay alert. But no sooner had I resolved myself to a careful vigil than I became distracted by the tension radiating from Claire Bellefontaine. Something had displeased her and she made little effort to conceal her irritation.

"What are *you* doing here?" she demanded as the two men approached. The emphasis on the pronoun jarred me and I stared at her for a moment before refocusing my attention on the newcomers.

"That's a fine greeting," Rance Duvall said jovially. "Did you or did you not ask me to meet you out here?"

"I asked *you*." She glared at Devlin and in that moment, she could not have looked less like a woman in love. Her fury was evident in the thinning of her lips and the jutting of her chin, and I thought with a shudder that Claire Bellefontaine was not someone I'd ever want to cross.

I stood quietly by and watched in fascination as the drama unfolded.

Devlin responded in an equally chilly tone. "Your brother said he was headed out here this afternoon so I thought I'd tag along. You don't mind, do you?"

"You said you had meetings for the rest of the day."

"Change of plans." Devlin moved in then and bussed her cheek. Her hand fluttered to his chest, not to draw him closer, but to hold him at arm's length. The rebuff didn't appear to bother him.

His low laugh as he pulled away sent a chill down my spine.

How extraordinary this all was to me and how utterly bewildering. I was no expert in kinesics, but their body language seemed to speak volumes.

Devlin didn't glance at me again. He had eyes only for Claire, but I had the strangest feeling that he was *watching* her. He made no move to touch her again or she him. I couldn't detect even the slightest hint of warmth between them. Their behavior made me wonder about the nature of their relationship, but I told myself not to go there. Speculation was a dangerous pastime for an ex-lover. Almost as treacherous as the imagination and wishful thinking.

While Devlin watched Claire, I observed him, and I couldn't help but note again how very much he had changed since we'd been together. Gone was the brooding police detective I'd been drawn to that first night he'd stepped out of the mist to confront me. Instead of the bespoke suits and fitted dress shirts, he wore jeans and a black wool jacket with the collar turned up. A lock of unruly hair fell across his forehead and I could see the shadow of his beard on his lower face. He was still a handsome man, perhaps even more so than I remembered, but the darkness within him had roughened his physical appearance and deepened his reserve. Maybe he and Claire Bellefontaine made a match after all.

Beside me, she said, "Miss Gray, I'd like you

to meet my fiancé, John Devlin. Miss Gray is the restorer we hired to clean up the cemetery."

Devlin said without inflection, "I know who she is." His gaze moved over me once more, igniting embers I'd tried to smother for well over a year. "Hello, Amelia."

He might look a stranger, but the soft drawl of my name hadn't changed one iota nor had my reaction to it. "Hello," I said as memories vibrated through me.

Claire said, "Oh, that's right. You did mention that Miss Gray—Amelia—had once helped you on a case."

Had he really explained our relationship by reducing it to a police investigation? I somehow doubted Claire would have accepted such an innocuous explanation. If Devlin's grandfather had uncovered my family's deepest secret, surely his fiancée would have found out about our time together.

Rance Duvall stepped forward then, offering his hand and an amiable smile, but I found myself once again repelled. He searched my face as we shook, his gaze narrowing in deliberation. I could smell the leather of his jacket and an undercurrent of musk that made me think of something feral and rapacious.

"Amelia Gray," he murmured. His drawl was deep and cultured and yet it reminded me nothing of Devlin's. He cocked his head slightly. "We've met before, haven't we? I can't think when or where but I never forget a face."

"We've never met," I said, trying to hide my distaste. "Not that I recall anyway. But I saw you last night at Rapture. I was there with a mutual friend. Dr. Temple Lee?"

Recognition flared and his smile widened, displaying a pair of boyish dimples. "Ah, yes. That must be it. And now that you've prodded my memory, I do recall Temple saying that your work involved cemeteries. I just never put it together that you were our Woodbine restorer."

"Small world," I said.

"And getting smaller every day," he agreed. How charming he seemed, how open and friendly his demeanor. And yet like Claire Bellefontaine, he aroused an aversion that was hard to explain. There was something in his eyes that made me think of all those dark things that crawled through the veil at dusk, that made me want to scurry toward the nearest hallowed ground and hunker down until dawn.

Instead, I reached for Rose's key, fingering the cool metal as I wondered why Devlin would associate with these people. But, of course, I already knew the answer. He was one of them now.

I shot him a glance but he was still fixated on Claire.

"Did Temple tell you about the excavation she and her crew are conducting on Duvall Island?" Rance asked.

Reluctantly, I tore my attention from Devlin. "Yes, she's very excited about the findings. And she's grateful for your cooperation. That isn't always the case."

He grinned. "Property owners tend to get a little nervous when a bunch of strangers show up with shovels and wheelbarrows."

"But not you."

"I'm a historian, so I see the bigger picture." He paused. "Temple says you also have a background in archeology. You used to work for her, I believe."

I didn't like the idea of being the topic of their conversation, much less the object of Rance Duvall's interest. "That was a long time ago, before I came to Charleston to start my business."

"It's still in the blood, I imagine. Once a digger, always a digger. Or so I'm told." Another guileless smile. "You should come out to the site sometime. Duvall Island was under siege in both the Revolutionary and Civil Wars, so we're uncovering all sorts of things. Bullets, buckles, cannonballs, breastplates, buttons and the like. And below those layers, bones, arrowheads, clay shards. It's all very exciting."

"Yes, I well remember the exhilaration," I replied noncommittally.

"Transportation can be a bit tricky. There's no bridge or causeway, so the only way on and off the island is by boat." He fished in his pocket and produced a card. "If you decide to come out, call this number. My assistant will make all the arrangements."

"Thank you."

"If I'm on-site, I'll give you the grand tour. Duvall Place has been badly neglected for generations, but the house is still a historical masterpiece. My father and his father before him saw no value in maintaining the integrity of the property, so I'm desperately playing catch-up. The structure has withstood Union assaults and untold hurricanes, but I'm afraid the battle of time and neglect may be our undoing."

"A word to the wise," Claire put in. "Don't go out there in bad weather. I can't speak to the dig site, but the plantation house is spooky even in broad daylight. Trust me when I say that you don't want to be trapped on that island overnight."

"If I can clear my schedule, I'll make sure to pick a sunny day," I assured her.

"There's a small cemetery on the island," Rance said. "The graves date back to the early seventeen hundreds. Some of the headstones are in very bad shape, so perhaps you could give us some pointers as to how best to preserve them. And speaking of cemeteries…" He turned to scan his surroundings. "I had no idea Woodbine had fallen into such a disgraceful state. The neglect is always like a dagger through the heart, but unfortunately, there's never enough money to go around for these projects. A cemetery, a building…something always falls between the cracks, especially in a city as old as Charleston. The Woodbine Trust is fortunate to have received such a generous donation."

"Yes, very lucky," I agreed, wondering if he'd had anything to do with the anonymous contribution. "I'm sure the neglect is especially distressing when you have family buried here."

"She means the aunts," Claire said and then turned to me. "They were Bellefontaines, so no relation to Rance. He's my stepbrother, you see, which explains why he's so much older."

"And so much wiser, apparently." His dark eyes gleamed. "Claire and Sybilla weren't sisters. Only one of them was a Bellefontaine."

"I'm sure you're mistaken," Claire said with a frown. "I know their story well. I'm named for them, after all. Pearlie and I used to visit their graves every Sunday and she told me how close they were, how they both refused to marry because of their utter devotion to one another."

"She wasn't wrong about that," Rance said. "They were extremely devoted and lived together openly in a cottage on Limehouse Street. The relationship created quite a scandal and they were eventually disowned by their families and shunned from polite society."

Which probably explained their interment in Woodbine Cemetery. Their plight made me wonder what other secrets the Bellefontaine family had buried here.

During the whole of the conversation, Devlin had remained silent, but now he shifted restlessly, his gaze moving about the cemetery before coming to rest briefly on me. "We should go," he said. "It's getting late and we're keeping Amelia from finishing her work."

"Yes, we've taken enough of your time," Claire agreed. "And I've completely missed the light. I'll have to come back another day to get my shots."

"Perhaps next time we could impose upon you for a tour," Rance said. "I daresay there may even be some Duvalls buried here."

I sincerely hoped there would be no next time, but I smiled and nodded politely.

They lingered for a moment longer before heading back toward the entrance—Rance once more in the lead, Claire in the middle and Devlin bringing up the rear. I watched until they were out of sight, and Devlin never once glanced back in my direction. I tried to shake off a lingering melancholy. Devlin hadn't been in my life for a very long time and I had managed to make peace with his absence. Or so I told myself on all those sleepless nights. I would be a fool to allow a brief encounter to undo my hard-fought contentment.

Still…

I didn't know what to make of their visit, but I was fairly certain it had nothing to do with photographing the cemetery. And I was equally certain that Devlin had had an agenda apart from the other two. That was why Claire had been so incensed by his arrival. She had obviously wanted only her stepbrother to meet her at Woodbine Cemetery, but why?

It was all very puzzling and more than a little disquieting. And I couldn't help wondering what would have happened if Devlin hadn't made a point to tag along.

Fifteen

I remained at the enchanted garden until the sound of their voices faded in the distance. A few minutes later, I heard the slamming of car doors and the gunning of engines, but I still didn't return to the main entrance. What if one of them waited for me there? Instead, I decided to go out the side gate, through which, I suspected, the early-morning visitor had departed.

The footprints, the dead starlings and even my encounter with Jonathan Devlin seemed far removed from me now, little more than curiosities that paled in comparison to the real-world threat of Claire Bellefontaine and her stepbrother, Rance Duvall. I couldn't know for certain the pair meant me harm. I wasn't even sure they were members of the *Congé*, but I'd seen and heard enough to be on my guard around them.

As I gathered up my gear, I tried to recall everything that Dr. Shaw had told me about the nefarious group. They recruited from the Order of the Coffin and the Claw, conscripting the elite from the elite to form a brigade of warriors to do battle against the supernatural. And now they'd gone mainstream, he'd said, spreading their influence into banking, finance and every level of government.

It sounded like the plot of a very bad movie, but my life was all about the incredible. As much as I wanted to discount such a threat, chalk it up to fairy tale and fantasy, I knew better. I'd long ago accepted that nothing was impossible in my world.

Slinging my backpack over one shoulder, I headed east through the cemetery as dusk seeped in from the river and settled like fine linen over the gravestones. The light had deepened to violet and soon the veil would be at its thinnest. The ghosts would come through, drawn to the living world by their hunger for human warmth and by the light inside of me that beckoned them.

Already I could feel the chill of the dead world in the breeze that undulated through the bushes and trees and in the frosty breath that blew down my collar. Zipping my jacket against the cold, I gazed up into those rippling leaves where I imagined ghost eyes peering back at me. Where I could hear unearthly voices whispering down to me.

Something happened then, unnerving even by my standards. The wind carried the whiff of a familiar scent and suddenly I was transported to a different time and place. I was trapped in a watery cocoon that had once kept me safe. The distant and rhythmic thumping that had once soothed me had gone silent and the soft walls that had cradled and protected me had become a death chamber. I knew nothing but hunger and darkness and a lurking presence that lured me deeper into the Gray, promising me succor and shelter as it claimed me for its own.

Whether memory or portent, the vision left me shaken. There were those who believed in a pre-birth consciousness, and what I had just experienced seemed like a fleeting recall of my birth mother's death and the terrifying aftermath of her silenced heartbeat. I knew that she had been murdered with me in her womb and so it wasn't hard to imagine that such a dramatic moment could have somehow been imprinted upon my brain. But like my dream about my mother and aunt, why had it surfaced now?

For the first time in a long time, I thought of Asher Falls, the place where I had died and then been born. I thought of that lurking evil that had seduced and entrapped my birth father's family for generations, the same malevolent presence that still lay hidden in the pastoral foothills of the Blue Ridge Mountains. I now knew my time in that withering town had been carefully orchestrated, perhaps even preordained once my father's rules were broken. I had been lured to that place where the evil was strongest when my defenses were at their weakest.

After escaping from Asher Falls, I'd chosen to believe that only there could I be touched by the evil. It needed the portal of my birthplace to influence my thoughts and behavior and to seduce me back to the other side. But the entity could watch over me from anywhere and I had no doubt that it waited for me still. It might even invade my dreams from time to time, but I was safe so long as I stayed away from Asher Falls. So long as I remained vigilant and kept my defenses strong.

But I could have sworn I sensed that fiendish presence now—or one like it—in the rising wind that tore at my clothes and whipped at my hair. In the distant howl that blew in with the twilight.

Peeling away the loose strands from my face, I clutched Rose's key for protection against an unexpected assault.

"I'm not afraid of you," I whispered.

You should be, the leaves seemed to taunt me.

I glanced out over the cemetery, skimming the headstones and peering into all the dark corners. The ghosts were coming through. I could see the shimmer of their manifestations and the faint glow of their auras in the fading light. I could hear the chatter of ethereal voices in my head, could feel the tug of all those unseen hands. I wondered if the evil was there among them, a nameless, formless presence that gathered strength from their energy and fed off their lost souls as it slithered over graves and around headstones, creeping closer. Ever closer.

It was bad enough that the ghost of a murdered child had latched on to me. Worse still that I found myself in the crosshairs of the deadly *Congé*. Now it seemed an old enemy may have come calling. An ancient evil that had watched me since before my birth, biding time until it could ooze underneath the veil while I basked in the false security of my evolving gift and heightened senses.

Tucking Rose's key into my shirt, I hurried my steps, refusing to glance over my shoulder as I pulled open the iron gate and stepped through to the road. The ghost voices didn't follow me as they once would have done, nor did the entities swarm me as they had in Kroll Cemetery. But I could hear a voice in my head, a familiar missive that grew stronger and more insistent as I moved away from the gate.

Mercy.

I could feel the ghost child's presence behind me, but I didn't turn. Instead, I took stock of my surroundings, ever mindful of Prosper Lamb's warning that an unsavory element invaded the cemetery after dark. I didn't want to be caught unaware by the living or the dead.

To my right, the narrow lane dead-ended at a broken barricade, behind which I could make out the silhouette of a car shrouded in kudzu. The vine grew over the fence and up a telephone phone, as insidious and voracious an invader as the gathering darkness behind me.

On my left, I could see a ramshackle house set back from the road, no doubt the caretaker's property. I knew that Prosper Lamb lived near the cemetery, close enough that—according to him—I could holler if I got into trouble. But from my vantage point the place looked deserted. I saw no sign of life. No lights in the windows, no vehicle parked in the front. And yet I had the eerie sensation that eyes watched me from that house.

I swept my gaze along the sagging front porch and then over each window and up to the tin roof. My heart thudded as I caught sight of a figure outlined against the deepening horizon. A cold, dark thing that moved quickly along the peak, pausing briefly to glance in my direction before disappearing over the ridge board, long coat flapping in the wind.

Whether illusion or reality, there was familiarity in the silhouette's stealth, in the way it melted so seamlessly into the darkness. I had seen that figure before, perhaps in Asher Falls, perhaps in a dream. I had seen it.

Prosper Lamb was right. People and animals were behaving not as they should. Someone was about to pass, but the door had opened too soon, allowing all manner of menaces to crawl through.

I started down the road toward the house, then stopped and whirled back to the cemetery. The pull from Woodbine was suddenly so powerful that I felt incapable of escape. No matter how much I craved the safety of my sanctuary, I couldn't put one foot in front of the other. Something held me fast.

The leaves started to whisper my name, the

sound coiling like the coldest of tentacles around my brain. *Amelia... Amelia...*

Shaking off the shackles of my imagination, I backed away, proving to myself that I could bolt whenever I chose. Why I didn't do so at that moment, I couldn't quite say. Maybe I need to prove something.

"You're not real," I said aloud. "You can't hurt me."

I will protect you. All you need do is come back to me...

Once again I resisted the urge to put hands to my ears as another image came to me, born not of a memory but of the story Papa had told me of my birth. I had been cut from my dead mother's womb, brought into the living world cold and silent until my grandmother had breathed life into my lungs, wresting me from the same evil that had tainted the Asher family for generations. The same evil that now sought a way into Woodbine Cemetery.

Come back to me...

I lifted my chin defiantly. "You can't touch me here."

As if to taunt me, the wind whipped open the gate and flung it back against the fence. I could see the crumbling necropolis inside, the crosses and angel wings eerily silhouetted against the horizon.

Come back to me...

I could hear the tinkle of a thousand chimes and

the eerie moan of the rising wind. All around me leaves shivered and quaked.

Come back to me...

Suddenly, the ghost child appeared inside the cemetery. She was dressed in white, blonde hair streaming behind her, eyes softly glowing in the fading light. But there was something different about her manifestation. The rage and surly demeanor had dissipated and now the apparition seemed more pitiable and lost. She was beautiful to look at, so airy and fragile, but I didn't trust this incarnation even as her innocence wrenched at me.

She made no attempt to follow me through the gate. It was almost as if she were chained to Woodbine, but she had once wandered as far as my garden and even farther to the restaurant's courtyard. She seemed to possess the ability to manifest wherever she wished so what bound her to the cemetery at that moment?

As if sensing my confusion, she drifted closer, hovering just inside the gate. Her face was pale and translucent, her hands unbearably dainty as she reached out to me beseechingly.

I didn't react to those outstretched hands. I *wouldn't.*

But the lure of her manifestation was so powerful it was all I could do not to go to her.

I saw it then. A nameless, formless shadow. A creeping darkness that devoured the graves and monuments as it glided toward the ghost child. Toward me.

I smelled it then. The dank, fetid odor of its essence. Not the scent of death, but the perfume of pure evil.

I knew it then. Knew the tricks that it would employ to trap me, seduce me, even going so far as to use the ghost child as bait.

Grasping Rose's key, I said harshly, "Get away from her."

A foul gust knocked me back. I stumbled in the road as the gate slammed shut, blocking the apparition from my view.

The episode was over so quickly I wondered again if I had imagined the shadow, the smell, that sinister voice in my head. Perhaps my subconscious had conjured the formless entity as a way of warning me away from Woodbine Cemetery and all the old secrets that were buried there.

But a trace of that stench lingered, a revolting combination of decaying flesh, wormy earth and sulfur that seemed to seep through my pores like poison, tainting my bloodstream and infecting my senses. My stomach recoiled and I bent double, coughing and retching until I expelled the venom into the dirt.

I hunkered on the road, spent and trembling, as I waited for the nausea to pass. When the heaving subsided, I dug in my backpack for a bottle of water to rinse my mouth and a tissue to wipe my clammy face. I dug even deeper and more frantically for a tin of mints, popping a handful in my mouth to mask the putrid taste.

Had I not lingered searching for those mints, I might never have noticed the footprints in the soft earth before me. Faint tracks made by a woman's shoes with a strange mark across one of the heels.

I rose on shaky legs and followed those footprints all the way to the ramshackle house where they halted at the edge of the yard just as they had halted that morning at the edge of the copse.

Sixteen

As I stood beside those footprints, I imagined the unknown visitor right there with me, gazing up at that dark, disintegrating house. With the approach of nightfall, the place took on an even more sinister air.

Was it haunted? Setting aside my belief that ghosts were attracted to people, not places, I could well believe the house had fallen prey to diabolical forces—from this world or the next. I was picking up some very strange vibes as I stood there.

Why had the cemetery visitor come here? I wondered. Or at the very least, why had she paused to stare across the yard at the crumbling house? What was her connection to this place, to Prosper Lamb and to the unnamed crib grave in Woodbine Cemetery?

I felt a strange kinship with the visitor even though I didn't know her name or if our paths had ever crossed. But coincidences were rare in my world, and a case could be made that everything happened for a reason. Even this creepy old house could be a piece of my larger puzzle.

The light was almost gone by now, but enough filtered down through the trees that I could easily trace the clapboard facade. The structure was narrow in the Charleston style with both front and side entrances and wooden shutters over the windows that could be closed during inclement weather.

Rickety steps led up to a porch that ran the width of the house. Long windows flanked the front entrance, but I could detect no movement through the glass, no prying eyes behind the lace curtains. A rusted-out car rested on blocks in the driveway, and the yard was littered with various castaways. By all appearances, the place had long been abandoned to spiders and lizards, but I couldn't shake the notion that someone was inside watching me at that very moment. I only hoped it was the caretaker.

I lifted my gaze to scan the shingles. I saw nothing on the roof. No predatory shadows. No menacing silhouettes. And yet…

The porch swing creaked in the breeze and I scampered to the other side of the road, hiding in the deep shadows while I continued to reconnoiter. I told myself there was no reason to linger. Even if Prosper Lamb did live there, he might not welcome an uninvited guest. There was no guarantee he would tell me anything more about Woodbine Cemetery than he'd already disclosed upon our first meeting.

But surely he'd had a specific reason for believing that a guilty conscience had facilitated the restoration. I had a feeling he knew the identity of the donor and he might even know the person who had visited the cemetery that morning. He most definitely knew about the birds.

But all those questions and the endless speculation might best be saved for another time. I'd had a long day with too many dramatic encounters and unnerving discoveries. I needed to be home in the shelter of my safe haven to regroup. I was already late. Angus would be waiting for me at the door, eager for his dinner and an evening walk.

Still hugging the shadows, I turned to leave. I even took a few steps down the road toward the front entrance of the cemetery when the faint strands of a familiar melody drifted out to the street. Not the ephemeral tinkling of the wind chimes this time, but the scratchy sound of a needle in the groove of an old record.

The sound was faint but the tune enveloped me. I had come to think of it as the ghost child's song, but as I closed my eyes, a memory broke loose and I realized the melody had a more personal association. Once more I was transported to a different time and place. I was a child now, curled up on a rug beneath an open window as I listened to my mother and aunt out on the front porch. The house was so quiet I could hear the creak of their rockers and the tinkle of ice in their glasses. The scent of roses, dreamy and hypnotic, drifted in from the nearby cemetery. I lay half asleep, cocooned by familiar surroundings but still lonely. Still alone.

"That song—" My aunt sounded stricken. "I haven't heard it in ages. Where is it coming from?"

"It's the radio," Mama told her. "I'll go turn it off."

"No, don't. I want to hear it." She hummed along for a moment. "I remember dancing to that song by moonlight once. It was the most romantic night of my life. We'd gone to the beach and the evening was so warm and balmy I didn't even need a shawl. He took off my shoes so they wouldn't be ruined and I can still remember the way the sand felt between my toes. I can still smell the woodbine from the sprigs I tucked in my hair before I left the house." I heard a shiver in her voice. "Honeysuckle was once my favorite scent, but I can't bear it now. Even after all these years that smell always takes me back."

"Father chopped down the vines after he sent you away," Mama said.

"The garden was never the same without it."

"Nothing was ever the same. The house was so quiet after you'd gone and I was so lonely. I used to sneak into your room after Mother and Father had gone to bed and listen to your music. It made me feel close to you. Father caught me one night and flew into an awful rage. He broke all of your records and gave away your phonograph. I don't remember there being music in our house ever again."

"Or laughter," my aunt said sadly. "Oh, Etta, we were both so young to have suffered so much heartache. I wonder how we stood it. At least you had Caleb and later Amelia."

"You could have married and had a family of your own," Mama said. "I always wondered why you didn't."

"I couldn't. Not after what I did. I didn't deserve happiness."

"What nonsense," Mama scolded. "You always get maudlin after you've been to the cemetery."

"It wipes me out for days, but I can't *not* go."

"I know. But don't think about it anymore, at least for the rest of the evening. Let's just sit here and watch the moon come up. Pretend that we're young and innocent again and we have our whole lives ahead of us…"

The memory spun away, leaving me drowning in a terrible sadness.

Once more, I berated myself for lingering. Leave well enough alone, *at least for the rest of the evening*. I needed to be home with Angus and my dark thoughts. I wouldn't go knock on Prosper Lamb's door, I wouldn't seek out the source of that music. I wouldn't leave the safety of the road no matter what happened.

But even as I hardened my resolve, my gaze strayed to a small outbuilding at the back of the house. The door hung open and the music seemed to be coming from inside.

A thrill rippled along my spine as I peered

through the shadows. The structure was small and nondescript, white like the house, with a tin roof and long windows on either side of the gaping door. I could detect no movement or light, but I knew the music emanated from somewhere inside.

Was that dark presence waiting for me in there? I wondered. Had it found a new way to lure me back to the dead world?

I cast an uneasy glance toward the cemetery. With a little perspective and distance, it was easy enough to pretend that my imagination had gotten the better of me earlier. That particular presence was a long way from me tonight, still trapped in the hills and hollows of the Blue Ridge Mountains. It couldn't get to me here. There was no doorway in Woodbine Cemetery. No portal through which it could crawl. All I need worry about was the real-world danger from the *Congé* and the familiarity of that song. The melody was connected to me somehow, connected to my mother and aunt. The haunting refrain might well be a clue to a child's murder.

I stood there for another moment still trying to talk myself out of what I had in mind to do. But the memory of my mother and aunt listening to that song was so strong I couldn't ignore it. I couldn't walk away without at least trying to ascertain their link to that dead child.

Easing across the road, I jumped the shallow ditch to stand at the edge of the yard, once against scouring the front windows. I knew better than to trespass on private property without at least finding out whether or not anyone was home. Prosper Lamb had made a point of letting me see that he was armed, so it was probably best not to catch him by surprise. I walked across the yard, climbed the porch steps and knocked on the door. I even called out to him.

"Mr. Lamb? Are you in there? It's Amelia Gray. I'm sorry to bother you like this, but I wonder if I might have a word about the cemetery."

No answer.

I felt foolish standing on the porch shouting through the door when I didn't even know for sure that the caretaker, or anyone, lived there. But as I turned back to the steps, I noticed a pair of work boots near the porch swing. The mud in the treads looked fresh, leaving me to conclude that someone had removed them before entering the house. I couldn't be certain, but they looked very much like the boots Prosper Lamb wore to the cemetery.

Crossing back over to the door, I rapped harder and called out to him again. Still unable to rouse anyone, I ran down the steps and made for the corner of the house. I could still hear the music. The hypnotic notes floated through the twilight as mournfully nostalgic as the memories it stirred.

Halfway around the house, I stopped with a start. The tin roof popped as if from a misplaced step. I had the disquieting notion that someone— something—was on top of the house tracking my progress. I told myself the sound was nothing more than a pinecone falling from one of the loblolly pines that surrounded the property. Nobody was on the roof. No *thing* stared down at me in the darkness.

I moved on and as I approached the outbuilding, I called out once more. "Mr. Lamb? Are you in there? Hello?"

I removed a flashlight from my backpack and flicked on the switch as I stepped up to the doorway. It was dim inside the building. Very little illumination came through the dusty windows or even through the doorway. I swept the beam inside and the light was reflected back to me from dozens of glowing eyes.

The hair at the back of my neck quilled. For a moment I wanted to turn tail and run, but instead I gripped the rubber casing of the flashlight as I splayed the light over the walls, over all those eyes, over feathers and paws and creatures in all manner of poses. The eyes were not real, but glass facsimiles set into the frozen faces of long-dead animals.

Slowly, I moved the beam around that strange menagerie, capturing a squirrel here, a raccoon there, but mostly what I saw were birds. Owls. Starlings. Crows. Even a sparrow. Apparently Prosper Lamb was not only a cemetery caretaker but also a taxidermist.

A chemical scent permeated the area to quell—I suspected—the odor of decomposition. At the far end of the space was a worktable filled with an assortment of tools and cans and an old-fashioned record player. As the last of the notes faded, the arm lifted and repositioned the needle. A moment later, the song started over.

The stool behind the worktable wobbled slightly as if someone had just gotten up. The caretaker must have left by way of the back door when he heard me coming, but why? Why not stay and talk to me?

"Mr. Lamb? Are you around? It's Amelia Gray. I'm really sorry to disturb your work, but I need to talk to you about the cemetery. There was a visitor this morning. A woman, I think. I wondered if you had seen her."

While I talked, I continued to move the light around the room. A burlap bag lay crumpled in a corner near the worktable and as I focused the beam, I saw the folds of the fabric twitch as if something alive remained inside. The floor around the bag was littered with black feathers and I thought at once of the dead starlings in the cemetery. Prosper Lamb had assured me they were all dead, but the movement inside the bag told me otherwise.

I had remained in the doorway this whole time, but now I eased inside to kneel beside the bag. If the caretaker or anyone walked in on me at that moment, I wouldn't be able to justify my presence. But how could I turn away knowing that one of those starlings had survived and remained trapped inside the bag? That kind of cruelty was abhorrent to me, even though rescuing animals had a tendency to get me in trouble. So be it.

Loosening the ties, I scrambled away in case something more dangerous than a wounded bird popped out.

Nothing happened. The bag remained motionless as if the trapped starling was now too badly frightened or hurt to try to escape. I gave it another try, gently upending the bag on the floor. A pile of black feathers floated out, nothing more.

You're losing it, Amelia. Time to go.

My instincts warned that I had waited too long and as if to punctuate that caution, the tin roof crackled overhead. Another pinecone, I told myself. But the sound came again and again, so many times that I lifted my gaze to track what I could only imagine were footfalls. The steps moved across the building right over my head and then halted abruptly. After a moment, I heard an odd swishing sound and then a more distant pop.

I rose and exited the building. Outside, twilight had deepened to nightfall and the moon was just coming up. The space between the shed and the house lay in deep shadows. I tried to gauge the distance, wondering if someone could have jumped from roof to roof. As my eyes became accustomed to the dark, a silhouette slowly took shape.

He—it—was perched on the roof of the house just above the eaves, resting on haunches, hands draped over his knees, long coat flapping in the breeze. His silhouette mimicked the lines of a predatory bird or a vulture perhaps, drawn by the scent of death.

Whoever—whatever—I saw was not Prosper Lamb, of that I was certain. I didn't think it human at all, rather one of those netherworld in-betweens. As I gazed up at the creature, my thoughts once again turned to Asher Falls and to an unlikely guardian that had reeked of decaying animal carcasses.

I stood there enthralled by the thing, trapped by the spellbinding quality of its luminous eyes. I sensed more than heard another nearby presence and I realized too late that someone had slipped up behind me.

Seventeen

Before I could flee or even reach for the pepper spray in my pocket, an arm snaked around my waist, holding me fast as a hand clapped over my mouth.

I had a sudden and terrifying image of my captor. Beady eyes, gaping beak. I could hear the rasp of his breath in my ear as he pulled me back against him. I froze but only for an instant, and then instinct and adrenaline took over and I squirmed and bucked and elbowed him as hard as I could in the rib cage. I heard a satisfying grunt as he tightened his hold.

Unable to retrieve the pepper spray from my pocket, I kicked at his shins and clawed at his arms. I may even have bit his hand. The ferocity of my defense must have caught him by surprise because his hold finally relaxed and I nearly got away before he wrapped both arms around me to subdue me.

"Will you stop?" he drawled against my ear. "It's me, for God's sake."

Recognition seeped in but the adrenaline was still pumping and before the rational side of my brain reclaimed me, I reached up and raked my nails down the side of his face.

He swore viciously beneath his breath and it was his language more than anything else that made me drop my arms limply to my sides in surrender. In the whole of my time with John Devlin, I couldn't remember ever hearing him utter even the mildest of swear words. His old-world courtliness and Southern manners had always charmed me even if at times his overprotectiveness had irritated me. Hearing *that* vulgarity from his lips stunned me.

As soon as the fight went out of me, he released me and I spun out of his grasp, intent on berating him for giving me such a fright. But before I could let him have it, he put a finger to his lips to silence me. Then he glanced around, taking in the looming facade of the house, running his gaze over all those rear windows and into the shadowy hiding places in the yard. I had a feeling he'd summed up in one split second any number of dangerous areas that might have escaped the attention of a normal person.

I wasn't *normal*, however and I had also taken note of all those windows and doors, all those concealed places. I had learned a thing or two since we'd been together, and the last person I needed watching over me was Claire Bellefontaine's fiancé. No matter how tough and menacing he looked in the dark.

Trembling, I locked my arms around my middle as I glared up at him. He stood in front of me, mere inches away, but the moon was so thoroughly blocked by the house and trees that he was little more than a shadow.

"What do you think you're doing?" I demanded furiously.

He didn't answer, but instead cocked his head as if listening for those telltale footfalls on the tin roof. I lifted my gaze, but the figure I'd seen earlier was gone or at least in hiding. I glanced around uneasily at our surroundings. The thing could be anywhere, lurking just over the peak of the roof or in a nearby treetop. I had an image of it now swooping down from the branches to grab me up in its talons.

Devlin spoke at last, still in that ominous half whisper. "It's not safe here. We should get back to the road."

What did he mean, not safe? Had he seen what I'd seen? Would he even admit it if he had? He had always had an aversion to the supernatural. It was only since last year that I was coming to understand why.

A dozen questions bubbled in my head and my first inclination was to stubbornly refuse to comply until he explained himself. But something came to me as we faced off. The music inside the building had stopped. Whoever had been in there earlier must have returned while Devlin and I had struggled outside the door. The caretaker—or someone—might be inside watching us at that very moment.

I nodded and pointed toward the street to let him know that I concurred.

Hoisting my backpack to my shoulder, I eased away from the building, keeping my eyes peeled for moving shadows or lurking figures. Devlin fell in behind me and, as he had earlier, he moved in complete silence. I didn't hear so much as a snapped twig or a hitched breath, but I had no trouble picturing him back there, eyes sharp, nerves steady.

I was still buzzing from the adrenaline, and as we progressed through the shadows, I couldn't help but analyze my reaction to the situation, how I had automatically struck back at my assailant. Finding myself in such a dire situation might once have paralyzed me with fear, but my recent experiences had taught me a lot about survival and base instincts and the lengths I would go to in order to protect myself.

Devlin wasn't the only one who had changed. I might not be a hero, but neither was I the same person I'd been even a year ago, let alone the girl who had once sequestered herself away from the rest of the world behind cemetery gates. My gift had evolved along with my senses. I was stronger, more resolved and, yes, still a bit foolish at times. Where capitulation and begging for mercy might have been the smarter moves, my natural inclination had been to fight back. I didn't know if this was a good thing or not.

We rounded the corner of the house and moved quickly across the yard, where we jumped the ditch to the road. Only when we were safely away from the house did I turn once more to confront him.

Whatever I'd been about to say flitted away as I took in his countenance. Now that we were out in the open, I caught my first good look at him. His features were blanched by moonlight, the planes and angles defined by light and shadow. I was still astounded by the changes the last year had wrought in his appearance. The stubble, the casual attire, the longer hair were the least of it. His suaveness had given way to an air of ruthlessness that I found unnervingly attractive. Even the timbre of his voice was more menacing.

But what gave me pause at that precise moment were the ugly red marks I'd left on his face. Four long scratches across his right cheek, all of them beaded with blood.

I stared at him aghast. "Your face—I can't believe I did that to you."

He wiped at his cheek with the back of his hand. "At least you missed my eye."

"Yes, thank goodness for that." Still, I was deeply disturbed by the evidence of my violence as I awkwardly tried to explain myself. "I didn't know who you were at first and even after I recognized your voice, the adrenaline was still pumping…" I trailed away. "I'm a bit reactionary these days."

"Yes, I got that."

I glanced away, not at all comfortable with my actions or Devlin's proximity. I wanted to take a step back from him, but I also didn't want to appear thrown by his presence. I had my pride, after all. "What were you doing back there, anyway?"

"I might ask you the same thing." He turned so that the moonlight was now full upon him. A shiver raced up my spine and tingled at my nape.

"You first," I said. "What did you mean we aren't safe?"

He glanced over his shoulder at the house and then swept his gaze through the trees and along the fence line of the cemetery. He seemed collected and controlled, but something had obviously put him on alert.

"I asked you a question—"

"I heard you, but keep it down, okay?" A frown fleeted across his features as he turned back to me.

"You're starting to scare me."

"Somehow I doubt that," he muttered as he pulled me to the edge of the road where we could blend into the shadows. He was standing even closer now. So close I could see the gleam of his eyes—as hypnotic as ever—and I told myself to glance away, erect whatever defenses necessary in order to protect myself from old memories and his dark charisma.

But despite my best intentions, my gaze drifted

to his mouth. His lips were parted as though he meant to kiss me and I closed my eyes briefly as I fought for poise along with my dignity. He belonged to someone else now and I would not be that woman. I would not.

But the memory of that mouth…those hands… what he could do to me in the dark with just the whisper of my name…

"You okay?" he asked softly.

His fingers were still wrapped around my arm and I could feel the warmth of his skin through my jacket. I shook off his hold as I moved away from him.

"Yes, I'm fine, but I need you to tell me right now what's going on. Something has obviously spooked you." I returned his stare, daring him to tell me about the *Congé*, willing him to confess the real reason he had come back to the cemetery. Strangely, even knowing what I knew about him, I didn't feel threatened. Not physically, anyway. Emotionally was another story.

"Take a look around," he said. "Do you have any idea how dangerous this area can be after dark? Do you have any idea the kind of people that hang out in deserted houses like that? You walk in on the wrong situation and you're as good as dead."

"Like a drug deal, you mean." Even though we were talking in hushed tones, he had made me paranoid and now I worried how far our voices might carry.

"Not only drugs. There are a lot of dangerous people doing a lot of dangerous things out there."

I suppressed another shiver as I thought about that silhouette perched on the edge of the roof. "So you thought it a good idea to sneak up on me and grab me from behind? You've no idea how close you came to getting pepper sprayed."

"Don't I?" He grimaced as he again ran the back of his hand across his damaged cheek.

"Sorry," I murmured. "Anyway, for your information, the house isn't deserted. At least, I don't think so. I believe the cemetery caretaker lives there and he apparently uses the outbuilding for taxidermy."

"That would explain the smell," Devlin said. "But it doesn't explain why you were there."

"I went looking for him. He told me to holler if I ever needed his help and so I did."

He canted his head, watching me in the dark. "Why did you need his help?"

I shrugged. "Not that I feel the need to explain myself, but I went to see him on cemetery business. There was a visitor this morning. She left something on one of the graves. I wanted to know if he had seen her. Satisfied?"

"For now. But we're not done yet."

"No, we are not," I agreed. "You still haven't told me why you came back to the cemetery."

His gaze strayed to the house. "Let's get back to the cars. We'll have a better sight line on the main road."

A better sight line? Who or what had him so worried?

Obviously he wasn't telling me everything, but then, I hadn't come clean with him, either. Communication had never been our strength as a couple.

Nevertheless, I fell into step beside him as we headed down the road, but I maintained a safe distance between us. I didn't want to take a chance that our shoulders might accidentally brush or our hands connect.

The moon was so bright I didn't bother with my flashlight. No use taking a chance on drawing attention. But the ruts in the gravel road were challenging and I had to concentrate on my step. Even so, I found myself glancing over at Devlin, surreptitiously studying his profile as we hurried along. How strange it was to be alone with him after all this time. I felt uneasy and off-kilter and I couldn't seem to quiet my heart.

We came to the end of the gravel road and turned left onto the paved street that ran in front of the cemetery. I could hear traffic on Morrison Drive now and it made me feel closer to civilization and a little less vulnerable.

"I'm parked just ahead," I told Devlin. "On the left side of the entrance."

"Yes, I know. I'm parked beside you."

That surprised me. The way he was acting, I half expected that he had hidden his car in the bushes somewhere. "Do you think it's a good idea for us to be seen together? You aren't worried that someone else could come back to the cemetery?"

"I'm more worried about you being out here alone after dark," he said.

"Because the area isn't safe?"

A slight hesitation. "Yes. Because the area isn't safe."

He didn't fool me. His precautions had nothing to do with the neighborhood and the miscreants that inhabited vacant houses. I suspected the threat was personal and far deadlier.

As soon as we cleared the cedar trees, I saw his car—sleek, black and gleaming in the moonlight. He took out his remote and the lights flashed as the doors unlocked. "Get in."

I turned in surprise. "Do you really think *that's* a good idea?"

"Nothing about this night is a good idea," he said. "Just get in."

Eighteen

To my credit, I balked. My defenses held. I told myself to get in my own vehicle and drive away. *Just go and don't look back.* More than ever, I needed to be home safe and sound in my sanctuary, protected from ghosts and evil and the man who stood staring down at me in the moonlight.

I got in.

The interior of Devlin's car was just as I remembered, close and luxurious with lots of supple leather, chrome and sleek mahogany. I sat with my legs dangling from the open door so that I could kick off my work boots.

"Don't bother. I'll have someone clean it tomorrow. Get in and close the door."

Yes, of course, there would be someone to clean his car. Now that he had reclaimed his place as the Devlin heir, he undoubtedly had people to cater to his every whim. The juxtaposition of the Devlin I had known then and the man I saw before me now was jarring. The deeper he sank into the lap of luxury, the rougher his outward appearance. I wondered if his perpetual five-o'clock shadow was his unconscious way of rebelling against all those heavy expectations.

I leaned back against the seat. With the door closed, the overhead light faded and the interior became an opulent cocoon, one that I in no way found protective. Particularly with Devlin so near, so shadowy and watchful.

With those dark eyes upon me, the strangeness of our situation hit me anew. I must have imagined a similar scenario a dozen times over during our estrangement, wondering how I would react to him, what I would say to him. How I would feel in his presence. Our parting conversation had become almost epic to me, one that I had used to convince myself of his noble intentions. He'd left to protect me, and even after our breakup, he'd found an extraordinary way to warn me of the treachery I'd faced at Seven Gates Cemetery.

If I truly believed in Devlin's virtue, then the flush of anger I felt now was petty and unjustified. But there it was. Anger at how easily he'd walked away, resentment for all those sleepless nights and more than a trace of bitterness at how quickly he'd found someone else.

Beyond those emotions, something more perilous lurked. Smoldering passion ready to flare up at the most inopportune time.

He draped an arm over the steering wheel as he turned to me. I wondered if he could hear the pounding of my heart. Did he have any idea of the tempest raging inside me? Did he even care what his nearness did to me?

Despite my anger, I wanted to touch him, *needed* to touch him, and so I curled my hands into fists at my sides and dug my nails into my flesh.

"You have questions," he said in that low drawl.

I closed my eyes briefly. "I watched you leave the cemetery earlier. I heard your car drive off. And yet here you are." The nails dug deeper into my palms. "Why did you come back?"

"I wanted to make sure you were all right. We kept you out here talking until almost dark and I knew you wouldn't leave until you'd finished whatever task we interrupted."

"You think you still know me that well?"

"Some things don't change."

"True enough. But you could have just called."

"You turn off your phone when you're in a cemetery. That hasn't changed, either, I'm assuming."

"No." Evidently, he did still know me that well.

"I circled back and saw that your car was still parked in the same location, so I knew you were around," he said. "When I couldn't find you in the cemetery, I went looking for you. I spotted you out on the road in front of that house. You kept glancing over your shoulder as if you thought you were being followed."

I gave him a look. "Turns out, I was."

"That's why I didn't call out to you. I didn't know who else might be around. I kept my distance and followed you because you were acting strangely and I didn't know what you might be walking into. I'm still wondering."

"I already told you. I went looking for the caretaker."

He leaned in, peering at me so intently I couldn't hold his gaze. "Why don't I think that's the whole story? What aren't you telling me? What have you gotten yourself into this time?"

It was the "this time" that tweaked my anger, and I pulled myself up by the bootstraps of my hardened resolve. "Maybe you should ask your fiancée. But perhaps the better question is—what has she *dragged* me into?"

He went very still as his cold, hard gaze searched my face. "What does she have to do with your being at that house?"

"She didn't tell you about the anonymous donor? Wait. I don't like to be presumptuous. Before we go any further, we should probably clear something up first. You are still engaged, aren't you?" I couldn't help taking a perverse pleasure in calling him out on what I'd witnessed in the cemetery. "You'll forgive the question, but earlier when we were all together, I could have sworn the two of you detested one another."

There was a painfully long pause. "I wouldn't read too much into that. Things aren't always what they seem."

How well I knew.

"Tell me about this anonymous donor," he pressed.

"I just found out about it today. I'm surprised your... Claire didn't tell you herself. She's more familiar with the details than I am, but apparently, the donation for the restoration was made anonymously to the Woodbine Cemetery Trust with two stipulations. The work had to be done in a certain time frame and only I was to be awarded the contract. She seemed to think the conditions eccentric but inconsequential. Although she did make a point of telling me about them."

"What do you think?"

"I'm troubled," I admitted. "I was led to believe others were vying for the project, but I'm the only one who received an invitation to bid. I had another project that was scheduled to begin within a week and then all of a sudden, that job got postponed. Maybe the delay was legitimate. It happens. Maybe this whole thing is just one big coincidence, but it has the feel of a setup to me. Someone is pulling strings and I don't like it."

"Then walk away."

I stared at him in surprise. "What?"

"Break the contract and walk. If there are any legal complications, they can be handled."

"Handled how—never mind. I'm not breaking the contract. It's unprofessional and could ruin my reputation. And anyway, I like to finish what I start."

His voice grew terse. "Even if it means putting yourself at risk?"

"Yes, even then." I studied him through narrowed eyes. "You keep talking about danger, but you've yet to identify a specific threat. All you've really succeeded in doing is making me uneasy. I've worked in far more questionable areas than this. You know that. Almost every graveyard I restore is isolated, and I always take precautions. You know that, too. So why don't you tell me what you're really worried about?"

He didn't answer, just sat staring through the windshield, scouring shadows and bushes and all those dark corners. When he finally turned back to me, his expression was inscrutable, but I caught a glimpse of something in his eyes that left me chilled. "You need to stay away from Claire and her stepbrother."

"Why?" I said on a breath.

"If they come back to the cemetery, avoid them or leave," Devlin said. "Don't take meetings, don't give tours and whatever you do, don't go out to Duvall Island even if Temple invites you to the site herself."

My heart thudded and I felt a terrible foreboding closing in on me. My gaze darted to the cemetery. I didn't know what I expected to find lurking inside the arched entrance. The ghost child? An evil presence? Claire Bellefontaine? I wasn't certain which threat I dreaded the most.

I almost clutched Devlin's arm until I thought better of it. "Tell me why."

"They're not good people. Is that specific enough for you?"

"I need to know *why*. If they're not good people, why were you with them earlier? Why are you with *her*?"

"I told you, things aren't always what they seem."

His wording was the same as before, but now he seemed to contradict his previous insinuation about his relationship with Claire Bellefontaine.

"Is your engagement real?" I asked bluntly.

"Yes."

"You really mean to marry that woman?"

"Yes."

"Then things are exactly as they seem."

The confines of the car were overpowering at that moment, the intimacy of our conversation almost more than I could bear. Images bombarded me as my memories betrayed me and I found myself wincing as my nails pressed into my palms.

"Don't," he said harshly.

"Don't what?"

"You need to stop looking at me as if you're torn between kissing me and killing me."

I felt as though the wind had been knocked out of me. He had summoned up my contradictory emotions perfectly.

"Maybe I don't feel either of those things," I said. "Maybe I'm having trouble figuring out why you still feel the need to protect me. Why you would go to the trouble of coming all the way back out here just to check up on me. Why do you even care?"

He said impatiently and without finesse, "Don't be ridiculous."

I tried not to read beyond the surface of that comment, but I wanted to believe I could detect a hint of tenderness around the edges. "Does she know you're here?"

"Not unless she had me followed."

"Is that a possibility?"

"Anything is possible with that pair. But I know what I'm doing. I may not be a cop anymore, but I'm still capable of spotting a tail."

"What if she doubled back first? Isn't that really what you're worried about?"

"I'm worried about a lot of things," he said. "Stay away from Claire and her stepbrother so I don't have to worry about you."

"I need some air," I muttered and before he could stop me, I opened the door and climbed out.

He didn't immediately follow. Maybe he sensed I needed time to collect my composure. Maybe he did, too.

Seconds and then minutes ticked by. I began to think that Devlin might just up and drive away without another word, and maybe that would have been for the best. I wasn't safe out here alone with him. *He* wasn't safe with me. My thoughts had taken a risky turn. Despite his insistence to the contrary, I didn't believe in the legitimacy of his engagement to Claire Bellefontaine, which in turn made me wonder about his true feelings for me.

Don't be ridiculous, I berated myself in Devlin's drawl.

I'd gone around to lean against the front of my vehicle, but I could sense him back there in his car, dark and brooding, perhaps even fuming that I refused to accept his warning without question.

I was stunned he'd said as much as he had, actually cautioned me away from Claire and her stepbrother. It made me wonder what bad things he knew about them and why he continued this dangerous charade of an engagement. It made me more certain than ever that they were all members of the *Congé*.

What a strange night this had turned out to be.

Through the cemetery gates, I traced the silhouette of angel wings and the outline of live oaks with their eerie outstretched arms. The landscape looked even more ominous now that darkness had fallen and the ghosts were fully manifested. There were a lot of them tonight and I was glad that I had Rose's key to keep them at bay. I could see the shimmer of their auras as they glided over graves and through the trees, forever restless and ravenous and searching. Was the ghost child out there with them? I wondered. Or was she even closer, hiding in the shadows as she plotted her revenge?

The ghosts—even the spirit of a murdered child—were the least of my worries tonight.

Finally, I heard the car door open but I still didn't turn. Even when Devlin came over to join me, I kept my gaze trained on the cemetery. He didn't touch me, but I could *feel* him there beside me. It was like in the old days when I'd had a sixth sense about his presence. There had been times when he'd seemed so much a part of me that I knew if I closed my eyes and concentrated hard enough, my heightened senses could pick up the beat of his heart and synchronize it with my own.

Those days were gone, but all of a sudden my memories had taken on a new life. I cast him a sidelong glance as an image unfurled in my head and I drifted back to a rainy Saturday afternoon. We were lying in my bed, front to back, his hand on my breast, my head against his shoulder as we basked in the afterglow.

"Do you ever think about the first time we met?" I murmured. *"Where each of us would be right now, at this very moment, if you hadn't found me walking on the Battery that night?"*

"I would have found you regardless," he said in that tantalizing drawl.

"How can you be so sure?"

"Because some things are meant to be."

I shivered and pulled myself back from the brink. Neither of us said anything for a very long time, but I sensed that our moods had shifted. Maybe it was just mine. Devlin had taken a big chance on warning me about his fiancée and her stepbrother and now I felt it was time for me to lay my cards on the table.

"I know who they really are," I said, my focus still on the cemetery. "Claire Bellefontaine and

Rance Duvall. I know *what* they are and why you've warned me to stay away from them."

He said very quietly, "What is it you think you know?"

"They're members of an old and deadly faction known as the *Congé*. Their mission, perhaps even their raison d'être, is to eliminate those they deem a threat to the living world. People with unnatural abilities. People…like me." I heard the sharp intake of his breath, but I turned to him before he could respond. I even laid my hand briefly on his sleeve. "We don't need to pretend. Not after Kroll Cemetery. So let's skip the parts where you claim you don't know what I'm talking about or you gently call into question my sanity."

"You're not crazy," he finally said. "I've never thought that even for a second. And, yes, I know of the *Congé*, but it's nothing more than a legend. The kind of grim folklore we Southerners thrive on because it feeds our fascination for the macabre."

I sighed. "Are we really going to do this? Then let me remind you that I was once told the same thing about the Order of the Coffin and the Claw. *That* secret society was nothing more than a legend, people said. If it had ever existed, it had long since fallen from favor. Yet you continue to wear that symbol around your neck. I've never once seen you remove it."

He shoved his hands in the pockets of his jacket as he leaned against the car. He didn't seem particularly defensive, but I definitely sensed wariness.

"You seem convinced you're on to something so I'll play along. What makes you think the *Congé* are real? What do you know that I don't?"

"I know that they can be traced back to the early days of Charleston, when some of the city's most prominent citizens formed an alliance to do battle against the influences of a powerful witch doctor."

He said nothing.

"I know they were considered guardians against the dark forces of black magic and witchcraft, but over time, they became fanatical in their pursuits. Not unlike the puritanical zealots that participated in the Salem witch hunts, I might add.

"I know that as recently as twenty years ago, the *Congé* murdered at least twelve men and buried their bodies in a circle of caged graves in Beaufort County. I found those graves during the restoration of Seven Gates Cemetery."

Still, he remained silent.

"I know that a list of members exists, comprised of the oldest and most powerful families in Charleston. I've been told the name Devlin appears prominently on that list."

That finally roused him. "Told by whom?"

"I'd rather not say. But I'm certain a perusal of said list would also turn up the name Bellefontaine and quite possibly Duvall. I could go on, but contrary to what you wish me to believe, I wouldn't be telling you anything you don't already know."

He gazed straight ahead, hands still in his pockets, but he was far from relaxed now. I could feel the tension pouring off him in waves. For a moment, I thought about clearing my mind to see if I could enter his thoughts or a memory, but that was a dangerous endeavor and I wasn't certain I wanted to learn the secrets that lay hidden in his subconscious.

"Have you told anyone else about this?"

I moistened suddenly dry lips. "Who would believe me?"

"You've talked to someone," he said, still in that deceptively soft drawl. "I would very much like to know who has been filling your head with this nonsense."

The way he turned slowly to stare down at me... that dark glint his eyes...

In that moment, I was sharply reminded of how long we'd been apart. As much as I wanted to believe we still had a connection, John Devlin was a virtual stranger to me now. A dangerous interloper who might no longer have my best interests at heart. "Does it matter?"

"Oh, it matters." He cocked his head, still studying me. "Someone has managed to convince you that I'm somehow connected to a group of murdering zealots. I think I have a right to know the identity of my accuser."

I knew that he wouldn't relent, so I chose the safest option. "I have a number of sources, but Essie Goodwine is the one who told me about the twelve caged graves."

The mention of his dead wife's grandmother seemed to give him pause. "Essie?"

"Her brother was one of the men buried in that circle. But something tells me you already knew about that, too."

"I haven't seen or talked to Essie in a long time," he said. "I don't doubt that she told you about those graves, but as to the rest, I sense the heavy hand of Rupert Shaw."

I shrugged, but my heart was still pounding and I wondered if it had been a mistake to come clean. Where did Devlin's allegiance really lie? "I still don't understand why it matters. Especially if the *Congé* is nothing more than a fable, as you claim."

"You know our history. Rupert Shaw has had an ax to grind with my family for years. You have to look at everything he says through that filter. I'm sure he'd like nothing more than to drive a wedge between the two of us."

Your engagement to Claire Bellefontaine has pretty much done that already.

I frowned. "Dr. Shaw has an ax to grind? It seems the other way around to me. He's always spoken very highly of you and he regards your time at the Institute with genuine fondness."

"Because he knew how much my working with him would get under my grandfather's skin."

"Why would he care about that?"

Devlin shrugged. "They go back. I don't know the details of their original falling-out, but Dr. Shaw's work became another bone of contention between them. My grandfather is the one who had him dismissed from Emerson University for conducting séances with the students."

"At least he didn't have him killed," I muttered, thinking of those twelve caged graves.

"No, of course not. But Dr. Shaw lost everything—his career, tenure, his good name. Is it really so hard to believe that he'd try to use you to get back at me?"

"What purpose would it serve? You weren't the one who crossed him. And anyway, you have it all wrong. Nothing Dr. Shaw said convinced me of your involvement with the *Congé*. You did that yourself. Think back to our last conversation in Kroll Cemetery. Your grandfather was very ill and you'd just learned something about your family that had clearly distressed you. You told me your grandfather was involved with some very bad people and because of that alliance, you couldn't be with me. It was too dangerous, you said. I didn't understand what was at stake until I learned about the *Congé*."

I waited for a denial, but he was as silent as the ghosts that floated through the cemetery gate. Could he see them? Could he feel their cold?

The uncanny quiet made me restless and I kept talking to fill the void. "You saw something while we were at Kroll Cemetery. We both did. First in the guest cottage and then later in Rose's burning house. Those manifestations convinced you of what I am and you knew that our continued re-

lationship could attract the attention of the *Congé.*
So you ended it. You had to for my sake."

He laughed softly, the same sound I'd heard earlier when Claire Bellefontaine pushed him away.
"You think I'm that noble?"

"I want to."

"Well, I'm not. There are some who might even
call what I'm about to do self-serving."

I swallowed. "What are you about to do?"

His gaze burned into mine. "I'm about to take
away the one friend you thought you could trust
above all others. The one person you've always
been able to turn to."

"I don't understand."

He spoke in a subdued tone, but his words had
the sting of a thousand needle pricks. "Have you
never wondered about the timeliness of your association with Rupert Shaw? You told me once
that he had contacted you through your blog, be-
friended you at a time when you were new to the
city, alone and vulnerable. He even found you a
place to live. Have you never wondered about the
convenience of his assistant leaving the country
so suddenly just when you were searching for suitable accommodations?"

"So?"

"Do you know who owns the house on Rutledge Avenue? Your rent and the upkeep of the
property are handled through a management company, am I right? I'd go so far as to wager you've
never met your landlady or even spoken with her

on the phone. All correspondence goes through a service."

"What are you getting at?"

"Rupert Shaw has owned that property for years. Don't you find it passing strange that he never saw fit to tell you?"

Something unpleasant burrowed under my skin and picked at my doubts. "How do you know this?"

"It was recently brought to my attention."

"By whom?"

"It doesn't matter. What matters is that you know the truth. He didn't tell you about the house because he needed to maintain distance in order to foster your friendship. Would you have been as comfortable or as open if you'd shared a business relationship with him? He wanted your trust and your confidence so that he could continue watching you... Studying you..."

"I don't—"

"You talk about all those names," he went on in that softly brutal tone. "A perusal of that same list would undoubtedly uncover the name Shaw. Oh, yes," he said at my shock. "His ancestors go back to the founding of Charleston just as mine do. He is as likely a member of the *Congé* as I am."

"He is the exact opposite of the *Congé*," I insisted.

"Maybe that's what he wants you to believe."

I reached for the key at my neck. "Why are you doing this?"

"It's high time you accept the truth about your

so-called mentor. I told you from the very start that Rupert Shaw couldn't be trusted. He's not the man you think he is. He has an agenda. Just as we all do."

Nineteen

Angus was beside himself by the time I got home that night. I found him pacing in the kitchen and as soon as I opened the door, he dashed out into the side yard. I dropped my belongings on the floor and grabbed his leash.

He came eagerly when I called and I took him out the side gate to the street, mindful as always of our surroundings. I knew the area well and we went out so often for nighttime walks that I recognized many of the faces we met along the way, but I didn't let down my guard. Complacency invited trouble.

Look what happened at Woodbine Cemetery.

Just when I thought Asher Falls was nothing more than a distant memory, evil had found its way back to me.

I was still shaken by the episode at the cemetery gate. Almost as stunned as I'd been by my encounter with Devlin, but I wasn't ready to think about that yet. Our conversation was too fresh and raw and disturbing. Better to concentrate on an old foe and the reason for its reemergence in my life.

No matter how hard I tried to convince myself that I had imagined that encounter or how often I reminded myself that evil was still trapped in Asher Falls, hopefully confined deep within a mountainous cave or in the drowned cemetery that rested beneath Bell Lake, I couldn't dismiss that smell nor could I quell the taunting voice in my head. Something had made contact with me earlier and I thought once more of Prosper Lamb's door. If left open too long, bad, bad things crept through.

But why now? It almost seemed as if the entity had sensed a weakness in me, but despite my harrowing adventures at Seven Gates Cemetery, I didn't feel especially vulnerable. If anything, I had come through that episode stronger than ever— ready, willing and able to defend myself against aggressors from this world and the next. Hadn't I proven that earlier with Devlin?

Something else must have drawn the evil. Was it possible that some*one* had brought it here?

Prodded by my agitation, I picked up the pace, allowing poor Angus little time to enjoy the sights and smells of an autumn evening. I found myself going back to the beginning of my day and the discussion with Jonathan Devlin about the negative energy inside his house. The possibility had crossed my mind that the ghost child from Woodbine Cemetery might haunt him, but I didn't yet know how the two of them were connected. Nor did I understand why Prosper Lamb—if he, indeed, lived in that old house—could know about the song that was attached to the ghost child and evidently to my mother and my aunt.

Mostly I didn't understand what any of these things had to do with Asher Falls and the evil that resided there, but I was frightened by the implications. This was no longer a simple murder mystery—if the killing of a child could ever be considered simple.

This wasn't about vengeance or justice so the girl's spirit could finally rest in peace. There were greater forces at play here. Deeper repercussions. If evil truly had come calling, if that dark force intended to use the ghost to somehow get to me, then a child's eternal soul could be at risk.

That seemed a little dramatic even for me, but I didn't think it overstated.

I shivered and drew my jacket more tightly around me. I didn't smell evil in the wind now. I didn't hear voices in my head. But I had a sense that darkness was gathering and devastation loomed.

Ever sensitive to my mood, Angus hugged my side as we walked along. We went as far as the lake, but we didn't linger in the park. The shadows were too thick and I was too jumpy. Traffic was still heavy on Rutledge, and the restaurants teemed with people, but the night had become a disturbing place. I kept glancing over my shoulder to make sure we weren't followed and I searched the sky for signs and portents. Even the call of a songbird put me on edge, and I couldn't wait to get back home to the safety of our sanctuary.

I'd left lights on in the house, and the glowing windows were a welcome sight when we turned up the drive. I let us in the side door, then removed Angus's leash and filled his food and water bowls, but he remained at my heels as we made our rounds through the rooms.

Satisfied that nothing was amiss, he trotted out to the kitchen to eat while I went to shower. By the time I came out of the steamy bathroom, he was curled up in his favorite corner, but he rose when he saw me and went to the door, wanting out again. I made him wait while I put on the kettle, and then pulling a cardigan over my pajamas, I followed him out to the back garden.

The moon was breathtakingly brilliant, obliterating all but the faintest outline of the Big Dipper. Even so late in the season, the artemisia thrived along the walkways, providing a silvery backdrop for the gardenias. The smell trickled through my senses, stirring nostalgia and awakening old memories. It was a beautiful evening tainted by premonitions.

With the perfume of my garden filling my senses, evil seemed a millions miles away at that moment, but I knew from experience that my yard was not a safe haven. Hallowed ground ended at the back steps. I didn't see the shimmer of apparitions or the dark silhouette of netherworld beings, but I could feel the chill of a nearby manifestation.

Somewhere out there in the dark, a ghost made its way to me.

I went back inside to fix my tea and then sat on the steps, cradling the warm mug in my hands. I felt a bit lost tonight. Restless and wary as if I didn't quite belong in my own garden. At the cemetery with Devlin, I'd felt more alive than I had in a long time, but now the tug of the dead world was stronger than ever. In those quiet moments, my premonitions deepened.

Struggling under the weight of my foreboding, I called to Angus, but his attention was caught by something at the edge of the garden. He wasn't given to digging as some dogs were, but I could see his paws working frantically in one of my flower beds. I called to him again and he came to me reluctantly, allowing me to scratch behind his ear nubs, but he whimpered impatiently as I did so.

"What have you found over there?" I murmured. He returned my affection with a resigned look, but tried to squirm away when I ran my hand over his scarred head. "Fine then. Go do your thing. But please leave the gophers alone."

Ever the obedient companion, he darted back to the same flower bed and resumed his digging. I thought about scolding him or making him go inside, but he was only reverting to his true nature. I could hardly begrudge him his instincts, but I did hope the gopher managed to tunnel fast enough to get away from him.

As I sat sipping my tea, I finally allowed myself to think about Devlin, *really* think about him and the impact of our meeting. Of all the day's occurrences, the one that niggled the most was his assertion that he wasn't a noble man. *Some might even call what I'm about to do self-serving.*

I wasn't surprised that he still harbored ill will toward Dr. Shaw. Even though Devlin had once worked at the Charleston Institute for Parapsychology Studies, he'd never made any bones about his contempt for Dr. Shaw's work. The two men had a long and troubled history, evidently going back even farther than I realized. I also wasn't surprised that the bad blood had started with Jonathan Devlin. He was imperious and controlling and I didn't trust him for a moment.

I wasn't sure I completely trusted Devlin, either—not after tonight. Whatever his motive, he'd succeeded in stirring qualms about the one person I'd always thought I could turn to in times of ghostly disturbances.

But the accusations against Dr. Shaw could only be considered self-serving if Devlin stood to gain personally from creating a rift. Maybe he'd only meant to counter Dr. Shaw's claims about the *Congé*, but I couldn't help wondering if he had a deeper provocation and a more insidious agenda.

To find out that Dr. Shaw had owned the place that I considered my sanctuary was troubling, to say the least. If he'd owned the property for years, then he must know its history and the hallowed ground upon which the original structure had been built. Had he known about my gift even before our first meeting?

Jonathan Devlin had been able to uncover my family's legacy, so it wasn't much of a stretch to assume Dr. Shaw had done so, as well. I was suddenly reminded of all those times early in our friendship when I had so carefully skirted the issue of ghosts to keep from revealing my true nature. He'd observed my struggle and had never once let on that he knew the truth about my gift.

He had deceived me by omission and now I wondered what else he had kept from me and why he had been so keen for me to accept the Woodbine restoration when he knew that Claire Bellefontaine could be a danger to me.

Why, why, why? So many questions, so many loose threads. I hardly knew where or how to piece them together. Maybe it would be best if I distanced myself from this mystery. Just walk away, as Devlin had suggested.

But then I thought about that spreading darkness in the cemetery. The shadowy presence that had crept closer and closer to the ghost child as if it meant to swallow her.

I was so caught up in my musings that I forgot about Angus and his prey. A low growl jerked me from my reverie and I called out to him. When he didn't come, I half rose in alarm, but he was still busy in the flower bed, pawing and sniffing at something that lay on the ground.

"Leave it be, Angus. Come!"

Whatever he'd uncovered lay motionless and I shuddered in dread at what I might find in the morning.

"Angus! Come away from there!"

He came but he refused to leave behind his prey. Something dangled from his teeth and I cringed.

"Angus, drop it!"

He paused in confusion, gazing at me across the yard with those deep, soulful eyes before trotting over to deposit his kill at my bare feet. I braced myself, expecting to find a maimed gopher or a frightened mouse, but instead he had dropped a mutilated teddy bear on the step.

I let out a breath of relief. I even managed a shaky laugh until I realized the significance of Angus's find. Despite the battered condition, I recognized the keepsake at once. Someone had placed that very toy in the bed of the stone crib only that morning and now Angus had dug it up in my garden.

The button eye had been torn loose and the stitches pulled apart as if in a fit of rage. But the more disturbing aspect of the discovery was the scent that emanated from the mohair. The smell had a greasy quality that reminded me of frying meat. I wondered if some animal product had been rubbed into the fabric and sprinkled in the flower bed to attract Angus's keen sense of smell.

Lifting my gaze, I scoured the bushes and shrubbery, searching for what or who, I didn't know. The culprit would surely be long gone by now. At least I hoped so.

Reluctantly, I returned my gaze to the step. Someone had taken that well-loved teddy bear from a baby's grave, mangled it beyond repair and buried it in my backyard.

This was not the work of an angry spirit or the negative energy of a poltergeist. This was not a sign or a portent from the other side. This was something dark and twisted. A human hand had wrought this damage and the warning couldn't have been plainer.

Don't go digging up secrets that are best left buried.

Twenty

I turned in early, certain that I would spend the night tossing and turning, but surprisingly, I dozed off before I made it through the first chapter of a new novel. With the security system activated and Angus snoozing in his bed beneath my bedroom window, I allowed a false sense of security to lull me. Pulling the covers to my chin and nestling my head against the pillow, I drifted off, and even my REM dreams were harmless before I sank into a deeper slumber.

I had no idea how long I'd been sleeping when a sharp knock on my front door awakened me. I lay still for a moment, groggy and disoriented, until the sound came again and then I bolted upright in bed as my gaze shot to the bedroom door.

Even as I listened intently, even as I glanced at the clock to check the time, I still had that dazed feeling of being trapped in a dream. I didn't know if the sound had been real or the remnant of a nightmare, because all was silent now. Swinging my legs over the side of the bed, I perched on the edge as I tried to orient myself to the darkness.

When no other sound came to me, I might have been able to persuade myself that the knocking had been imagined. But Angus was up, too, and his behavior roused me from my indolence. Head and tail erect, he stood in the hallway just outside the bedroom door, his gaze trained on the foyer.

When he heard me stir, he momentarily left his post to pad over to the bed to make certain that I had heard the noise, too, and that we were both still safe and sound.

I gave him a reassuring pat as I grabbed my phone and the pepper spray from my nightstand. Slipping the phone into the pocket of my pajamas, I clutched the canister in front of me as I eased across the room on bare feet, pausing at the door to glance both ways before following Angus toward the foyer.

The house was too quiet, the abnormal hush of a tomb. I took stock of my surroundings as I crept down the hall. Behind me, the bathroom, kitchen and my office. Across the hall, the guest bedroom. Straight ahead the foyer. Just off the entrance, the darkened parlor.

I hated to turn my back on any of those shadowy rooms even though I felt certain the house was still secure. The alarm hadn't been triggered and hallowed ground would keep the ghosts at bay.

We're safe, I said to myself and then repeated

the mantra as I paused in the archway, pepper spray lifted and at the ready.

I turned on a lamp and the shaded light threw my shadow against the wall, startling me. Hysteria bubbled a little too close to the surface. I swallowed it back. *We're safe, we're safe, we're safe...*

Nothing was amiss in the foyer and I could see nothing out of the ordinary in the parlor. But that *quiet*. Utter and unnerving.

I moved across to the front door, once again pausing to listen. I heard no sounds from outside. No more knocking. No footfalls across the porch. Yet I sensed a presence. A *thing*.

No one I knew would come calling at this hour, much less pound on my front door as if they meant to raise the dead. A disturbance in the middle of the night never boded well, but I would have welcomed a human emergency at that moment. A frantic neighbor. The sound of a siren. Instead there was nothing but that wearing silence and a deep certainty that something waited for me on the other side of the door.

Already I'd worked myself into a state. My heart flailed and my knees trembled so badly I had to put a hand to the wall for support. Taking a moment to settle myself, I rose on tiptoes to peer out the peephole. Nothing. I moved over to the front window. I saw nothing. Heard nothing. And yet...

I scoured the shadows on the porch and in the front garden and then I moved my gaze along the street. It was possible someone had knocked on my door and then fled by the time I got up.

Yes, that must be what happened. It was a prank, nothing more. It wasn't unusual for neighborhood adolescents to get up to mischief. I desperately wanted to believe that no one or no *thing* waited just beyond my line of sight, but my quilled nerves told me otherwise.

I remained at the front window for several minutes, searching the bushes along my walkway and peering into the shadows in the alley across the street. Just when I was about to give up my post, the knocking came again, so hard and rapid I had the image of someone out there pounding on the door with both fists, demanding to be let in.

I eased back up to the peephole. Nothing. Over to the window. *No one was there.*

Backing into the foyer, I placed my hand on Angus's spine, as much to calm myself as him. He was clearly agitated. So was I. And I didn't know how to end this. A button on my alarm would summon the police, but what could they do? Whatever had invaded my front porch had no substance or form. It couldn't be seen. It wasn't real, and yet the pounding was all too real.

The hair on Angus's back bristled and he growled, curling his lip and tucking his tongue as he bared his teeth. He stood at attention, his gaze fixed on the door as he pressed forward on his front paws, ready to spring, ready to do battle for me as he had in Seven Gates Cemetery.

"We're safe," I whispered.

The pounding grew louder and more urgent. I half expected the door to be flung wide at any moment. I had a sudden image of a dark figure with beady eyes and a gaping beak standing on the threshold glaring in at me.

Don't think about that now, I warned myself. *Don't think about what might come through that door if it opens. Steady yourself and get ready to run.*

I still grasped the pepper spray, a totally useless weapon against dead-world invaders, but I couldn't seem to let go. My fingers were frozen around the canister. My heart knocked against my rib cage and a pulse throbbed at my temples. I could smell something seeping under the front door now, an odor that did not come from the living world. I lifted my gaze to the brass knob, and almost as if I had willed it, the orb began to turn, slowly at first and then more frantically.

The rattling seemed to mesmerize me. I stood immobile for what seemed an eternity. Then I lunged across the foyer, dropping the pepper spray as I grasped the knob with one hand and the dead-bolt lever with the other. I could feel the lock turn in my fingers and the door seemed to swell inward from an invisible force. I put my shoulder against the wood and then my back as I planted my bare feet on the floor and pressed.

Angus growled and paced and flung himself at the door. We had faced a lot of bad things together, but I had never seen him more stressed. I wondered if he recognized the smell. I wondered if, like me, he associated the threat outside our door with Asher Falls.

My heart was thundering by this time, my pulse leaping so erratically I could hardly breathe. The door bulged inward and I heard wood splinter. I didn't know how long the frame or the deadbolt would hold. For the first time in my life, I wished for a gun, but even a silver bullet couldn't stop the force that had laid siege to my sanctuary.

"What is it?" I whispered to Angus. "What's out there?"

He gave a loud bark, a warning, and just like that, the pressure on the door eased. The rattling subsided and once again an uncanny silence fell over the foyer.

My back was still to the door, my breath still coming hard and fast. I wanted nothing so much as to dash down the hallway and hide in a closet or jump back in bed and pull the covers over my head. But I wouldn't leave my place at the door. The moment I let down my guard, whatever was out there would find a way inside my house.

After a few moments, I turned to have a look through the peephole and then I slipped back over to the window. The sight of my own reflection in the glass startled me and my hand flew to my heart.

"Easy, easy," I whispered. "We're safe."

I moved back to the door and put a hand on the

knob. I didn't have the courage to flip the dead-bolt and have a look around on the porch. Instead I put my ear against the wood and concentrated my senses.

Outside my sanctuary, the night was very still. No traffic sounds came to me. No blaring horns, no gunning engines. The neighborhood slumbered, but the silence seemed loaded and waiting. Portentous.

Squeezing my eyes closed, I tried to focus only on the porch. The entity was still out there, I felt certain. I imagined it hunkered in a dark corner, watching and waiting. I could have sworn I heard the rasp of its breath and the scratch of claws across the floorboards. Then I heard a sort of rushing sound and a hard thud as if something had dropped from one of the trees onto the roof.

I lifted my gaze to the ceiling, once again pooling my senses as I tried to peer through the layers of plaster and shingles. I could hear nothing now beyond the sound of my own breathing. Even Angus had gone very still. But something was up there. Crouched and ready, beady eyes gleaming in the dark.

The upstairs apartment was directly above me, but I didn't think my neighbor had made the sound. Macon Dawes worked long hours at the hospital and his car wasn't in the drive. Besides, this was not the sound of someone casually walking through his apartment. The noise was fainter, stealthier. The softest of footfalls as if the thing tiptoed across the shingles, not wishing to be heard.

I followed the sound with my gaze, turning to track the furtive steps across the foyer roof and into the parlor. I zeroed in on the fireplace and a thought fleeted through my head that the flue might still be open.

Springing across the foyer, I tripped and stumbled through the archway, then righted myself as I dashed for the fireplace. Light spilling in from the hallway seemed to illuminate a path for me, but the rest of the room lay in deep shadows. Dropping to my knees before the hearth, I reached up into that cold, dark place for the handle of the damper.

An icy draft streamed down through the chimney, bringing the smell of human decomposition and rotten eggs. I thrust my hand higher, searched frantically for the lever. Something clamped onto my wrist and tugged so fiercely that for a moment, I thought I might be pulled up through the flue and into the night, into the Gray where my soul would be lost forever.

Angus growled as he left his place by the front door and rushed toward me. He planted his front paws on the hearth as he barked into the fireplace. The sound echoed up the flue and out through the chimney to the roof, where I could have sworn I heard an answering growl.

In the grip of full-blown panic, it took me a moment to realize that my pajama sleeve was caught on the handle. The fabric ripped and then I was released so abruptly I sprawled backward against the floor. I bolted up immediately and scrambled back to the fireplace, reaching in and up, searching, searching, searching until I finally grasped the lever and then I pushed it upward until the damper closed with a clank.

I allowed myself a breath. It seemed as if we'd been in the throes of battle for hours, but only a few moments had elapsed since the knock on my front door had awakened me. I wanted to believe it was over for now. We had withstood the assault and the rest of the night would pass peacefully. But I knew that it was still up there…out there… searching for a way in.

I struggled to my feet and hurried back into the hallway, calling for Angus to follow. I checked the deadbolt and glanced through the peephole. I still couldn't see anything, and the smell in the foyer had faded. I cocked my head, listening. I didn't hear anything at first. I thought again that maybe it was all over for the night. But as I settled my nerves and concentrated my senses, I heard the footfalls again. Still on the roof but now running toward the rear of the house.

Angus was at my heels as I raced toward the back door. The urge to flee the house was almost overwhelming, but I knew better than to go out into the night. Leaving my sanctuary was exactly what that thing wanted. If it could get inside, it would have by now. The banging on the front door, the footsteps across the roof…ploys to lure me away from hallowed ground.

After checking the lock on the back door, I padded into the kitchen and then out into my office, where I had a view of the garden. I hung back, combing the shadows from a distance before finally moving up to the windows.

I stood shivering as my gaze traveled along the flower beds and walkways. Even with security lights, there were so many shadows. So many hiding places. But now that I realized it couldn't get in, I felt safer and somewhat calmer. I was under siege, no question, but the attack was over for now.

Angus didn't seem as certain. He stood at my side, eyes peeled on the garden. When I touched his back, the hair along his spine bristled.

"We're safe," I said—for now. But we both knew evil would be back, because the ultimate prize was not the ghost child's soul, but mine.

I remained at the windows for a very long time, but I detected nothing untoward. Which, looking back, was strange. The thing was right there before me, hiding in plain sight, blending so well with the night that it seemed like nothing more than another amorphous shadow.

Maybe the eyes had been closed before, which was what had kept it hidden. They were open now and softly glowing.

Beside me Angus tensed as if he had just spotted it, too. Neither of us moved a muscle or uttered a sound as we stared at the figure in the garden.

It was humanlike but not alive, I didn't think. Not a living being as we knew it, though I could make out features. Eyes, nose, a mouth.

The thing hung upside down from a gnarled branch of a live oak, staring through the windows into my house. At me.

Twenty-One

I spent the rest of the night curled up on the chaise in my office with Angus on the floor at my feet. We were calm now, but neither of us could sleep. Pulling a wool throw to my chin, I stared wide-eyed into the garden as I clutched Rose's key in my fist. I couldn't see the hanging creature from my vantage, but if anything came to the window—or flew up to the roof—I felt certain I would see it. The deadbolts and chain locks kept the doors secure, and the alarm system remained activated.

"We're safe," I whispered. Angus answered me with a wide-eyed stare before he turned back to the windows.

Toward morning, I managed to doze off only to awaken with a start and scramble to my feet to check the house again. Angus followed me, sniffing at doors and prowling restlessly through darkened rooms. I allowed the steady glow of the activated light on the security console to lull me and I went back to the chaise, wrapping myself in the throw as I listened for any unusual sound.

When dawn finally broke, I arose as if nothing had happened and went about my normal routine. I filled Angus's food and water bowls, let him into the side yard for his morning ritual and then I dressed and headed out for my usual jaunt.

The air was still cool but the sky was clear and I knew the temperature would rise by midmorning. Accelerating my pace, I turned down Tradd, heading toward the water with the bells of St. Michael's at my back. I walked all the way to the end of the peninsula, pausing only for a moment to watch the sun crown the horizon. But I didn't wait for the full show as I usually did. Instead, I turned on my heel and headed home without glancing back at the harbor, without pausing to search the third-story balcony of the Devlin mansion.

When I returned, I came in by way of the front gate. I had avoided the porch on my way out and I hadn't yet gone into the garden to explore. Normally, I would have allowed Angus free rein inside the fence while I went for my walk, but what if that thing still hung from the oak tree?

Whatever it was, I didn't think it the same entity that had come pounding on my door, trying to find a way into my house. I didn't think it evil at all, but rather one of those strange watchers or guardians that sometimes slipped through the veil. It had arrived at an opportune time, just when my sanctuary was under attack. It may even have been the force that had chased evil away from my front porch.

Or maybe the thing had no purpose at all except to hang from a tree in my garden. *People and animals don't act as they should.*

Now with the sunrise at my back and the perfume of gardenias beckoning me up the walkway, I managed to convince myself I would find nothing more threatening than a sparrow gazing in my window.

The first thing I noticed was the smell. The stench hit me as I came up the walkway and climbed the porch steps. It was the same putrid combination of earthworms and spent matches that I had experienced at the edge of Woodbine Cemetery.

My stomach revolted and I very nearly fled back to the street, but I braced myself and climbed the steps slowly, stunned by what I saw when I reached the top.

Four deep gouges ran across the porch, and I had a sudden vision of the scratches I'd left on the side of Devlin's face. But the marks were not the superficial abrasions made by human nails. The grooves were so deeply embedded in the wood that they could only have been dug by a routing tool or by razor-sharp talons or claws. I'd seen scars like that once before on the face of a man in Asher Falls. He'd been disfigured by an attack in the woods, but he had no recall of the event.

A gelatin-like substance crisscrossed the porch, reminding me of the slime of a snail. Maggots had already invaded the secretion and it was from this ooze that the smell emanated.

I turned and stumbled down the steps, leaving the remnants of last night's dinner in the grass. When the nausea finally passed and my knees stopped trembling, I pulled the garden hose around to the front of the house and rinsed off the porch. Then I got a bucket and scrub brush and scoured every single floorboard. I kept at it until even my calloused hands were raw, and then afterward I went inside and stood under the shower until the water turned tepid.

Dressed for work, I finally went out to the back garden to have a look around. Nothing hung from the oak tree, thankfully, and I smelled only the gardenias and the faintest hint of bleach that clung to my skin. The sun was up now, spangling down through the trees and turning the dewdrops to diamonds. A green anole sunned on a flagstone. A fragrant breeze tinkled the wind chime. The sky was cloudless and already a soothing robin's egg blue.

It was a glorious day in my beloved Charleston.

I wondered what horrors awaited me in Woodbine Cemetery.

Twenty-Two

The first thing I saw when I pulled up to the cemetery entrance was a sleek black car. I thought at first it was Devlin's, but then I realized the vehicle was longer and wider, a luxury sedan like the one that had stopped in front of my house two nights ago. I recognized the man leaning against the front fender as the one who had come up my porch steps.

I killed the engine and got out, taking my time to gather my belongings from the back of my vehicle. I had no wish to talk to Jonathan Devlin or his associate. I was still reeling from the night's events and the morning's discoveries and I had things to do, personal missions to carry out.

Removing a plastic zip bag from the back of my vehicle, I carefully stored it in my backpack. Inside was the mangled teddy bear that Angus had dug up in my backyard. A cemetery rule had been broken—take nothing, leave nothing behind—and before I tended to anything else, the offering had to be returned to the stone crib.

After that, I intended to find out if Prosper Lamb actually lived in the tumbledown house across the street from the cemetery and if he had been responsible for the record that had been playing in the outbuilding last evening. I wanted to know if he could identify the female visitor to the cemetery and the anonymous donor who had arranged for the restoration. One way or another, I meant to get those answers.

On top of all that, a full day's work awaited me, and I was already getting a late start. So, no, I didn't have time for a lengthy conversation with Jonathan Devlin about the entity that had invaded his home or his imagination. I had problems enough of my own.

I slammed the back door as a way of signaling I meant business. Strapping on my backpack, I headed for the entrance with only a nod and a passing glance in the driver's direction.

He was dressed in a sports coat, slacks and loafers, but his innocuous attire and nonchalant demeanor didn't fool me. I hadn't missed the covert way he'd watched me as I climbed out of the vehicle or the subtle scrutiny of our surroundings. He stood with arms folded, feet crossed, head slightly bowed, but I could tell he was on full alert.

He hadn't moved or spoken during the whole time I'd been busy with my preparations. Now as I started toward the entrance, he straightened from the car and took a step toward me.

I tried not to let him see my wariness as I gazed

up at him. He was even taller than Devlin, and the lines of his sport coat did nothing to disguise the bulk of his muscles. Despite his size, he moved quickly and gracefully—like a trained fighter— and I had no doubt he was armed. Unlike Prosper Lamb, however, this man valued discretion.

"Miss Gray?"

I slid my hand in my pocket so that the pepper spray was within easy reach. "Yes?"

"My name is Knox. I work for Jonathan Devlin."

"What's that to me?" I started to move away, but he took another step toward me, stopping short of catching my arm.

"He'd like a word, if you don't mind."

I shot a glance at the car. I could see nothing through the tinted windows, but I imagined Jonathan Devlin inside, watching our every move.

"I'm sorry, but I do mind. I'm already late for work so…" I tried to move around him, but this time he stepped directly in front of me, blocking my path.

"Mr. Devlin is a strong-willed man," he said almost apologetically. "He always gets what he wants, so why not save us all a lot of time and trouble and hear him out? Then you can get on with your day."

I glanced back at the car with a frown. "Fine."

Dropping my backpack to the ground, I followed the driver around to the side of the vehicle, and when he opened the door, I bent and glanced inside. The sight of Jonathan Devlin huddled in the corner gave me pause. It was hard to believe I'd ever been intimidated by this thin, frail man. He seemed to have withered since our last meeting. And yet I would do well to remember who he was—not just the patriarch of an old and powerful family, but in all likelihood a member, perhaps even the leader, of the deadly *Congé*.

He was as well-dressed as always in a dark three-piece suit, his gray hair perfectly combed and his pocket square precisely folded. Beyond the surface, however, were the telltale signs of distress. His complexion was ashen and his eyes seemed overly bright, almost feverish. His hands trembled and his breathing seemed labored. Jonathan Devlin was not a well man and no amount of careful grooming could disguise his fragility and his almost tangible fear.

Once I was settled inside, the driver closed the door and I sat for a moment, taking in my immediate surroundings. Like Devlin's car, the sedan was luxurious, perhaps even borderline indulgent. It smelled of rich leather, old money and a hint of the basil and lime I'd noted from our previous meeting. The buttery seat seemed to engulf me and for a moment I had a bout of claustrophobia that set my pulse to racing.

I drew in a deep, calming breath, scolding myself for giving in to an old weakness. A chink in my armor was the very thing Jonathan Devlin would take note of and use against me.

"Thank you for agreeing to see me," he said, and I thought that even his voice sounded weaker.

I clasped my hands in my lap and tried not to stare at him. "I'm afraid I don't have much time. There's a lot to be done in the cemetery today and I'm getting a late start as it is."

"Woodbine has been badly neglected for years. Surely a few more minutes won't matter." He paused, giving me a long scrutiny, and I once again had a mental image of how he must see me—a woman just shy of thirty, attractive but far from beautiful with all the scrapes and scars and sunburned skin that came with a rugged profession.

I had on my work attire of boots, brown cargoes and denim jacket, and my hair was pulled back in the usual ponytail. The style undoubtedly highlighted the strain in my face and the dark circles underneath my eyes from lack of sleep. I was no Claire Bellefontaine and I wondered if the same thought had crossed Jonathan Devlin's mind.

He said almost kindly, "Are you all right? You don't look well this morning."

"I had a bad night."

"I worried something might have happened when you didn't show up in the park this morning."

I glanced at him in disbelief. "You were worried?"

"Does that surprise you?"

"You barely know me."

"I think we've established that's not quite true."

I shrugged, but I was far from complacent. "So you came looking for me here. Why?"

"The incidents have escalated since last we spoke. The ghost, the poltergeist, the entity…whatever one wishes to call the energy in my home has grown bolder and far more dangerous. The situation has become quite dire. I'm not a man given to dramatics or overreaction, but it's no exaggeration to say that you are my last and only hope."

"That's a lot of pressure to put on me first thing in the morning," I muttered.

He made a helpless gesture with his hand. "Desperate men, Miss Gray…"

It would have been easy to write him off as delusional. The glittering eyes, the trembling hands, the pulse that throbbed at his temple…all signs of a deeply troubled man. But I believed Jonathan Devlin to be sane and in control of his faculties. I also believed him to be haunted and highly manipulative.

"What happened?" I asked with reluctance.

"I was nearly killed last night, murdered in cold blood by a ghost."

The stark statement sent a chill shuddering through me, but before I could react, he put a handkerchief to his mouth, suddenly overcome by a coughing fit. The attack was so severe I worried that he was on the verge of collapse.

"Should I call for Knox?" I asked anxiously.

He waved off my concern and fumbled in his

pocket for an inhaler. Once he'd pumped medicine into his lungs, he let his head fall back against the seat and drew in air.

"Mr. Devlin—"

"I'm fine," he rasped. "Please, just give me a moment."

I nodded, wishing to be anywhere but inside that car. It was not my place. Jonathan Devlin wasn't my family. We were barely acquainted. Devlin should be at his grandfather's side, not I. But here I sat.

After a moment, he put away the inhaler and straightened, still dabbing at his mouth with the handkerchief. "My apologies."

"None necessary. But perhaps we should do this at another time."

"Without your help, there may not be another time. Please," he said. "Just hear me out."

I nodded with an inward sigh. "Go on."

He turned to stare out the window as he gave himself another moment to recover. "I was alone in the house. My grandson had gone out before dinner. The housekeeper had retired to her quarters in the carriage house and my assistant had gone home for the night. I had reading to do, so I went up to bed early. But the quiet unnerved me. I couldn't concentrate. Neither could I sleep. I lay awake for a very long time just listening to the tick of the grandfather clock on the landing. I felt uneasy…oppressed, as if something wasn't right. I suppose one could say I experienced a premonition, but outwardly nothing seemed amiss in the house. At some point I got up and took a sleeping pill. The next thing I knew, a sound awakened me."

Except for the sleeping pill, he might have been describing my night. "What time was this?"

"Just past midnight. I have a habit of looking at the clock as soon as I awaken. I assumed Jack had come home and perhaps had gone into the study for a nightcap. I thought I might join him. I wasn't afraid. Not then. I put on my robe and slippers and went out to the landing to call down to him. He didn't answer but I could hear someone walking about. I tried to pinpoint where the sound came from and I even started down the stairs to investigate. Then I paused only a few steps down, frozen again by that terrifying premonition. That's when I knew. My grandson hadn't come back and my housekeeper was still in her quarters, undoubtedly fast asleep. I was alone in the house, but not truly alone."

He was visibly shaken, the hand resting on the seat between us trembling. I said softly, "Are you sure you want to do this now?"

"Yes, yes, you must hear everything. It's a relief to be able to get it all out. Even if nothing else comes of our meeting…if you still won't agree to help me…at least someone will know…"

He certainly wasn't above playing on my sympathies. "Go on, then. But take your time."

He nodded absently. "The house grew cold. You know the cold I mean." He turned, his gaze burning into mine. "The kind of chill that settles in the bones and seeps down into one's soul."

The frost of the dead, I thought.

"I couldn't seem to move. It was as if my muscles had atrophied and I remained suspended on the stairs more terrified than I'd ever been in my life. Because I knew, you see. I *knew*. I'd glimpsed her before, *felt* her before, but in that moment, I realized without a single doubt who she was and why she had come back." As he spoke, he seemed to sink deeper into the leather seat, as if he were fading away right before my eyes. It was a strange effect and I blinked to bring him back into focus.

He rallied and his voice grew sharper. "I tried to convince myself otherwise, of course. One does. Even under extraordinary duress, the mind tries to reason and cope. The cold was only a draft, I told myself. Someone had left a window open in the house and a sea breeze had whipped through. My muscles were stiff from sleep and the night air. I knew better, of course, but I didn't want to face the impossible reality of a ghost. Of *her* ghost."

"She was fully manifested?"

My terminology seemed to perplex him. "She had form but no substance. I could see through her. Is that what you mean?"

"Did she appear to you as she had in life? Could you make out her features, her clothing?"

"For the first time, I saw her clearly. She stood at the end of the hallway staring straight at me. Even then, I tried to convince myself I was seeing things. She was a mirage created by failing eyesight or even the product of a mental breakdown. I was dreaming, hallucinating…anything but the truth." He rubbed a hand over his eyes as if trying to erase the ghost's image from his mind.

"One moment she was in the hallway and in the next instant, she hovered above me on the landing. Her arms were outstretched as if she were reaching out to me and I thought for a moment… Then I saw her eyes and I knew what she had come to do." He trailed away on a deep shudder. "I felt a force, almost like a storm gale. A wind so strong that it blew me back and I lost my footing. If I hadn't managed to hang on to the bannister, I would have tumbled down those stairs. The fall would have killed or maimed me and I have no doubt that was her intention."

"Why you?" Now it was my gaze that burned into his. "Who was she to you and why would her ghost want to harm you?"

I saw a flash of the old Jonathan Devlin, an imperious, secretive man who'd never felt compelled to answer to anyone, least of all someone like me. "Our history doesn't matter."

Of course it mattered. How else could one appease a vengeful ghost? But I didn't press the point because I wasn't certain I wanted to know the truth. Not here, not now. The cemetery was empty and isolated and I was in a precarious position, especially with his driver so nearby. Jonathan Devlin might well be a haunted man, but I still didn't trust him. I had a feeling the less I knew about his past, the better for my well-being.

How quickly things had changed, I thought. In the space of a night, I had reverted from the fearless warrior who'd aptly defended herself against an unknown assailant to someone who wished to keep her head buried in the sand.

When Devlin had grabbed me from behind at the outbuilding the evening before, I'd fought him with a ferocity that had surprised both of us and I had taken no small amount of pride in my instincts. But hubris was always going to bite me. Just when I thought my evolution had made me invincible, evil had come calling, reminding me that in the scheme of things, I was still puny and human and in need of my cemetery walls.

"Have you told John about any of this?"

He lifted a brow. "Do you really think my grandson would believe me?"

After our time together in Kroll Cemetery and after everything he'd learned about his family and their history with the *Congé*, yes, I had no doubt Devlin's mind had been opened to the supernatural. "You shouldn't be alone from now on."

"There's nothing Jack can do. You're the only one who can save me."

"You're still laboring under a misconception about my abilities, it seems."

"I assure you I am not. I know what happened at Kroll Cemetery."

I stared at him in shock, wondering for one dizzying moment if he had read my mind. "What do you know about Kroll Cemetery?"

"I told you before, there is very little about you that I haven't uncovered. Kroll Cemetery was a very haunted place before you arrived."

"If there were ghosts in Kroll Cemetery, they moved on because a killer was exposed. It had nothing to do with me." Which wasn't entirely true.

"I didn't kill her," he said quickly.

It took me a moment to realize what he meant. Then *I* said quickly, "I never meant to imply—"

"If a crime was committed, mine was of silence."

I drew a quick breath, trying to calm my thudding heart. "If a crime was committed, all the more reason to bring John into it. He was a cop not so long ago. He can help you."

Something changed in Jonathan Devlin's demeanor then. He still looked old and sick and feeble, but slyness had crept into his eyes, perhaps even a hint of triumph that reminded me yet again he was not a man I wished to cross. "You still think highly of my grandson, don't you, Miss Gray?"

"He's a good investigator."

"Oh, I think your admiration goes beyond the professional." He gave me a shrewd assessment. "Be honest. You're still in love with him."

Somehow the game had changed without my knowing. The elder Devlin had seized control.

He'd sensed my vulnerability and was now trying to press his advantage. "My feelings don't matter," I said with ice in my voice. "This isn't about me."

"You're wrong, young lady. You have no idea just how wrong you are. You are connected to everything that's happened in ways you can't begin to imagine."

I took a moment to absorb that. "What do you mean?"

He gave me a chilling smile. "You have *so* many questions. About my grandson, about me. About Woodbine Cemetery. How badly do you want those answers, I wonder?"

My heart flailed and I felt a surge of panic. Outwardly, I remained collected, but I knew without doubt that I was in the presence of a very dangerous and cunning man.

He leaned in. "Come to my house this evening and I'll tell you whatever you wish to know."

"I don't think that's a good idea."

"It's the only way. I'll send everyone out. The housekeeper…my grandson. We'll talk in private and I promise you I won't hold back. In return, you'll deal with the ghost."

"That sounds like blackmail," I managed, still astounded to be sitting in the same car with Jonathan Devlin, let alone discussing ghosts and extortion.

"I prefer to think of it as an exchange. A simple barter, if you will. Information is the only thing I have of value to someone like you. You aren't like the others. You're not motivated by greed or lust for power. But you don't like secrets, do you, Miss Gray?"

"What *others*?"

He lifted a brow as if surprised by my takeaway from his pitch. "My grandson is an extraordinary man in many ways, an intelligent and sophisticated man. But his choice of companions has invariably caused a lot of problems. Mariama Goodwine. Claire Bellefontaine. You."

I drew myself up. "I have faults, a lot of them, but I hardly think I deserve to be put in the same league as Mariama Goodwine. I would never drive my car over a bridge, deliberately trapping my four-year-old daughter inside so that I could appease one man and torment another."

"Mariama was trapped, too," he pointed out.

"Only because her seat belt malfunctioned. Perhaps it was divine intervention," I added a bit cruelly.

Both brows lifted. "Do you really believe that? The authorities ruled their deaths accidental, but I take it you don't agree with the official conclusion."

"I have my reasons."

He was silent for a moment. "Mariama Goodwine was a very beautiful woman who had a talent for arousing strong emotions and impulses. Think how easily she manipulated Ethan Shaw."

"What does he have to do with any of this?"

"I mention him only as an example of how expert Mariama was in pushing buttons. He was no match for her." His smile sent another shiver down my spine. I had the distinct impression he'd taken no small amount of satisfaction in the demise of Dr. Shaw's only son. Perhaps he'd even had a hand in it, though I couldn't think how.

Jonathan Devlin watched me carefully. "I, too, have thought about that malfunctioning seat belt. It's logical to conclude that Mariama would have swum her way to safety if she hadn't become trapped. But is it really so far-fetched to imagine that someone tampered with the mechanism before forcing her car over that bridge? Perhaps it was the child, and not Mariama, who was meant to be saved."

Why was he telling me all this? Why now? It almost sounded as if…

No. Don't even think that.

Jonathan Devlin wasn't responsible for what happened to Mariama and little Shani. It was too horrible, too terrifying to even contemplate. Losing his daughter had very nearly snapped Devlin. I could only imagine how he would react if he suspected even for a moment that his grandfather had been complicit.

Just stop.

Mariama alone had been responsible for their daughter's death. If anything, this was a ploy to catch me off guard or a subtle threat to warn me of what might happen if I didn't cooperate.

As dangerous and manipulative as I'd always

imagined Jonathan Devlin to be, I'd never once considered the possibility that he had been behind Mariama's death, let alone Shani's. I wouldn't entertain that possibility now. I would not.

Perhaps it was the child, and not Mariama, who was meant to be saved.

If a crime was committed, mine was of silence.

He watched me shrewdly as I tried to mentally scrub my face free of emotion.

"We'll never know what really happened," he said. "But the one thing I can tell you with certainty is that had she lived, Mariama Goodwine would have destroyed my grandson, utterly and completely. So perhaps you're right. The accident was divine intervention."

"And the child?"

"Children have a way of becoming collateral damage, I'm afraid."

That silenced us both and I wanted desperately to open the door and bolt, run as far and as fast I could from Jonathan Devlin. I was no longer certain that he was even haunted by a ghost. Perhaps a guilty conscience had driven him over the edge.

"Don't you want to know about Claire Bellefontaine?" he asked, still in that deceptively soft voice.

"What about her?"

"On the surface, she seems a perfect match for my grandson, wouldn't you agree? Smart, cultured, incomparably beautiful. But where Mariama was driven by passion and emotion, Claire Bellefontaine is cool and calculating. She plots and plans with infinite patience. She leaves nothing to chance. She is a woman without conscience, incapable of remorse. A true black widow."

I looked at him aghast. "Why are you telling me all this?"

"You must be curious about the woman my grandson has promised to marry."

"It's none of my business."

"If only that were true," he said. "But their arrangement is very much your concern. You see, each has something the other wants or can provide. Claire is an ambitious woman. What she craves above all else is power. Her family has an illustrious history in Charleston, but in recent generations, the Bellefontaines have been tainted by scandal, as have the Duvalls. In the circles that Claire wishes to rule, tradition and reputation are still everything. The Devlin name would give her the ultimate redemption."

"What does John get in return?" I couldn't help asking.

The elder Devlin smiled. "Come to my house this evening. Come at twilight. Help me get rid of the ghost and you'll know everything by nightfall."

Twenty-Three

My conversation with Jonathan Devlin tormented me for the rest of the day. His nebulous confessions and vague revelations were disturbing on so many levels and I couldn't help but think they'd been maliciously planted. He knew those questions would endlessly niggle, poking and prodding at my curiosity until my defenses were completely worn down.

I told myself I wasn't about to give in to his manipulations. I didn't know what had happened to him on that stairway. Maybe a malevolent entity had attacked him or maybe he'd let his imagination get the better of him, but in either case, he wasn't my problem. I had to worry about my own safety. Any further interaction, much less going to his home, would be asking for trouble.

Yet I couldn't stop brooding about Devlin's relationship with Claire Bellefontaine as I finished laying out the grid that morning. If the engagement was nothing more than a business alliance, what would Devlin get in return for marrying that woman?

His first marriage had ended in tragedy, but I still couldn't bring myself to accept that Jonathan Devlin had had anything to do with Mariama's and Shani's deaths. Was I turning a blind eye to the obvious? Maybe I didn't want to believe that Devlin's grandfather could be capable of such cold-blooded malice. Maybe I didn't want to see the monster that lurked beneath that withering persona.

Regardless of my feelings for Devlin and my doubts about his grandfather, one thing seemed certain to me now. The Devlins had secrets, dark and well buried.

My family had nothing on them.

With so much turmoil swirling around me, I found it impossible to lose myself in work. Nevertheless, I labored on until the sun started to slide beneath the treetops, and then I gathered my belongings and left the cemetery without a backward glance.

I told myself to go home to Angus and hide in my sanctuary until morning. I would disregard any further overtures from Jonathan Devlin just as I would ignore any knocks on my door. I would hunker down in my private domain until the crisis had passed, and if that made me a coward, so be it. Better safe than sorry.

But, of course, nothing was ever that simple in my world. The questions, as compulsive and tenacious as the ghost voices in my head, continued to beleaguer even as I walked through the cemetery gates.

After storing my gear in the back of my vehicle, I climbed behind the wheel and drove slowly down the gravel road that Devlin and I had traveled the previous night. Despite my better judgment, I still wanted to talk to Prosper Lamb. I couldn't shake the feeling that he knew more about Woodbine— about a lot of things—than he'd let on, and right now I felt more comfortable getting answers from him than I did from Jonathan Devlin.

I hadn't seen the caretaker in the cemetery all day and I found his absence curious. I wondered if he knew about my visit to his workshop last evening, and if so, why had he bolted when he heard my voice? Was he still avoiding me?

The evening was warm and I drove with my window down so that I could detect any unusual sounds or scents drifting over the fence from the cemetery or from the tumbledown house. I went all the way to the dead end and turned around. Then, after pulling to the shoulder, I got out and took a moment to reconnoiter my surroundings. The side gate was closed and the footprints that I'd followed were all but invisible. No one had come or gone this way since the evening before, and I didn't know if I should feel reassured or alarmed by the absence of humans.

I stood listening for a moment, hearing nothing more than a faint tinkle of the wind chimes from the cemetery. I hadn't seen anything of the ghost child all day, but it was still early. I knew from previous encounters that she could manifest before twilight, but only in the sheltering shadows of the willow copse.

With the task that lay ahead of me, I didn't want to think about the evil that had loomed over her diaphanous form, creeping steadily toward her as if it meant to consume her or to somehow use her to lure me back into the cemetery. I didn't want to think about the knock on my front door or the subtle footfalls across my roof. I didn't want to think about the creature hanging from a tree in my garden or the scratches across my front porch. But the images were all there, floating through my mind as I squinted into the light of the dying sun.

If a door had truly been opened, things were crawling through at an alarming rate. Beings and entities that I'd never seen before. I didn't know how to make them go away or even if I should. Not all of them were evil. Some might even have come through to help me.

It was tempting to believe that everything was connected to the ghost child and once I solved her murder, the door would close and all would be normal again. Normal for me, at least.

But no mere haunting afflicted me. Her manifestation was a symptom, not the catalyst, of gathering forces.

Satisfied that no imminent threat lurked, I locked the car doors and then patted the side pocket of my cargoes to make sure my phone and pepper spray were at the ready. Senses on high alert, I walked back to the house and hovered in the shadows at the edge of the road, surveying the dilapidated facade as I'd done the evening before.

I watched for several moments, concentrating my focus along the roofline, but I didn't see anything out of the ordinary, other than the structure itself. As I swept my gaze over the sagging balcony, I had the uncanny sensation that the house watched me back. Not someone or some thing but the place itself. It was as if the house were a living, breathing entity, a personification of whatever dark presence had taunted me through the cemetery gate and again later through my front door.

The sun hovered just above the horizon and the daylight shimmering down through the trees bolstered me. Even so, time was slipping away. The shadows had already lengthened, and they crept across the yard toward the house.

The wind had picked up, and behind me I could hear the discordant clang of the wind chimes in the cemetery. In front of me, the treetops undulated. The sky was clear but a storm was coming. In every direction, the dead world seemed to crowd in on me, warning me away even as it lured me closer.

I remained in the shadows for several more minutes, watching for any sign of life as I gathered my courage. It didn't take much. As wary as I was of Prosper Lamb and his ramshackle house, I was more frightened of the unknown and all those unanswered questions.

Crossing the road, I jumped the ditch and then paused yet again at the edge of the yard to survey the property. Satisfied that nothing lurked in the shadows or upon the roof, I walked up the porch steps and knocked on the door. As I stood waiting for someone to answer, I recalled Devlin's warning about the criminal element that hung out in derelict properties.

"Can I help you?"

I whirled at the sound of the raspy voice behind me. I thought I'd been on guard, but Prosper Lamb had managed to come across the yard or around the house without making a sound. He stood at the corner of the porch staring up at me through a ragged camellia bush. He was dressed in much the same attire as I'd seen him in before—dark jacket, tattered jeans, worn work boots—but this time he also wore cotton gloves, the fingers stained with something that looked very much like dried blood. All those preserved animals in his workshop flashed before my eyes and a shudder went through me even as I tried to give him a polite smile.

"Mr. Lamb, you startled me. I didn't hear you come up. I'm sorry for dropping by like this." I gave an absent wave toward the door. "I wasn't even sure you lived here. I'm relieved to know that I'm at the right place."

He didn't seem amused by my babbling nor

did he try to put me at ease. Something flickered across his face as he watched me. Surprise? Suspicion? Bewilderment? As usual, he was hard to read and I felt certain he wanted it to stay that way.

"I told you I lived nearby and this is the only house around so…" He shrugged.

"True. It was a fair bet. You also said that I should holler if I ran into trouble."

"Let me guess. More dead birds?" I might have mistaken his question for a taunt except for the alarm that flashed in his eyes. I left my place at the door and went quickly down the rickety steps to meet him. Somehow, I felt safer standing on solid ground as I faced him.

His sudden appearance had thoroughly unnerved me. Maybe it was those bloodstained gloves and the weapon I knew he wore at his hip. Or the creature I'd seen perched on top of his house and the dead animals he kept in his workshop.

I dropped my hand to my side so that my fingers could easily close around the pepper spray. "No more dead birds, thankfully. At least none that I've found. I still haven't gotten over all those starlings falling from the sky like that."

"It wasn't a pretty sight," he agreed.

"Thank you for taking them away," I said. "What did you do with them, anyway?"

"Why do you ask?"

"I know this may sound odd, but…" I paused. "I came by here yesterday looking for you. I saw your workshop in the back. I…couldn't help wondering if you had a use for them."

"Not those birds, no way. Those birds needed to be buried."

"Why?"

"I told you, they were signs. They'd already served their purpose."

"Where did you bury them?"

"There's a spot I use at the edge of the cemetery for the dead animals I come across."

I flashed again to all of those stuffed carcasses in his workshop and all those gleaming glass eyes. "Do you find a lot of dead animals around here?"

"Enough." He turned to glance across the road at the cemetery. "Not all of them are signs, but some are, if you know how to read them."

"And you do?"

"My mother did. I reckon she passed on some of her ways."

I knew all about legacies.

My gaze dropped to those darkly stained gloves and it was all I could do to suppress my own shudder. "It's nice of you to take the time to bury them. The animals, I mean."

"The smell gets bad if I don't. Not to mention the flies. But that's not why you're here, is it?" He removed the gloves and stuffed them in his back pocket. I couldn't help noticing the scar on his hand and I wondered again if he came from a violent past. And what or who had brought him to Woodbine Cemetery.

"I'm here on cemetery business," I said. "If you have a moment, I'd like to ask you some questions."

"About what?"

"You said something the first day we met that struck me. You said you thought a guilty conscience might be responsible for Woodbine's restoration."

"So?"

"I've recently learned that a donation was made anonymously to the Woodbine Cemetery Trust with the stipulation that I be the one to do the work. I know it's a long shot, but I'm wondering if you have any idea who may have made that donation. If that's why you said what you did about a guilty conscience."

He put a foot on the bottom step and folded his arms on the railing, but his casual stance was hardly reassuring. There was an odd glint in his eyes, not unlike the one I'd noted when he examined the dead birds. I'd had a feeling then as I did now that there was a lot more to Prosper Lamb than he let on.

"I'm just the caretaker," he said. "The Woodbine Cemetery Trust pays my salary, but I don't know anything about the donations."

"But you had a strong opinion about the motivation behind the restoration and you seem to know an awful lot about Woodbine in general. I get the impression you keep a sharp eye on things, so I'm sure you would take note of repeat visitors or any unusual activity. This is a roundabout way of saying that the donor may be someone with a personal connection to Woodbine. Someone who may have been coming to the cemetery on a regular basis for years or someone who just started to visit. Either way, someone with a guilty conscience."

"People come, people go. The gates are left open, so visitors wander in at all hours. So long as they're respectful and not up to mischief, I try to stay out of their way. And anyway, the dead don't care where the money came from. Why do you?"

"Maybe I'm just being paranoid, but I can't help thinking there's something suspicious about how things were handled. I wasn't given all the facts before I signed the contract. Certain things were kept from me and I don't like being misled or manipulated."

"I can't help you with that."

He straightened as if he meant to end our conversation, but I said quickly, "No, wait. I understand about respecting privacy, but I need to ask you about someone who came to the cemetery yesterday. A woman. She came early, before sunrise. I didn't see a car around, but I noticed her footprints in the soft ground. The tracks must have been made after the rain stopped. I think she visited the crib grave and then she left by way of the side gate when she heard me approach. You were in the cemetery early. Did you see her?"

He rubbed his hand across the scruff on his

lower face. "You were the only person I saw in the cemetery yesterday."

He hadn't seen Claire Bellefontaine and her stepbrother? He hadn't seen Devlin? "I noticed the footprints again when I exited the side gate. I followed them here. Did she come to see you?"

"I just said I didn't see anyone but you in the cemetery."

"You said in the cemetery. I'm asking if she came to your house."

His eyes darkened and I wondered if I had pushed him too far. "How do you know they were even the same prints?"

"One of the heels had a distinct mark like a cut or indentation. It was most definitely made by the same shoe."

He said nothing to that, merely glared at me until alarm skittered along my backbone.

I took a breath and said in an appeasing tone, "I don't mean to badger you and I'm not trying to pry into your private affairs. But there are things going on in Woodbine Cemetery that concern me. It's more than just the dead birds. Or the signs, as you call them. I'm just trying to find out what I've gotten myself into."

He was silent for a long moment, those cold eyes taking my measure before he shrugged. "I don't know her name. She's never said and I don't ask. She comes to the cemetery a few times a month. We have the same arrangement she had with the previous caretaker."

"Which is?"

"She slips me a few bucks every now and then to clean up around the stone crib. Sometimes she asks me to plant a certain flower, depending on the season. She leaves toys and coins and whatnot on holidays and sometimes she just sits beside the grave reading a book. She always comes early and she goes to a lot of trouble not to be seen."

"What do you mean?"

"I've never seen a car anywhere near the cemetery when she visits. I figure she takes a taxi. Or maybe someone drops her off and comes back to pick her up." He gave me a shrewd look. "She's not the only one, you know. Plenty of people sneak in and out of Woodbine to pay their respects or quiet their conscience. What makes this woman so special?"

"I'm wondering if she could be the anonymous donor."

"She respects the dead, but I doubt she has the kind of money to hire someone like you."

I thought about that for a moment. "Do you know who Jonathan Devlin is?"

I watched him closely, but his facade of surly indifference never wavered. "I know the name. Be kind of hard to miss in this city with all the Devlin this and Devlin that."

"He came to the cemetery this morning," I said. "We spoke briefly. I wondered if you'd ever seen him here before."

"How should I know? He could walk up the

porch steps and knock on my front door and I doubt I'd recognize him. If he visits Woodbine, chances are I never noticed him. Like I said, the gates are left unlocked. Easy enough to slip in and out without calling attention." He paused. "You sure have a lot of questions."

"Yes, and I'm sorry about that. I don't mean to sound as if I'm grilling you. I've wanted to talk to you for a while about all this. As I said, I came by here yesterday after I finished in the cemetery. When I first walked up, there was a song playing in your workshop. It sounded familiar. Haunting. I wonder if you remember the name of it."

For the first time, I seemed to have cracked his wall of indifference. Something flared in his eyes. "You may have heard music, but it wasn't coming from my workshop. Must have been a car radio. I wasn't around yesterday and I always keep the place locked up when I'm gone. Too many nosy people around."

I wasn't sure if that was a dig at me or not. "The door was wide open. I could hear the music all the way to the road. There wasn't any traffic, so it couldn't have been a car radio. I didn't just go snooping around your property," I assured him. "I knocked on your door just as I did today. When you didn't answer, I assumed you were in the workshop. I called out to you, but I thought you might be unable to hear me over the music. As I said, the door was open, so I had a look inside. There was a record playing on an old phonograph."

"Phonograph?"

"You know, a record player."

"I know what a phonograph is and there's one back there all right, but it's a piece of junk. I found it when I moved in and never got around to throwing it away."

"It was sitting right there on your worktable. I even heard the click of the arm as it reset itself and started the record over." I glanced up at the house. "Do you live here alone? Could someone else have been in the workshop playing records?"

"Not unless they broke in and even then…" He trailed off, his gaze sliding back across the yard toward the cemetery. "What time did you say you were here?"

"Dusk or a little after. It was pretty dark around back where your shop is. I didn't see anyone inside, but I had the impression that someone had bolted when they heard my voice. Maybe I interrupted a break-in. Have you been back there today? Is anything missing?"

"Maybe we'd better go have a look." His hand slipped under his jacket as if he were making sure he could get to his weapon. I did the same with my pepper spray.

Investigating the workshop with Prosper Lamb probably wasn't the best idea. I'd had some very dangerous encounters in the outbuildings of old properties. But I'd come here for answers, hadn't I?

My gaze darted back to the cemetery. I could still hear the wind chimes over the fence. Maybe it was my imagination, but I thought I could detect a melody now. The haunting strands that heralded the ghost child's manifestation seemed like a warning, a sign that I should seek sanctuary before it was too late.

Prosper Lamb had already rounded the corner of the house. I hesitated for only a moment before I hurried to catch up with him. Daylight was still upon us and so long as I kept a sharp eye, I'd be fine. As wary as I was of the caretaker, I couldn't imagine that he meant me any harm. I'd been alone with him in the cemetery and nothing had happened.

"How long have you lived here?" I asked as I came up behind him.

"Nearly a decade."

"That long? Did you know the previous owner?"

"There was no previous owner, just a previous caretaker. The property belongs to the trust. The house comes with the job. It's not much to look at but it suits my needs."

"Have you…" I trailed away as the hair at my nape quilled.

"Have I what?"

"Have you had any strange experiences since you've been here?"

He glanced over his shoulder. "What kind of experiences?"

"Unusual sounds, bad smells."

"Bad smells are why I bury the animal carcasses."

"I'm not talking about decomposition. Have you smelled sulfur?"

That stopped him cold. He turned, cocking his head to one side as he stared at me. "*Sulfur?* Is that a joke?"

"It's not a joke. I smelled it last evening when I came through the side gate of the cemetery. I wondered if it might be sewer gas in the area or some kind of bacteria in the water. You've never noticed it?"

His face was shadowed by the house, but I could feel his gaze on me, dark and intent. "If I smelled sulfur, I doubt I would have forgotten." He turned and started toward the workshop.

I didn't know why I felt the need to press him. Maybe his comments in the cemetery about signs and omens made me wonder if he was a kindred spirit. Maybe I wanted to believe he could help me figure all this out so that I wouldn't have to go see Jonathan Devlin. "Have you seen anything strange around here?"

"Like what?"

"Anything you couldn't explain."

"I live across the street from an old cemetery. I see strange things all the time. It's like I told you before, places like Woodbine attract a certain element."

"But you were talking about a human element."

He seemed to falter but he kept walking. "What else would I mean?"

The workshop was just ahead. Even with the

sun still hovering on the horizon, the building lay in deep shadows. My gaze lifted to the roof and now I faltered, too. If something was up there, I couldn't see it, and yet the breeze sweeping through the treetops drew a shiver.

Prosper Lamb had stopped once again. His gaze followed mine along the roof and then he turned to face me once more. My heart was suddenly pounding, not because of the suspicion in the caretaker's eyes, but because I knew that something watched us. I couldn't see it, I couldn't hear it, but something was near.

"Have you ever heard anything on your roof?" I asked softly. "Have you ever seen anything up in the trees?"

Even in the fading light, I saw the color leach from his face. "What are you talking about?"

"I just—"

His voice sharpened. "What did you see here last night? What did you hear?"

"I already told you about the music."

"No, you heard something else." His gaze darted to the roof as he took a step toward me and I took a step back. His eyes were gleaming now, feverish and demented, and I was all too aware of the gun he wore at his hip. "What did you hear? What did you see? Tell me!"

I slid my hand into my pocket and closed my fingers around the pepper spray. "It may have been nothing. Just my imagination or pinecones dropping from the trees—"

"Tell me!"

His harshness startled me. I put a hand to my throat. "The tin roof popped. First on the house and then on the workshop. It sounded like footsteps. Like someone had jumped from the house to the workshop and then back to the house."

His eyes still blazed but his voice had softened in disbelief. "That's impossible."

"I know."

He scanned the lines of the house and then turned to scour the workshop. "What did you *see*?"

"When I came out of the workshop, something was perched on the edge of the roof. A vulture maybe or an owl. That's the logical explanation. Only…" I still wasn't sure why I was telling him all this. For so many years I'd guarded my secrets and now here I was confessing my connection to the dead world to a virtual stranger.

But Prosper Lamb wasn't just any stranger. Despite my distrust of the man, I'd sensed something in him from the first. He knew things. He saw things. Just like me.

"Only *what*?" he asked in a near whisper.

I reached for Rose's key, tangling my fingers in the ribbon. "It looked human. And I could have sworn it watched me just like the sparrow in the cemetery watched me."

He said nothing for the longest moment. I wondered if he was trying to process everything or trying to discern my mental state. Maybe he was quiet for so long because he didn't want to risk setting off an unbalanced woman.

"Mr. Lamb, are you right?"

"What did you bring to my house?"

His outburst frightened me so thoroughly that I could only gape at him. He had been looking up at the roof, but now he whirled back to me, pressing so close that I could see that strange glint in his eyes and the glisten of spittle at the corners of his mouth.

I put up a hand to stop him. "Don't."

He seemed to catch himself then. He didn't creep closer, but neither did he back away. Tension radiated between us. Then he drew a sharp breath, lifting his gaze skyward as he asked in a calmer tone, "What did you bring here?"

I clutched Rose's key tightly to my breast. "I didn't bring it. It was already here."

"I don't believe you."

"It's true. I saw it on the roof from the cemetery gate." As I spoke, I inched away, my fingers closing over the pepper spray. I tried to keep my tone even so as not to provoke him. Maybe it worked. He made no move to follow me. Then I stepped in a hole and went sprawling backward to the ground. He loomed over me and I tried to scramble away before I realized he'd reached his hand down to help me up.

"You need to go," he said. *"Now."*

"Why? What do you know? What aren't you telling?"

"I said go!"

"All right, I'm going." I studied his expression in the waning light as I slipped the pepper spray back into my pocket. "But you need to be careful. We both do. Whatever I saw on your roof could come back."

"Shush." Once again he lifted his gaze to the sky.

I heard a sound then, like a distant whispering. The breeze blew through the trees, stirring the woodsy scent of pine and cedar and an undercurrent of something I couldn't name.

The whispers grew progressively louder and more insistent. For a moment, I even imagined that I could hear my name on the breeze. Then I realized those strange, muted utterings came not from the wind or the leaves or even the ghosts in Woodbine Cemetery, but from the flap of a thousand wings.

I scrambled to my feet as a shadow drifted over me. Not a cloud passing over the setting sun, I realized in awe, but a formation of starlings. I almost expected to see dead birds drop all around us and I braced myself for the coming death storm.

Beside me, Prosper Lamb stood immobile, his gaze fixed on the sky. As we watched in frozen astonishment, the flock separated and then came back together, all those starlings swirling and dipping as one, creating extraordinary patterns against the deepening sky—ocean waves, a seashell and then a human face with beady eyes and a beak-like mouth.

The face seemed to dip lower, as if that gaping mouth meant to devour us. I clutched Rose's key, stunned by the eerie formations. We watched the sky until the starlings flew on and the whispering faded.

Then I turned to the caretaker, my pulse still racing. "What just happened?"

"It's called a murmuration," he said. "I've only witnessed it one other time in my life."

"What does it mean?"

He tore his gaze from the sky and stared down at me in pity. "You still don't get it, do you?"

"Get what?"

"All these birds… I told you before, they're coming to you for a reason."

"Yes, I remember and I've done some research. The crow we found that first day…you called it a corpse bird. A death omen. You said it meant someone else is likely to pass. In certain beliefs, sparrows are considered soul catchers and starlings are messengers. I'm trying to figure out what it all means, but I have a feeling you already know."

"It's not the birds you need worry about," he said darkly. "The danger lies in what comes through the door after them."

Twenty-Four

I was shaken by my encounter with Prosper Lamb and what we had witnessed in the sky, and even more unnerved by his reaction. He obviously had sensitivity to the dead world and I didn't take lightly his warning about what might come through the door after the birds. I was frightened, yes, but I also felt an urgent need to solve the dead child's murder so that her ghost could finally move on. It pained me to think of her eternally earthbound, but her killer's trail had undoubtedly grown cold years ago. All I had to go on was the vision she'd shown me, but were there clues in that disturbing vignette that I hadn't picked up on? Hints in my dreams that I'd yet to cue into?

I thought about what I did know. The haunting music. The smell of woodbine. A woman's footprints in the cemetery.

Jonathan Devlin's desire to rid himself of a ghost.

The ghost child's rage. Her apparent attachment

to the stone crib. Her scream as she'd fixated on Claire Bellefontaine.

Perhaps I knew more than I realized. The puzzle pieces were all there and now it was time to start putting them together.

Before time ran out.

Research had always been my strong suit and as eager as I was to get home to my computer, I tarried at the cemetery gate. The breeze picked up and the wind chimes beckoned. The notes of that haunting melody drifted down from the trees and floated out over the graves, whether summoning me or warning me, I could no longer be certain.

I didn't give in to my fears, however. Bracing myself against a possible assault, I opened the side gate and stepped through. The cemetery still basked in the golden light of the sunset. Burnished angel wings beckoned, and the light shimmering down through the Spanish moss cast an ethereal glow over the enchanted garden. I looked for the ghost child among the cockleshell headstones, and not finding her there, I moved quickly along the winding path to the willow trees.

As I parted the fronds and stepped into that hidden enclave, I almost expected to find a sparrow staring at me from the stone crib. Or the ghost child glaring at me from the shadows. But all was quiet in that sad little glen. My only company was the forlorn teddy bear I'd returned to the crib that morning.

After everything I'd witnessed, the silence seemed weighty and portentous. The premonition that had dogged me since I'd found the unnamed grave deepened.

I sank to the ground beside the stone crib and drew up my knees. The day was coming to an end and I needed to keep an eye on the light. As much as I wanted answers and as eager as I was to solve an old murder, dangers lurked in Woodbine Cemetery after dark. Threats from this world and the next. I was cautious, but more resigned than frightened, and as I sat there beside that hidden grave, loneliness had never settled more heavily.

The wind shifted and the wind chimes tinkled. The smell of woodbine drifted over the graves, sweet and distinct.

But a darker note lurked. I didn't let it frighten me away. Instead, I lifted my head and searched the shadows. The ghost child was nearby. I could sense her presence in the shiver that ran up my spine.

"Where are you?" I whispered. "Who are you?"

Silence, deep and abiding.

"I know what happened to you. I know about the music and the woodbine and the footsteps. You've been leaving clues from your very first manifestation, but I haven't wanted to follow them. I've been too frightened by what I might find. But I'm ready now."

The wind picked up, tangling the loose strands of hair around my face, and for a moment I could have sworn I felt the chill of her fingers sifting through the tendrils at my nape, the gentle brush of her hand against my cheek. *Home*, she seemed to whisper.

The poignancy of her missive tore at me, but the moment was fleeting. In the next instant, I sensed her anger and her impatience at my lack of understanding.

Mercy, she demanded.

"Mercy," I whispered.

Loosened by the wind, a shower of colorful leaves rained down upon the clearing, settling like a patchwork quilt over the stone crib. Shivering, I tucked my hands in my pockets and waited, but the ghost child was gone.

Twenty-Five

After leaving the cemetery, I went straight home and took Angus for a quick walk before hopping in the shower and then dressing to go back out. I didn't relish the idea of a visit with Jonathan Devlin, particularly in his domain, but I needed answers and he claimed to have them.

I'd had a suspicion since our first conversation in White Point Garden that the Woodbine ghost haunted him, as well. He was somehow connected to the murder of that child. He may not have been directly responsible for her death, but the entity obviously held him accountable. She may even have tried to kill him. And if she had tried it once, who, besides me, could stop her from trying it again?

I parked near the waterfront and made my way down East Bay Street as dusk slipped in from the sea. The air had cooled and I hugged my jacket around me as I approached the Devlin mansion. Like most of the houses along Battery Row, a wrought-iron fence enclosed the property and I expected to have to ring the bell to be admitted, but the gate hung open and waiting.

I placed my hand on the brass lever and pushed the gate wider, then paused halfway through as a strange sensation overwhelmed me. I felt as if I were stepping into a different world, into a glitzy, dangerous world that I'd ever only glimpsed from afar.

I glanced over my shoulder to the exact spot on the Battery where I'd stood watching Devlin on that rainy day. I could see myself there now, a once lost and lonely young woman, toughened from experiences and the weight of an unwanted legacy but still clinging to an impossible dream. Still hoping for a future that was never going to be.

I hadn't asked for this life. I'd never wanted the ghosts. Never desired to entangle myself in their mysteries, much less to relinquish my warmth and energy to their hunger. With each new encounter, I told myself that if I could find a way to close the door to the dead world forever, I would finally be free. If I could find my great-grandmother's long-lost key, a normal life would be mine.

But as I hovered in the gateway of the Devlin estate, I felt a shift. An almost peaceful acceptance of who I was and what I was. There was no magical key, no way to run or hide from my legacy. This was the life that had been given to me. What I made of it was up to me.

I stepped through the gate and latched it behind me.

As I moved up the walkway, I could hear waves crashing against the seawall and the tumultuous swirl of waters where the Ashley and Cooper Rivers joined in the harbor. But I felt calm inside.

Perhaps I should have taken my unnatural serenity as another sign. At that precise moment, however, my mind was on the night bird that trilled from a treetop and the scent of gardenias that drifted over the garden gate.

History was there with me, too. History and the weight of all those Devlin secrets.

I paused on the brick walkway to stare up at the looming facade, trailing my gaze along all those magnificent columns and balustrades, along the rooftop promenade and then back to the third-story balcony where I had seen Devlin. No one was up there tonight, but I had the same feeling standing on the walkway that I'd experienced on the road in front of Prosper Lamb's house. The house watched me back.

And just like that, fear and dread returned. Tranquility fled and I had a momentary desire to turn back before it was too late. I had a very strong feeling that whatever I learned tonight might help free the ghost child, but it could cost me everything.

I took several deep breaths, striving for that elusive calm, but a single moment of weakness had eroded my composure. I wouldn't have been at all surprised to see a dark figure in a long coat perched like a gargoyle on the edge of the promenade or a nebulous form hanging upside down from one of the balconies.

The house was beautiful, an architectural layer cake, but as twilight settled, it became oppressive, and I had the terrifying thought that the Devlin home might be a gateway. A portal through which dark and inhuman things had once crept.

Shaking off those murky fantasies, I stepped up on the checkerboard entryway and rang the bell. When no one came, I waited a moment and then pressed the button again. Still no one came.

Jonathan Devlin had assured me that we would be alone, so perhaps that explained why no one answered. The staff had been sent away and he hadn't heard the bell. Placing my finger over the button, I pressed one last time and then knocked for good measure. The heavy wooden door swung inward without so much as a creak.

Entering any home without an invitation was never a good idea, let alone one of the mansions along Battery Row. I had no idea if an alarm had already been triggered. For all I knew, I was being monitored at the very moment. What would I do or say if the police came? Hopefully, Jonathan Devlin would back me up, but what if his invitation was nothing more than a ploy to somehow entrap me? A reach, perhaps, but what was I to make of his strange innuendoes about Mariama Goodwine's death?

I glanced over my shoulder to scan the street as I furtively pushed open the door with my foot.

I didn't consider myself impulsive or one to take unnecessary risks. I usually had good reason for my behavior even when I knowingly put myself in danger. But apart from a niggling suspicion that something was very wrong inside the house, I found myself curious about Devlin's ancestral home. How could I pass up the opportunity for at least a quick peek?

I pressed my foot against the door and let it swing wide enough so that I could slip through, then I braced myself for an ear-shattering alarm. The silence held and I let out a relieved breath as I glanced around. Sconces were lit on either side of the doorway, but the long hallway beyond lay in deep shadows.

The checkerboard pattern from the outer entry continued into the foyer, and tinkling glass drew my gaze to the vaulted ceiling, where a chandelier of Venetian crystals stirred in a draft. A wide staircase curved up to the second-story landing and I had a sudden vision of Jonathan Devlin up there in the shadows, chilled from the ghost's manifestation, paralyzed by fear and yet somehow clinging to the banister as he endured her assault.

I stood motionless for the longest moment, peering up those stairs and searching the shadows as the feeling of being watched came over me once more. I wasn't alone in the house, but whether the voyeur was real or imagined, I didn't know.

The front door was still open and the normal sounds from the street drifted in. I closed my eyes for a moment and let them wash over me. The gun of car engines. The laughter of tourists as they strolled along the street. The clop of horse hooves from the carriages. And more distant, the crashing waves against the seawall.

I turned my back to the ordinary world, to the real world, as I hovered on a threshold and a *threshold*. It was not too late, I told myself. Despite my resolve, I could still turn and run away. I could go home to Angus and wait out the night. I could hunker in my sanctuary, clutching my great-grandmother's key until daybreak, when the ghosts and in-betweens drifted back through the veil. I could keep wondering about the murdered child and her connection to my family and I could keep pondering Devlin's relationship with Claire Bellefontaine. I could hide behind my cemetery gates and let the living world pass me by or I could call out to Jonathan Devlin and demand that he give me the promised answers to all my questions.

I closed the door and moved deeper into the foyer but I didn't call out. There was still the matter of being watched. I lifted my gaze once again to the landing, peering as far as I could along the upstairs hallway. Then I turned in a circle in the foyer, glimpsing mostly closed doors and another dark hallway. I could feel a slight breeze on my skin, undoubtedly from the same draft that stirred the chandelier. But I saw nothing suspicious. I heard nothing out of the ordinary. No stealthy footfalls. No labored breathing.

With the outside noises muted by the heavy door, I realized the house wasn't so silent after all. I could hear the creak of settling floorboards and the pop of ancient timber. I could hear the tick of the grandfather clock on the landing and an electrical hum from somewhere deep in the house. The noises registered and then receded into the background as another sound captured my attention.

A music box played somewhere in the house.

I turned my ear to those tinkling strands as my scalp prickled and the hair at the back of my neck lifted. Dread descended and perhaps a fleeting triumph. I had been right after all. The entity that haunted Jonathan Devlin was the same ghost child that had manifested in Woodbine Cemetery. I had no idea the part he'd played in her murder, but it must have weighed heavily on his conscience all these years. And it had made the entity seek him out for revenge.

If a crime was committed, mine was of silence.

What had he covered up and for whom? And why had he kept quiet all these years?

Following those haunting strands, I slipped down that long hallway, glancing through open doors and over my shoulder. The house seemed at once cavernous and claustrophobic. The weight of all that history and all those dark secrets pressed down on me and I had to battle panic as the walls seemed to close in on me.

I was well past the staircase now and those prying eyes from above, but I could still hear the tick of the grandfather clock on the landing. The pendulums seemed to measure my trepidation. *Go. Back. Go. Back. Go. Back.*

But it was too late to flee now. Already, I'd passed the point of no return.

Another door stood ajar at the end of the hallway. As I crept closer the music grew louder. I proceeded in an almost dreamlike state, on and on, closer and closer, deeper and deeper into Jonathan Devlin's lair.

Pausing again outside the door, I turned an ear to the opening and closed my eyes, concentrating my senses. The music tinkled on as I listened for footsteps or the murmur of voices. I heard nothing, saw nothing, and yet for the longest moment, I couldn't lift my hand to push open the door; I couldn't make myself take that first step.

As I hesitated, the blackest premonition descended and I knew that destiny awaited me inside. The sparrow and the starlings had come to me for a reason, to warn me of this moment. Someone else was about to pass. Someone close to me.

I thought of Devlin then and the bargain he'd made with Claire Bellefontaine. I thought about the contempt with which she'd looked at him in the cemetery and I wondered what she might be capable of if he crossed her.

That alone prodded me forward. I pushed open the door and the scent of woodbine came rushing out, along with a metallic smell that might have been blood.

I stepped across the threshold and froze as my gaze traveled over the unfamiliar space. A lamp had been turned on to ward off the coming darkness. I took in the tall bookcases, the heavy desk, the French doors that opened into a garden. One of the doors stood open and I could feel the chill of the evening breeze as I entered the room.

Despite the dim light, I had the impression of opulence. Thick rugs. Gilded paintings. Leather furnishings. Beneath the scent of the woodbine, I detected a hint of whiskey and a tantalizingly fresh fragrance that seemed out of place in that room.

The entity hovered nearby. The scent of woodbine deepened as the room grew colder.

"Mr. Devlin?" I called softly. "Are you in here? It's Amelia Gray. You asked me to stop by at twilight. You haven't forgotten, have you?"

The ghost's anger was palpable, pulsing and throbbing like a heartbeat. She had manifested in the same white dress, with a bow in her hair and another at her waist. So sweet. So innocent. But she was not the spirit of a passive child. Even in life, she'd been dark. I sensed that now as images from her past strobed in my head. Somewhere in all those flashing memories was the visage of her killer.

"I know what happened to you," I said. "Someone pushed you down those stairs. He hid your body, didn't he? All these years you've been waiting for someone to find you, to free you so you can finally go home."

I spoke softly, as if addressing a flesh-and-blood child. Could a ghost be soothed? Perhaps so. Unlike before when my attention seemed to embolden and imbue her, she remained transparent, wavering in and out of this world until I took a step toward her. "I'll find you," I promised. "I won't rest until I do."

She faded then as I inched around the desk. Perhaps her quick departure was another warning, but I didn't understand the full extent of her anger until my foot bumped up against an obstacle and I glanced down. The light was so faint that it took me a moment to realize I was gazing at a body. Then I saw his pale face...

I gasped and stumbled back, putting a hand on the desk to steady my balance before I realized I shouldn't touch anything.

Jonathan Devlin lay sprawled on his back, a silver letter opener protruding from a scarlet bloom on his chest. His eyes were open and glazed.

I took a breath and moved in closer, avoiding that cold gaze as I knelt beside the body to check for a pulse. Light sparked off a gold locket he clutched in his fist. Even in my state of high agitation, I noted that the chain was broken as if it had been snapped from his killer's neck.

Across the end panel of his desk, Jonathan Devlin had scrawled a devastating clue in his own blood: "Mercy."

Panic quickened my breath. I knew that I needed to call the police. Someone had murdered Devlin's grandfather in cold blood and the longer I dithered, the colder the trail.

But I crouched beside the body unable to move, not out of fear but because I knew I was meant to find something. Another clue or a sign.

Emotions swirled in the room. I closed my eyes and tried to focus as a wave of rage swept over me, along with stinging notes of betrayal and disbelief.

The woodbine had faded with the ghost and now another scent drifted up from the body. That out-of-place fragrance that smelled of gardens and cedarwood and fresh linen. It was a scent straight from my childhood and it rocked me back on my heels, smothering me in all those clean notes as I stared down at Jonathan Devlin's cold body.

That locket...all I had to do was open it and glance at the photograph inside. That would tell me something. Perhaps even show me the face of the killer. I would know my connection to all this. I would know what Jonathan Devlin had meant to tell me tonight.

A sound deep in the house stilled me yet again. I'd forgotten my earlier sensation of being watched, but now it came back, along with a certainty that the killer had not yet fled.

I crouched beside the body listening to those stealthy noises. Closing my eyes, I concentrated my senses as I tried to identify the sounds. The slide of a drawer. The click of a door. Then footfalls on the stairway. Footfalls in the hallway.

All this time and I had yet to call the police.

Now the killer was returning to the scene of the crime and I would be found hunched over the body.

The footsteps drew closer.

I became desperate and fear made me clumsy and dull. The thought crossed my mind that I should crawl under the desk so that I could see whoever came into the room, but that seemed too risky.

My gaze darted around the study, searching for concealment. I spotted the open French door. For all I knew the killer had entered the house through that very door and might plan to leave the same way. But I had to do something and the garden beckoned.

I scrambled to my feet, taking care as I stepped over the body. After slipping through the French door, I darted into the garden and found a hiding place behind a planter as I waited for the killer to follow me.

No one came through the door.

I hunkered in the shadows, willing my pulse to slow as I peered through the foliage. I could see nothing inside the house and tried to maneuver into a better position. Suddenly a silhouette appeared in the open door, blocking the light from the study. I caught my breath and ducked behind the shrubbery. A moment later, light once again spilled into the garden as the figure retreated from the doorway. I heard the office door close and then the distant click of the front door. I remained hidden as footsteps hurried past the garden wall.

Somewhere down the street, a car engine started up and only then did I rise and slip back through the French door.

The lamp was still on and I noticed two things simultaneously. The lid on the music box was closed and the locket that Jonathan Devlin had clutched in his hand was gone.

Twenty-Six

I noticed a third curiosity as I moved toward the desk—drops of blood on the surface near the music box. I didn't know if they had been there before or not. I'd been in shock over my discovery and might well have missed them. Now I wondered if the blood had dripped from Jonathan Devlin's wound before he fell or if the killer had sustained an injury during the struggle.

Still taking care not to touch anything, I knelt beside the body to see if the locket might have slipped from his hand rather than been taken. As I scanned the room for any other anomalies, I unlocked my phone to call 911. I had my finger on the phone icon when I realized once again that I wasn't alone in the house. The drops of blood and the missing locket had distracted me and I'd grown careless. I'd been too certain the killer had already fled the scene.

I couldn't see the door, but I had a sense that someone hovered on the threshold. A few steps inside the room and I would be discovered. If I tried to flee, the intruder would be on me. My best bet was to remain still. Maybe the killer wanted one last look at the crime scene before he bolted. Maybe he'd flee without coming over to the desk.

Strange that I should think of the murderer as male when the clues had a distinct feminine touch. The missing locket, the music box, even the choice of a murder weapon—a letter opener grabbed in the heat of the moment. A male assailant could easily have subdued his frail victim, taking him out in any number of ways, including strangulation or blunt-force trauma. There was something about that letter opener that spoke of a crime of passion.

All of this spiraled through my head in the space of a heartbeat as I caught my breath and waited. In that interminable silence, I tried to focus on sounds and scents, anything that might give away the killer's identity, but fear blunted my senses. The only thing that came to me was the smell of Jonathan Devlin's blood, so strong I could taste it on my tongue.

The room had grown warm despite the open French door. Sweat beaded on my brow and my muscles started to tremble. I didn't know how much longer I could remain immobile.

Why would the killer linger so nonchalantly without fear of being caught? Unless the person knew that Jonathan would be all alone for the evening. Unless my presence had already been detected.

My muscles screamed for relief as a drop of

perspiration roll down the side of my face. I didn't dare wipe it away.

I still clutched my phone, but it was useless because a lit screen would shine like a beacon in that dim room.

As I huddled there trying to wait out the killer, a whispery sound came to me and then another and another. Soft footfalls moved quickly across the thick rug.

Fueled by panic, my instincts took over and I scrambled to my feet to dash for the open French door. A strong arm snagged me from behind and a hand clapped over my mouth. It was a repeat of the night before, complete with Devlin's drawl in my ear. "Stop. It's me."

I went still and he let me go at once. I whirled to find him staring down at his grandfather's body.

"What happened?" he asked in a ragged voice.

"I don't know. I found him like this."

"*You* found him." He lifted his gaze to mine. "What are you even doing here?"

"Your grandfather invited me."

His tone sharpened. "My grandfather invited you *here*?"

"Yes. I know it sounds strange, but he's been seeking me out. He came to Woodbine Cemetery only this morning."

"Seeking you out? Why?"

"He said he needed my help."

"With what?"

I hesitated. "That will take some explaining and

we really should call the police. But I need you to know…" A hint of desperation crept into my voice. "I swear to you, I had nothing to do with this."

"I never thought you did."

Relief swept over me. "You believe me? Just like that?"

A frown flitted. "Of course I believe you. Why wouldn't I?"

"Because I must be the last person you expected to find here. And aren't you wondering how I got in?"

"I assume you came in through the front door. It wasn't locked."

"Yes, but no one let me in. I just…entered. You don't find that suspect?"

"You said you were invited. I believe you. Why are you working so hard to arouse my suspicion? Is there something you need to tell me?"

"No. Not about this."

"Then we'll talk about the rest later. We've other things to worry about at the moment."

He knelt then, sweeping his gaze over the body and around the room. He seemed very cool and collected—not at all the expected behavior of a stunned and grieving grandson. But then, he'd been a police detective for many years. His training and instincts wouldn't evaporate overnight. At least that's what I told myself.

"Did you touch anything?" he asked.

"Just the desk. There." I pointed to the corner. "I was about to call 911 when you came in. I thought you were the killer returning to the scene of the crime. That's why I stayed hidden. But someone was here before you. They took something from the bo— From his hand."

Devlin's head came up. "What was taken?"

"When I found him, he was clutching a gold locket. The chain was broken as if it had been snapped from someone's neck. I heard footsteps in the hallway and so I slipped through the door to hide in the garden. When I came back, the locket was gone and the lid on the music box was closed. And I saw those drops of blood on the desk. Maybe they belong to the killer. He or she may even have left prints on the music box."

"You didn't get a look at this person?"

"No, I couldn't see anything from the garden. But I thought I heard the front door close and then footsteps out on the sidewalk. A few moments later, a car started up down the street." I hesitated as I studied his face. "You didn't see anyone when you came in?"

"No. I must have just missed him."

"Or her."

Devlin glanced up. "Or her."

He rose so quickly I took an instinctive step back and caught my breath. I wasn't afraid of him and yet there was something about his conduct that set off an alarm. I told myself he was probably in shock. I was. And he was undoubtedly thrown by finding me here.

But I couldn't help remembering my earlier conversation with the elder Devlin and his insinuation about Mariama and Shani. My first thought then had been of Devlin's reaction should he ever find out of his grandfather's complicity in his daughter's death.

I shoved all that to the back of my mind as I glanced down at Jonathan Devlin's body.

"We should call the police," I said again.

"I'll handle the police," Devlin said. "You need to go. You shouldn't be found here."

Something echoed. A remnant of a dream came back to me. *You don't belong here.*

He stood very close. I had my back to the French doors and I told myself the cool breeze blowing in had raised the chill bumps on my arms. The way the fragile light struck his face caused the strange glow in his eyes.

I was overreacting. He was still Devlin. *My* Devlin. But we hadn't been together for a very long time and I no longer knew him—if I ever really had.

I hugged my arms around my middle because I was still shivering and because I needed to do *something.*

"I can't flee the scene of a crime," I said. "You know better than anyone how that would look. And besides...you shouldn't be here alone."

I'd barely known Jonathan Devlin. I hadn't liked or trusted him. He'd been a cold, ruthless man and he'd done bad things, probably more than I would ever know. But no one deserved this. And Devlin shouldn't have to deal with the aftermath alone.

The backs of my eyes burned as I said quietly, "I'm sorry this happened. I'm sorry you had to see him like this."

Devlin's reaction to my sympathy surprised me yet again. "Did anyone know you were coming here? Did anyone see you enter the house?"

"I didn't tell anyone, but there were people on the street…tourists…"

"You didn't notice anyone watching you?"

He'd taken hold of my arms and I winced as his grasp tightened and his fingertips inadvertently dug into my flesh. "No, but we can't hide my whereabouts from the police. They'll find out. You know they will."

"They won't find out. Not if you do as I say. You have to trust me. I know what I'm doing." His grip eased as he searched my face. "The last thing I'd ever do is knowingly put you in harm's way. You believe that, don't you? I'm trying to protect you."

"But why do I need protecting? I didn't do anything."

"There's more to this than you know and I don't have time to explain. We have to get you out of here so I can call it in. There'll be questions, a lot of them, and I'll have to give a statement. I don't know how long it'll take. If I don't see you later tonight, just keep quiet until we can talk. Make sure your doors and windows are locked and keep Angus nearby."

I stared up at him with widened eyes. "You're scaring me."

"I want you to be scared so that you won't be tempted to do something foolish. Now go. I'll call the police as soon as you're safely away. Go through the garden and make sure you aren't seen leaving through the gate."

He leaned down and brushed his lips across my forehead. His fingers slid up and tangled in my hair, and as our gazes locked, I forgot that Devlin was a betrothed man.

For one breathless moment, I even forgot about the dead body at our feet.

Twenty-Seven

For the next few hours, I paced. From my office to the kitchen. From the kitchen to the front window and then back to my office. For a while, Angus had followed at my heels, but then he'd tired and watched me forlornly from his bed in my office.

At some point, I fixed a cup of tea and carried it out to the garden while he moseyed around the flower beds. I felt bad for not giving him a proper walk, but I didn't want to stray too far from the house. As soon as we went back inside, I resumed my pacing.

Finally around midnight I stretched out on the chaise and managed to doze off, but I'd only been asleep for a few minutes when I heard a tap at my front door. I rose silently, padding on bare feet down the hallway and then pausing in the foyer before I crossed over to the door. What if the evil had returned, softly this time so as to lull me into letting down my guard?

I reached down and smoothed my hand along Angus's backbone to see if his hair was ruffled.

He appeared alert but not overly excited and so I called out, "Who's there?"

"It's me."

I recognized the drawl even through the door, but I glanced through the peephole before letting him in.

Devlin entered quickly, bringing a cool draft of night air with him. "What happened here?" he asked with a scowl as he nodded toward the gouges on the porch.

"Another long story," I said. "And I believe we have more pressing business at the moment."

He traced a finger along one of the scratches on his cheek where the marks from my nails remained. "Yes," he said with an odd note in his voice. "It seems we have a lot to talk about."

I hadn't turned on the foyer light, but enough illumination streamed in from the hallway to highlight his features. He seemed on edge, and the gleam in his eyes made me shiver.

I said on a breath, "What happened after I left? You called the police?"

"They came." Absently, he reached down to give Angus a pat. "This may be a long night. We should probably settle in. And I could use a drink if you have something stronger than tea."

He followed me out to the kitchen, where I retrieved the bottle of whiskey I'd bought the previous winter to make hot toddies for a bad cold. I served it neat and he didn't complain. He carried his drink to the kitchen table and sat down. I followed with the bottle and another glass. I had never acquired a taste for hard liquor, but it was one of those nights.

I poured some into my glass and sipped tentatively. I still didn't care for the taste, but the fortifying burn helped to calm me. "Tell me what happened with the police," I said.

He shrugged. "It was mostly routine."

"Mostly?"

Now that I could see him clearly, I noted the fatigue in the lines around his eyes and the exhaustion that pulled his mouth into a thin, hard line. His beard was thicker than I'd ever seen it and the curl of his hair at his nape took my breath away. I sipped again, bracing myself now against the impact of his nearness.

"They came, they asked questions and they examined the crime scene."

"Did you have to go to headquarters to give a statement?"

"Not yet, but I will. I spoke at length with the detectives, though. They know they can count on my cooperation."

"I'm sure they do. Did they find anything useful? Do they have any suspects?"

"We'll get into all of that later, but right now I want to hear your story. You said you went to the house because my grandfather asked you to."

"Yes. I'll tell you everything I know, but some of this may not be easy for you to hear. I don't know how skeptical you remain..." I paused. "All

I ask is that you keep an open mind. There can't be any more secrets between us."

"I agree. No more secrets."

I drew a breath and began. "I first spoke with your grandfather two mornings ago in White Point Garden. He was waiting for me in a spot where I sometimes go to think or watch the sunrise. He had had me followed and researched to the point where he could surmise where I would be that morning. That is a very deep investigation," I said.

Devlin showed not the slightest hint of emotion. "Grandfather was nothing if not thorough."

"You don't seem surprised. Did you know about his investigation?"

"If I'd known, I would have shut it down. Or tried to. It wasn't until this past year that I had any influence on Grandfather. And not much even then. He was a stubborn man until the bitter end."

"I gathered as much. Stubborn and persistent. He told me there was very little he didn't know about me, including where I came from and who my people were. He even knew about my gift."

"Your gift?"

I wavered. Coming clean was no easy thing for someone who had kept secrets for most of her life. "I think you know what he meant. Even if he didn't tell you about his findings, you surely had suspicions after Kroll Cemetery."

Devlin returned my scrutiny for the longest time, and then placing his arm on the table, he leaned toward me. "I have suspicions. I've had them for a long time. But I need to hear you say it."

"I see things. I hear things."

"What kind of things?"

"Things that are not of this world. Ghosts, entities, beings that are no longer alive, but not altogether dead. I call them in-betweens."

He looked taken aback by my honesty. "Do you see them now?"

"No. This house is built on hallowed ground. It protects me."

"How long—"

"Since childhood. I saw my first ghost when I was nine years old. I didn't really understand what was happening to me until Papa explained about our sight. He told me the ghosts were dangerous and he taught me ways to protect myself. Rules that I lived by for the longest time. But now..." I trailed away. "My journey is another long story. I could go on and on and one of these days I'd like to tell you the rest. I meant what I said about secrets. But how I came to this point doesn't really matter. Suffice to say that Papa's rules can no longer protect me. The ghosts come to me now. They want things from me."

"Like what?"

"It varies."

He shook his head as if still trying to take it all in. "You see things, you hear things..."

"As do you," I said. "Remember Kroll Cemetery?"

He passed a hand across his face. "I remember Kroll Cemetery, but I still don't know what I saw there. I tried to convince myself that the shadow in the cottage was just that—a shadow. And the woman I saw in the flames at Rose's house was an illusion. But those lights… I couldn't find an explanation for the lights no matter how hard I tried."

"What lights?"

He stared at me for a moment. "The lights that came out of the woods. They floated up out of the trees, dozens of them and they seemed to enter you, to pass right through you." He took another swig of his whiskey. "Is that what happened?"

"I can't explain what happened. You saw lights… I saw the ghosts of those buried in Kroll Cemetery. I think uncovering their killer somehow released them, but it was as if they had to pass through me to get to the other side. I've never experienced anything like it before or since. I don't always know what my purpose is…if I have a purpose. Sometimes the entities use me as a conduit to the living world. Sometimes they need me to solve old mysteries or to help take care of unfinished business. But mostly they want to feed off my warmth and energy so they can feel human again. It can be terrifying."

"And you've lived with this terror since childhood?"

"Yes."

"You never told me." I heard the deepest regret in his voice.

"You wouldn't have believed me until Kroll Cemetery. And then you didn't give me a chance. You said—"

"I know what I said."

I had to glance away from those dark, probing eyes. I clasped my fingers together because my hands were suddenly trembling. "Anyway, your grandfather somehow found out about my gift and that's why he came to me. He said there was a ghost in his house. He wanted me to try and make contact so that we could find out what she wanted and make her go away."

"She?"

"He used the feminine pronoun. At that point, he'd only caught glimpses of the ghost from the corner of his eye, but he was convinced the entity meant him harm."

Devlin polished off his drink and poured himself another. "Did he give you a name?"

I said nothing for a moment as I reflected on his reaction. "You're accepting all of this far more easily than I would have ever dreamed."

"I don't know how much I accept. But I am trying to listen with an open mind."

"I appreciate that. I know this must be difficult for you. In more ways than one. I said it earlier and I'll say it again—I'm truly sorry for what happened."

His gaze dropped to his drink as if he suddenly had a hard time meeting my eyes. "I know you are. But let's just get through this. This ghost…"

I nodded. "Yes, the ghost. He said he had a suspicion of who she was and why she was there, but he wouldn't tell me anything more unless I agreed to help him."

"And did you?"

"No, not then. I told him he was misinformed about me and there was nothing I could do. I realize how coldhearted that sounds now, but you have to look at it from my point of view. I didn't know your grandfather. He'd never shown the slightest interest in me and then suddenly he comes to me for help. I had no way of knowing if he was telling me the truth. For all I knew he could have been setting a trap."

"What kind of trap?"

"Remember the list I told you about? I had every reason to believe that your grandfather was a member of the *Congé* and that his true purpose for making contact was to expose me."

"Did you tell him that?" I heard a note in Devlin's voice that jolted me.

"No. I only said that I couldn't help him."

He fell silent once more, staring yet again into the amber depths of his drink. But I had to wonder what was going through his mind. Was he really listening with an open mind or was *this* a trap?

Don't. Now was not the time for doubts and insecurities. Now was not the time to retreat behind my walls when we were finally clearing the air. Before Kroll Cemetery, I could never have been so open, but things had changed since we'd last been together. Devlin had changed and I could only wonder about his experiences during our estrangement. What had he seen, what had he heard?

"Go on," he finally said.

"Your grandfather wouldn't take no for an answer. He came to see me again at the cemetery the next morning. He was very upset and he seemed so frail, I worried that he was on the verge of collapse. He told me that the ghost had tried to kill him the night before."

Devlin drew a quick breath. "How?"

"He was alone in the house. He heard a noise and got up to investigate. He felt a powerful wind, a gale force that nearly knocked him down the stairs. Somehow he managed to cling to the bannister. He saw her then. He saw the ghost, fully manifested. He knew who she was and why she'd come."

Devlin leaned in. "And?"

I sighed. "He still wouldn't tell me about her unless I came to his home. He said I should come at twilight. He would make sure that you and the housekeeper were out for the evening so that we could speak in private."

"That explains all the errands," Devlin muttered. "So you went to see Grandfather to find out about the ghost?"

"Not just about the ghost." I took another quick sip of my drink. "He also said he would tell me why you've agreed to marry Claire Bellefontaine."

"He promised that, did he?" Devlin got up and

went over to the door to glance out into the side garden. The whiskey had relaxed him for a time, but now he seemed nervous and edgy. Obviously, we were getting to the part of the story that made him uncomfortable.

He turned back to the table, propping a shoulder against the door frame as he regarded me for another long moment. "You say you went to see my grandfather to find out why I agreed to marry Claire. But you already know the answer, don't you?"

"I think it goes back to our last conversation in Kroll Cemetery. But I'd still like to hear you say it."

"And I will. I'll tell you everything. No more secrets. But…"

I lifted a querying brow.

His gaze deepened, drawing me once more into his orbit, making me breathless with awareness as he stood there gazing down at me. "I need to hear the rest of your story first. What happened when you got to the house?" He returned to the table, brushing a hand so lightly against my shoulder that I wondered if I had imagined his touch.

I shivered as he once more sat down across from me. "The front door was open and I let myself in. I can't explain it, but I had a feeling, a premonition that something was wrong. I could hear the music box playing and I followed the sound back to your grandfather's study."

"That's when you found him?"

"I didn't even see him at first. I was distracted by the ghost."

A slight hesitation. "You saw the ghost in Grandfather's study?"

"Yes. The spirit of a child, a little girl. I'd seen her before in Woodbine Cemetery. I think my presence in the cemetery somehow awakened her."

"How?"

"I don't know. After all these years, I still don't know how or why they come to me. Papa says I have a light inside me that draws them. They come because they have to, like a moth to flame. As I said earlier, they sometimes want things from me."

"What does this ghost want?"

"I can only guess. I still don't know her name or when she died, but she appears to have been around ten when she passed. She had long blond hair and blue eyes. A very pretty child, but not a happy one. Do you have any idea how she might have been connected to your grandfather?"

Devlin shrugged. "I don't know of any relative who would fit that description. My father was an only child, as am I." He paused. "You didn't answer my question. What does she want from you?"

"I think she wants me to find her killer."

He looked stunned. "She was murdered? How can you possibly know that? You said you don't even know her name or when she died."

"She showed me."

"She showed you…how?"

I made a helpless gesture with my hand. "I can't really explain it, but I sometimes have visions."

"You're clairvoyant?"

"No, it's not that. It's more like glimpses into memories. She *let* me see how she died. She was pushed down a flight of stairs and the fall broke her neck. The killer carried her away and I think he hid her body. It's not just a matter of exposing her murderer. It's not just a matter of justice. She needs me to find her remains so that she can have a proper burial. So that she can finally rest in peace."

For the first time, Devlin seemed to struggle to remain receptive.

"You must know how all this sounds to me."

"Yes."

"All these years, you've kept this to yourself."

"Not completely to myself. I've confided in Dr. Shaw from time to time."

His gaze flickered. "Him, but not me."

"You didn't really want to know any of this, did you? You never made any bones about your disdain for Dr. Shaw's work. What was I to think your reaction would be to all this?"

"I was wrong," he said. "I never realized how wrong until this past year, but we'll get to that. We'll get to everything. God." He ran a hand through his hair. "There's so much to say, isn't there? So much time has been wasted with all these secrets. But we can't think about that right now. We can't let ourselves get distracted. This child…this ghost. You said you saw her in Grandfather's study. You don't think she had anything to do with his death, do you? Could a ghost even do that?"

"I've no idea. I do know the dead can influence the living, but I don't think that's the case here. Your grandfather said something to me that last morning at Woodbine Cemetery. He said that if a crime had been committed, his was one of silence. Maybe he knew what happened to that child. Maybe he was the only living person besides the killer who did know. That's why the ghost child came to him. Not to harm him, but because she needed his help. His guilty conscience misinterpreted her visits."

Devlin picked up his glass and swallowed the contents in one gulp. Then he poured himself another. When he saw my concern he said, "Don't worry. I walked over. I'm not about to get behind the wheel tonight."

"You can stay here if you like. In the guest room, I mean."

He smiled at that. "Thank you, but I'll need the cover of darkness when I leave. I can't be seen here."

"By Claire?"

His gaze instantly darkened. "I suppose it's my turn now."

"Yes. And I promise I'll try to remain as open-minded as you were."

"You'll need to be," he said. "It would also help

not to underestimate the evil that can reside inside a human soul."

"I never underestimate evil."

He glanced around as if suddenly remembering the scratches on my front porch, and I could have sworn I saw him shudder. "I told you that Claire and her stepbrother are not good people."

"Your grandfather said the same thing. He said that your engagement to Claire is a business arrangement. You each have something the other needs or can provide. For her, it's the Devlin name."

"And for me?"

"You told me yourself in Kroll Cemetery, didn't you? You said you'd learned things about yourself and about your grandfather that made it dangerous for us to be together. You weren't just talking about the *Congé*, were you? You'd already met Claire and you were trying to protect me."

Another fleeting smile. "You still think you know me that well?"

"I think I don't know you at all," I said. "You seem more of a stranger to me now than you did when we first met. And yet…" His devastating gaze made me shiver.

"There's still a connection," he said.

"So strong that at times I can feel your presence before you ever enter a room. I can hear your voice in my ear when I know you're miles away. Sometimes I wonder…"

"Say it." His voice was husky from the whiskey, but his drawl was like velvet.

"You told me once that you would have found me no matter what because we were meant to be together. In spite of everything, do you still believe that?"

"Yes."

"Even though you're engaged to another woman?"

He reached across the table and took my hand. "Since that first night on the Battery, there's never been anyone but you. I can't envision a time when there ever would be."

"And yet...you *are* engaged to another woman."

He held my hand in both of his for a moment before letting me go. I felt bereft.

"I'd like to tell you about that now," he said. "If you still want to hear it."

"I do."

"It's a sordid tale," he warned. "One that involves blackmail, murder and the occult. And that's only the beginning."

Twenty-Eight

I pushed my glass away. I'd had enough whiskey. It was making me fuzzy-headed and I needed a clear mind. But Devlin seemed to have no such compunction. He sipped in silence for a few moments as if trying to decide where to begin.

"You'll remember last year before you left for Kroll Cemetery I was already concerned about my grandfather's health and mental state," he said. "That's when he first started to tell me things about our family's history and legacy and about the organization that he had been involved in years ago. An organization immersed in ritual and secrecy."

"Not unlike the Order of the Coffin and the Claw," I pointed out.

"The Order has always been about tradition and connections. The rituals and secrecy were a way to foster an air of exclusivity. The group that Grandfather spoke about had a far darker history."

"The *Congé*," I said. "So you do know about them."

"Oh, yes," he said grimly. "I know about them. Unlike the Order, they did more than dabble in the occult. The other night you compared them to the Salem witch hunters. You're not wrong. I've heard them called sentinels, vigilantes, you name it. But until last year, I never considered them anything more than an urban legend. Parts of the South, especially here in Charleston, remain steeped in superstition and tradition. There have been rumors about underground organizations for centuries."

"Not all of them are rumors," I said.

"No, but for the most part, secret societies belong to another era. At least that's what I thought. During my time at Emerson University, even the Order of the Coffin and the Claw was in decline. But last year, Grandfather told me that the rumors about the *Congé* are true. They're a very old and wealthy organization, and as you said, their origin dates back to the city's founding. They were once thought of as powerful guardians, but over the years, their purpose became corrupted, first by zealots and then by greed. They fell out of favor and mostly went dormant except for a few of the most extreme fanatics. The story Essie Goodwine told you about the twelve caged graves you found—that's all true."

"Was your grandfather involved in that?"

"No, but he knew about it. As I said, most everyone had left the organization by then, including my grandfather. Now it seems the group is on the rise again."

"Why now?"

He shrugged. "These are turbulent times and the *Congé* know how to exploit fear and superstition. They feed on human frailty. People like my grandfather—the old guard—were coerced into returning to the fold in order to lend clout and legitimacy to the movement."

"Coerced how?"

"Intimidation, bribery." Devlin paused. "They came to my grandfather with a proposition. Either he return and help with recruitment or certain things from his past would be made public."

"What things?"

"Incidents like the twelve caged graves. He wasn't personally involved, but even the slightest connection could have been devastating to him, not to mention the legal ramifications. But there was something else they had on him, something personal. He wouldn't confide in me so I started digging and discovered that Claire Bellefontaine and Rance Duvall were behind the threats and behind the movement. The *Congé* is just the sort of organization to appeal to their sense of entitlement and thirst for power."

"But you must have already known them. Charleston is a very insular city, especially among the elites."

He nodded. "I knew each of them by reputation. I'd heard talk about Rance Duvall for years."

"What kind of talk?"

"Mostly about the decadent parties he threw on

Duvall Island and later his proclivity for stalking and abusing underage girls. At one time, the rumors were rampant. Apparently, some of his victims even filed charges, but their families were paid off. One of the girls disappeared without a trace."

I stared at him aghast. "*Disappeared* as in murdered?"

"We don't know that. Her family may have been bought off, too. If the police ever conducted a formal investigation, the records have since disappeared. I couldn't find so much as an unpaid parking ticket on Duvall. He knew how to cover his trail. Time after time I hit a brick wall, so I decided the best way to bring him down and expose the *Congé* was by working from the inside. I resigned from the police department and my grandfather withdrew his membership so that I could be inducted in his stead."

"And Claire?"

"As I said, I knew her by reputation, too." Devlin's gaze was dark and steady. "Her first husband died under suspicious circumstances, but nothing could ever be proven."

"The rich really are different, aren't they?" I murmured.

"Yes," Devlin said without inflection.

"You know all this and yet you still plan to marry Claire Bellefontaine."

"If it comes to that."

"Why?"

"You know why. She and Duvall found out about you. I don't know how. Maybe they got to Grandfather's investigator or maybe they hired their own. Once they knew about you, they had me."

"This is crazy," I said in a daze. "I would never ask you to sacrifice your life for mine."

"You didn't ask," he said. "It's a simple exchange. My name for your safety. If I do as they say, they won't involve the *Congé*."

"And you trust them to keep their bargain? What happens after you're married and Claire has what she wants?"

"I expect she'll try to kill me. If I don't kill her first."

"You say that so calmly," I said on a shiver.

"Because I don't plan to die. Not by her hand."

A pressure headache throbbed at my temple. I rubbed the aching spot with my fingertips. "I find this whole conversation terrifying. That you would put yourself in this kind of danger to protect me…" I closed my eyes briefly. "I don't want this. I can take care of myself. I'll go away for a while, take another out-of-town job. I'll remove myself from the equation."

"That would only be a temporary fix," Devlin said. "The very worst thing you can do is to underestimate them. For now, keep a low profile and let me handle the situation. Sooner or later, I'll find what I need. No crime is perfect. Something always gets left behind."

I dropped my hand to the table as I stared at him. "Do you think Claire and Rance are responsible for what happened to your grandfather?"

"That seems the logical conclusion. Once Claire had me on the hook, they no longer needed Grandfather. But a letter opener doesn't fit their MO. They plot and they plan. They leave nothing to chance. This seems like an impulse. A crime of passion."

"I thought so, too. The killer didn't go to the house with the intention of taking your grandfather's life. But maybe that's what they want us to think."

"We'll know more after the autopsy. My grandfather was a difficult man. He made a lot of enemies over the years."

"Including Dr. Shaw?"

Devlin lifted a brow. "Why do you bring him up?"

"Not because I think him capable of murder," I rushed to explain. "But he is an example of people who found your grandfather difficult, isn't he? You mentioned the other night that they had a history."

"It goes back to when they were young men. I don't know the details, but I've always thought it had something to do with Dr. Shaw's wife. My grandfather had a penchant for acquiring the unattainable. Whether he seduced Sylvia Shaw or she rebuffed him, I've no idea. But both men harbored a grudge for years. I'm certain that's why my grandfather went after Dr. Shaw's job and reputation. That and the fact that he wanted to prove a point to me. He hated my involvement with the Institute. He despised even more my relationship with Mariama. He blamed Dr. Shaw for both. And Dr. Shaw still blames my grandfather for Ethan's death."

"What? Why?" I asked in astonishment. "Your grandfather had nothing to do with Ethan pulling that trigger."

"Dr. Shaw thinks my grandfather manipulated Ethan's infatuation with Mariama to try and break up my marriage."

"You've talked to him about this?"

"He and my grandfather had a recent run-in. Things got heated. It was an ugly scene," Devlin said. "I've never seen Dr. Shaw so irrational."

"When was this?"

"A few weeks ago."

"Is that why you tried to turn me against him?"

Devlin sighed. "I wish it hadn't come to that, but I had to open your eyes. His investigation into the *Congé* is like poking a hornet's nest. If he doesn't stop asking questions, you could both end up dead."

"He's doing it because I asked him to."

"Then you need to tell him to stop."

"He says he's pulled back already."

"I hope that's true,"

"I've no reason to think otherwise. And you know as well as I do that Dr. Shaw isn't capable of murder."

Devlin gave me a long, hard stare. "Anyone is capable of murder given the right circumstances. As I said, we'll know more once we have the autopsy and lab reports."

"Because something always gets left behind," I said.

"Exactly."

"This is a lot to take in. My head is spinning." I pushed back my chair and stood. "I'm going to make some tea. Or would you prefer coffee?"

"I'll stick with whiskey," he said, swirling the liquid in his glass.

I busied myself with the kettle. I filled it with water and then moved to the stove. When I turned, Devlin had followed me.

"It's been a long night." His eyes were slightly bloodshot, but he appeared steady on his feet. And determined.

I drew a breath. "Yes, it has."

"It's been a long year, Amelia."

The drawl of my name almost did me in. "Yes." I leaned back against the counter and folded my arms. "I understand why you did what you did. Still…"

"You can't forgive me."

"There's nothing to forgive. There never was. But I did try to forget you. I tried to move on."

"I know."

I looked up at him. "What do you know?"

His eyes on me were dark and deep and his closeness, even more than the whiskey, dizzied me. "I heard about the police detective down in Beaufort County."

"*Him*," I said with contempt. "He was a diversion. A lapse of judgment. He tried to kill me."

His eyes went even darker. "I know that, too."

I studied his features, focusing my gaze on that tiny scar beneath his bottom lip. Still a mystery to this day. "You did more than hear about it, didn't you? You were there."

Devlin cocked his head. "What do you mean?"

"No more secrets, remember?"

"Okay," he said slowly. "What am I missing?"

"Dr. Shaw told me about a young man he once knew who had the ability to separate his spiritual self from his corporeal body. On one of his travels, he saw something that so badly frightened him he managed to convince himself it had been a dream." I paused, still gazing up at him. "During my time at Seven Gates Cemetery, I could feel you there with me, watching over me."

Devlin's tone turned grim. "I only wish I had been there."

"But you were. Maybe you don't even realize when you travel. It could happen in your sleep. But I know you were there. I heard your voice in my ear as plainly as I hear you now."

"Whatever you heard, whoever you heard, it wasn't me." He reached around me and turned off the burner. Then he placed his hands on my shoulders, gazing down at me in a way that I'd been dreaming of for a very long time. "I wasn't there," he said. "But I'm here now."

I put my hands on his chest, not to push him away or even to draw him close, but simply to *feel* him. He cupped my neck and then threaded his fingers through my hair as he kissed my forehead, my eyelids, the tip of my nose and then finally my lips. "I'm here, Amelia."

Yes, he was here, but for how long? Soon enough he would have to go back to his new life, back to his secret investigation and a fiancée who might even now be plotting his murder. Fear and panic seized me and I wrapped my arms around his neck, kissing him back with a fervor that seemed to stun him.

He pulled away, staring deeply into my eyes as he dropped his hands to my waist. Then he drew me back against him, not gently, as he nuzzled my neck and whispered in my ear, "It's been so long. God, how I've missed you."

"I've missed you, too."

"You don't know how many times I wanted to pick up the phone and call your number just to hear your voice. But I couldn't. I had to keep my distance."

"I know."

"I used to drive by your house, hoping to catch a glimpse of you in the garden or through a window." His low laughter throbbed in my ear. "I shouldn't have admitted that. It makes me sound like a stalker."

"I understand the compulsion. I used to stand on the Battery and stare across the street at your house."

"Yes, I know. I saw you there once."

"The way you looked at me that day…it was so intimate…so powerful. It was almost as if I could feel your arms arm me. I could feel your lips at the back of my neck…"

"Like this?" He turned me and then pulled me against him, pushing my ponytail aside as he trailed kisses along my nape.

I shivered and let my head fall against his shoulder. "Is this a good idea?" I said with a sigh.

"No. But when has that ever stopped us before?"

"Never." I turned in his arms, kissing him again as my fingers fumbled with his belt.

"So the kitchen, then?" he whispered against my ear.

It was tempting. I had an image of him now, shoving everything aside and lifting me to the counter as he knelt before me. But I was nothing if not practical. The kitchen had too many windows and there were too many monsters—human and otherwise—that would like nothing more than to intrude upon our intimacy. My bedroom was dark and cozy. The curtains at the window blocked even the moonlight. We would be safe there, sequestered from prying eyes and protected by hallowed ground.

I took his hand and led him down the hallway. We closed the door against the hallway light, blocking traffic noises and Angus's soft snores. We were alone in the dark and the quiet. Intimate strangers.

He tugged off my shirt and then his own. Pulling me to him once more, he ran his hands up and down my bare back and then slid them between us to find my breasts. "I've missed touching you."

"Then don't stop. Don't ever stop," I said on a shudder.

We struggled out of the rest of our clothing and then stumbled to the bed. I didn't want to think about anyone but Devlin. I didn't want to think about anything beyond this moment. But somewhere in the back of my mind I heard a phantom knocking. I told myself it was just my imagination. No one was there. Nothing could get to me here, not even the evil that sought a way into my world. But the knocking persisted.

"Did you hear that?" I whispered.

Devlin lifted his head. "Hear what?"

"I thought I heard someone knocking on the door."

He listened for a moment. "You're imagining things. But I'll go have a look around if you want."

"No. Don't leave me. Don't…" I caught my breath on a gasp as he trailed his lips lower.

But even as he moved over me…in me, something niggled at the back of my mind. Even as my world exploded in a shuddering release, I couldn't quite dismiss a persistent worry. Something was out there in the dark. Something from the other side.

A door had opened because someone close to me was about to die.

Devlin left before daybreak. I stood at the kitchen door and watched as he went through the side gate and disappeared into the night. As soon as I heard the gate latch close, I locked up the house and returned to my bedroom, leaving the door open this time so that Angus could take his spot near the window.

I shoved back the curtains to allow in the moonlight and stood for a moment in the silvery spill as I searched the darkness. I wanted nothing so much as to bask in the afterglow of my reunion with Devlin, but I was too uneasy. I felt more strongly than ever that things were coming to a head. A door had opened and forces were gathering. The evil that had stalked me since before my birth still watched and waited. Even now it was searching for that door, searching for my weaknesses.

I climbed back into bed and drew the covers up to my chin. But no sooner had I closed my eyes than a knock sounded again at my front door. Angus rose with a whimper and trotted over to the bedroom door to peer down the hallway. I swung my legs over the side of the bed and watched him.

"What is it?" I whispered.

He pivoted back to the door and emitted a low growl that had me rising and reaching for my robe.

I followed him silently down the hallway and then we paused as one in the archway to stare at the front door. The knock came again, followed by a strange howl that quilled Angus's fur.

I'd never heard anything like it. Not even from the ghost child. Not even during my stay in Asher Falls. The sound was distant at first, and then grew steadily louder as the pounding on the door intensified.

Something was coming. Not stealthily, but boldly. It wanted me to know that it was there. It wanted me to know that it was getting closer and closer to that doorway.

I moved across the foyer and glanced through the peephole. The porch light was on, illuminating all but the darkest corners. Nothing was there. I moved to the window and searched the shadows. I didn't see anything at first, but I wasn't fooled. Unnatural beings knew how to blend with the night. I kept searching, trying to detect shapes and anomalous shadows. Once I spotted the first, the others became more apparent.

Something was perched on my neighbor's roof and another form crouched behind a trashcan at the curb. I watched in fascination. I had no idea the nature of these entities, but I knew they were real. They weren't figments of my imagination, but otherworldly beings that were gathering around my house.

I wanted to believe they would protect me, but I couldn't help remembering Prosper Lamb's warning about birds. I needn't worry about why they were coming to me. The danger lay in what followed them through the doorway.

Twenty-Nine

I went to see Dr. Shaw the next day. After everything Devlin had told me about his recent conduct, I was very worried about him. He had seemed distracted and a little gloomy during our last visit, but the behavior Devlin had described didn't at all sound like the man I knew.

However, my visit was not altogether selfless. I wanted to talk to Dr. Shaw about the persistent knocks on my front door and all those strange entities I'd seen in the dark last night. Years ago, Dr. Shaw had harbored a fascination with lingering death. His wife had suffered from a terminal illness and he'd believed that in her final hours, it might be possible for him to glimpse the other side through the door that had opened for her.

He hadn't spoken about his late wife in a very long time, not since before his son's death. But I'd always had the impression that theirs had been a deep and abiding love. If Jonathan Devlin had tried to destroy that relationship, I could see why

Dr. Shaw might still hold a grudge after all these years.

The parking area at the back of the Institute was empty when I arrived, and silence enveloped me as I entered the lobby. The quiet seemed strange for a weekday and I felt chilled all of a sudden, not from a ghostly manifestation but because someone watched me.

Heart thudding in apprehension, I peered down the shadowy hallway. Dr. Shaw stood motionless in a doorway. I could feel his gaze fixed upon me and yet I had a feeling that he wasn't really seeing me at all.

"Dr. Shaw?" I called softly. "Is that you?"

He didn't answer. He made no move to acknowledge my presence, much less to come down the hallway to greet me. The way he hovered on the threshold—half in, half out—seemed portentous, perhaps even sinister, and yet I couldn't imagine that he would ever mean harm to me or anyone else.

I took a step toward him. "Dr. Shaw? Is something wrong?"

"What are you doing here?" His voice sounded strangely hollow, as if he were calling up to me from a very deep well or from inside a very dark tomb. It was an unnerving effect and one I chalked up to the strangeness of the situation and my oversensitivity.

"It's me, Amelia. I called earlier, remember? You said I could come by today."

"Amelia?"

"Amelia Gray."

"I know who you are, my dear. Of course I do." I was relieved to hear that his voice sounded normal now. "And, yes, I do recall our appointment but time got away from me, I'm afraid."

"No worries. I can come back later if you like."

He glanced over his shoulder into the room and then pulled the door closed behind him as he stepped into the hallway. "No, please, come back to my office. A visit with you is just what I need."

"Are you sure? It seems as though I've interrupted something."

"Nothing that can't wait." He motioned toward his office, a casual gesture, but I heard a strange note in his voice that I couldn't quite decipher.

I followed him down the hallway and through the double pocket doors, but instead of sitting down at his desk, he walked over to the window to gaze out into the garden for a moment. "Lovely day, isn't it? Even so late in the season, Sylvia's roses are still blooming. She had a green thumb. Everything flourished under her care. I'm not an accomplished gardener, but I have managed to do right by her roses."

"The smell is intoxicating," I said. "Even after all these years, you must still miss her."

"My dear, you have no idea. It's the one thing…" He trailed away, his gaze going back to the garden.

"What were you about to say?"

"Nothing of consequence. Shall I put on the

kettle?" he asked as he turned back to his desk. He motioned me to my usual chair and we both took seats.

"No, thank you. I've already had my limit this morning, but don't let me keep you."

He regarded me with kindly eyes as he folded his arms on his desk. I could see a slight tremor in his hands and with the morning light slanting in through the windows, the lines and creases in his careworn face seemed more prominent. He wasn't a young man and it struck me anew that the day might come all too soon when I would no longer have the pleasure of his friendship and counsel. Losing his only son had taken a toll. He was not the same man I'd met when I first moved to Charleston. But then, if Devlin was right, maybe that man had never existed at all.

"You look troubled," he observed.

"Have you read the paper or listened to the news this morning?"

"I've heard about Jonathan Devlin if that's what you're asking. A regrettable passing, but he lived a long and, by his standards, productive life. One can't ask for much more."

A regrettable passing? What a strange way of putting it. "Still, murder is distressing no matter the age or status of the victim," I said.

"Of course, you're right. I don't mean to dismiss what happened. What did happen, do you know? The news reports have been sketchy, but then I imagine the police have barely begun their investigation. I gather no arrests have been made."

"No, not that I'm aware of." I thought about the letter opener protruding from Jonathan Devlin's chest and the seep of blood across his shirt. For some reason, my gaze went to the silver letter opener in Dr. Shaw's pencil cup, and I couldn't help remembering the way he'd run his thumb along the blade the last time I'd sat in this very chair. He had seemed troubled then as he did now, and I wondered again about the source of his anguish.

I shook off the memory and said, "I'm afraid I can't offer much enlightenment. I haven't spoken with John since last night."

One snowy brow rose and I could have sworn I heard his breath catch. "You've been in touch with John?"

"Only briefly."

"My dear…" Dr. Shaw's expression turned somber. "Do you think any contact wise?"

"Because of his engagement or because of his involvement with the *Congé*?"

His hand fluttered nervously. "Both."

"Actually, that's one of the reasons I'm here. The last time we spoke, you said you'd dropped your inquiries into the *Congé*. I hope that's true. I think it's imperative that we both keep a low profile."

"Yes, I think it is for the best," he agreed. "But

has something happened since our last meeting? You sounded upset when you called earlier."

I hesitated as I watched him closely. "I'm a little on edge," I admitted. "I've had some strange experiences lately, but before I get into all that, I'd like to talk to you about another matter. I've found out something about the restoration that has me puzzled."

He waited silently.

"Claire Bellefontaine told me that you gave the board a glowing recommendation on my behalf. But if you knew about her position with the Woodbine Cemetery Trust, why would you even put forth my name? Did you not consider that her involvement might make things tricky for me?"

"Yes, of course, I considered it. But I was under the impression their minds were already made up. Perhaps I'm a bit too cautious these days, but I wondered if seeking my approval was some sort of test. I've never been hesitant to voice my opinion to that board or any other body that asks for my advice. Nor have I ever made any bones about my admiration for your work. When I was specifically asked to give a recommendation, I thought withholding my endorsement might seem suspicious. If that makes me paranoid, so be it."

I wasn't certain I completely bought his explanation, but what other reason could he have for wanting me in that cemetery? "I'd also like to talk to you about the house on Rutledge Avenue. My house."

"What about it?" His expression remained that of gentle concern, not at all the countenance of a man who had secrets.

"John told me that you own the property. Is it true?"

"Technically, the Institute owns the property," he said. "We once investigated a disturbance at that address. There were reports of strange noises and sightings from the downstairs tenant. The cause turned out to be benign—the house is built on hallowed ground, after all—but the owner was so spooked, he offered to sell the place to the Institute. It seemed a good investment. We were often in need of accommodations for staff and visiting investigators. When I met you, I knew the place would be perfect for someone with your gift."

"But you didn't know about my gift then. I never really talked to you about the ghosts until we were at Kroll Cemetery last year."

"Yes, but think about our previous discussions. You came to me with hypothetical situations involving shadow creatures, thought forms and any number of supernatural beings. I tried to provide rational explanations because that's what you seemed to need. But from the moment I laid eyes on you, I knew you had a unique sensitivity to the unseen world. I just didn't know to what extent."

"I still don't understand why you withheld information about the house. Why all the subterfuge?"

"I didn't want to frighten you away. You seemed

so determined to protect your secret, and the hallowed ground beneath the house was the only way I knew to keep you safe. And it has served you well, has it not?"

"For the most part."

"We had an instant bond, you and I, and over the years, I've come to care for you a great deal. In many ways, you've become a surrogate daughter to me. But I would be lying if I said my actions were completely unselfish. I wanted to keep you close. A person in my line of work rarely—if ever—comes across someone with your abilities. But there was never a nefarious purpose in hiding the ownership of that house. I hope you can accept that."

I nodded, but in truth, I was disquieted by all these revelations. For so long, Dr. Shaw had been the one person I thought I could count on and now the very foundation of our relationship had been shaken. "And then there's the list," I said.

He frowned. "The list?"

"The *Congé* membership. You made a point of telling me about the prominence of the Devlin name on that list, but John implied that your name might also be there."

He looked dumbfounded. "John told you that I'm a member of the *Congé*?"

"He said your family goes all the way back to the founding of Charleston just like the Devlin family. He said it is just as likely that your name would be on that list as his. He even implied that you might be trying to drive a wedge between us because of a grudge you held against his grandfather. Is it true that Jonathan Devlin was behind your dismissal from Emerson?"

"He was responsible for a good deal more than my dismissal." The edge in Dr. Shaw's voice drew a shiver. "He convinced my son to pursue Mariama Goodwine. He tried to use Ethan to drive her away from John. I don't blame Jonathan Devlin for my son's ultimate demise, but I do fault him for preying on Ethan's weaknesses and obsessions." He turned to stare out the window for the longest moment before he said, "I've never thought John was anything like his grandfather, but the timing of his revelations is interesting, don't you think?"

"What do you mean?"

"When did he speak to you about all this? How long before his grandfather's passing?"

"The night before."

"Has it not occurred to you that he might have a reason for raising doubts about me? For creating a viable suspect for his grandfather's murder?"

I stared at him in shock. "You can't think he had anything to do with his grandfather's death."

"I don't. But see how easy it is to plant suspicion? Doubt can become insidious because in the backs of our minds we know that seemingly good people commit murder every day. Something snaps and you become a different person."

Devlin had said much the same thing, but I didn't want to believe that anyone I cared about could be capable of murder. It was far easier to pin the blame on people like Claire Bellefontaine and Rance Duvall. Far preferable to search for monsters beyond our own front door.

Dr. Shaw regarded me across his desk. "Have I answered all your questions?"

"Yes, and I'm sorry if I upset you. But I knew that I wouldn't rest until we cleared the air."

"I'm glad to have it all out in the open," he said. "It would distress me to think that any bad feelings festered between us, especially now."

"Why especially now?"

His gaze faltered before he glanced away. "Death always makes one appreciate those close to us."

"Yes, that's true. And that's the reason I'm here. I've come to talk to you about death. You told me the other day that a corpse bird needn't be interpreted literally. It might not mean that someone is going to die. But I've seen more signs. Starlings literally falling from the sky. Dr. Shaw…" I leaned forward in my chair as I gripped the armrests. "I'm very much afraid someone close to me *is* about to die."

He frowned. "Someone has already passed."

"I don't think the signs were warning me about Jonathan Devlin. We weren't close. I barely knew him. And it's more than signs. The caretaker told me when someone is about to die, a door opens to allow the soul to pass through. If the door opens too soon or the person lingers too long, bad things can come through. I've seen them. Strange beings perched on roofs and hanging from trees. And for the past two nights, someone—something—has knocked on my front door in the middle of the night. When I look through the peephole or out the window, nothing is there. I think it's another sign or another warning. Something is trying to find its way through that doorway. Something is coming for me."

"What do you think is coming for you?"

"Do you remember our conversation last year before I left for Kroll Cemetery? I told you about the circumstances of my birth and about the evil that my grandmother sensed as she brought me back from the other side. I thought as long as I stayed away from Asher Falls, I would be safe. Evil couldn't touch me here. But now it senses a weakness in me and it's seeking a way into my world. It's searching for that doorway. The longer the door stays open, the greater the danger."

Dr. Shaw steepled his fingers beneath his chin as he watched me worriedly. "If the door has opened because someone is about to die, then theoretically it would close again as soon as the soul passes through."

"Theoretically."

"It's an interesting concept," he said. "And one that has long held my interest. I've done a lot of research into terminal illnesses."

"Yes, I know."

"My wife lingered for years."

"I'm sorry."

He waved aside my condolences. "She's been at peace for a very long time. That's how I wish to think of her. But this doorway—"

"Dr. Shaw," I said in alarm.

"What is it, my dear?"

"Your nose is bleeding. Are you okay? Here, let me help you."

I rose quickly and went to his side. I handed him a tissue and he held it to his nose as he leaned his head against the back of his chair.

"Are you all right?" I asked again.

"It's no cause for alarm," he said. "Just a simple nosebleed. A rather messy one, though. Excuse me for a moment while I go clean up."

"Of course, but should I leave and let you rest?"

"No, stay," he said. "I want to think more about this doorway and how to go about closing it for you."

"I don't think it will close until someone near to me passes."

"Perhaps that's the answer," he murmured.

But I barely heard him. My gaze had lit on an envelope on his desk. I recognized the MUSC Medical Center logo from my mother's stay there. But what caught my attention now was the blood.

Three pristine drops in the exact formation as the drops I'd seen on Jonathan Devlin's desk.

Thirty

I didn't see or hear from Devlin for the next few days, nor did I contact him. I took his advice—the same advice I'd given to Dr. Shaw—and tried to keep a low profile. I worked all week in the cemetery and kept my head down. But every day before twilight, I visited the stone crib in the willow copse. I would sit quietly in the grass and wait for another sign or manifestation to help guide me in my investigation. I had expanded my database search to include the surrounding counties, but I'd yet to turn up any record that matched the birth and death dates on the crib. And I still couldn't connect the ghost girl—a ten-year-old murder victim—to the buried infant. My best guess was still a sisterly bond, but how were they connected to my mother and aunt? To me?

The ghost didn't try to make contact with me again, either, although I almost always sensed her presence inside that copse. Sometimes I would see her diaphanous form in the enchanted garden, drifting among the seashell headstones or sitting on the ground with her legs pulled up, hugging her knees. The aura of loneliness that radiated from her manifestation tore at me. I knew that loneliness. I knew what it was like to feel lost and forsaken. It seemed to me that she was starting to fade. Had she given up hope of ever being found? Of ever having justice?

"Show me a sign," I murmured. "Tell me where I should look."

Nothing came to me. No fluttering wings or whispering leaves. Other than the child's ghostly form, I didn't see or sense anything out of the ordinary in Woodbine Cemetery. Maybe Jonathan Devlin's death really had closed a door.

One day, visitors came to the cemetery. I had finished photographing and logging all the headstones and graves and had just begun hauling off trash and clearing the overgrowth along the fence line. The extra help that I'd hired had already gone home for the day and I was alone once more in the willow copse. I heard voices nearby, but I didn't rush from my hiding place to investigate. Instead, I found a place where I could peer cautiously through the leaves without being seen.

Claire Bellefontaine and Rance Duvall were walking among the headstones, talking in low tones, but their voices carried in the quiet. They appeared to be looking for something. Or someone. I remembered everything Devlin had told me about them. The rumors that had swirled for years about Duvall Island, the girl who had come forward with accusations and then later disappeared. The mysterious circumstances that had claimed Claire's first husband. I'd sensed darkness in each of them, but I'd had no idea the extent of their evil. I shivered now as I watched them move toward me.

A hand fell on my shoulder and I jumped but didn't make a sound. I turned to find Prosper Lamb lurking in the shadows behind me. He put a finger to his lips and we both turned to watch the pair in silence.

Once Claire and Rance were out of earshot, Prosper Lamb said ominously, "You best get going before they double back."

"What makes you think they're looking for me?" I asked, my gaze moving again to the scar at his neck and then to the one on his hand. Our recent interaction had only deepened my suspicions about the caretaker. He was more than he seemed. Like me, he had a connection to the other side, but I still didn't know if he was friend or foe.

"They're bad people," he said, echoing Devlin's sentiments.

"How do you know?"

He moved around me so that he could keep watch while we talked. "They offered me money to keep an eye on you."

"They wanted you to spy on me? Why?"

"You would know their motive better than me," he said.

I frowned. "Did you take their money?"

"I know enough not to bargain with the devil," he said sagely.

I shivered at the look in his eyes. I turned back to search the graveyard. I couldn't see or hear Claire and her stepbrother, but I knew they were still out there. Why they'd come I could only imagine. Surely, they wouldn't attempt to harm me until Claire had what she wanted—the Devlin name. But they could certainly try to intimidate me and they could send Devlin a powerful warning about double-crossing them.

I wondered where they'd been on the evening of Jonathan Devlin's murder. And I wondered if they knew that Devlin had spent the waning hours of that tragic night in my arms.

"I can show you a secret way out of the cemetery," Prosper Lamb said behind me.

I turned. "I know about the side gate."

"Not the side gate. An opening in the fence no one else knows about." He motioned for me to follow. I hesitated as I had in his yard that one evening. Then I took off after him.

We left the cover of the copse as the sun sank beneath the horizon. We had enough light to guide us through the headstones, but the deep shade along the fencerow gave us cover. I felt like a shadow being, slinking through the gloom. We slithered through a hole in the fence and I found myself on a footpath that tunneled through the overgrowth on the other side.

The last of the light shimmering down through

the canopy cast a strange glow in the thicket. A mild breeze stirred tendrils of ivy and morning glory and I could smell the fecund perfume of damp earth and rotting leaves. I swatted a mosquito that had vectored in on my neck. There was something strange and otherworldly about the place. I stopped and called softly to the caretaker.

"Where are we? I've lost my sense of direction."

"Don't worry," he said. "I know the way out."

"I'd like to know."

He stopped and faced me. "We're headed toward the front of the cemetery. That's where you left your vehicle, isn't it?"

"Yes. But I need to know something before we continue. Why are you helping me?"

"Why wouldn't I help you?"

"After our last meeting, you didn't want anything to do with me. In fact, you ordered me off your premises. What changed?"

His eyes were shuttered. "Nothing's changed. I still don't want you at my house. It's nothing to do with you personally. It's what you are. It's what you bring."

That sounded pretty personal to me. "What do you mean?"

"I've been in war," he said. "I know what comes through that door when a life lingers too long. You've got something inside you that draws them. Maybe I do, too. I spent some time in a psych ward because of what I saw over there. I learned not to talk about it much. But you…" He trailed away, glancing over his shoulder as if to make certain no otherworldly creature had crept out of the underbrush to observe us. "You're different from me. It's like you're one of them somehow."

I felt a chill go through me at his words. "A living ghost," I whispered.

He nodded. "Maybe that's why they're here. Maybe they've come to take you back."

My conversation with Prosper Lamb haunted me all the way home. I'd managed to elude Claire Bellefontaine and Rance Duvall, but I couldn't outrun my fears. Even Angus couldn't soothe me, though he tried his best.

I sat on the back steps and watched him mosey through the garden. He didn't stray far. He kept coming back to my side, nuzzling my hand and pressing his snout against my knee as if to reassure me that all would be well. But he was upset, too. I could tell his senses were on high alert. Maybe he was picking up on my negative vibes or maybe he knew those things were out there in the dark, hiding among the shadows. Maybe he knew they were coming for me. Whatever the reason for his agitation, we cut short our evening constitution and hunkered down behind locked doors for the night.

I worked in my office for a while and then tried to watch a television program that I enjoyed. My mind kept wandering and I lost track of the plot. Clicking off the set, I turned in early, but I didn't sleep. I waited.

Just after midnight, the knocking sounded at my front door. As usual, Angus rose to investigate, but I pulled the covers over my ears and pretended to sleep.

Thirty-One

Jonathan Devlin's memorial was held the following week. Despite his stature, the service was to be low-key, by invitation only. I had no intention of crashing the event, but I felt compelled to be near so that I could at least offer Devlin my silent support even if he never knew I was there.

I found a shady and inconspicuous spot across the street and watched from afar as the mourners filed into church. Devlin was one of the last to arrive, and as much as I wanted him to know that I was there for him, I backed even deeper into the shadows.

Claire Bellefontaine was at his side. The two made a striking couple, both elegantly dressed in somber black. To casual onlookers, they would appear the perfect couple, but even before Devlin had told me about their relationship, I'd seen the cracks. I'd witnessed firsthand the chill between them. Now it wasn't at all difficult to detect the stiffness in his posture and the way he pulled away when she slid her arm through his.

They were almost at the entrance when he turned suddenly and glanced across the street as if he had sensed my presence. He couldn't see me. I was certain of that and yet he had somehow intuited my nearness. Or maybe he just knew me that well.

Claire turned, too, sweeping her gaze along the street. My heart jumped painfully as her gaze seemed to linger and I could have sworn I saw her smile.

Then they both turned and disappeared inside the church.

I told myself not to loiter. I could still be noticed and I didn't want to call attention to myself. And anyway, I needed to get back to work. Between the weather and my own detective work, I'd fallen behind.

As I left my position, I saw someone emerge from a recessed doorway across the street. She had on sunglasses and a wide-brimmed hat, but I recognized my aunt at once. I started to wave and call out to her, but something froze me. The way she stared across the street at the church sent a warning tingle up my spine.

So many things flashed through my head in that moment. Bits and pieces of that last overheard conversation between her and my mother came back to me.

"Oh, Lyn, you can't confront him. Not in your state."

"Why not? You don't think it would be interest-

ing to hear what he has to say for himself after all this time?"

"It's been nearly fifty years. Half a century. How can anything about that man possibly matter to you now?"

"He's old and sick. It's never too late to develop a guilty conscience."

Like Devlin, Aunt Lynrose seemed to sense my scrutiny. She turned for a moment to scour the sidewalk and then she whirled to hurry away, disappearing around the next corner as I remained stunned by her presence and by the implication of all those memories.

And then I rushed after her.

I wasn't certain I had the courage to confront her with my suspicions, but as it happened, I never got the chance to find out. I turned the same corner and collided with Rance Duvall.

He wore dark glasses so that I couldn't see his eyes, but his smile was as open and charming as ever. He put his hands on my shoulders to steady me, but I backed away, repelled by his touch.

"Well, hello," he said warmly. "Amelia, right? Our cemetery restorer."

I didn't at all care for his use of the possessive pronoun. "I'm sorry. I wasn't looking where I was going...if you'll excuse me..." I took another step back from him.

"No, don't run off. I'm glad we bumped into each other. You're a hard woman to find these days."

"You've been looking for me?"

"I drove out to Woodbine the other day, but I somehow missed you. I did see the caretaker, though. He's a strange fellow, isn't he? He said he hadn't seen you all day, but your car was still parked at the front of the cemetery."

"Maybe he was occupied elsewhere. I don't see him every day."

"Well, let's hope he earns his keep somehow." Rance Duvall took off his sunglasses, folded them and put them in his pocket. He was still smiling, but his eyes were as cold as ice.

"Why were you looking for me?" I asked, keeping my tone even.

"The cemetery on Duvall Island could use someone like you. Some of the headstones have very nearly crumbled to dust. I wondered if you would be interested in taking on the project once you're finished with Woodbine."

"I don't know," I hedged. "My schedule is full through the next year. I wouldn't want you to wait that long. Time is of the essence in those kinds of situations."

"Sounds like business is booming. That's good for you, bad for me," he said with another smile. "Perhaps you could at least spare an afternoon to give me some advice. I would really love for you to see the cemetery. I don't believe there's another like it. You're the only other person I know of who could appreciate its hidden charms."

I suppressed a shudder as his dark gaze took me in. "I'll try to make some time," I murmured.

"Then I'll call you in a week or two. I'll be out of town for a few days. I'm leaving right after the service, but you don't need to wait for my return to visit Duvall Island. The excavation is winding down. I know Temple will be disappointed if you don't make it out to the dig before she closes the site."

"I'll see what I can do." I glanced up the street, but Aunt Lynrose was nowhere to be seen. "I really should go. I'm keeping you from the service."

"You aren't going?"

"I didn't really know Jonathan Devlin well."

"That surprises me. He spoke very highly of you."

"Of me?" I stared at Duvall in astonishment. "I doubt that. We only met a couple of times."

"He must have known you by reputation then. He told me once that you were a woman of rare talents and abilities. I believe he was a little in awe of you."

I frowned. "Maybe he meant someone else."

"Oh, no. He was specific." He paused thoughtfully. "I belong to an organization that's very interested in people like you."

My heart bounced painfully. "People like me?"

"You won't have heard of us, but we've been around for ages. You might call us a preservation society. Membership is usually legacy and always by invitation only. But perhaps I'll mention your name to the others. We're always on the lookout for new blood."

The exchange with Rance Duvall chilled me even more than the sighting of my aunt. His friendly tone didn't mask his subtle threat. He knew about me. He knew all about my gift. If I tried to interfere with his and Claire's plans, he would give my name to the *Congé*. I didn't see how else to interpret his words.

I watched him until he was out of sight and then I hurried back to my car. By this time, Aunt Lynrose was long gone. I had no hope of finding her downtown so I decided to see if she'd gone home.

A little while later, I pulled to the curb in front of her house, noting the absence of her car in the driveway. Where she might have gone to after she'd rushed away from the church, I had no idea. I tried her phone and when she didn't answer, I wondered if she was avoiding me. Not one to be easily discouraged, I settled in to wait for her.

Minutes passed and then half an hour. I tried her phone again. Still no answer.

I began to grow antsy. I got out of the car and paced up and down the sidewalk for a few minutes, trying to talk myself out of a bad idea. I knew where Aunt Lyn kept her spare key. I'd used it any number of times to check on her house when she was out of town. I kept fixating on those old memories that had surfaced, particularly the one involving the locked door at the end of her hallway and that blue porcelain box on the floating shelf. It had been years since I'd seen her place the key inside. For all I knew, she could have hidden it elsewhere by now.

I told myself I should keep my nose out of my aunt's affairs, but this was more than idle curiosity. I had been dragged into a mystery through no action of my own. I hadn't asked for the ghost child to manifest in my presence. I never meant for the sound of that haunting melody or the scent of woodbine to awaken so many memories. But now that it was all coming together, I had to see it through. The ghost child wouldn't rest until I found her.

Glancing around for any sign of prying eyes or my aunt's car, I turned and strode up the walkway, bending quickly to extract the key from underneath a flowerpot.

The house was as immaculate as ever, serene on the surface, but as I stood in the foyer gazing around, I experienced another of those strange premonitions. This wasn't a happy house. This was a place of secrets.

The locked door beckoned. I eased down the hallway and put my ear to the door. I didn't hear anything inside, not even the faint tinkle of the mobile. Taking the blue porcelain box from the shelf, I opened the lid.

The key to the locked door had been placed in a separate compartment, as had other hidden treasures, among them a folded newspaper clipping and a gold locket with a broken chain. The same locket I had seen clasped in Jonathan Devlin's cold hand.

My heart thudded as a wave of dizziness washed over me. I bent double, dragging air into my lungs to quell the nausea that curled in my stomach and clogged my throat.

Aunt Lyn had been in the house the night of Jonathan Devlin's death. She had taken that locket from his hand before fleeing the scene of his murder. I didn't want to believe she'd had anything to do with his death. I was desperate to come up with another explanation for the presence of that locket in her house. Maybe it wasn't the same necklace. Maybe all of this was just some strange coincidence.

But it all made sense now. My aunt and Devlin's grandfather.

Something came to me as I clutched the locket. I remembered once when Aunt Lyn and I were sitting on the porch at my parents' house in Trinity. I'd just met Devlin and I asked if she knew anything about his family. She'd told me that his parents had died when he was a teenager and his grandfather had taken him in. She'd referred to the elder Devlin as Bennett rather than by his first name, Jonathan. The slip hadn't registered at the time. Only now with the obituary of Jonathan Bennett Devlin fresh in my head did I recall it.

And now I remembered something else—the aberrant trace of white flowers and fresh linen in

Jonathan Devlin's study the night he died. A scent that had, even in my shock at finding his body, taken me straight back to my childhood.

I knew without a doubt that Aunt Lynrose had been in the Devlin mansion. I even had an inkling of her motive. But still I needed more proof.

I pressed the locket release and the lid popped open, revealing a miniature replica of the infant portrait embedded in the stone crib in Woodbine Cemetery. My aunt's baby must have been buried in the unnamed grave, but what about the ghost of the murdered child? I still didn't understand the connection.

Returning the locket to the porcelain box, I unfolded the clipping. The headline and accompanying photo nearly bent me double again. I instantly recognized the child's face because her ghost had been visiting me since my first day in Woodbine Cemetery.

The headline read Search Halted for Ten-Year-Old Mercy Duvall.

Mercy.

According to the article, the child had gone missing from Duvall Island during a storm. She was presumed drowned when her older brother, Rance, had found a capsized dinghy.

Only I and her killer knew the truth. Mercy Duvall hadn't died in that storm. Her neck had been broken after she'd been pushed down a steep set of stairs.

My heart twisted at the very thought of her murder, still hidden after all these years. But at least now I had a place to start my search. And I had a suspect. No wonder I'd had such a visceral reaction to Rance Duvall.

I put everything away and then went into my aunt's bedroom. I found what I was looking for at the back of her closet—a pair of boots with an indention in the right heel.

She said from the bedroom doorway, "I wondered if you had seen me at the cemetery that morning."

I closed my eyes briefly and then returned the boot to its mate before joining her in the bedroom. "I saw your footprints. There's a mark in the heel of your boot. I'm sorry for invading your privacy this way, but I had to know."

She nodded. "I assumed you'd put it together when I saw you across from the church. Those dreams you've been having. Your recall of those old conversations I had with your mama. You must have a lot of questions."

"The infant buried in Woodbine Cemetery... was she your baby?"

Aunt Lyn folded her hands. "No one is buried beneath the crib. The grave is empty."

I could only stare at her in shock. "I don't understand."

"The grave and monument were never anything more than an elaborate deception to keep me in line."

I sank to the floor and drew up my knees. "Tell me what happened."

"It's a very sad story," she said. "Though hardly unique. A naive, romantic young girl meets a wealthy older man who happens to be married."

"Jonathan *Bennett* Devlin."

She glanced up.

"Don't you remember? You called him Bennett once."

Her smile was sad. "Ironic, isn't it? That name was meant as a safeguard so that I wouldn't slip up and give away his identity. His idea, of course." She sighed. "I remember now. We were on your mama's porch. You asked what I knew about the Devlins. You can't imagine my surprise and shock when you became involved with Bennett's grandson. Although I suppose there's no harm in referring to him as Jonathan now."

"You hid your shock well," I said.

"I've had years of practice. I was barely sixteen when I met him. Mother was his wife's dressmaker and I went with her to their house one day. He saw me. He pursued me. And I foolishly fell in love."

"And then you got pregnant. That's why you were sent away."

"Father threatened to have him arrested. I was still underage, you see. The charges would never have stuck. Not to a Devlin. But Father could have made things very unpleasant for everyone and so I agreed to go stay with my aunt. When the baby was born, Ben—Jonathan—arranged for an adoption with a good family, an old family. Wealthy and powerful like the Devlins. The child would never want for anything, he said. I told myself it was for the best. I was young. I had a promising future ahead of me. I thought I could put it behind me and move on with my life."

"You did," I said. "You became a teacher."

"But I never moved on. Not really. I couldn't forget. I ached for my baby. I imagined her crying for me at night and I cried for her, too. I finally confronted Jonathan. I told him that I needed to see her. Just a glimpse so that I would know she was healthy and happy. He talked me out of it, of course. He could do that at first. But I grew angrier as time went on and more determined. I threatened him. I told him I would go to his wife and tell her everything. I would go public. The statute of limitations wasn't yet up. I could still send him to prison if he didn't let me see our child."

"What did he say?"

"He told me that the baby had died. She was only two years old but she'd suffered from a heart condition since birth. That was the reason he'd refused to let me see her. He'd wanted to spare me the grief."

"You believed him?"

"Not at first. But he took me to her grave in Woodbine Cemetery."

"The stone crib," I said.

She nodded. "He told me that he had pulled strings and arranged for her burial in Woodbine.

There was another grave, an empty grave for her family in Magnolia Cemetery, but I shouldn't worry about the details. That little grave—unnamed and hidden—was just for us. Our special place where we could go and be with our little girl."

"Oh, Aunt Lyn." I put my hand on her knee and she clutched it.

"How stupid I was to accept such an explanation. But I was still very young and half-crazy with grief. That's my only excuse." She paused to draw a quivering breath. "In some strange way, that grave gave me comfort and closure. A little peace. A place where I could sit with my daughter and read her stories the way I'd always dreamed."

"When did you find out the grave was empty?"

"Not until a few weeks ago. Someone sent me an old newspaper clipping about a ten-year-old girl who had gone missing and was presumed drowned after a terrible storm on Duvall Island. I knew the moment I saw her picture that she was my daughter. She hadn't died as an infant. Jonathan lied to keep me silent. He watched me weep beside that empty grave knowing that our child was still alive. He stole those years from me. Robbed me of the time I could have had with her. Robbed me of the chance to keep her safe."

"Who sent you the clipping?"

"Jonathan."

"But why?" I asked with a frown. "If he wanted to come clean, why not just tell you?"

"Maybe he didn't think I would believe him. Or maybe he was too much of a coward to face me at first. But he was old and sick and he didn't want to die without me knowing the truth. After so many years, I suppose he finally developed a conscience. He's the one who arranged the Woodbine restoration, you know."

"If the crib grave is empty, why would he care about Woodbine?"

"I can only guess, but Woodbine was the only memorial we had of our daughter. The only place we could mourn her. We'd both shed tears there."

I thought about the locket at the bottom of that blue porcelain bowl. "Aunt Lyn, did you go see Jonathan Devlin before he died?"

She dropped her gaze. "Etta warned me not to. She thought it best to let the past stay buried, but I had to know the truth. And I wanted to hear him admit what he'd done. He owed me that much."

"What did he say?"

"He said he had no proof, but he'd never believed our child's death was an accident. The Duvalls had a grown son, Rance. A black sheep because of certain things he'd done. Terrible things that the family tried to keep hidden. Something happened on Duvall Island the night Mercy disappeared. Jonathan was convinced that she saw something she shouldn't have. Maybe she was trying to get away when her boat capsized. God only knows what could have happened. I think about her out there alone and frightened…" My aunt trailed away with a shiver. "I've dreamed about her every night since I received that clipping. I even went to the church today to confront Rance Duvall with Jonathan's suspicions."

I said, aghast, "You can't do that. Promise me you won't have anything to do with that man. He's dangerous."

She looked up in surprise. "You know him?"

"I've met him. Just stay away from him. Let Devlin handle him."

"Devlin? Your Devlin? What's he got to do with this?"

"He's investigating Rance Duvall and his stepsister, Claire Bellefontaine. You have to trust him to uncover the truth."

She shook her head helplessly. "I don't understand. Investigating them because of what happened to Mercy?"

"Among other things. It's complicated and right now I want to hear the rest of your story. You said Jonathan Devlin had suspicions. Did he go to the police?"

"And risk exposing his relationship to Mercy? He kept silent to protect his name and reputation. All those years, and he never said a word." Her eyes were as hard and brittle as ice.

"You said you went to see Jonathan Devlin the night he was killed. Was he alive when you left him?"

She didn't answer. She didn't say another word. But the ensuing silence chilled me more deeply than any confession.

Thirty-Two

My aunt got up and walked out of the room, leaving me to ponder her silence. *Had* Jonathan Devlin been alive when last she'd seen him? Or, in the heat of an argument, had she picked up the letter opener from his desk and plunged it into his chest?

I hated to even imagine such a scenario, but questions needed to be asked and answered. Better I try to get the whole story before she had to deal with the police.

When I came out of her bedroom, the door at the end of the hallway stood open. I heard the soft tinkle of the mobile from inside and followed the haunting melody, calling softly to my aunt as I approached the threshold. I hovered just inside, taking in the beautifully appointed nursery. The room was just as I remembered it. Soft pastels and a white crib. Shelves of toys and books. The butterfly mobile dancing softly in a draft.

My aunt stood at the window staring out.

"Aunt Lyn?"

She didn't turn. "You must think it stupid of me

to have kept a nursery all these years. I knew that she would never spend a night in this room, but it made me feel better knowing there was a place for her, a safe haven, if she ever needed it."

"I don't think it stupid."

"Not a day goes by that I don't ache for her. That I don't dream about her being home with me where she belongs. Had she lived, she would have had a home of her own by now, perhaps even children. It was unfair of me to say earlier that our time together was stolen from me. The truth is, I gave it away. Just like I gave *her* away."

"You were a child yourself," I said. "You did what you thought was right. It was a selfless act. You wanted a loving home for your baby. You couldn't have known what would happen to her."

"Cold comfort," my aunt said with a sigh. "Let this be a lesson to you, Amelia."

"To me?"

She turned to face me. "You and John Devlin belong together. Don't waste any more time apart over petty grievances."

Our estrangement had hardly been for petty grievances, but I understood her point. "Aunt Lyn, I need to ask you something."

She gave a weary shrug. "Go on."

"What happened when you went to see Jonathan Devlin?"

"You're asking if I killed him," she said bluntly. "I didn't."

"But you were there that night. You took something from the body. A locket."

She frowned. "How could you know that?"

I drew a breath and took a step into the room. "Because I was there, too. I saw the locket in his hand. Then I heard someone in the house and hid in the garden. When I came back in, the locket was gone. You took it, didn't you?"

She said with uncharacteristic heat, "It was mine! He gave it to me years ago, along with the portrait of our baby. He told me the photo had been taken on her second birthday, right before she died. Another lie. It was so easy for him. Just like breathing. He would have said and done anything to protect his precious name and reputation."

"How did he end up with the locket?" I asked carefully, remembering the broken chain.

"The clasp must have snapped. I didn't even realize I'd lost it until I was almost home. I went back for it. I found him on the floor with the letter opener in his chest. He was already dead. There was nothing I could do to help him so I took what was mine and fled."

"You left immediately? You didn't go upstairs?"

"Why would I?"

"I thought I heard someone moving about. It may have been the killer."

"Imagine that."

She was very calm, I noted. Perhaps the implication of her actions at a crime scene hadn't sunk in yet.

"The police don't know I was there," I admitted.

"Then we both have secrets."

"Aunt Lyn—"

"I'm tired," she said, turning back to the window. "And I think we've said all we need say on the matter."

For now, perhaps.

"Leave me be, chile. Leave me alone with my memories."

My thoughts were chaotic as I left my aunt's house. I desperately wanted to head home and settle in for the rest of the day with my computer. Now that I knew the ghost child's name, I was eager to start my research. But something niggled and prodded. A voice in my head insisted that time was of the essence.

I went back over the details of that newspaper clipping. Mercy Duvall had been presumed drowned when her older brother, Rance Duvall, had found her capsized boat floating off Duvall Island. Given the family's standing, no one had questioned the child's disappearance. Even if doubts had surfaced, the Duvall name and influence would have made those suspicions go away.

But Mercy had shown me the truth. She'd been murdered. And where better to hide the body than on the family's private island.

I checked the clock on my dash. The service would be over by now, but Devlin would likely be tied up for the rest of the day. Rance Duvall had said he was leaving town right after the memorial, but I didn't know whether to believe him. Maybe he was baiting a trap. Maybe he knew his absence would make Duvall Island irresistible to me.

I cautioned myself to wait for Devlin, but the little voice in my head prodded me once more. Time *was* of the essence. If Rance suspected I was on to him, he might do more than bait a trap. He might decide to move the remains from Duvall Island and then Mercy Duvall would never find peace. She would never have justice.

An image came to me of the ghost child lurking in the willow trees near the stone crib, wandering restlessly through the tiny graves in the enchanted garden because she had nowhere else to go.

We were connected, Mercy and I. Not just through my gift, not just through my aunt, but because of our shared loneliness. I had once been her, a living ghost, wandering alone through the headstones of Rosehill Cemetery, a forlorn child with nowhere else to go.

I had to find her. It was no longer a mission, but a compulsion. I *had* to find her.

To that end, I called Temple and asked her to arrange transportation to Duvall Island. We agreed on a time and place to meet, but only after I promised to explain everything once I arrived. Then I called Devlin and left a voice mail.

As I pulled from the curb, I glanced across the

street at my aunt's house. She remained at the window staring out. I lifted a hand to wave goodbye but she didn't return the gesture.

Thirty-Three

A little while later, I was in a boat headed for Duvall Island. Temple's driver steered us through a sea of sweetgrass, deftly avoiding the crabbers trawling with their dip nets. The marsh soon gave way to open water, where the dance of sunlight on the waves nearly blinded me. I sat back, enjoying the wind in my hair and the salty mist upon my face as I contemplated my risky endeavor.

Maybe it wasn't so risky after all. For all I knew, Rance Duvall really could be on his way out of town, and I'd taken precautions. I'd alerted Devlin of my plans via his voice mail, and Temple would be waiting for me on the island. She had a whole slew of archeologists and graduate students at her beck and call, so we'd hardly be alone.

Still, as the driver guided the boat eastward, a chill descended and a cloud moved over the sun, darkening the landscape.

Temple was standing on the dock as we pulled in. She put a hand down to help me from the boat, and we left the driver pushing off as she motioned toward a waiting golf cart. "Climb in," she said as she adjusted her hat. "The trail's a bit rugged, so you'd better hang on."

"I'll do my best."

She grinned. "Shall I give you a quick tour of the island or do you want to go straight to the dig site?"

"Neither, actually. I'd like to go to Duvall Place."

"You won't be able to see much," she warned. "I suppose you can wander around the grounds, but I don't have a key to the house."

"That's okay. Wandering around is what I do best."

As we bumped away from the dock, she turned down a trail lined with dwarf palmettos and wild hibiscus. "Mind telling me what this is all about?"

"It's a long story," I warned.

"I'm all ears."

I glanced around, still uneasy by our surroundings. The forest crowded in on us as we headed inland and claustrophobia gripped me. It seemed as though we were driving toward nothing but gloom. "How well do you know Rance Duvall?" I finally asked.

She shrugged. "Well enough, I suppose. His family has owned this island for generations. Duvall Place was once an indigo plantation, but the house and island were abandoned years ago. Rance is hoping to eventually open the place up to tours, or so he says, but I'm not sure if much can be done to make the buildings safe. As you can imagine, time and neglect have done a real number."

"That's the professional answer," I said. "I had the impression at dinner the other night that your relationship with him is also personal."

She hesitated. "We had a moment. But it didn't take long for me to figure out that he's not the sort of person with whom I want to spend my time."

I clung to the seat as we hit a hole. "What happened?"

"Nothing really. We just didn't click." She frowned. "Actually, it was a bit more than that. It's hard to explain, but I had a bad feeling about him. He's very suave on the outside. Very handsome and charming, but…" She slowed as the trail became even more rugged.

"But what?"

She shot me a glance. "Why all these questions about Rance Duvall?"

"I have a bad feeling about him, too. From the moment I first laid eyes on him at Rapture, I knew something was off about him."

"Why didn't you say anything?"

"What was there to say? It was just a hunch. And anyway, would you have listened to me?"

"Probably not," she admitted. "Sometimes it's best to discover these things for one's self."

I gave her a sidelong glance. "You've never heard any rumors about him?"

She thought for a moment. "I do remember a bit of gossip. When I was in college, there was talk about wild parties, orgies and whatnot on the island. Rance was long gone from Emerson when I was a student there, but his family still had a presence on campus. I believe he even sat on the board for a time, so some of the students knew him, at least by name and reputation."

"From what I hear, it was more than wild parties," I said. "He allegedly stalked and abused underage girls. One of them disappeared when she tried to come forward."

Temple stopped the cart and turned to me. "What are you saying, exactly?"

"It's possible Rance Duvall bought her off, but who really knows? Did he ever mention a younger sister to you?"

"You mean Claire Bellefontaine?"

"No, he had another sister who died at the age of ten. She was adopted. Her name was Mercy. She disappeared off the island one night during a storm. Her capsized boat washed ashore and she was presumed drowned."

"What was a ten-year-old child doing out in a boat during a storm? At night, no less?"

"I don't know. Maybe she was trying to run away from something. Or someone. But at any rate, she didn't drown. She was killed in the house and then buried somewhere on the island."

Temple cocked her head as she observed me. "And you know this how?"

"Call it another hunch. I wish I could give you a better explanation, but I don't know how much time we have. Rance told me earlier he was headed out of town after Jonathan Devlin's memorial service, but I don't know if I believe him. For all I know he could be on his way out here right now. I promise I'll tell you everything once this is all over. Right now we need to keep moving."

She looked as if she wanted to challenge me, but instead she nodded and pressed the accelerator. "You still want to go to the house?"

"No, take me to the cemetery instead."

"Another hunch?"

Not so much a hunch as a compulsion. The ghost child was here on the island. Already, I could feel her pull. I couldn't yet see her, but I sensed her presence beside me, guiding me to where I needed to be.

Temple and I were silent for the rest of the trip. We passed a set of ornate gates through which I could glimpse the white columns and sagging balconies of Duvall Place. A shiver went through me as I peered through the tunnel of live oaks. Twilight was hours away, but the cloudy sky deepened the gloom and I could sense the stir of more than one ghost. Duvall Island was a very haunted place. An inhospitable place for someone like me.

A rusted iron fence enclosed the small cemetery. The trees and bushes had encroached and many of the headstones had crumbled. A more eerie spot I could hardly imagine.

"What are we looking for?" Temple asked as we

left the golf cart and tramped through the weeds to the gate.

"Disturbances, signs, clues. Anything out of the ordinary." Although after half a century of wind and weather, any evidence would have long since been destroyed. Still, Mercy was here. I could feel her cold now. I could sense her anger.

"Can you be more specific?" Temple asked.

I didn't answer. I merely pointed to the far side of the cemetery where the ghost child had manifested, still in her white dress and bows. Temple couldn't see her, of course. But as I stood watching the ghost, she dropped to her knees beside a grave and started digging.

I remained enthralled for the longest moment until Temple said beside me, "What are you looking at? You seem transfixed."

"We're going to need tools," I said. "Shovels and spades. A screen. Can you get them from the dig site?"

She gave a little gasp. "Please tell me you're not planning on digging up graves."

"Just one."

"Need I remind you this is private property? And even if it weren't, there are procedures and protocol. Not to mention court orders."

I tore my gaze from the ghost child and her frantic digging. "The graves here are well over a hundred years old, so that puts them in your jurisdiction."

"Even the state archeologist can't exhume graves without the proper authorization."

I returned my focus to the ghost child. "You should probably call the county coroner. She knows you. She'll come out as a favor if you ask her."

"Regina Sparks is a busy woman," Temple said in exasperation. "She won't make a trip out here unless I give her a valid reason."

"She'll come. Better call the police, too, and bring back some of your people from the dig. We'll need witnesses."

"And just what am I supposed to tell the police?"

"Tell them you stumbled across a grave with exposed human remains."

"Look around," she said. "Do you see any exposed human remains?"

"There will be by the time the authorities arrive."

She gave me a long scrutiny. "This is crazy. You know that, right? If Rance Duvall gets wind of what you're doing—"

"Which is why we have to act quickly," I cut in. "We can't do this the proper way. He has too much power. Even if we could by some miracle get the police to listen to us, he'd have the remains removed before a judge could issue an order. I'm telling you, this is the only way."

She drew a breath and nodded. "I'll see what I can do. But for the record, I'm against this."

"I know. Just…trust me. I know what I'm doing."

"I hope you do," she said as she climbed back into the golf cart and drove off, leaving me alone with the ghost of Mercy Duvall.

I stood just inside the fence, shivering in the frost of her presence. She didn't seem to notice me. She just kept right on digging. But when I moved to her graveside, she rose and drifted over the headstone, floating so close that the brush of her ghostly fingers raised goose bumps.

I heard her in my head, whispering to me longingly: *Home.*

She moved past me to the gate, turning to glance over her shoulder as if willing me to follow. I wanted to start digging. The sooner we uncovered her remains, the sooner we could bring her killer to justice. But once again I felt compelled to do her bidding. It seemed as if I had no will of my own. I tried to shake off those unearthly shackles as I followed her through the gate.

She drifted through the underbrush, trailing the faintest trace of woodbine. Presently, we came to the sagging gates of Duvall Place. She floated through the rungs, but I had to pause and wrestle with the rusted hinges. The gates opened with a squeal and I stepped inside, bracing myself against the dark aura of that house.

The structure was plantation-style with heavy wooden shutters at the windows to block out the light and inclement weather. The house had been built on a raised basement and I could well imagine the condition of those dark, dank rooms. No doubt there would be several inches, perhaps even several feet, of murky water from the last rainstorm. There would be snakes, I thought with a shiver. And spiders by the thousands.

I moved down the drive beneath the spreading arms of all those live oaks. Then I paused once again at the base of a wide staircase that led up to the veranda. The house was in very bad shape. Decades of neglect and salt air had taken a discouraging toll. I wasn't at all sure the place was safe to enter, but the hazards of a dilapidated house had never stopped me before.

To my surprise, the front door was open. That should have been my first warning that all was not well inside. The trap had been set, but I couldn't turn back now. Mercy Duvall's ghost had come here for a reason. She needed me to see something, find something. She needed me to finish this.

I took a tentative step inside and then froze. The floorboards sagged beneath my weight, and I imagined myself falling through to the snaky water below. Steadying my nerves, I made my way over to the staircase, clinging to the banister as I gazed up at the landing. Mercy Duvall's ghost hovered at the top. I understood now why she had brought me here. This was where it had happened, where she had fallen. Where she had drawn her last breath.

I climbed the stairs slowly and when I got to

the top, she momentarily faded until I moved away from the landing. Pressing against the wall, I stared at her diaphanous form as I opened my mind to whatever message or clue she might want to send me.

As before, my attention seemed to embolden her and she once again appeared at the top of the stairs. I wanted to reach out to her, to somehow offer her comfort. But our surroundings had changed. We were still inside Duvall Place, but I knew instinctively that I was no longer gazing upon Mercy Duvall's ghost. Instead, I had entered her memory. She stood on the landing staring up at her killer. I could see his face now. I could hear his voice berating her.

"You miserable little brat. I warned you before about following me out here, but I'm the least of your worries. Father will have your hide for taking the boat without his permission."

"You won't tell him," she taunted. "Because if you do, I'll tell him about you."

Rance Duvall merely laughed. "As if he would believe a word out of your lying mouth. Blood is thicker than water, little girl. Hasn't anyone ever told you that? I'm a true Duvall. You're just a nuisance that no one wanted, not even your own mother."

"That's not true!"

"Oh, it's true all right. You're nothing more than a business arrangement."

Her eyes glistened with tears, but she lifted her

chin defiantly. "I know what you did to that girl. The one who disappeared. If Father won't believe me, I'll go to the police."

"And you think they'll believe you?" He laughed again.

"They'll believe me if I have proof!"

That seemed to stop him for a moment. Then eyes narrowing, he jerked her hands from behind her back and pried open her fingers, revealing a silver charm bracelet.

"It belonged to her," Mercy said. "You kept it as a souvenir, didn't you? That's what killers do."

"You're very clever," he said. "Too clever for your own good." He took her by the shoulders, lifting and shaking her until the bracelet fell from her hand. Her eyes went wide with shock and her arms flailed helplessly as he flung her down the stairs.

I gasped and ran to the banister, but she wasn't there, of course. Only her ghost remained.

"So it's true what Jonathan Devlin told me about you." I whirled to find Rance Duvall standing in one of the bedroom doorways peering out at me. I wasn't surprised to see him. I realized I had been bracing all along for this confrontation.

He came out into the hallway, smiling at me as if he were greeting an old friend. "Is she here with us now?" he asked.

"Who?"

"Let's not play games. I suspected all along that you could see her. Claire said you even whispered her name that day we came to Woodbine. And just now I saw you at the cemetery. You went straight to her grave. There's no way—no *humanly* way—you could have known where I buried her. Even Jonathan Devlin didn't know."

I swallowed past the fear that threatened to choke me. "But he knew you killed her. Is that why you killed him? Because he threatened to expose you?"

I could see his smile in the gloom. "You think I killed Jonathan Devlin?"

"You seem to have a knack for eliminating threats. Mercy knew you killed that girl. She found something that would have incriminated you."

"Such a clever girl, little Mercy. Always snooping into my private affairs. Poking her nose in places it didn't belong. I think Father was as relieved as I to be rid of her. He only agreed to take her in so that he'd have leverage over Jonathan Devlin. I'm not sure it was worth it. She was such an unpleasant child, even as an infant. Always sulking and glowering."

Anger pierced through my fear. "Perhaps she was unpleasant because she knew she wasn't wanted."

He shrugged. "No matter. All water under the bridge, as they say."

I pressed back against the wall, inching away from him.

"Oh, don't worry," he said. "I'm not going to kill you. Claire and I still need you. But you won't be returning to the mainland, I'm afraid. We'll stow you here on the island until she manages to get her reluctant fiancé to the altar. And just to prod things along, I'll send John Devlin a finger or a toe—perhaps an eye. There's nothing more pliable than a desperate man clinging to hope."

I had been easing away from him the whole time. He seemed to take note of the growing distance between us and moved toward me, only to halt at the top of the stairs. Mercy had manifested at his side. He turned, glancing around almost frantically.

"You feel her, don't you?"

Fear fleeted across his features. He said in awe, "She's here?"

"Right beside you."

He put out a hand, but his fingers went right through her. "Where?" he demanded.

"You're touching her."

He recoiled. "How do I know you're telling the truth? Maybe you don't have any special abilities. Maybe you're just good at reading people."

"Oh, I can read you all right. Mercy could, too."

A frigid draft swept down the hallway, blowing the tendrils of hair from my face as I moved back over to the railing. I could see down into the foyer where the floorboards had buckled. The whole house began to tremble under the weight of Mercy's anger. I grabbed onto the bannister as the floor beneath me shifted.

"Make her stop!" Rance Duvall screamed.

"Mercy," I whispered, but the wind only grew

colder. I dropped to my knees, clinging now to the railing as I watched the ghost's manifestation strengthen until I could have sworn she was flesh and blood. Rance Duvall screamed again and tried to run away from her, but she kept him teetering at the top of the stairs for what seemed an eternity.

Then arms flailing, he tumbled backward, bones snapping as he bounced off each step. His body rolled into the foyer as Claire Bellefontaine bolted through the front door. She stopped cold when she saw her stepbrother's body. Even in the murky light, I could see the dull glow of his open eyes, the odd angle of his neck.

Slowly, Claire lifted her glittering gaze to where I still hunkered on the landing, and I saw that she had a gun in her hand. "What have you done?"

"It wasn't me."

She took aim. "You killed him. In cold blood. I *saw* you."

"You don't know what you saw."

"*Liar!* Get up and face me!"

I rose slowly.

"Come to the top of the stairs where I can see you," she commanded. *"Now!"*

I moved to the landing. "If you kill me, Devlin will never marry you," I said, desperate to buy time.

"Oh, I won't kill you. At least not yet." She gazed up at me, eyes shimmering in the gloom. "But before this is over, you'll wish you were dead."

I drew a shaky breath. "You should probably just go while you still can. John is on his way here now, along with the police. They may already be on the island."

"How stupid do you think I am?" She gestured with the gun. "I made certain John would be occupied for the rest of the day before I followed Rance out here. He won't miss me."

"I wouldn't count on that."

For the first time, she allowed herself a smile. "John Devlin is all about doing the right thing. He won't leave until his last guest has departed. And even if you did manage to convince the police you've stumbled onto something, they won't be here for hours. So..." She moved to the bottom of the stairs. "Come down slowly and do as I say."

My mind raced as I started down the steps. Should I rush her? How good a shot was she?

"Don't try anything," she warned.

"What are you going to do with me?"

"Exactly what Rance wanted to do from the start. I'll put you away somewhere until I have what I want and then I'll turn you over to the others."

"The others?"

"You know who I mean."

The *Congé*, I thought.

"They'll know what to do with your kind."

"Claire!"

My heart leaped at the sound of Devlin's voice. He called again to her from the veranda. The front door hung open, but he didn't come through. "Put the gun down before someone gets hurt. The police are here with me. It's over, Claire."

She spun back to me, her eyes hard and gleaming. She knew it was over. I could see the defeat on her face. But she wouldn't go quietly. She wouldn't go until she'd had her revenge.

As if the house itself had intuited her intentions, the floor heaved and the walls shuddered. I fell to my knees, clinging once more to the bannister. Claire's eyes went wild as she crashed through the rotting planks. I heard a gunshot and then a split second later, a splash and a scream as she hit the standing water in the cellar.

The house quieted as Mercy Duvall's anger subsided. But something dark slinked out of the gloom. Shadowy forms surrounded Rance Duvall's body while others slithered through the broken floorboards to claim Claire Bellefontaine.

I watched it all as if from afar. I felt detached somehow. Calm. Then Devlin rushed into the house. He didn't make any attempt to rescue Claire. Instead he bounded up the stairs as he called out my name.

I couldn't respond. Something was wrong. I looked down at my blood-soaked shirt in awe. Then I looked back at Devlin. I put out a hand.

He called my name again as I crumpled. And then everything around me went white.

Thirty-Four

"Please, please, please," Devlin muttered. He sounded winded and frightened.

As I swam up out of that thick, white mist, I saw him running down the path toward the dock. I called out to him again and again, but he never looked back. He just kept running.

He carried someone in his arms and I realized that someone was me.

But…how was that possible? How could I be in his arms, and yet somehow looking down on him?

I watched from my strange vantage as he kept going, on and on, looking more panicked than I'd ever seen him.

The floating sensation bewildered me at first and then a moment of clarity astounded me. My heart had stopped beating and my body and spirit had separated. I was there…and here.

Now I knew why the birds had come to me. Now I knew why the evil from Asher Falls had knocked on my door. They knew something bad was about to happen. Someone close to me was about to die.

I was that someone.

Devlin kept running. I felt a very strong tug toward him, but an even stronger force pulled me backward into a thick mist. I found myself in a very strange place. Not in the Gray, not in the Dark or the Light, but in that gossamer space between the living world and the dead world.

Familiar faces peered at me through the haze. The thing hanging upside down in my tree. The birdlike creature on Prosper Lamb's roof. The old man in the overcoat from Asher Falls. I stared at them as if in a dream. And, indeed, maybe I was dreaming. Maybe I was trapped in a nightmare from which I would never awaken.

I still didn't understand the purpose of these entities. I thought they were guardians of sorts. They might even be protectors. But they did not welcome me into their domain.

The Gray welcomed me. The ghosts behind the veil beckoned. I belonged with them. I had been born in their world and now they wanted me back. *It* wanted me back.

I felt very frightened all of a sudden. Something lurked in the darkest part of the mist. A presence that had known me before I was born, before my mother's death had left me trapped in her womb. It was still watching, still waiting. I could hear it in my head.

You're in my world now, Amelia. No one can save you.

The voice was silky and seductive. So hypnotic I found myself floating deeper into the mist. A woman appeared at my side. She looked younger than I, but I somehow knew she was older, wiser. I was drawn to her, too. Her allure was even stronger than the waiting presence. I knew that she was a ghost, but when she took my hand, she didn't feel cold. Quite the contrary—she radiated warmth.

She moved in front of me, blocking my path, and the mist thickened and swirled, the gossamer strands weaving a cocoon of protection around us. The hush was so complete I could hear the sound of her heartbeat. But how could a ghost have a heartbeat?

"There's time," she said. "You can still go back."

Her voice was sweet and pure and I closed my eyes, letting it wrap around me like an embrace. "I don't think I can. I don't think it will let me."

She turned to peer into the murky space where the presence hid. "You're safe here with me. I won't let anything happen to you. But you can't stay." She had the kindest eyes and the saddest smile. "You have to find your way back."

She let go of my hand and I drifted away. Floating, floating through the in-between space, back into the living world, where I observed my body. I was hooked up to all kinds of machines and there was a tube down my throat. Doctors and nurses hovered over me, oblivious to my spirit looking down on them.

I drifted into the antiseptic hallway where my family had gathered. Head in hands, Devlin sat apart from the others, Mama and Aunt Lynrose huddled together. They were preoccupied with their thoughts and prayers, but not Papa. He looked right at me. He could see me. He could see my ghost.

"Child," he said softly. "You need to come back."

"I can't, Papa. It won't let me."

He looked stricken. "Yes, you can. You once broke free of its hold. You can do it again. You're strong. Stronger than my mother, stronger than me. Stronger than you even know. You have the power to come back, but you have to do it now before it's too late."

His voice faded as I drifted away, but I was still in the hospital looking down upon another gurney, upon a dear, familiar face. Dr. Shaw's voice said in my ear, "It's okay, my dear. It's for the best. It's what I wanted."

"But—"

"Hurry," he said. "The door is still open. You can come back through. But you must hurry."

I floated away again and when the mist parted, I saw that the young woman's ghost had waited for me on the pathway. "There's still time," she said. "But he's right. You should hurry."

"Why?"

I sensed her anxiety as she searched the shadows. "It's coming for you."

I looked beyond her to where the mist roiled like a storm cloud, moving ever closer. I could feel the cold now. I could smell the foulness of its essence. Terror seized me. This was no mere ghost; this was no mischievous entity. This was Evil. And it was looking for me. Once trapped by the manifestation of its talons and teeth, I would never break free.

I could see more faces in that turbid mist. Pel Asher and his sons—my blood kin that had succumbed to evil. But I was stronger than they. Papa's blood also ran through my veins. Tilly Pattershaw's blood ran through my veins. I had the power to end this now.

Even as I braced myself for battle, I was being pulled deeper and deeper into the Gray. But someone else had taken my hand. My great-grandmother Rose. Her blood also ran through my veins.

"I know you," I said, searching her familiar features. She was young again and her eyes had been restored. I might have been staring at my reflection in a mirror.

"We were very much alike," she said. "We shared the same gift."

Her use of the past tense chilled me. "You tried to help me once. You tried to tell me where I could find the lost key. The one that could close the door to the dead world forever. But your house burned down and the numbers you left behind were destroyed. Now there's no way to find your key," I said sadly.

"You already have the key. Here and here." She pointed to my head and heart. "All you have to do is go back through the door."

"I can't. It won't let me."

"You can," she said. "But you have to hurry."

The younger ghost was back at my side now, clutching my arm. "Yes, hurry," she said. "Someone is waiting for you."

I turned on the path to find a gate some distance from me. It was an illusion, of course, created by the limitations of my imagination.

Devlin stood on the other side, peering at me through the mist. I floated right up to the gate, but I couldn't pass through. I didn't have the key.

He clutched the metal pikes in desperation. "Come back, Amelia. Come back to me."

"I'm trying, but I can't pass through."

"Try harder. You don't belong there. It's a place for the dead."

"But I don't belong on your side, either," I told him. "You should go back."

"Not without you."

"You can't stay here." I felt the wrench of that awful presence. "It's not safe."

The young ghost took my hand. She looked tense and frightened. "It's coming."

"I know," I said with a shudder. "I can feel it."

"You have to go. Someone's waiting."

"I can't pass through the gate. Maybe I'm meant to be here with you."

"Shush." She put a fingertip to her lips. "Listen. Can you hear it?"

The rhythmic thud came to me faintly, but I was instantly comforted. I'd heard that sound once before a long time ago, before my birth. Before my mother's murderer had silenced it. "I hear a heartbeat," I said. "But why is it so faint?"

"You have to go," she urged.

"I can't. The pull is too strong."

"You're stronger." She took both my hands in hers. "You are as strong as you need to be, baby girl."

I gazed at her, awestruck. "You're my mother, aren't you? You're Freya."

"Shush. Just listen."

I could barely hear the heartbeat now. Somehow my presence in the dead world was causing her to fade away.

"Don't go," I pleaded. "I need you."

"You don't need me. You never needed me. But there's someone who needs you." She glanced beyond me to the gate.

"Devlin," I whispered.

"He can't stay here," she said. "It's too dangerous. The longer he tarries, the harder it will be for him to find his way back. But he won't leave without you."

"And I can't leave you."

"You have to."

"I *can't*."

"Baby girl, *listen*."

I could no longer hear the heartbeat. A terrifying hush engulfed me. I knew that silence. I had experienced it before at the moment of my mother's death.

"Go," she said.

"How?"

"A door has opened. Someone close to you has passed."

She nodded once more toward the gate and I turned to see Dr. Shaw. He hovered on the threshold as if he had just come through. Someone waited for him, too. His late wife, Sylvia. But he didn't go to her immediately. Instead, he gazed upon me.

"Hurry," he said.

"Dr. Shaw…" I wanted to go to him, fling my arms around him and tell him how much he'd meant to me, how much I had always valued our friendship.

"I know." His smile was warm and content. "I'm where I belong. I'm where I want to be. But you must go back, my dear. Come now. I'll close the door behind you."

I whirled back to Freya. "Mother…"

She was still there but fading. "Baby girl," she whispered. "Listen."

The heartbeat was faint but steady. And growing stronger…

* * *

I floated up out of the darkness and opened my eyes. For the longest moment, I didn't know where I was or even who I was. Machines surrounded my bed and I still had a tube down my throat. My first inclination was to claw myself free of all those tubes and wires, but I couldn't move my arms. Panic overwhelmed me and I wanted nothing so much as to sink back into oblivion.

I must have made an involuntary sound because a shadow was instantly at my side. I heard a familiar voice calling my name and then suddenly there were other shadows around my bed. One of them asked if I knew my name and what day it was. Another reminded me soothingly that I was in the hospital. I'd been badly hurt, but I was going to be fine. Just fine.

I closed my eyes and let the darkness claim me.

I drifted in and out any number of times until the haze began to lift. I remembered that Claire Bellefontaine had shot me. I even remembered my time on the other side, but all of it seemed like a dream.

The next time I awakened, I felt a sense of peace. Devlin was dozing in a chair at my bedside. When he heard me stir, he rose at once to peer down at me. "Can you hear me?"

I nodded.

He put his hand on my forehead and smoothed back my hair. "It was touch-and-go for a while, but the doctors say you'll make a full recovery. You're going to be fine. Do you understand?"

Another nod.

He took my hand in both of his and smiled at me tenderly. "Welcome back, Amelia."

The drawl of my name would always do me in. I sighed and went back to sleep.

Days passed. Doctors and nurses came in and out of my room at seemingly all hours, and my family took turns sitting with me. I was never alone. The haze continued to lift and my memories slowly returned, along with a niggling worry that there was something I needed to know.

Devlin and I were alone one afternoon when I said out of the blue, "Why hasn't anyone told me about Dr. Shaw?"

He sat on the edge of my bed and took my hand. "What do you mean?"

"I know he's dead. Why hasn't anyone said anything?"

Devlin said carefully, "How do you know?"

"I was dead, too. My heart stopped beating and I floated away for a while. I saw him. He came through the door, although it looked more like a gate. Then he waited to close it behind me. I don't think I'll see ghosts anymore."

Devlin gave me a bemused smile. "No?"

"The voices in my head are gone. I don't hear anything but silence."

"That's a good thing, right?"

"I think so."

His expression sobered. "About Dr. Shaw… there's something you need to know. He had an inoperable brain tumor. That's why he acted so erratically before he died."

"But the tumor didn't kill him," I said.

"No." Devlin's fingers squeezed mine. "There's no easy way to say this. He shot himself, Amelia."

I was shocked but not surprised. I remembered our last conversation and his speculation that once someone close to me passed, the door could be closed before evil came through. "He did it for me," I murmured.

Devlin frowned. "What do you mean?"

I shook my head. "It doesn't matter. I'm safe now."

"Yes, you're safe and I'm grateful. We all are. Your papa went back to Trinity for the night, but your mother and aunt will be by later. They stayed with you night and day. You're very lucky to have them."

"I am. I love them all very much. But there's something I need to tell you." I clutched his hand. "It's about my aunt Lyn."

"I know all about that."

I gazed up at him in surprise. "You do?"

"She told me that she'd gone to see my grandfather before he died. She was very angry with him for his deception and she had every right to be. But she didn't kill him. No one did. He died of heart failure."

"But the letter opener…?"

"Not a life-threatening wound."

I frowned. "But someone *tried* to kill him."

"Yes, but it may be a case that never gets solved," Devlin said. "No prints, no trace evidence."

"You said something always gets left behind." I was thinking of those drops of blood on Jonathan Devlin's desk.

His gaze flickered. "We'll let the police worry about that. In light of everything else that's happened, they're taking a long, hard look at Claire and her stepbrother."

"They're dead, aren't they?"

"Yes."

"Then you're free. We both are."

"There's still the matter of the *Congé*. My investigation isn't finished, not by a long shot. But I don't want to talk about that right now. We've too much to celebrate." He lifted my hand to his lips. "When I think how close I came to losing you…"

"I know."

"You seemed so far away. So unreachable. I didn't know how to bring you back."

"You came for me," I said.

"I did?"

"You don't remember? You were there waiting for me on the other side of the gate. You wouldn't leave without me. You were there with me in Seven Gates Cemetery, too. You may not remember it, but you were there."

He smiled. "If you say so."

"You were *there*."

He bent and kissed me gently.

I clung to him. "You brought me back. You and Freya."

"Freya?" He pulled back to gaze into my eyes. "You mean your birth mother?"

I took his hand and placed it on my flat stomach. "I mean Freya...our daughter."

* * * * *

AMANDA STEVENS

Against the ominous backdrop of Charleston's dark and forgotten cemeteries, The Graveyard Queen returns to unlock the secrets of the past.

Restoring lost and abandoned cemeteries is Amelia Gray's profession, but her true calling lies in deciphering the riddles of the dead. Legend has it that Kroll Cemetery is a puzzle whose answer has remained hidden within the strange headstone inscriptions and intricate engravings…an answer that may come at a terrible price.

Years after their mass death, Ezra Kroll's disciples lie unquiet, their tormented souls trapped within the walls of Kroll Cemetery, waiting to be released by someone strong and clever enough to solve the puzzle.

Amelia is summoned to that graveyard by both the living and the dead. Every lead she follows, every clue she unravels brings her closer to an unlikely killer and to a destiny that will threaten her sanity and a future with her love…

Available now, wherever books are sold!

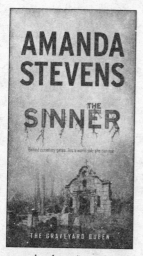

New York Times **bestselling author**

HEATHER GRAHAM

ups the ante in this suspenseful addition to her *New York Confidential* series.

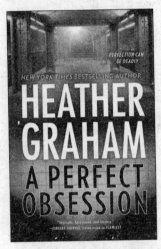

Someone is murdering beautiful young women in the New York area and displaying them in underground tombs. The FBI is handling the case, with Special Agent Craig Frasier as lead.

Kieran Finnegan, forensic psychologist and part owner of Finnegan's, her family's pub, is consulting on the case. Craig and Kieran are a couple who've worked together on more than one occasion. On *this* occasion, though, Craig fears for the safety of the woman he loves. Because the killer is too close. The body of a young model was found in the catacombs under an old church that's been deconsecrated and turned into a nightclub, directly behind Finnegan's in lower Manhattan. Craig and Kieran are desperate to track down the murderer, a man obsessed with female perfection. Obsessed enough to want to "preserve" that beauty by destroying the women who embody it.

Available now, wherever books are sold!

Be sure to connect with us at:
Harlequin.com/Newsletters
Facebook.com/HarlequinBooks
Twitter.com/HarlequinBooks

www.MIRABooks.com

MHG1987TALL

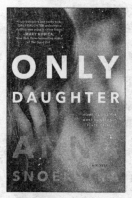

AMANDA STEVENS

31784 THE SINNER	___ $9.99 U.S.	___ $11.99 CAN.
31517 THE VISITOR	___ $9.99 U.S.	___ $11.99 CAN.

(limited quantities available)

TOTAL AMOUNT	$ _____	
POSTAGE & HANDLING	$ _____	
($1.00 for 1 book, 50¢ for each additional)		
APPLICABLE TAXES*	$ _____	
TOTAL PAYABLE	$ _____	

(check or money order—please do not send cash)

To order, complete this form and send it, along with a check or money order for the total above, payable to MIRA Books, to: **In the U.S.:** 3010 Walden Avenue, P.O. Box 9077, Buffalo, NY 14269-9077; **In Canada:** P.O. Box 636, Fort Erie, Ontario, L2A 5X3.

Name: _____
Address: _____ City: _____
State/Prov.: _____ Zip/Postal Code: _____
Account Number (if applicable): _____

075 CSAS

*New York residents remit applicable sales taxes.
*Canadian residents remit applicable GST and provincial taxes.

MIRA®

www.MIRABooks.com

MAS0417BLTALL